HAPPY!

WRITTEN BY
GRANT MORRISON

ART BY
DARICK ROBERTSON

CHAPTERS 1 & 2 COLORING BY
RICHARD P. CLARK

CHAPTERS 3 & 4 COLORING BY
TONY AVINA

LETTERING BY
SIMON BOWLAND

DESIGN & LOGO BY
DREW GILL

IMAGE COMICS, INC. / Robert Kirkman: Chief Operating Officer / Erik Larsen: Chief Financial Officer / Todd McFarlane: President / Marc Silvestri: Chief Executive Officer / Jim Valentino: Vice President / Eric Stephenson: Publisher / Corey Murphy: Director of Sales / Jeff Boison: Director of Publishing Planning & Book Trade Sales / Chris Ross: Director of Digital Sales / Jeff Stang: Director of Specialty Sales / Kat Salazar: Director of PR & Marketing / Branwyn Bigglestone: Controller / Kali Dugan: Senior Accounting Manager / Sue Korpela: Accounting & HR Manager / Drew Gill: Art Director / Heather Doornink: Production Director / Leigh Thomas: Print Manager / Tricia Ramos: Traffic Manager / Briah Skelly: Publicist / Aly Hoffman: Events & Conventions Coordinator / Sasha Head: Sales & Marketing Production Designer / David Brothers: Branding Manager / Melissa Gifford: Content Manager / Drew Fitzgerald: Publicity Assistant / Vincent Kukua: Production Artist / Erika Schnatz: Production Artist / Ryan Brewer: Production Artist / Shanna Matuszak: Production Artist / Carey Hall: Production Artist / Esther Kim: Direct Market Sales Representative / Emilio Bautista: Digital Sales Representative / Leanna Caunter: Accounting Analyst / Chloe Ramos-Peterson: Library Market Sales Representative / Marla Eizik: Administrative Assistant / IMAGECOMICS.COM

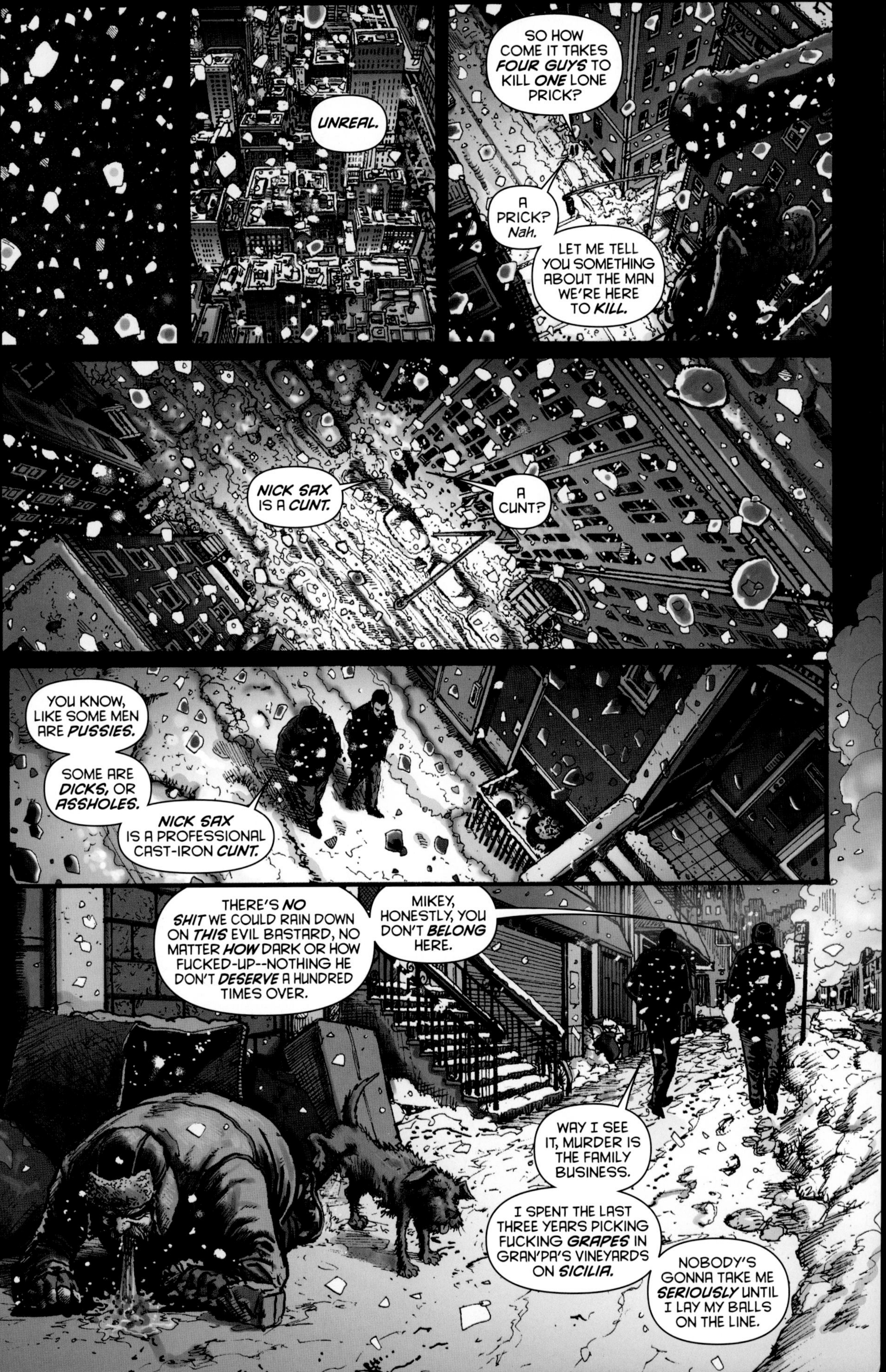
UNREAL.
SO HOW COME IT TAKES FOUR GUYS TO KILL ONE LONE PRICK?
A PRICK? Nah.
LET ME TELL YOU SOMETHING ABOUT THE MAN WE'RE HERE TO KILL.
NICK SAX IS A CUNT.
A CUNT?
YOU KNOW, LIKE SOME MEN ARE PUSSIES.
SOME ARE DICKS, OR ASSHOLES.
NICK SAX IS A PROFESSIONAL CAST-IRON CUNT.
THERE'S NO SHIT WE COULD RAIN DOWN ON THIS EVIL BASTARD, NO MATTER HOW DARK OR HOW FUCKED-UP--NOTHING HE DON'T DESERVE A HUNDRED TIMES OVER.
MIKEY, HONESTLY, YOU DON'T BELONG HERE.
WAY I SEE IT, MURDER IS THE FAMILY BUSINESS.
I SPENT THE LAST THREE YEARS PICKING FUCKING GRAPES IN GRAN'PA'S VINEYARDS ON SICILIA.
NOBODY'S GONNA TAKE ME SERIOUSLY UNTIL I LAY MY BALLS ON THE LINE.

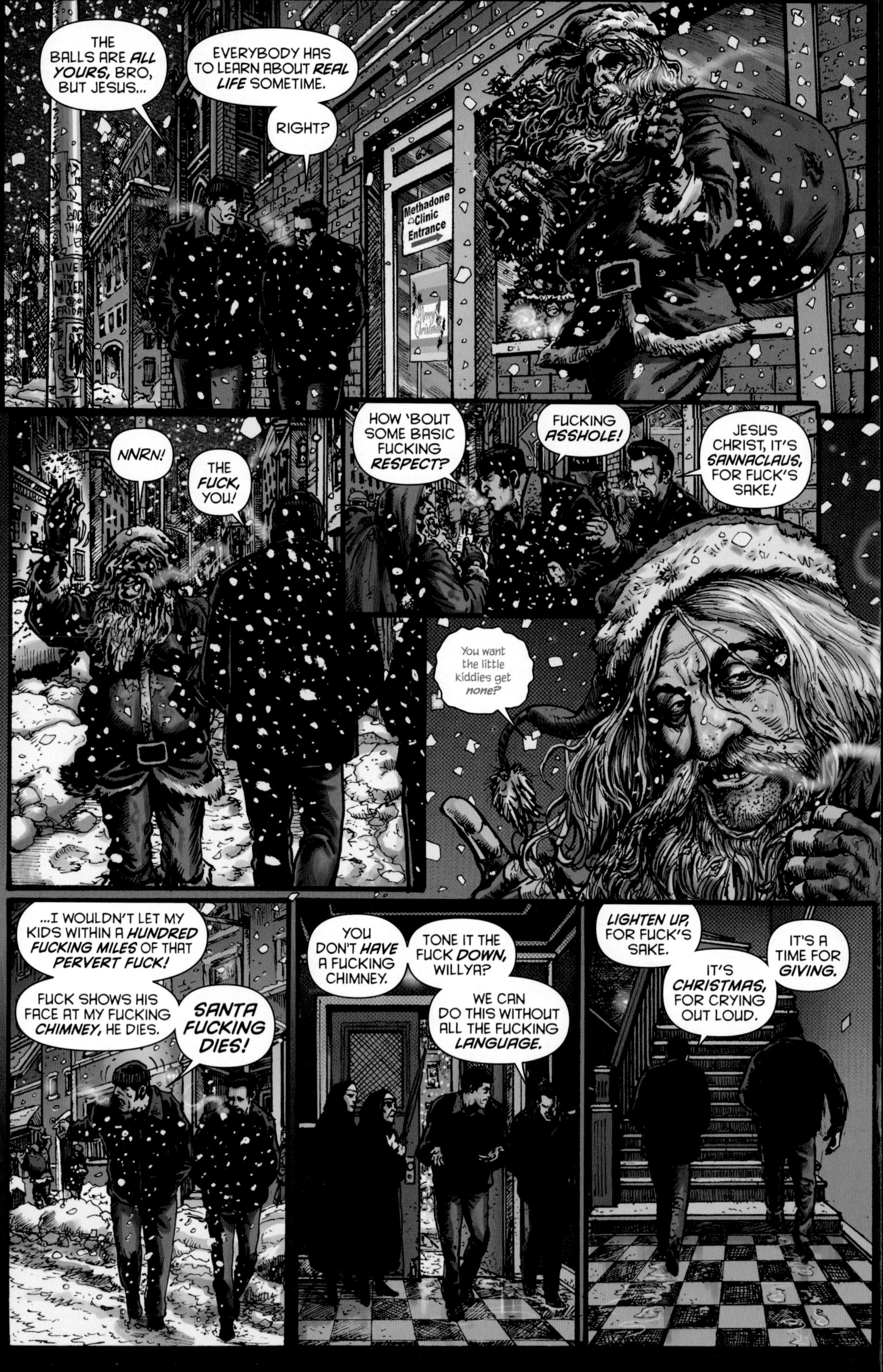

THE BALLS ARE ALL YOURS, BRO, BUT JESUS...
EVERYBODY HAS TO LEARN ABOUT REAL LIFE SOMETIME.
RIGHT?
Methadone Clinic Entrance
Merry Christmas
NNRN!
THE FUCK, YOU!
HOW 'BOUT SOME BASIC FUCKING RESPECT?
FUCKING ASSHOLE!
JESUS CHRIST, IT'S SANNACLAUS, FOR FUCK'S SAKE!
You want the little kiddies get none?
...I WOULDN'T LET MY KIDS WITHIN A HUNDRED FUCKING MILES OF THAT PERVERT FUCK!
FUCK SHOWS HIS FACE AT MY FUCKING CHIMNEY, HE DIES.
SANTA FUCKING DIES!
YOU DON'T HAVE A FUCKING CHIMNEY.
TONE IT THE FUCK DOWN, WILLYA?
WE CAN DO THIS WITHOUT ALL THE FUCKING LANGUAGE.
LIGHTEN UP, FOR FUCK'S SAKE.
IT'S CHRISTMAS, FOR CRYING OUT LOUD.
IT'S A TIME FOR GIVING.

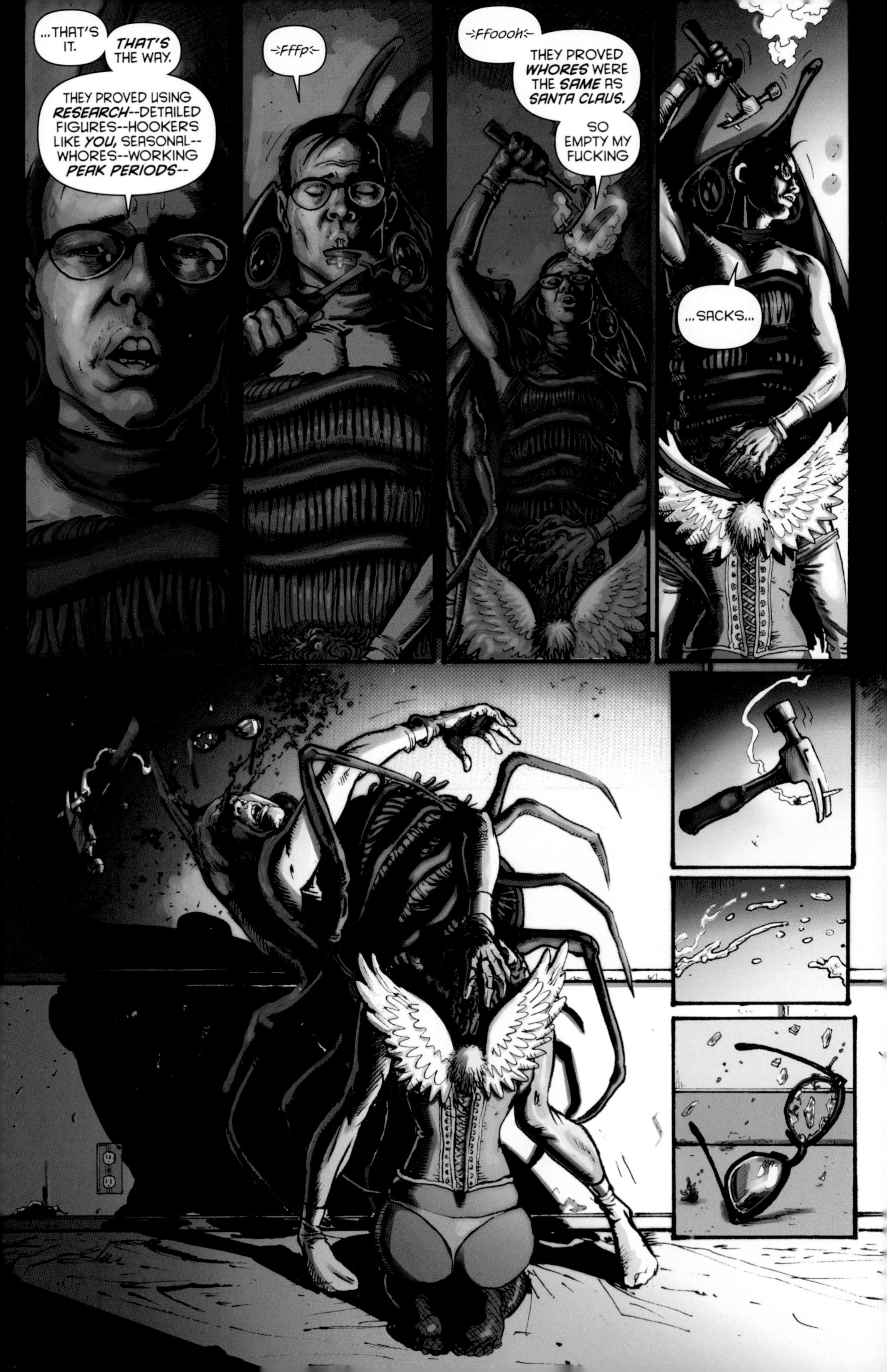
...THAT'S IT.
THAT'S THE WAY.
THEY PROVED USING ***RESEARCH***--DETAILED FIGURES--HOOKERS LIKE ***YOU,*** SEASONAL--WHORES--WORKING ***PEAK PERIODS***--
-Fffp-
-Ffoooh-
THEY PROVED ***WHORES*** WERE THE ***SAME*** AS SANTA CLAUS.
SO EMPTY MY FUCKING
...SACKS...

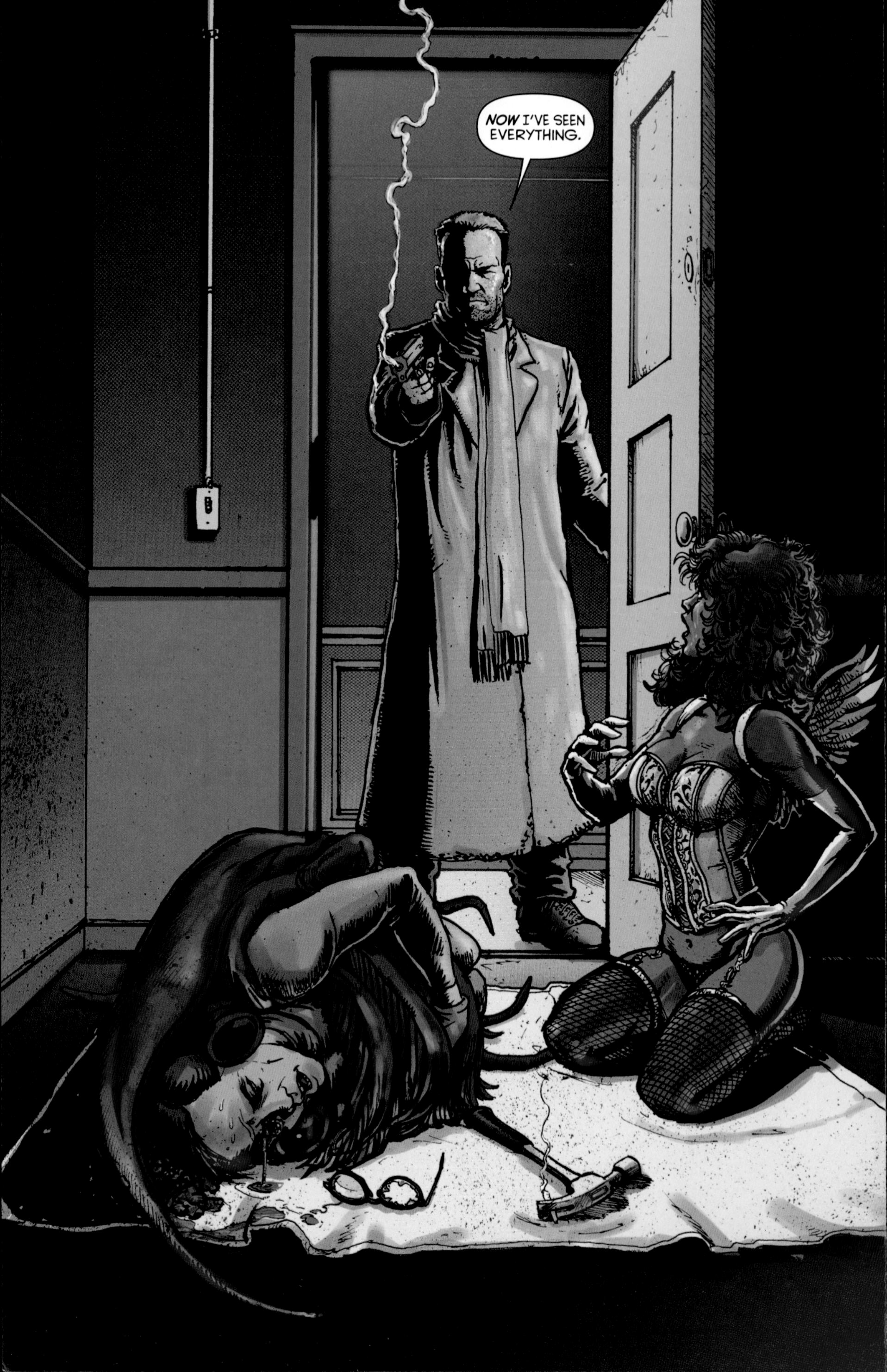
NOW I'VE SEEN EVERYTHING.

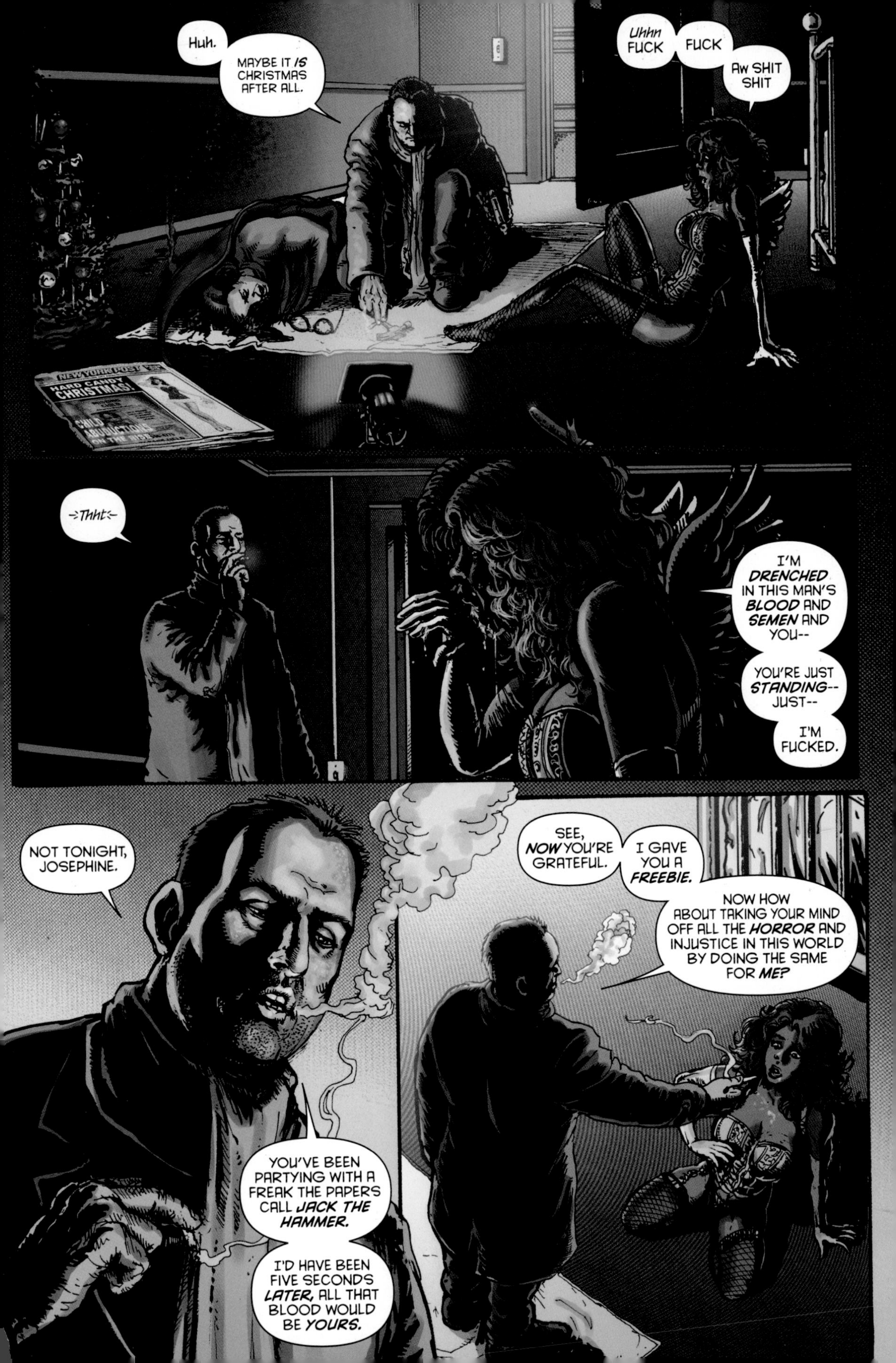
Huh.
MAYBE IT *IS* CHRISTMAS AFTER ALL.
Uhhn FUCK
FUCK
AW SHIT SHIT
NEW YORK POST
HARD CANDY CHRISTMAS!
CHILD ABDUCTIONS ON THE RISE
Thht
I'M ***DRENCHED*** IN THIS MAN'S ***BLOOD*** AND ***SEMEN*** AND YOU--
YOU'RE JUST ***STANDING***-- JUST--
I'M FUCKED.
NOT TONIGHT, JOSEPHINE.
YOU'VE BEEN PARTYING WITH A FREAK THE PAPERS CALL ***JACK THE HAMMER.***
I'D HAVE BEEN FIVE SECONDS ***LATER,*** ALL THAT BLOOD WOULD BE ***YOURS.***
SEE, ***NOW*** YOU'RE GRATEFUL.
I GAVE YOU A ***FREEBIE.***
NOW HOW ABOUT TAKING YOUR MIND OFF ALL THE ***HORROR*** AND INJUSTICE IN THIS WORLD BY DOING THE SAME FOR ***ME?***

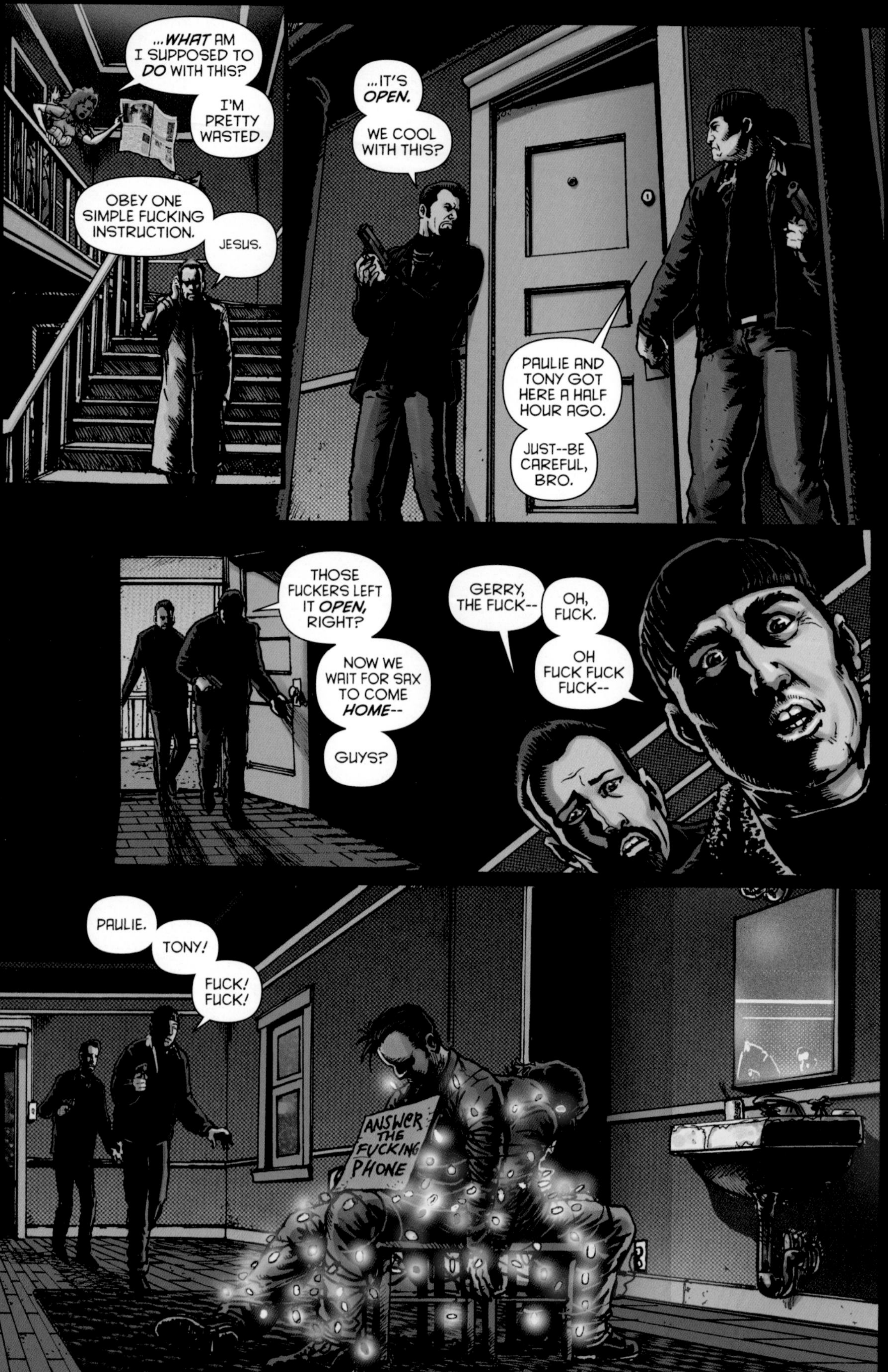
...WHAT AM I SUPPOSED TO DO WITH THIS?
I'M PRETTY WASTED.
OBEY ONE SIMPLE FUCKING INSTRUCTION.
JESUS.
...IT'S OPEN.
WE COOL WITH THIS?
PAULIE AND TONY GOT HERE A HALF HOUR AGO.
JUST--BE CAREFUL, BRO.
THOSE FUCKERS LEFT IT OPEN, RIGHT?
NOW WE WAIT FOR SAX TO COME HOME--
GUYS?
GERRY, THE FUCK--
OH, FUCK.
OH FUCK FUCK FUCK--
PAULIE.
TONY!
FUCK! FUCK!
ANSWER THE FUCKING PHONE

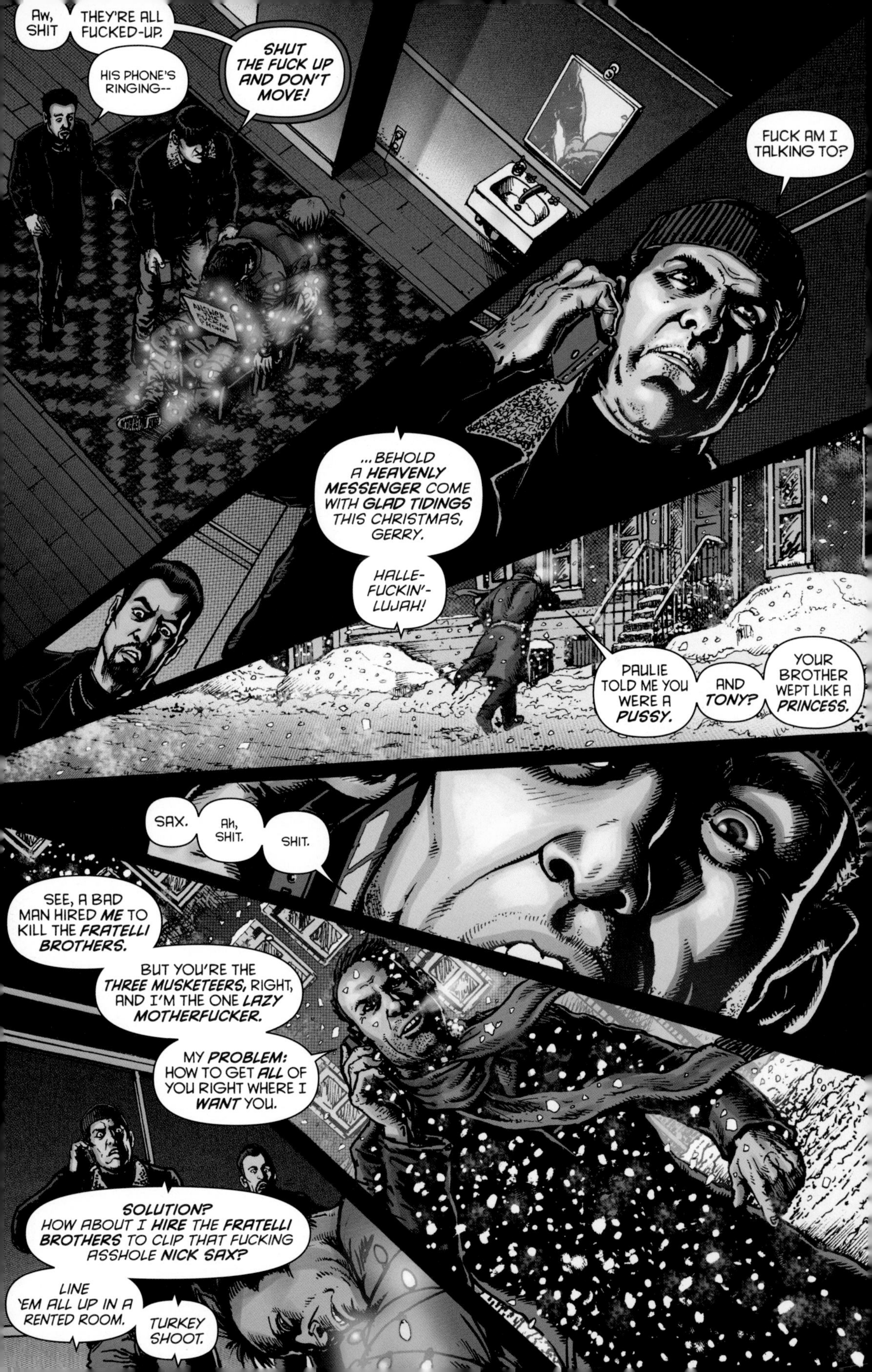
AW, SHIT
THEY'RE ALL FUCKED-UP.
HIS PHONE'S RINGING--
SHUT THE FUCK UP AND DON'T MOVE!
FUCK AM I TALKING TO?
...BEHOLD A HEAVENLY MESSENGER COME WITH GLAD TIDINGS THIS CHRISTMAS, GERRY.
HALLE-FUCKIN'-LUJAH!
PAULIE TOLD ME YOU WERE A PUSSY.
AND TONY?
YOUR BROTHER WEPT LIKE A PRINCESS.
SAX.
AH, SHIT.
SHIT.
SEE, A BAD MAN HIRED ME TO KILL THE FRATELLI BROTHERS.
BUT YOU'RE THE THREE MUSKETEERS, RIGHT, AND I'M THE ONE LAZY MOTHERFUCKER.
MY PROBLEM: HOW TO GET ALL OF YOU RIGHT WHERE I WANT YOU.
SOLUTION? HOW ABOUT I HIRE THE FRATELLI BROTHERS TO CLIP THAT FUCKING ASSHOLE NICK SAX?
LINE 'EM ALL UP IN A RENTED ROOM.
TURKEY SHOOT.

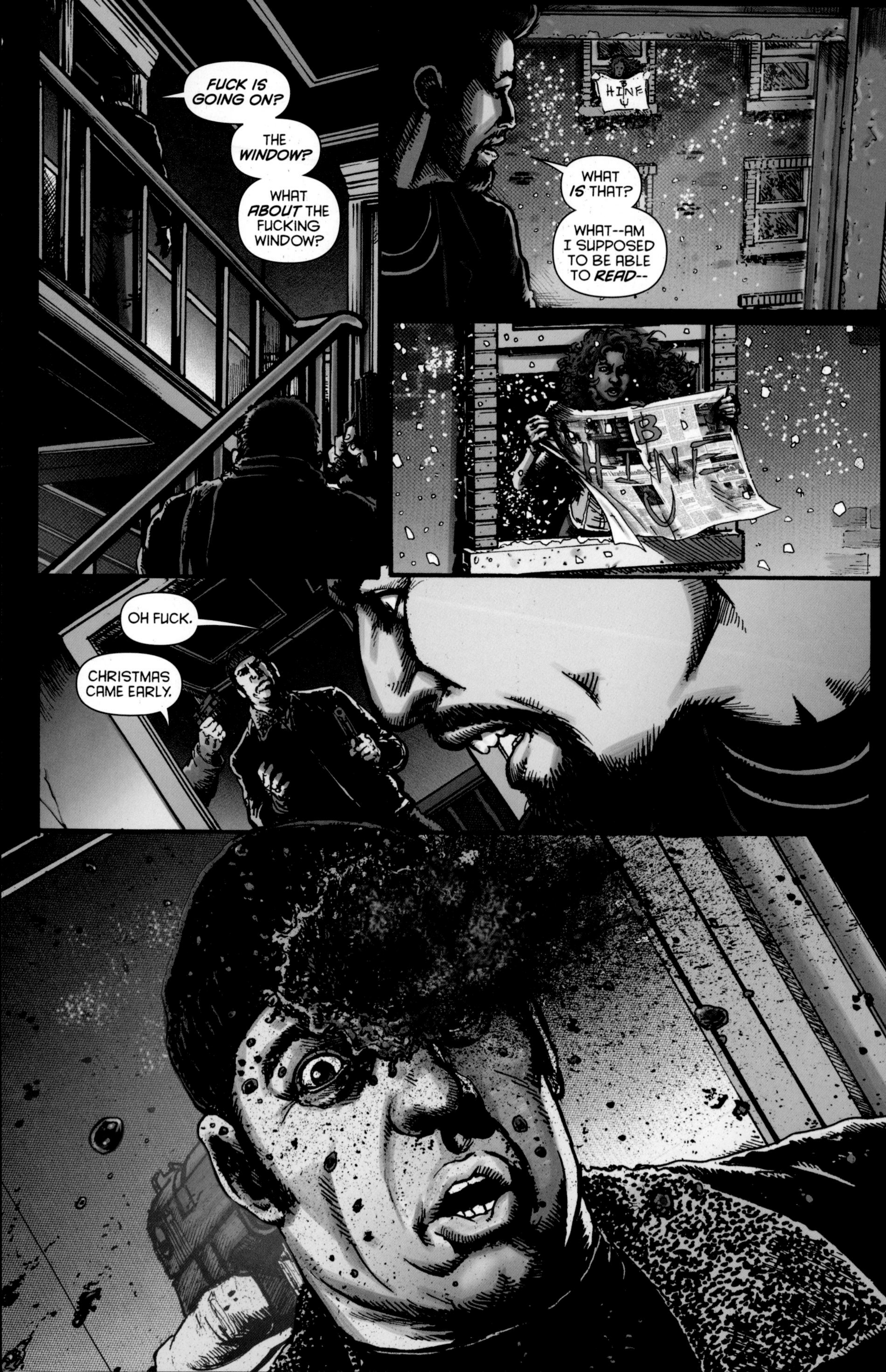
FUCK IS GOING ON?
THE WINDOW?
WHAT ABOUT THE FUCKING WINDOW?
WHAT IS THAT?
WHAT--AM I SUPPOSED TO BE ABLE TO READ--
OH FUCK.
CHRISTMAS CAME EARLY.

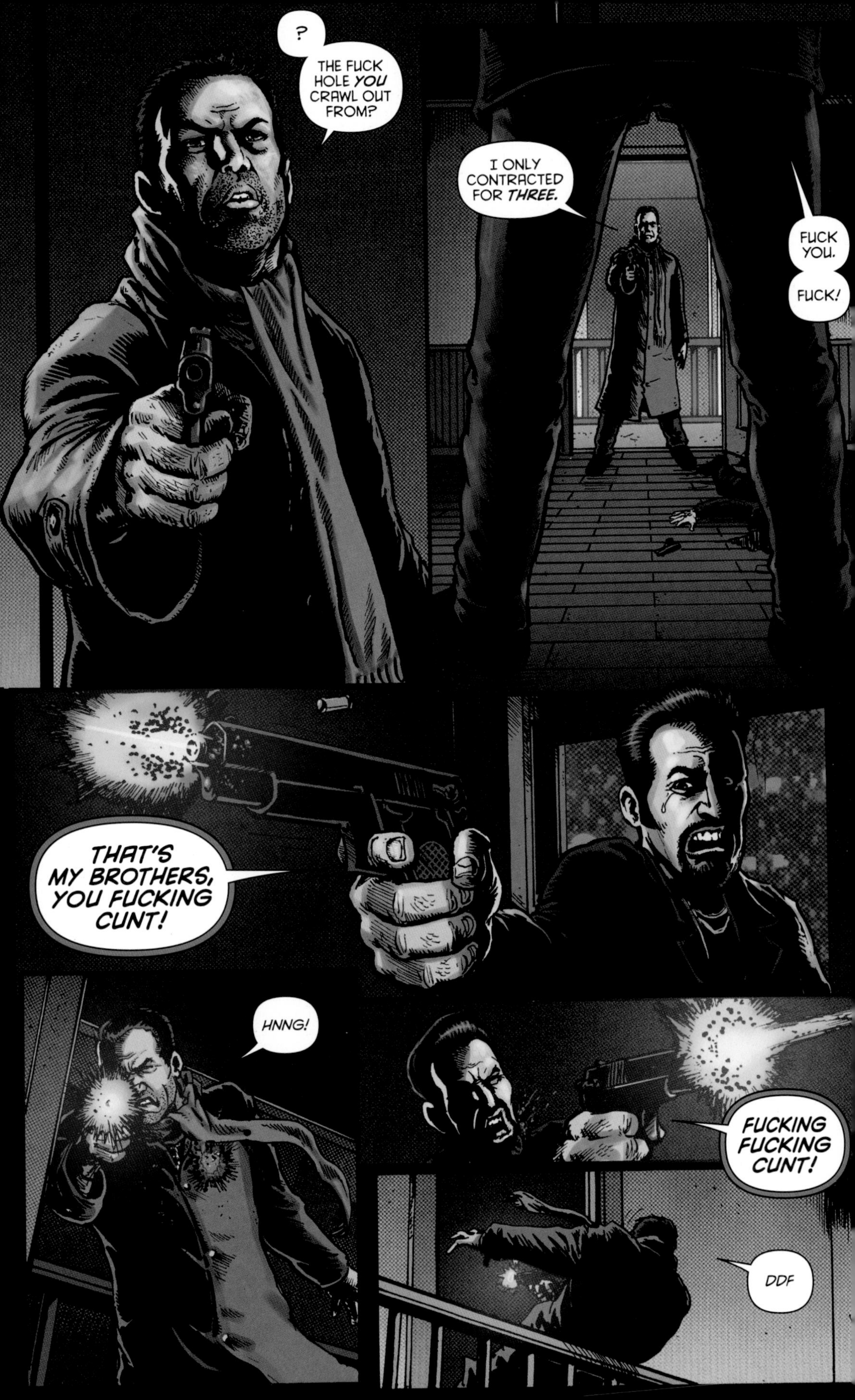
?
THE FUCK HOLE *YOU* CRAWL OUT FROM?
I ONLY CONTRACTED FOR *THREE.*
FUCK YOU.
FUCK!
THAT'S MY BROTHERS, YOU FUCKING CUNT!
HNNG!
FUCKING FUCKING CUNT!
DDF

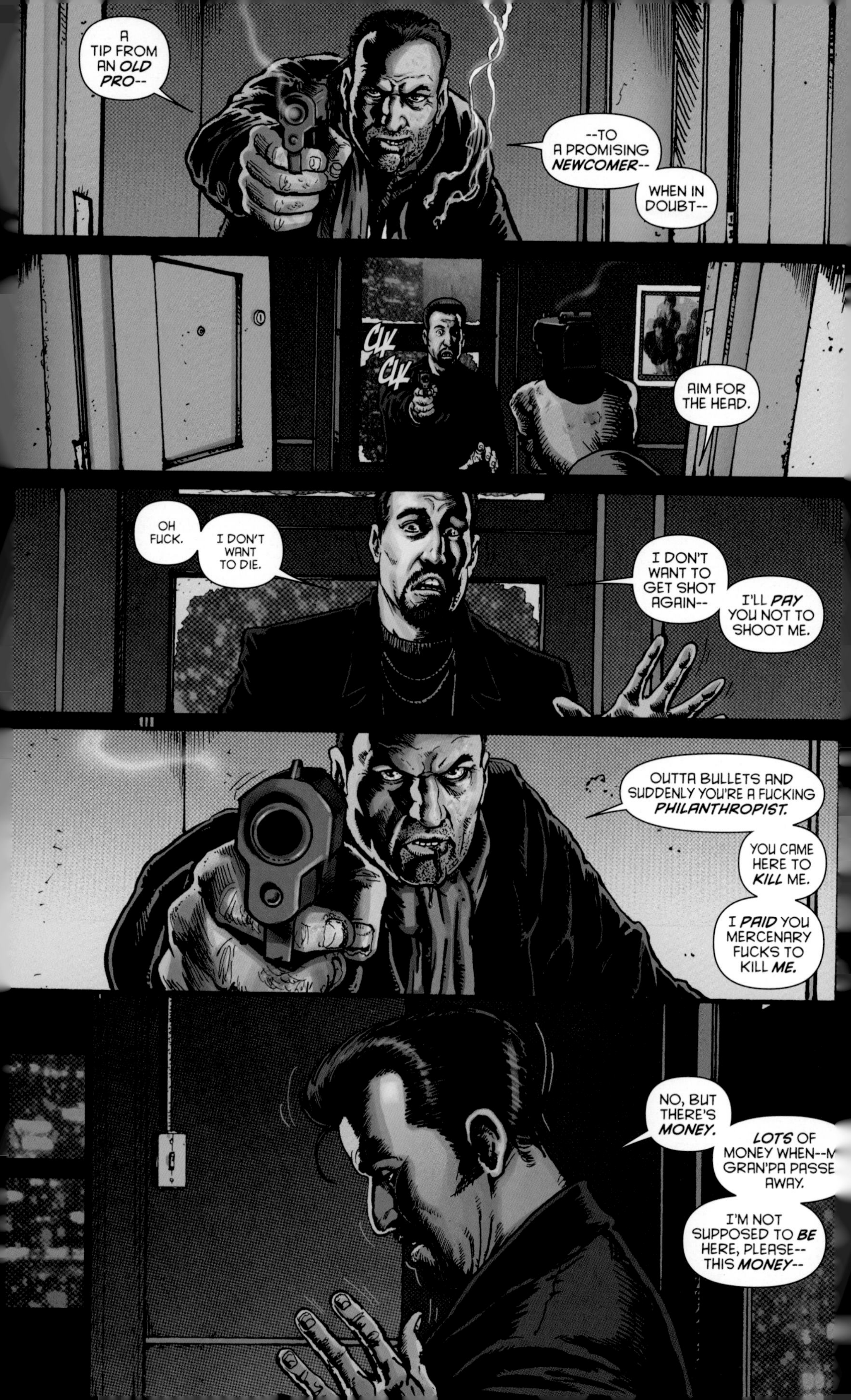

A TIP FROM AN *OLD PRO*--
--TO A PROMISING *NEWCOMER*--
WHEN IN DOUBT--
CLK
CLK
AIM FOR THE HEAD.
OH FUCK.
I DON'T WANT TO DIE.
I DON'T WANT TO GET SHOT AGAIN--
I'LL *PAY* YOU NOT TO SHOOT ME.
OUTTA BULLETS AND SUDDENLY YOU'RE A FUCKING *PHILANTHROPIST.*
YOU CAME HERE TO *KILL* ME.
I *PAID* YOU MERCENARY FUCKS TO KILL *ME.*
NO, BUT THERE'S *MONEY.*
LOTS OF MONEY WHEN--M GRAN'PA PASSE AWAY.
I'M NOT SUPPOSED TO *BE* HERE, PLEASE-- THIS *MONEY*--

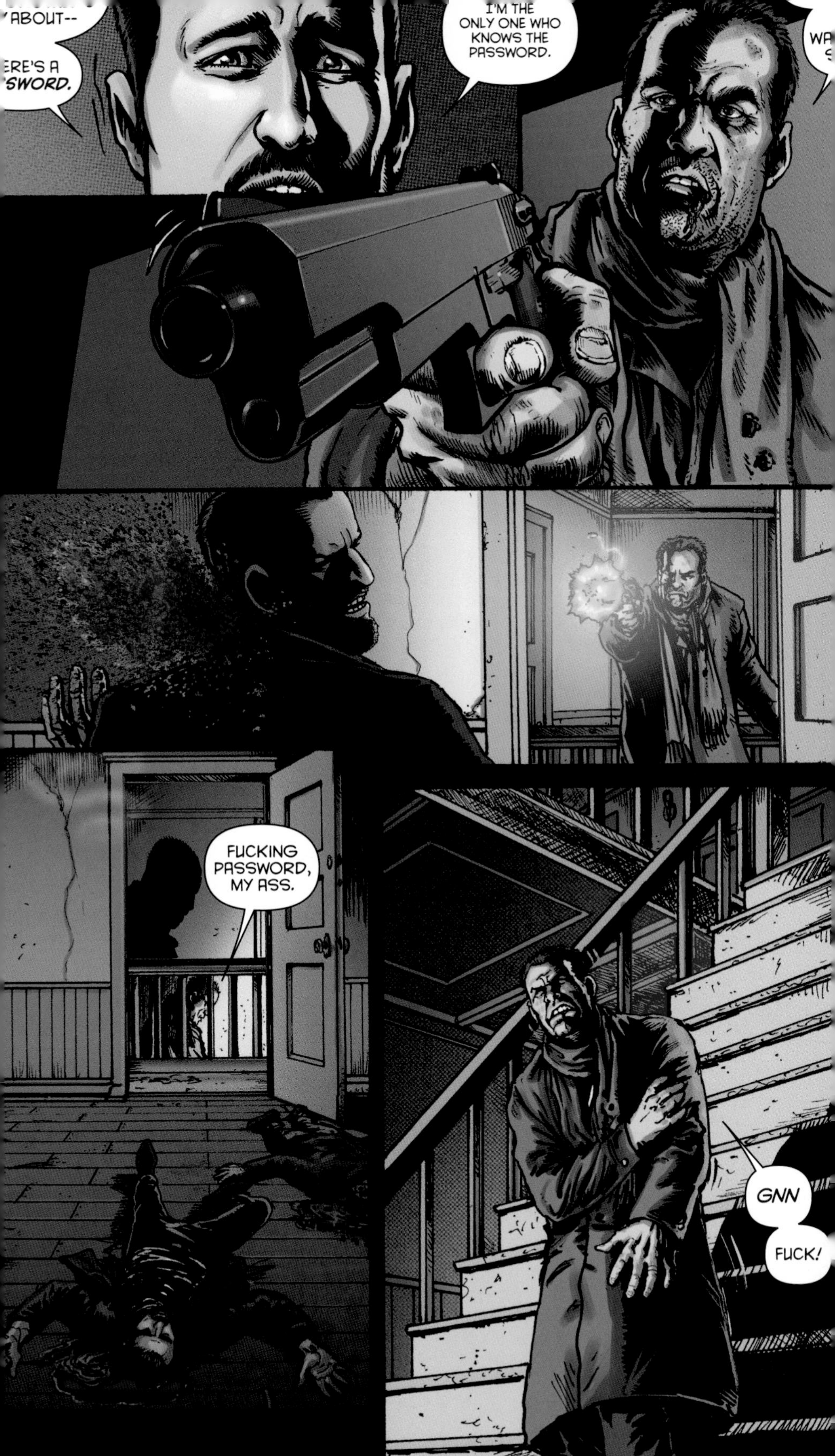
ABOUT--
I'M THE ONLY ONE WHO KNOWS THE PASSWORD.
FUCKING PASSWORD, MY ASS.
GNN
FUCK!

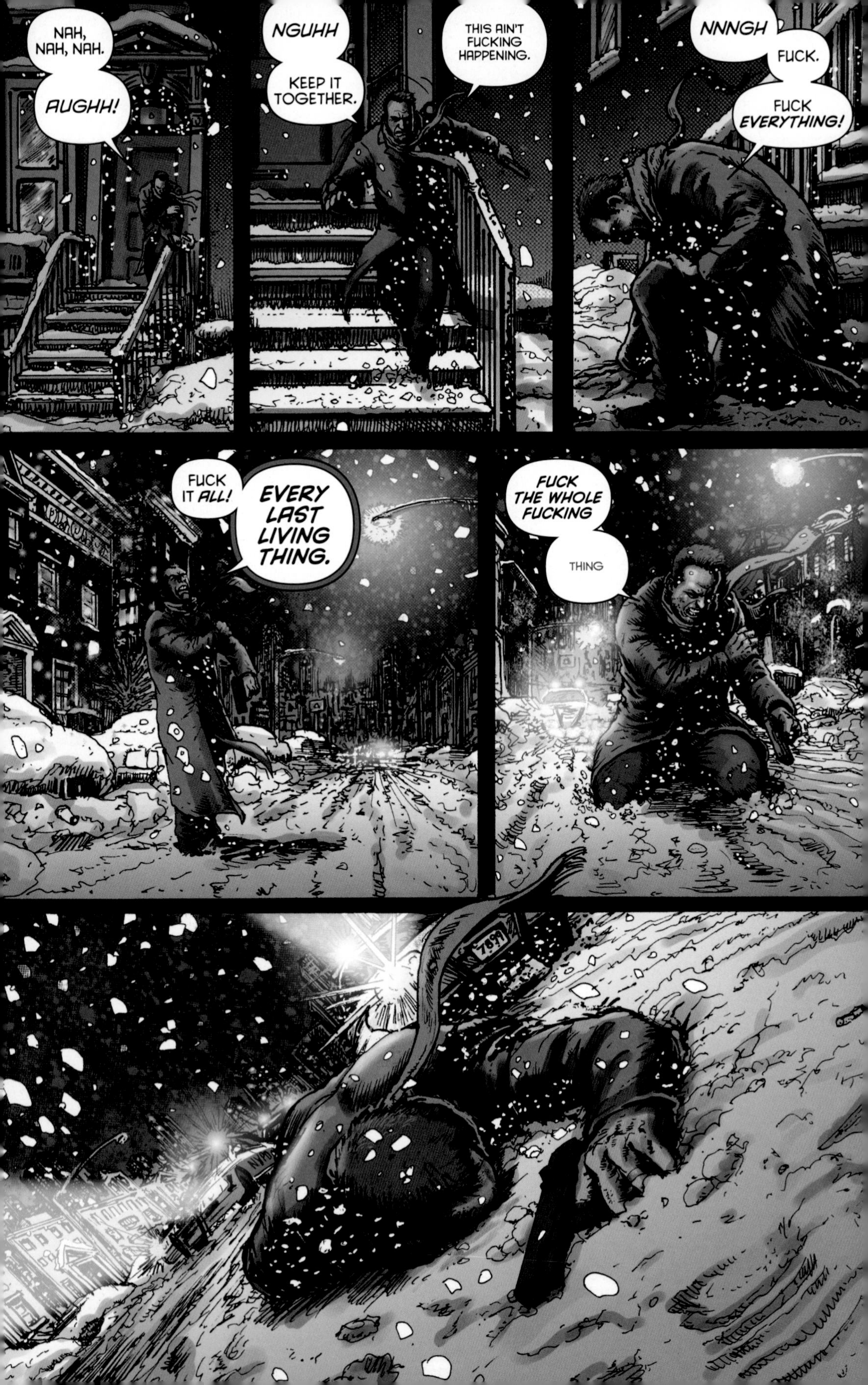
NAH, NAH, NAH.
AUGHH!
NGUHH
KEEP IT TOGETHER.
THIS AIN'T FUCKING HAPPENING.
NNNGH
FUCK.
FUCK EVERYTHING!
FUCK IT ALL!
EVERY LAST LIVING THING.
FUCK THE WHOLE FUCKING
THING

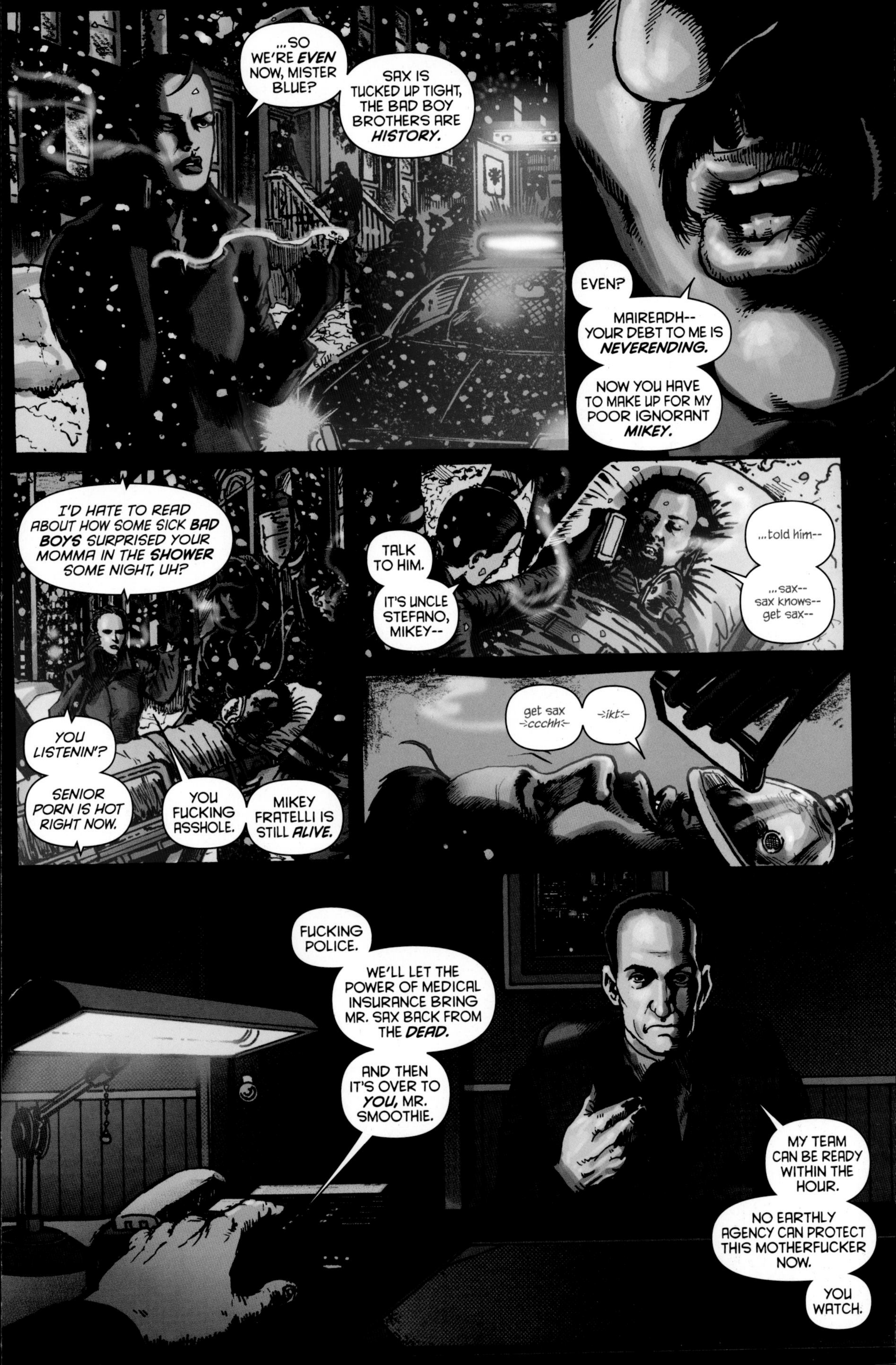
...SO WE'RE EVEN NOW, MISTER BLUE?
SAX IS TUCKED UP TIGHT, THE BAD BOY BROTHERS ARE HISTORY.
EVEN?
MAIREADH-- YOUR DEBT TO ME IS NEVERENDING.
NOW YOU HAVE TO MAKE UP FOR MY POOR IGNORANT MIKEY.
I'D HATE TO READ ABOUT HOW SOME SICK BAD BOYS SURPRISED YOUR MOMMA IN THE SHOWER SOME NIGHT, UH?
YOU LISTENIN'?
SENIOR PORN IS HOT RIGHT NOW.
YOU FUCKING ASSHOLE.
MIKEY FRATELLI IS STILL ALIVE.
TALK TO HIM.
IT'S UNCLE STEFANO, MIKEY--
...told him--
...sax-- sax knows-- get sax--
get sax ->ccchh<-
->ikt<-
FUCKING POLICE.
WE'LL LET THE POWER OF MEDICAL INSURANCE BRING MR. SAX BACK FROM THE DEAD.
AND THEN IT'S OVER TO YOU, MR. SMOOTHIE.
MY TEAM CAN BE READY WITHIN THE HOUR.
NO EARTHLY AGENCY CAN PROTECT THIS MOTHERFUCKER NOW.
YOU WATCH.

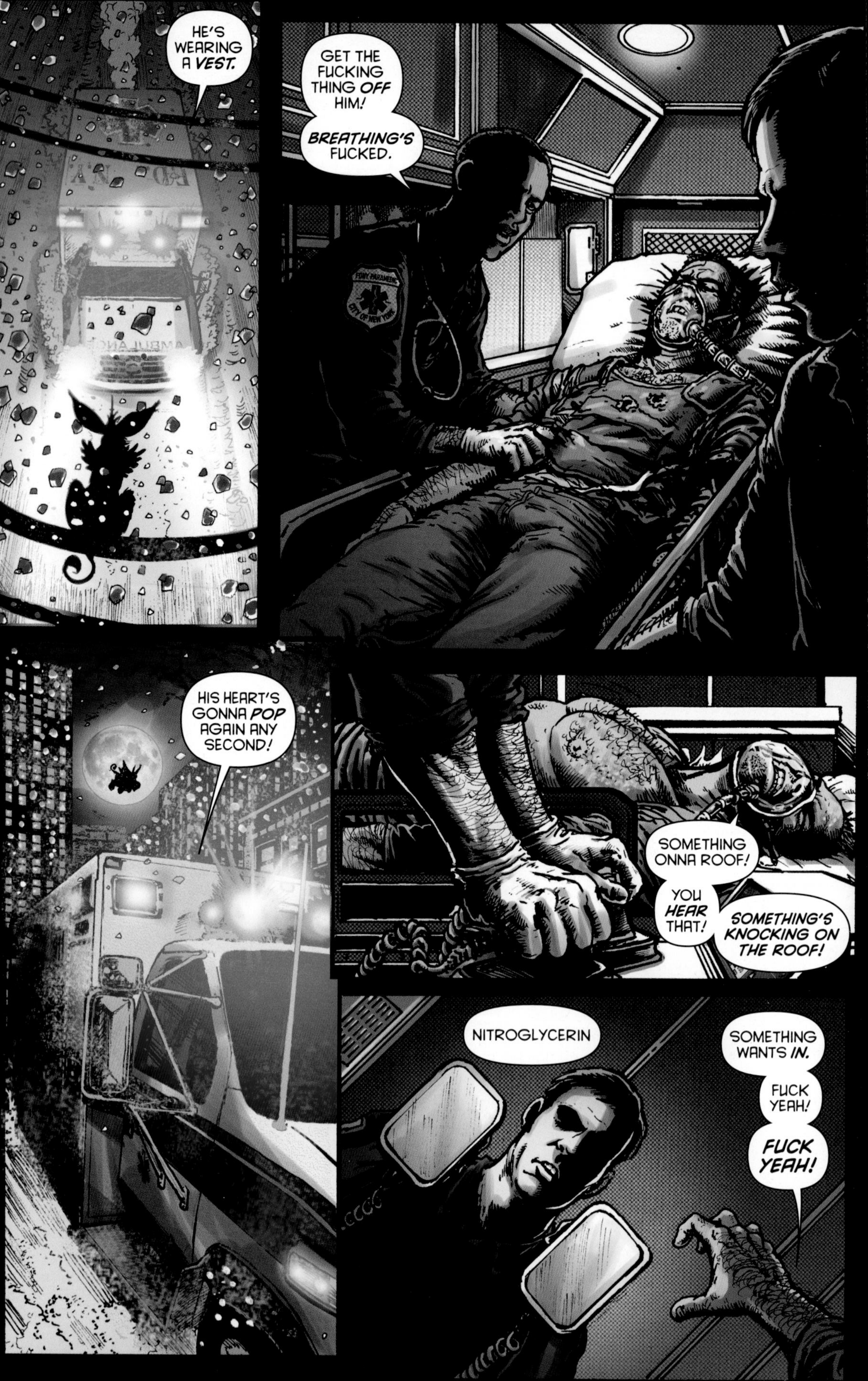

HE'S WEARING A *VEST.*
GET THE FUCKING THING *OFF* HIM!
BREATHING'S FUCKED.
FDNY PARAMEDIC CITY OF NEW YORK
HIS HEART'S GONNA *POP* AGAIN ANY SECOND!
SOMETHING ONNA ROOF!
YOU *HEAR* THAT!
SOMETHING'S KNOCKING ON THE ROOF!
NITROGLYCERIN
SOMETHING WANTS *IN.*
FUCK YEAH!
FUCK YEAH!

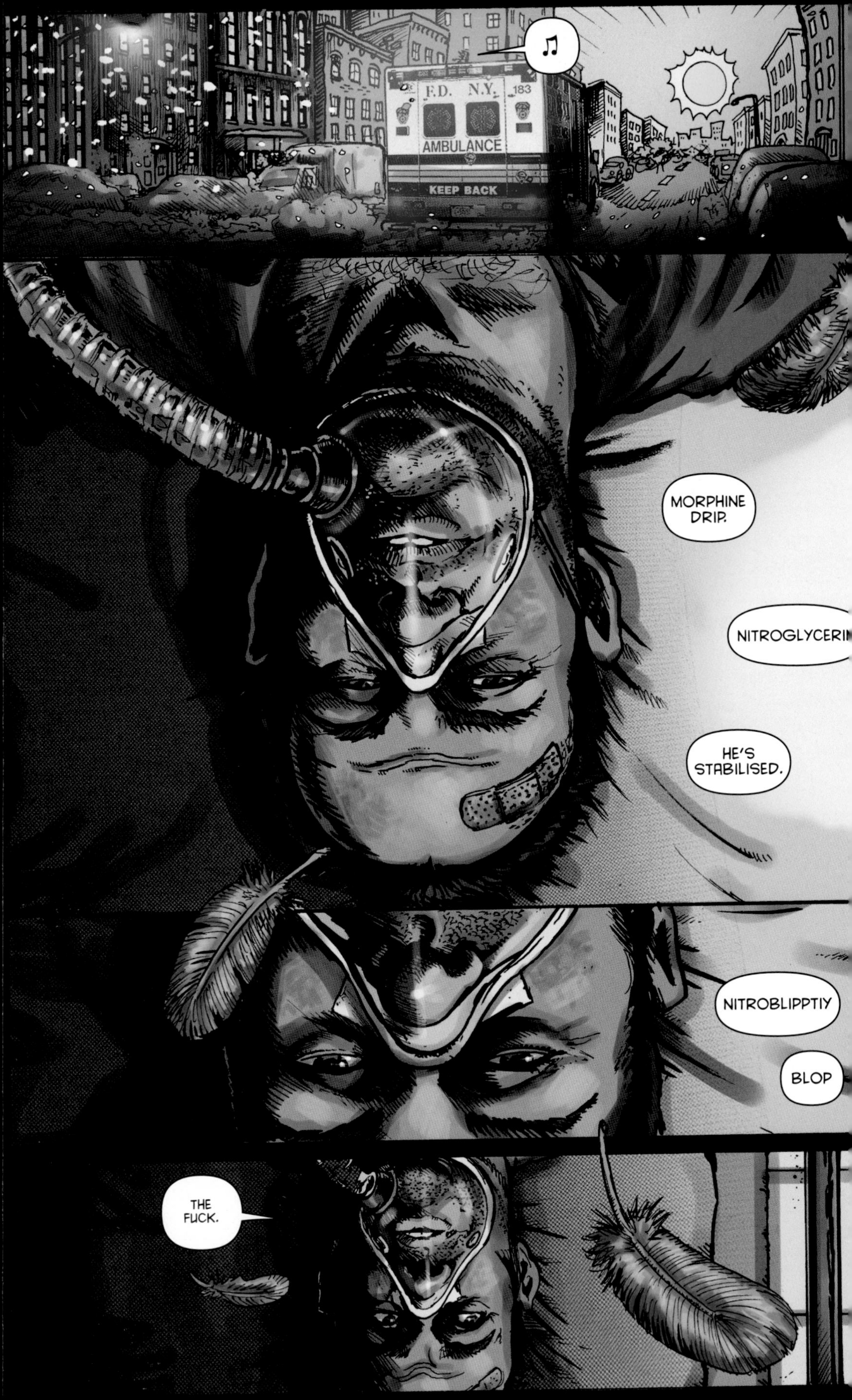

♫
F.D. N.Y. 183
AMBULANCE
KEEP BACK
MORPHINE DRIP.
NITROGLYCERI
HE'S STABILISED.
NITROBLIPPTIY
BLOP
THE FUCK.

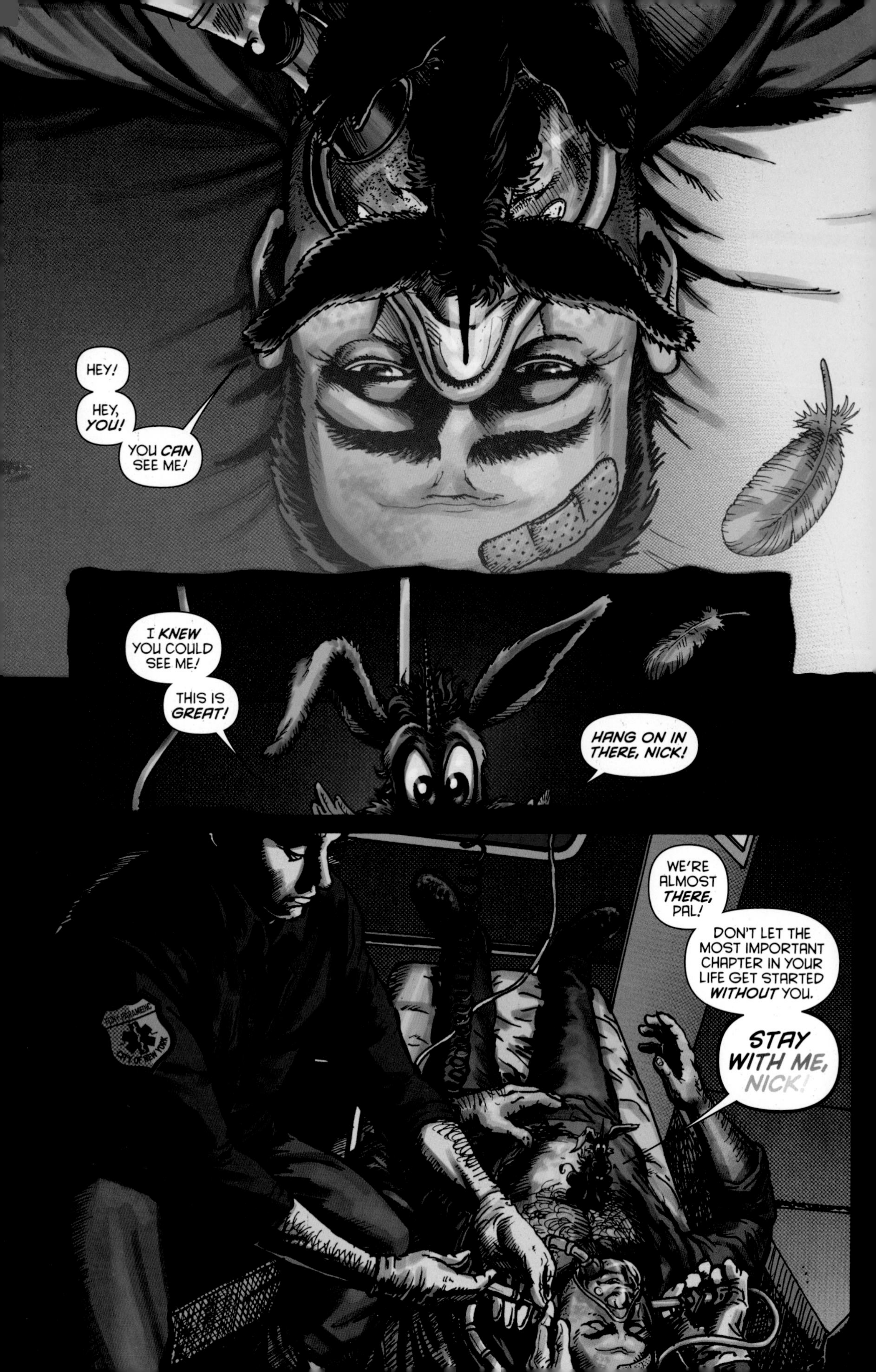
HEY!
HEY, YOU!
YOU CAN SEE ME!
I KNEW YOU COULD SEE ME!
THIS IS GREAT!
HANG ON IN THERE, NICK!
WE'RE ALMOST THERE, PAL!
DON'T LET THE MOST IMPORTANT CHAPTER IN YOUR LIFE GET STARTED WITHOUT YOU.
STAY WITH ME, NICK!

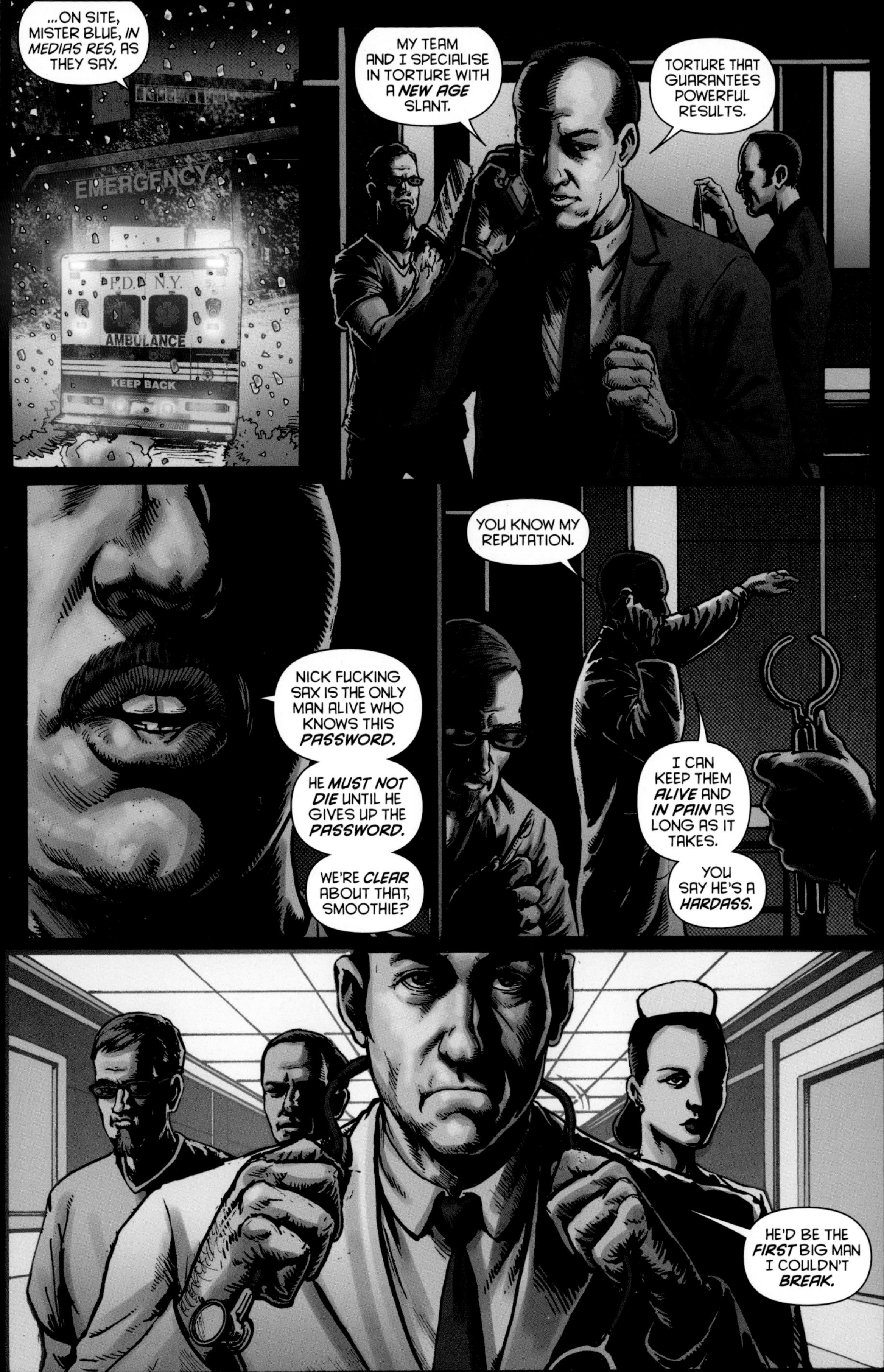
...ON SITE, MISTER BLUE, IN MEDIAS RES, AS THEY SAY.
EMERGENCY
F.D.N.Y.
AMBULANCE
KEEP BACK
MY TEAM AND I SPECIALISE IN TORTURE WITH A NEW AGE SLANT.
TORTURE THAT GUARANTEES POWERFUL RESULTS.
NICK FUCKING SAX IS THE ONLY MAN ALIVE WHO KNOWS THIS PASSWORD.
HE MUST NOT DIE UNTIL HE GIVES UP THE PASSWORD.
WE'RE CLEAR ABOUT THAT, SMOOTHIE?
YOU KNOW MY REPUTATION.
I CAN KEEP THEM ALIVE AND IN PAIN AS LONG AS IT TAKES.
YOU SAY HE'S A HARDASS.
HE'D BE THE FIRST BIG MAN I COULDN'T BREAK.

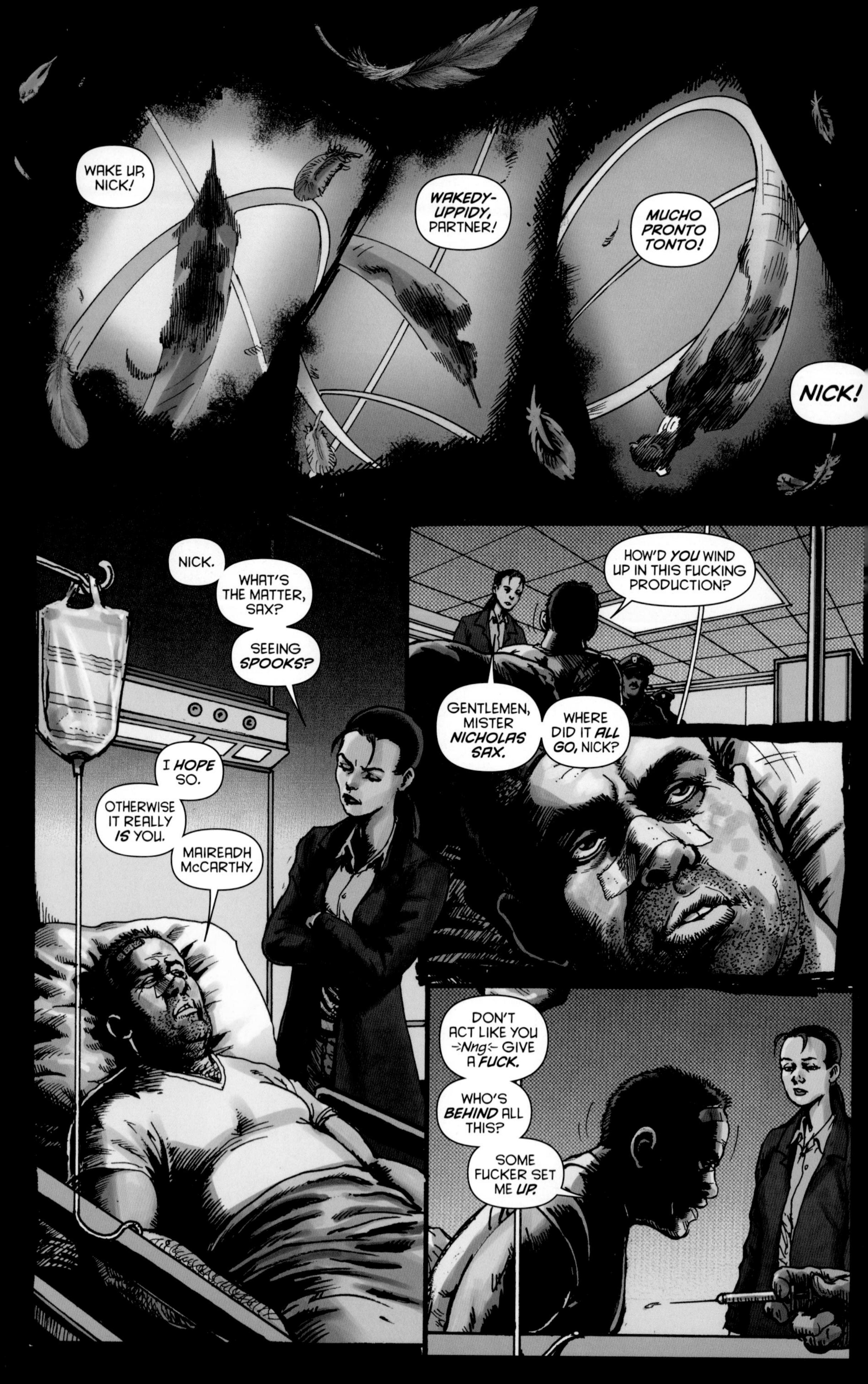
WAKE UP, NICK!
WAKEDY-UPPIDY, PARTNER!
MUCHO PRONTO TONTO!
NICK!
NICK.
WHAT'S THE MATTER, SAX?
SEEING SPOOKS?
I HOPE SO.
OTHERWISE IT REALLY IS YOU.
MAIREADH McCARTHY.
HOW'D YOU WIND UP IN THIS FUCKING PRODUCTION?
GENTLEMEN, MISTER NICHOLAS SAX.
WHERE DID IT ALL GO, NICK?
DON'T ACT LIKE YOU -Nng- GIVE A FUCK.
WHO'S BEHIND ALL THIS?
SOME FUCKER SET ME UP.

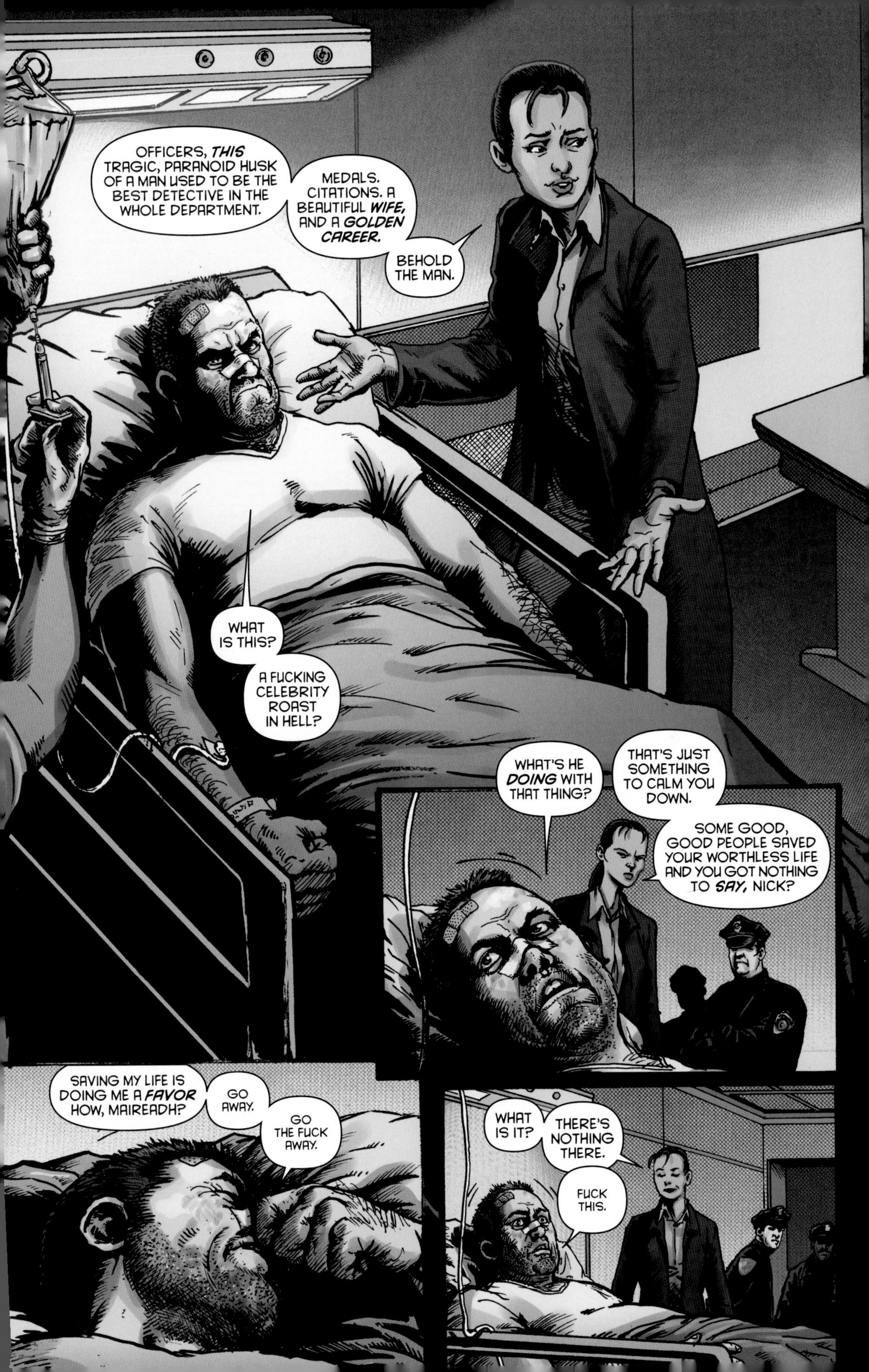
OFFICERS, THIS TRAGIC, PARANOID HUSK OF A MAN USED TO BE THE BEST DETECTIVE IN THE WHOLE DEPARTMENT.
MEDALS. CITATIONS. A BEAUTIFUL WIFE, AND A GOLDEN CAREER.
BEHOLD THE MAN.
WHAT IS THIS?
A FUCKING CELEBRITY ROAST IN HELL?
WHAT'S HE DOING WITH THAT THING?
THAT'S JUST SOMETHING TO CALM YOU DOWN.
SOME GOOD, GOOD PEOPLE SAVED YOUR WORTHLESS LIFE AND YOU GOT NOTHING TO SAY, NICK?
SAVING MY LIFE IS DOING ME A FAVOR HOW, MAIREADH?
GO AWAY.
GO THE FUCK AWAY.
WHAT IS IT?
THERE'S NOTHING THERE.
FUCK THIS.

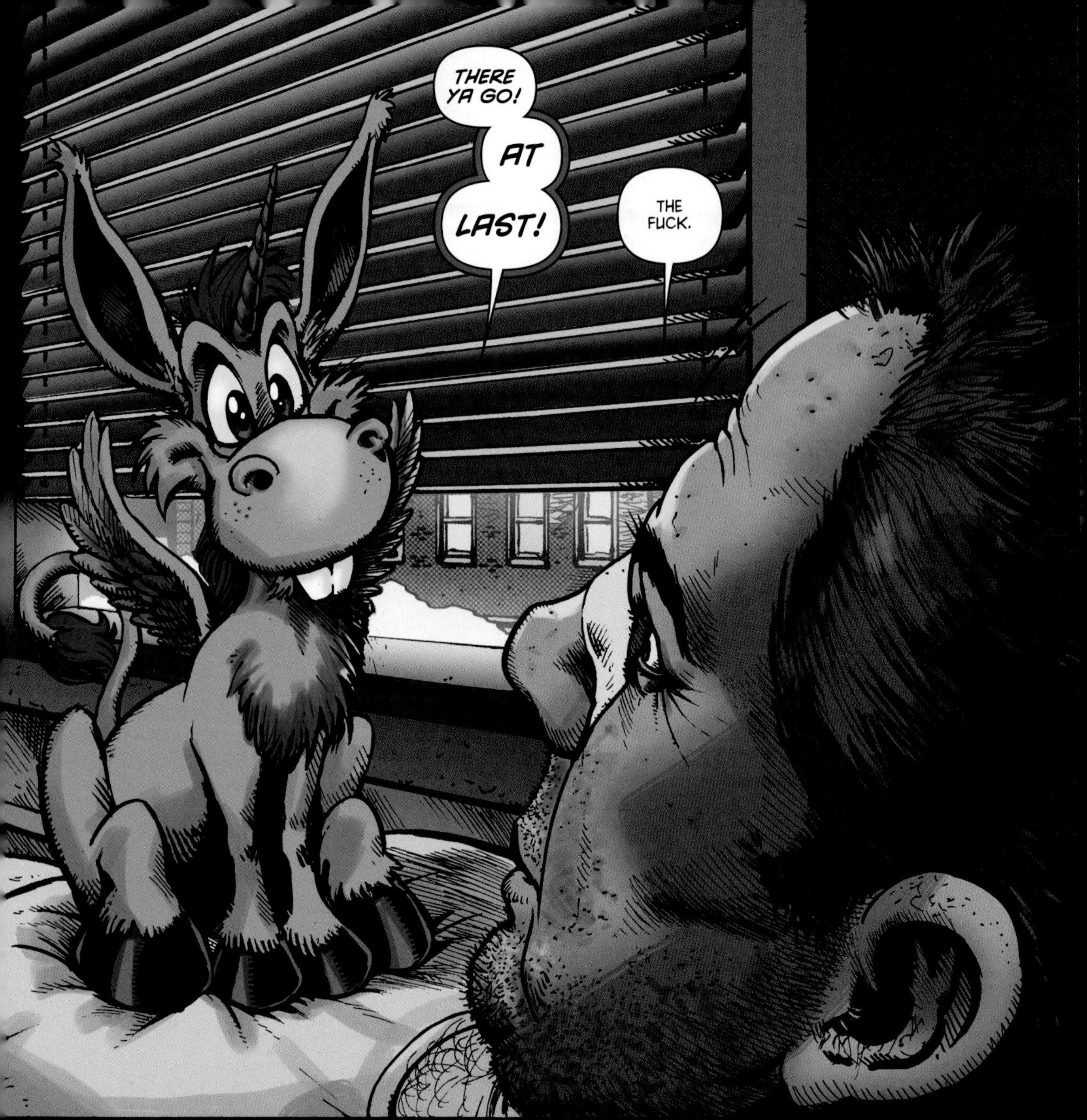
THERE YA GO!
AT LAST!
THE FUCK.

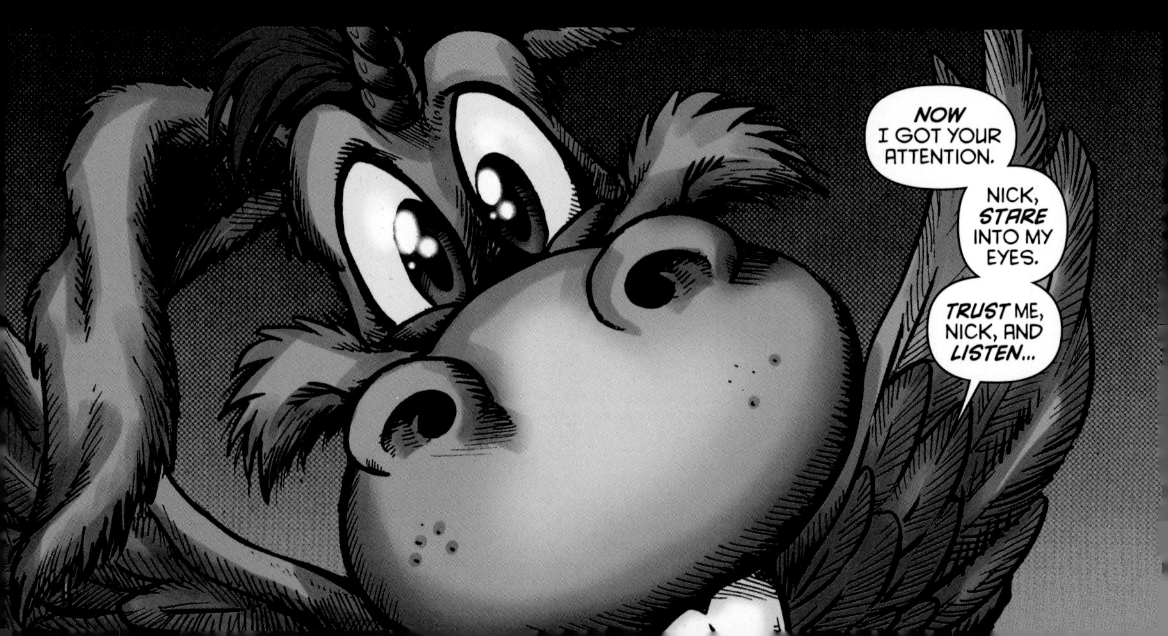
NOW I GOT YOUR ATTENTION.
NICK, STARE INTO MY EYES.
TRUST ME, NICK, AND LISTEN...

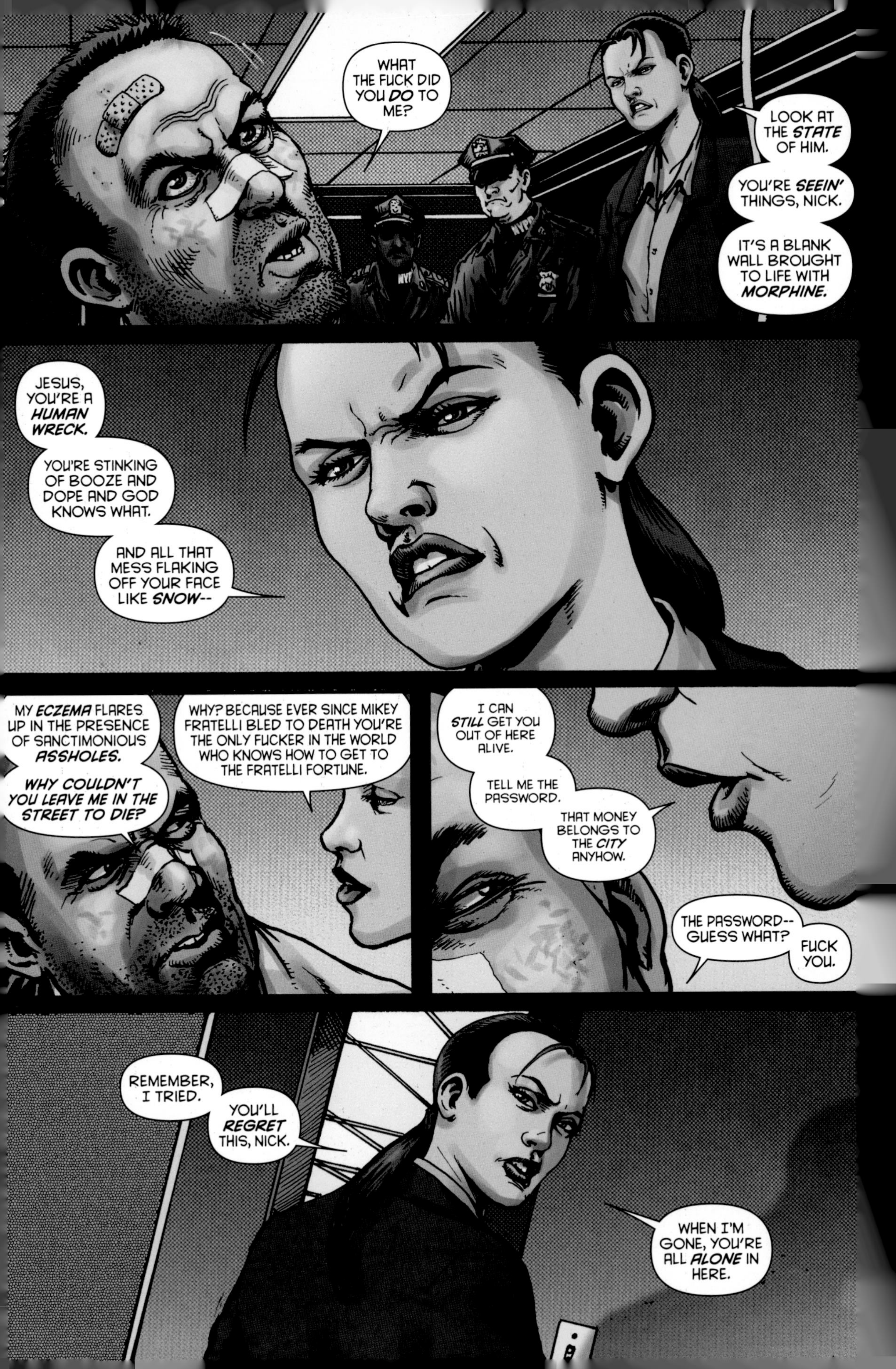
WHAT THE FUCK DID YOU DO TO ME?
LOOK AT THE STATE OF HIM.
YOU'RE SEEIN' THINGS, NICK.
IT'S A BLANK WALL BROUGHT TO LIFE WITH MORPHINE.
JESUS, YOU'RE A HUMAN WRECK.
YOU'RE STINKING OF BOOZE AND DOPE AND GOD KNOWS WHAT.
AND ALL THAT MESS FLAKING OFF YOUR FACE LIKE SNOW--
MY ECZEMA FLARES UP IN THE PRESENCE OF SANCTIMONIOUS ASSHOLES.
WHY COULDN'T YOU LEAVE ME IN THE STREET TO DIE?
WHY? BECAUSE EVER SINCE MIKEY FRATELLI BLED TO DEATH YOU'RE THE ONLY FUCKER IN THE WORLD WHO KNOWS HOW TO GET TO THE FRATELLI FORTUNE.
I CAN STILL GET YOU OUT OF HERE ALIVE.
TELL ME THE PASSWORD.
THAT MONEY BELONGS TO THE CITY ANYHOW.
THE PASSWORD-- GUESS WHAT?
FUCK YOU.
REMEMBER, I TRIED.
YOU'LL REGRET THIS, NICK.
WHEN I'M GONE, YOU'RE ALL ALONE IN HERE.

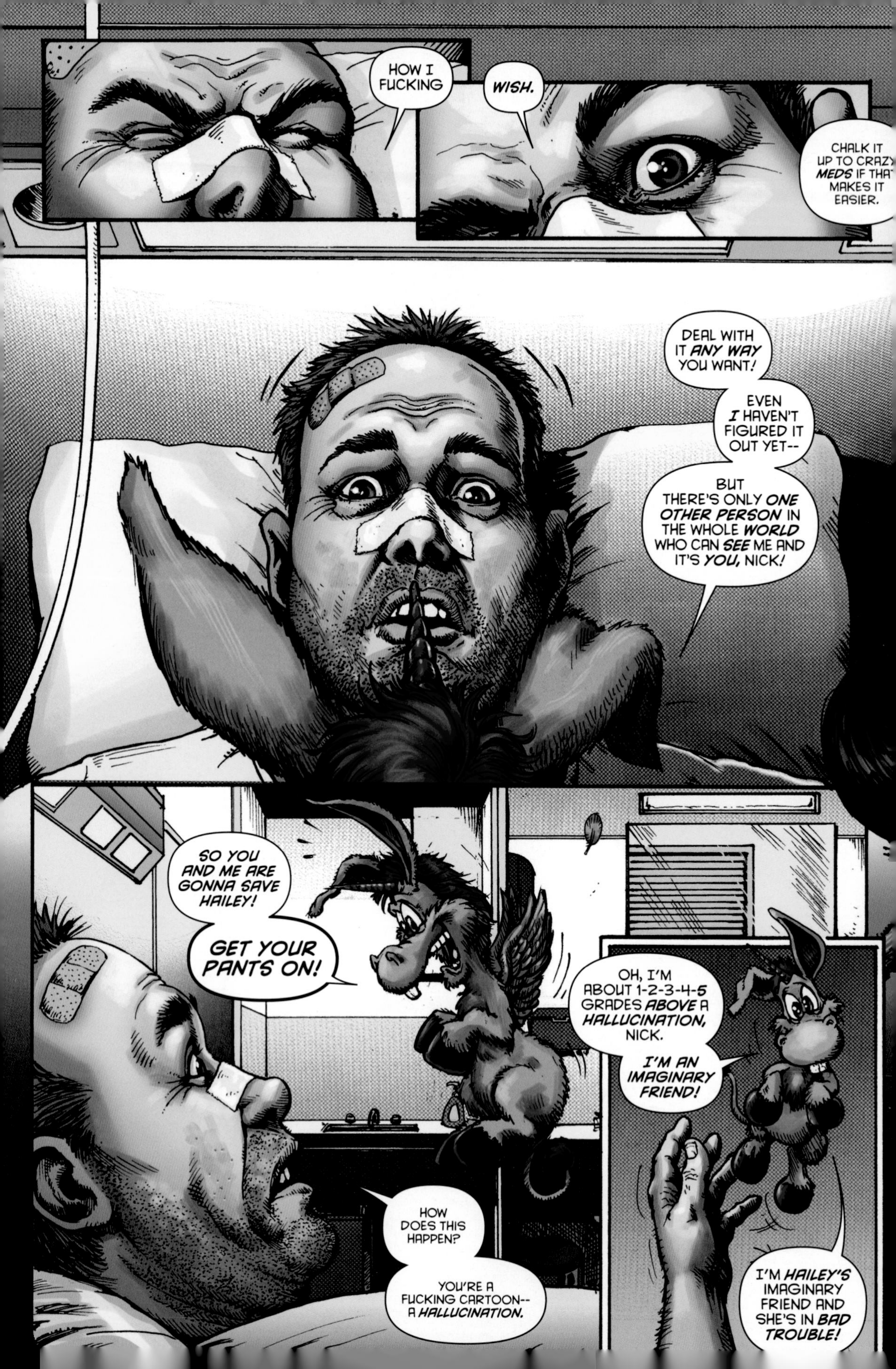
HOW I FUCKING
WISH.
CHALK IT UP TO CRAZY MEDS IF THAT MAKES IT EASIER.
DEAL WITH IT ANY WAY YOU WANT!
EVEN I HAVEN'T FIGURED IT OUT YET--
BUT THERE'S ONLY ONE OTHER PERSON IN THE WHOLE WORLD WHO CAN SEE ME AND IT'S YOU, NICK!
SO YOU AND ME ARE GONNA SAVE HAILEY!
GET YOUR PANTS ON!
HOW DOES THIS HAPPEN?
YOU'RE A FUCKING CARTOON-- A HALLUCINATION.
OH, I'M ABOUT 1-2-3-4-5 GRADES ABOVE A HALLUCINATION, NICK.
I'M AN IMAGINARY FRIEND!
I'M HAILEY'S IMAGINARY FRIEND AND SHE'S IN BAD TROUBLE!

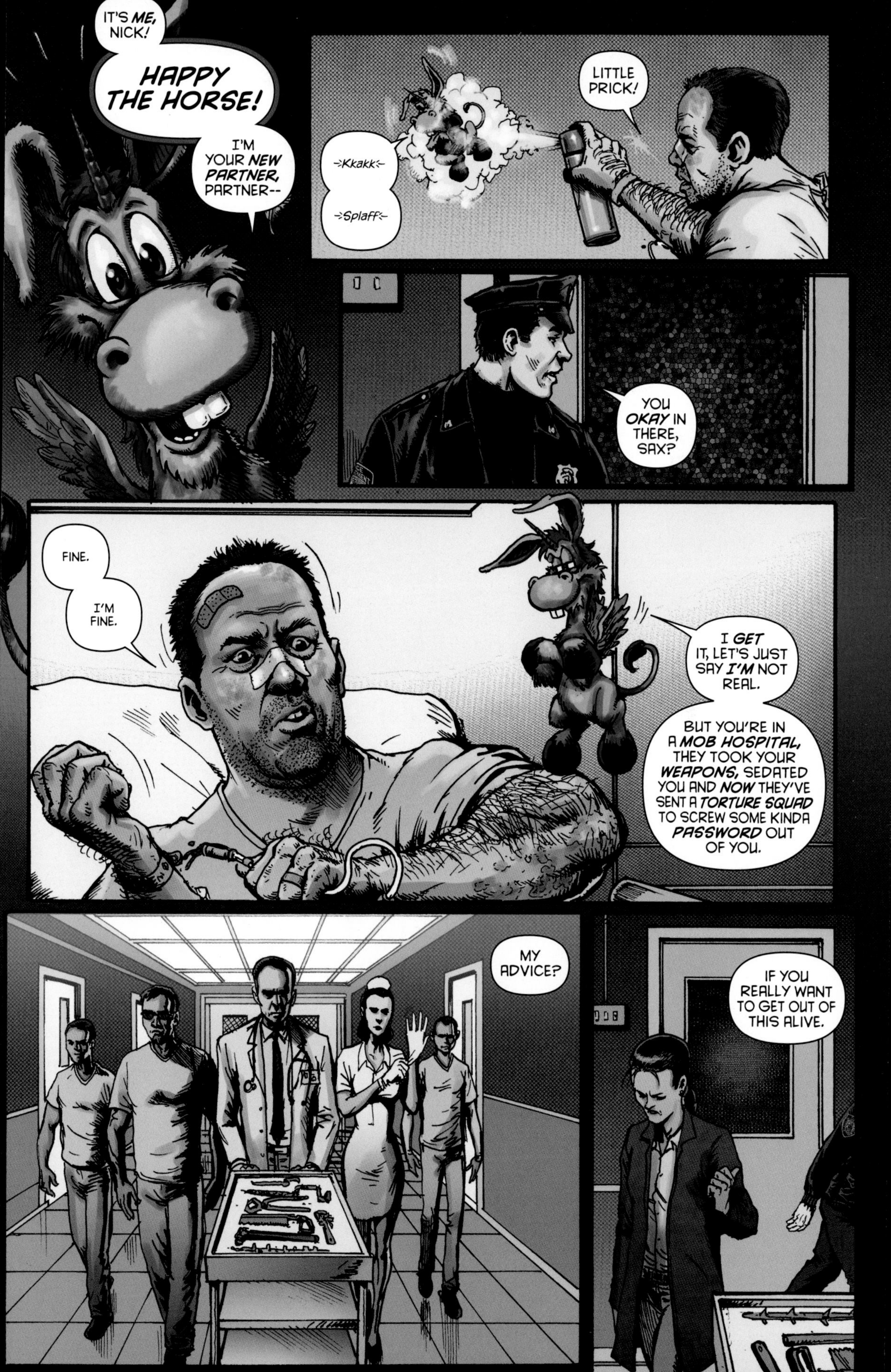
IT'S ME, NICK!
HAPPY THE HORSE!
I'M YOUR NEW PARTNER, PARTNER--
LITTLE PRICK!
-Kkakk-
-Splaff-
YOU OKAY IN THERE, SAX?
FINE.
I'M FINE.
I GET IT, LET'S JUST SAY I'M NOT REAL.
BUT YOU'RE IN A MOB HOSPITAL, THEY TOOK YOUR WEAPONS, SEDATED YOU AND NOW THEY'VE SENT A TORTURE SQUAD TO SCREW SOME KINDA PASSWORD OUT OF YOU.
MY ADVICE?
IF YOU REALLY WANT TO GET OUT OF THIS ALIVE.

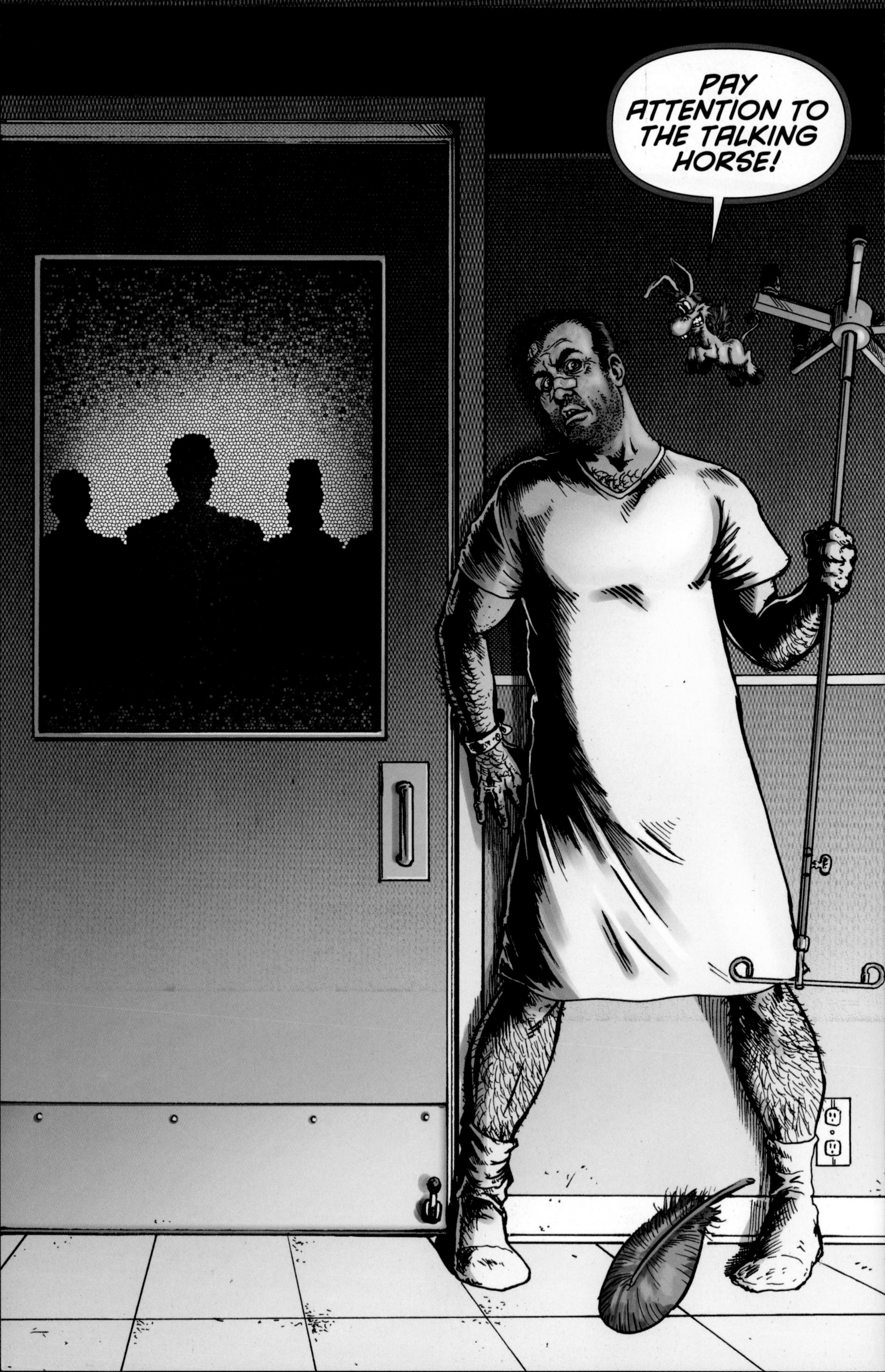
PAY ATTENTION TO THE TALKING HORSE!

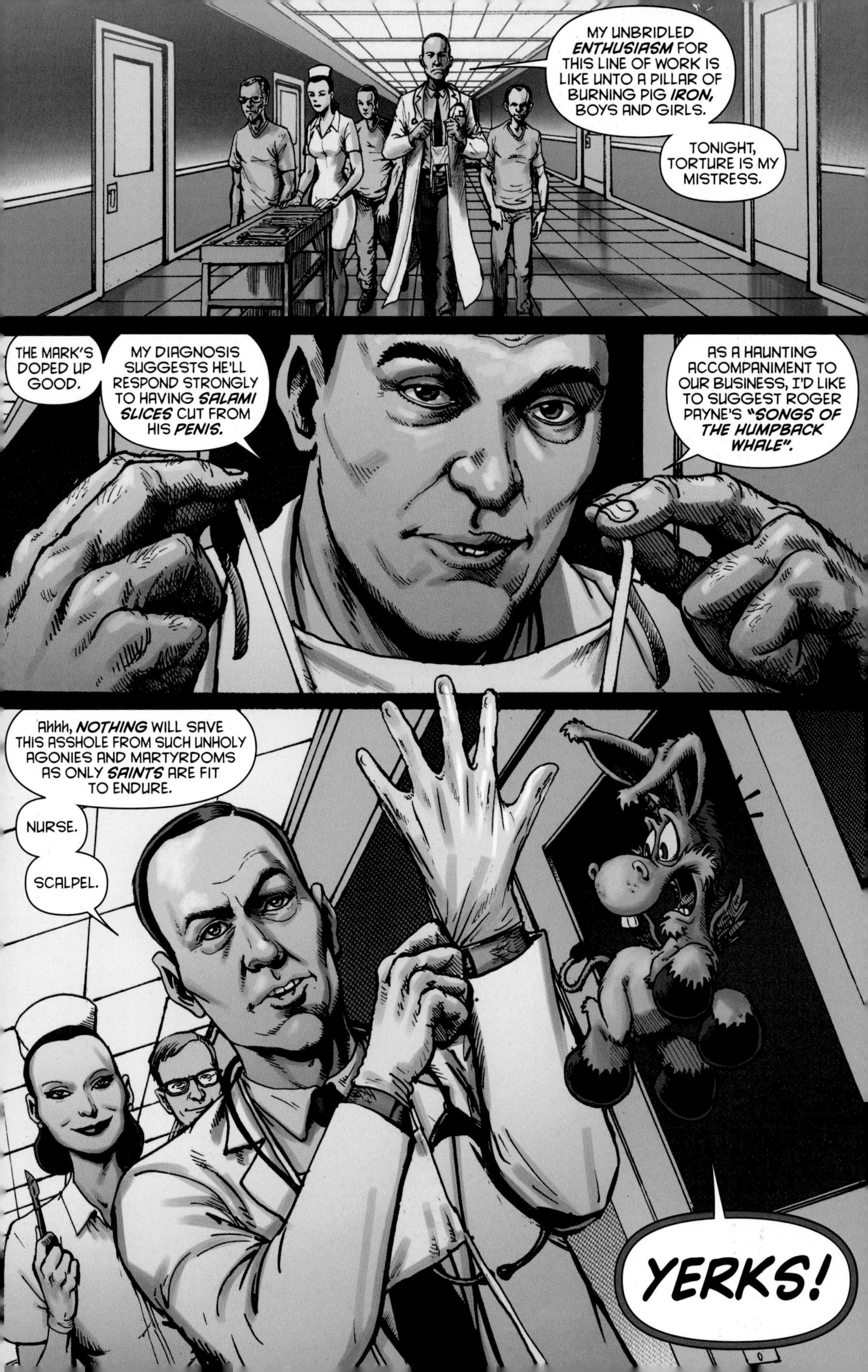

MY UNBRIDLED ENTHUSIASM FOR THIS LINE OF WORK IS LIKE UNTO A PILLAR OF BURNING PIG IRON, BOYS AND GIRLS.
TONIGHT, TORTURE IS MY MISTRESS.
THE MARK'S DOPED UP GOOD.
MY DIAGNOSIS SUGGESTS HE'LL RESPOND STRONGLY TO HAVING SALAMI SLICES CUT FROM HIS PENIS.
AS A HAUNTING ACCOMPANIMENT TO OUR BUSINESS, I'D LIKE TO SUGGEST ROGER PAYNE'S "SONGS OF THE HUMPBACK WHALE".
Ahhh, NOTHING WILL SAVE THIS ASSHOLE FROM SUCH UNHOLY AGONIES AND MARTYRDOMS AS ONLY SAINTS ARE FIT TO ENDURE.
NURSE.
SCALPEL.
YERKS!

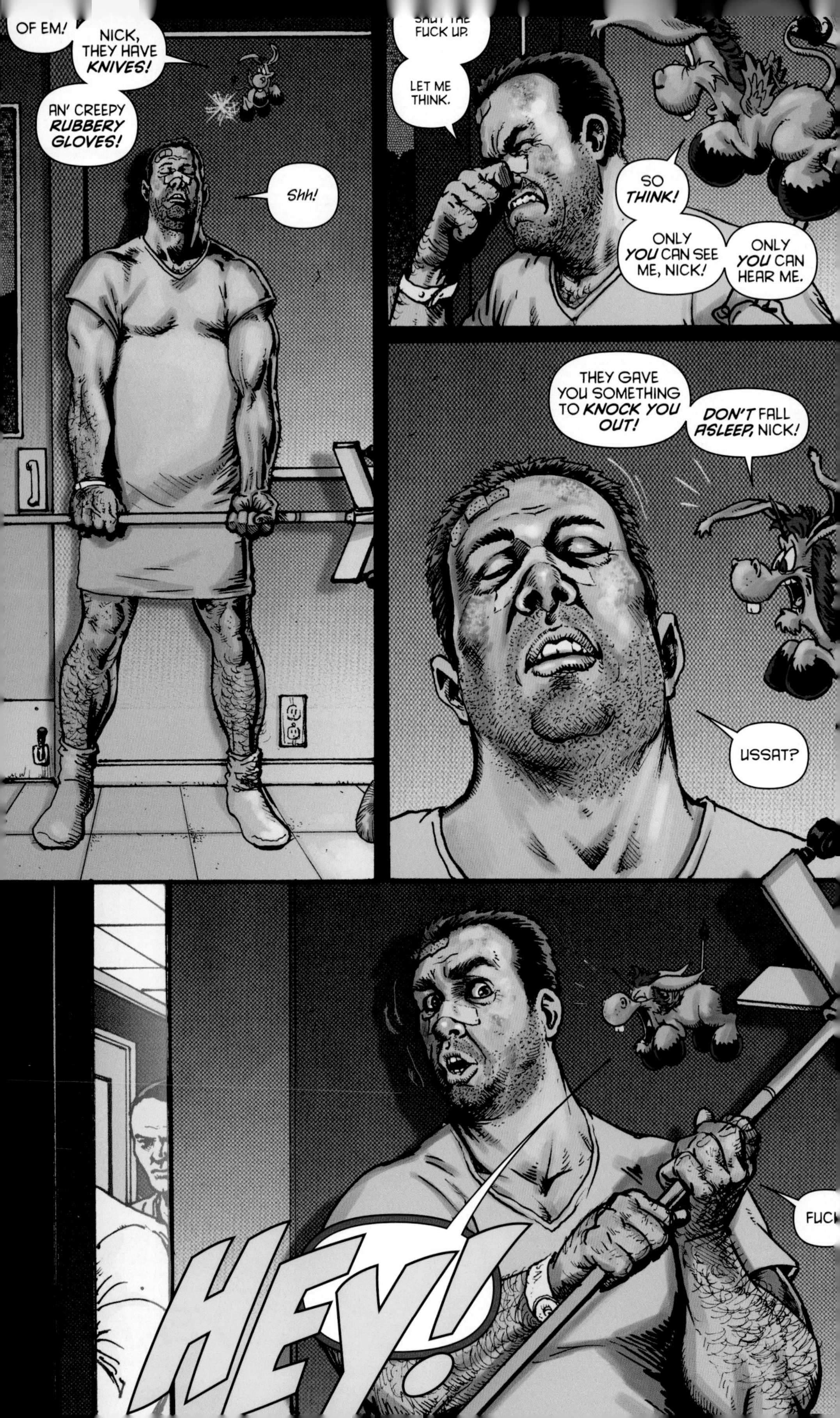
OF EM!
NICK, THEY HAVE KNIVES!
AN' CREEPY RUBBERY GLOVES!
Shh!
SHUT THE FUCK UP.
LET ME THINK.
SO THINK!
ONLY YOU CAN SEE ME, NICK!
ONLY YOU CAN HEAR ME.
THEY GAVE YOU SOMETHING TO KNOCK YOU OUT!
DON'T FALL ASLEEP, NICK!
USSAT?
HEY!
FUCK

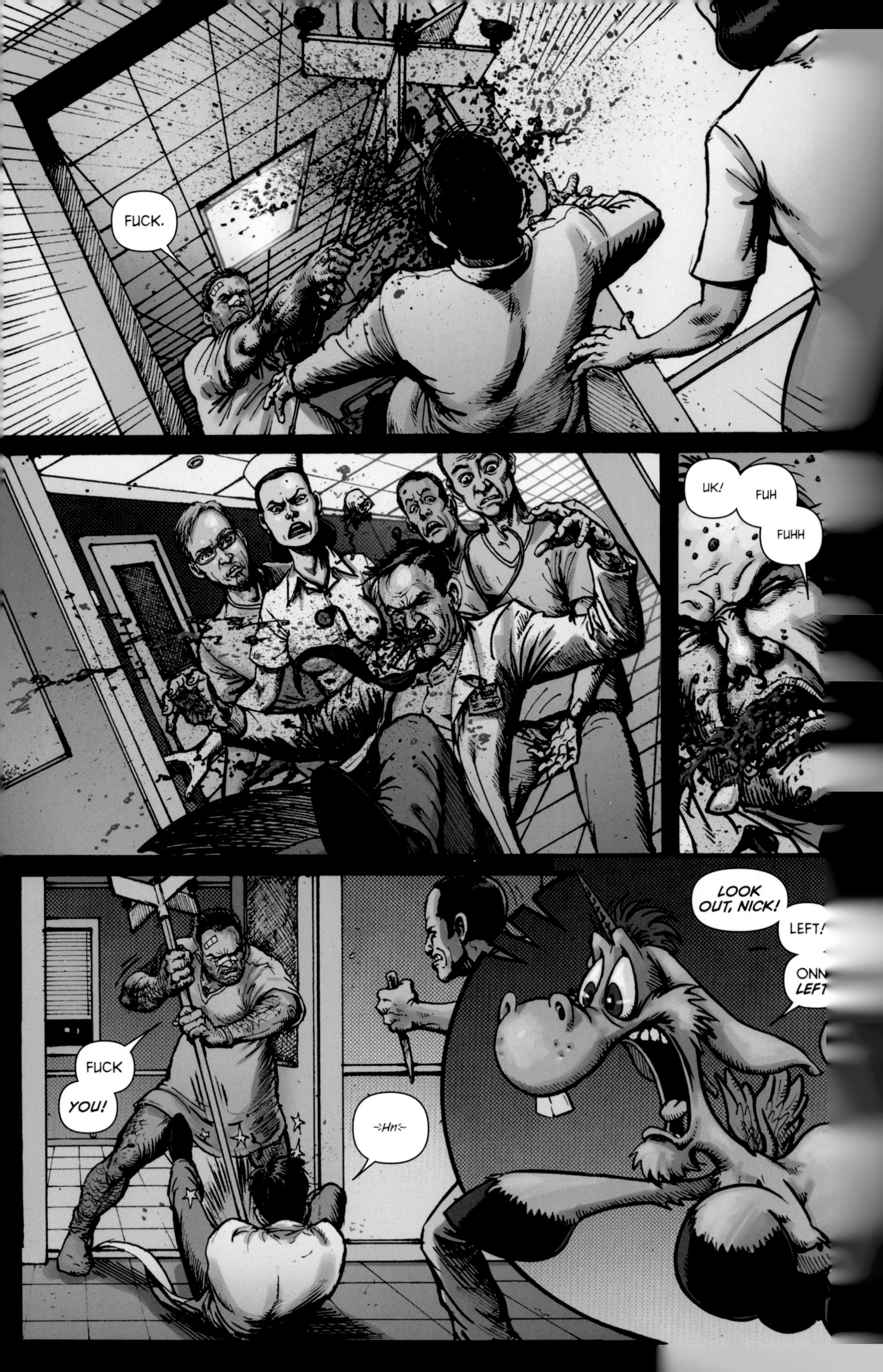
FUCK.
UK!
FUH
FUHH
FUCK
YOU!
-Hn-
LOOK OUT, NICK!
LEFT!

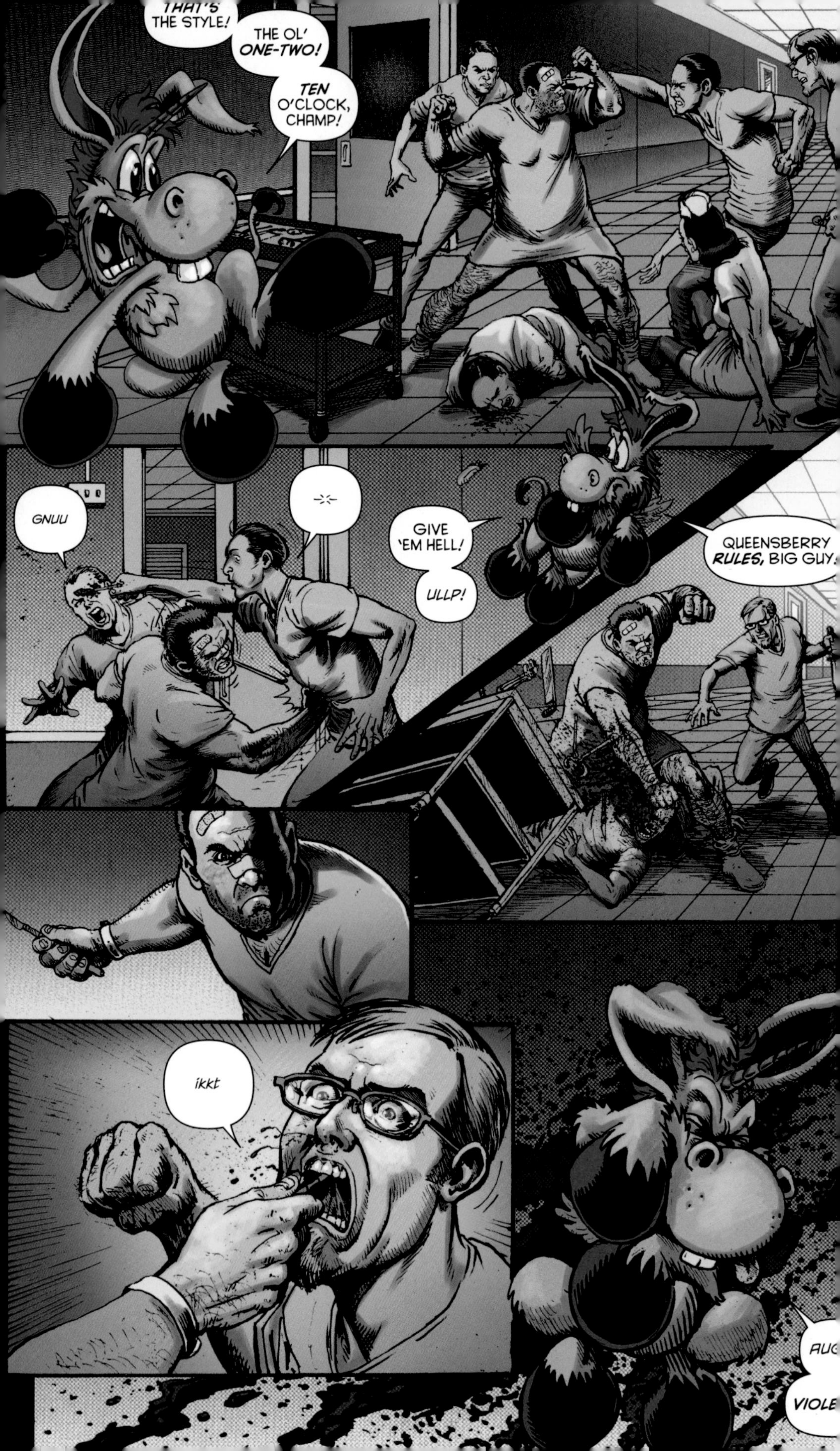
THAT'S THE STYLE!
THE OL' ONE-TWO!
TEN O'CLOCK, CHAMP!
GNUU
-¦-
GIVE 'EM HELL!
ULLP!
QUEENSBERRY RULES, BIG GUY.
ikkt

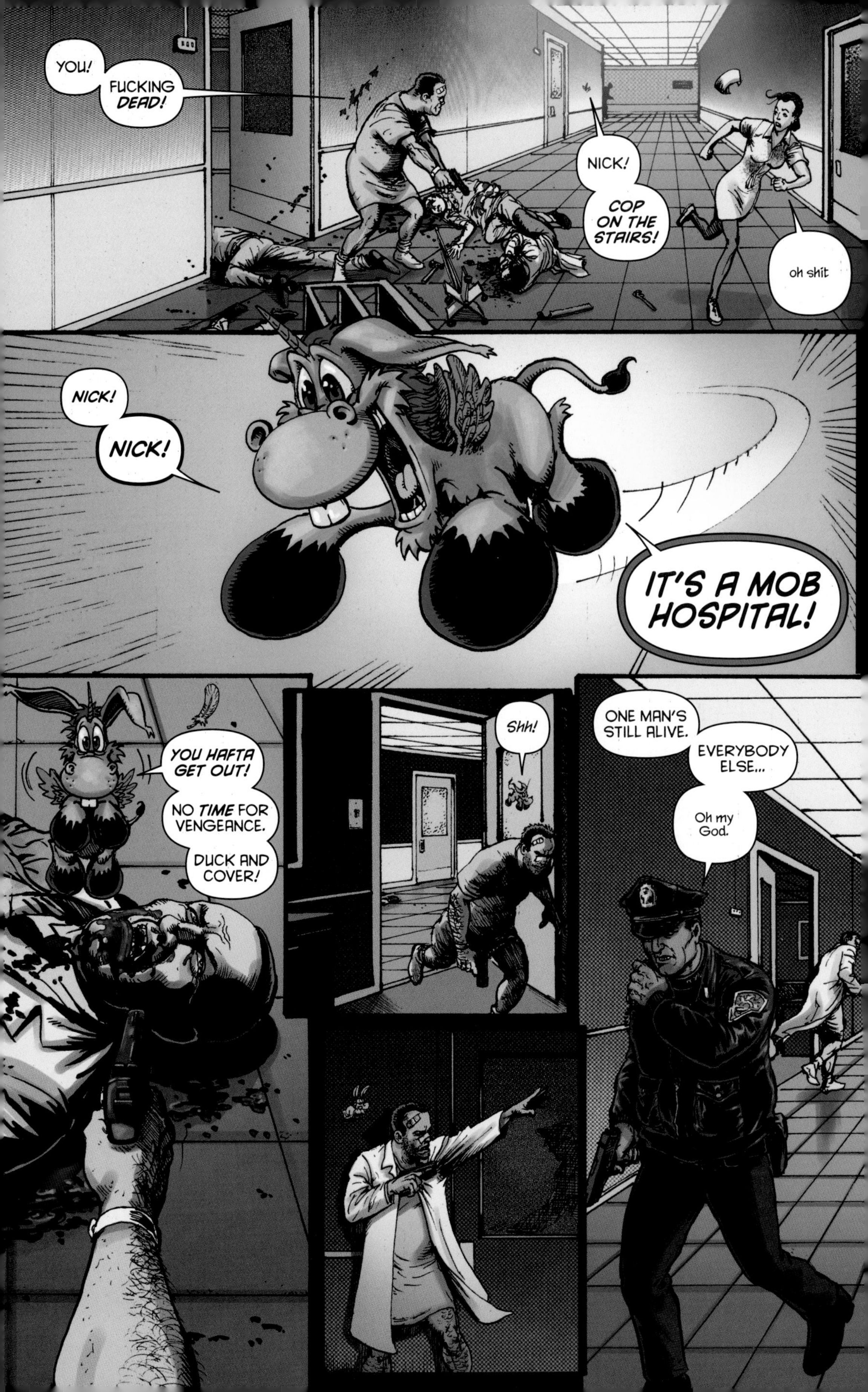
YOU!
FUCKING DEAD!
NICK!
COP ON THE STAIRS!
oh shit
NICK!
NICK!
IT'S A MOB HOSPITAL!
YOU HAFTA GET OUT!
NO TIME FOR VENGEANCE.
DUCK AND COVER!
Shh!
ONE MAN'S STILL ALIVE.
EVERYBODY ELSE...
Oh my God.

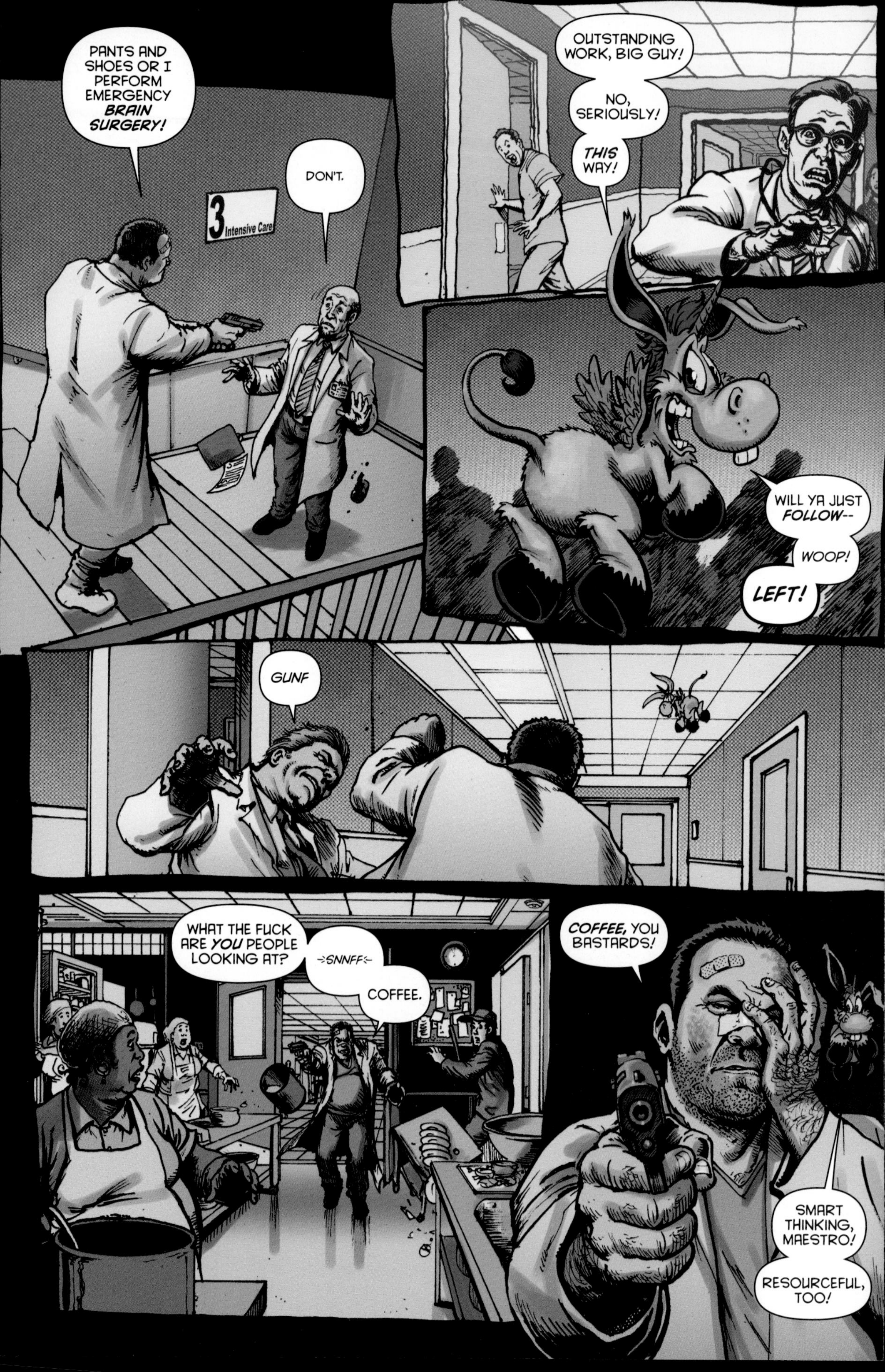
PANTS AND SHOES OR I PERFORM EMERGENCY *BRAIN SURGERY!*
3 Intensive Care
DON'T.
OUTSTANDING WORK, BIG GUY!
NO, SERIOUSLY!
THIS WAY!
WILL YA JUST *FOLLOW*--
WOOP!
LEFT!
GUNF
WHAT THE FUCK ARE *YOU* PEOPLE LOOKING AT?
SNNFF
COFFEE.
COFFEE, YOU BASTARDS!
SMART THINKING, MAESTRO!
RESOURCEFUL, TOO!

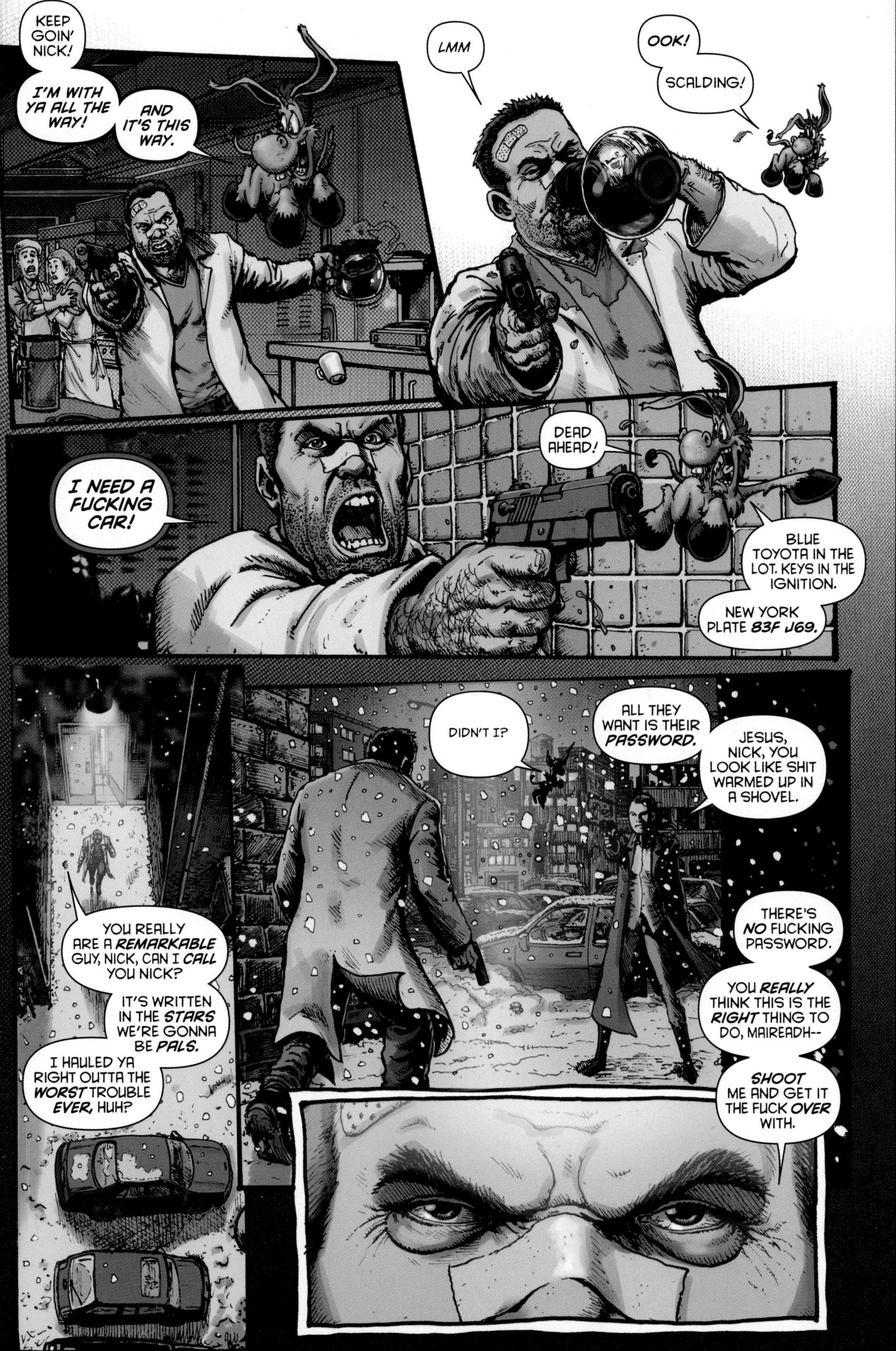
KEEP GOIN' NICK!
I'M WITH YA ALL THE WAY!
AND IT'S THIS WAY.
LMM
OOK!
SCALDING!
I NEED A FUCKING CAR!
DEAD AHEAD!
BLUE TOYOTA IN THE LOT. KEYS IN THE IGNITION.
NEW YORK PLATE 83F J69.
YOU REALLY ARE A REMARKABLE GUY, NICK, CAN I CALL YOU NICK?
IT'S WRITTEN IN THE STARS WE'RE GONNA BE PALS.
I HAULED YA RIGHT OUTTA THE WORST TROUBLE EVER, HUH?
DIDN'T I?
ALL THEY WANT IS THEIR PASSWORD.
JESUS, NICK, YOU LOOK LIKE SHIT WARMED UP IN A SHOVEL.
THERE'S NO FUCKING PASSWORD.
YOU REALLY THINK THIS IS THE RIGHT THING TO DO, MAIREADH--
SHOOT ME AND GET IT THE FUCK OVER WITH.

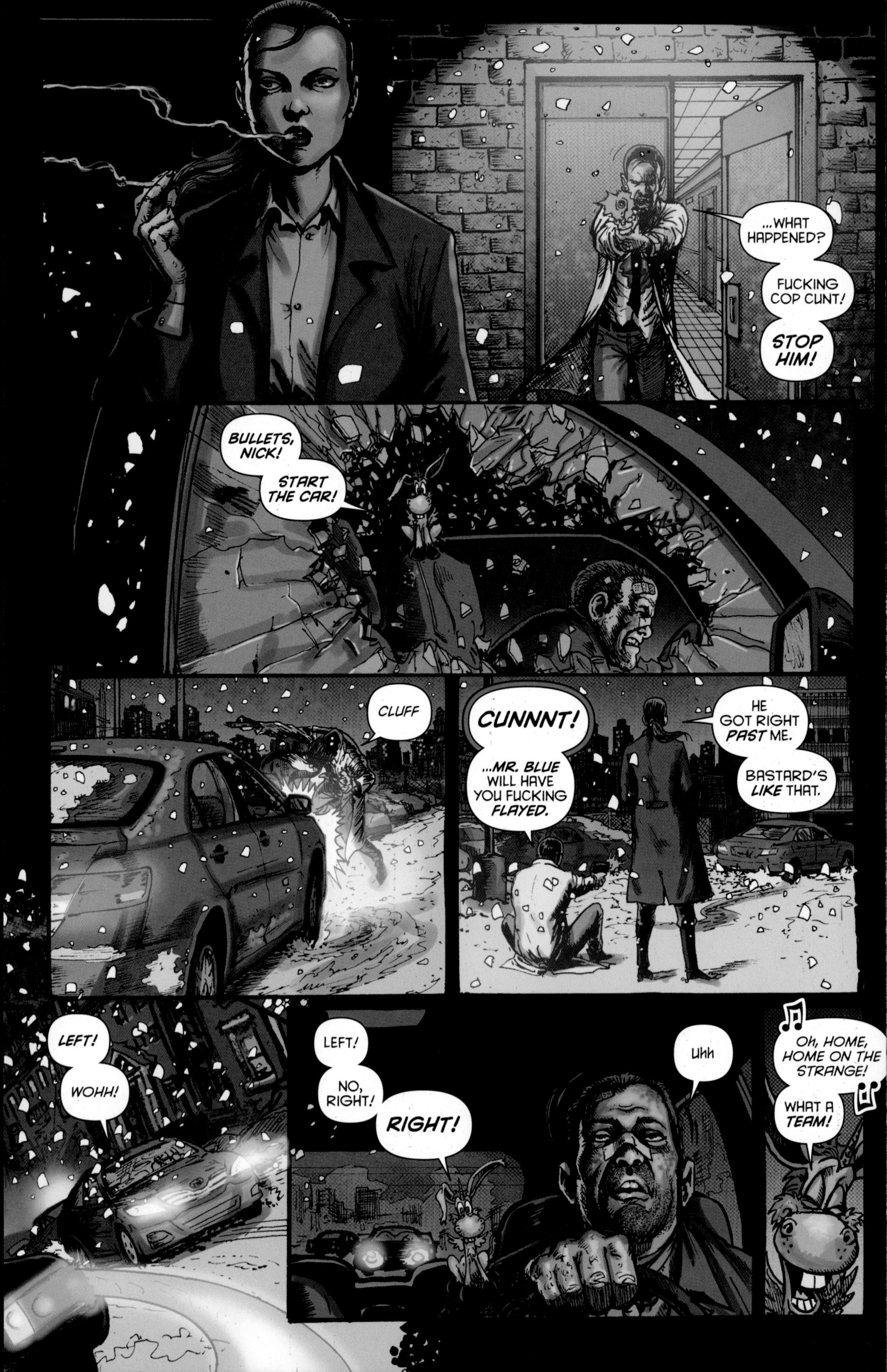
...WHAT HAPPENED?
FUCKING COP CUNT!
STOP HIM!
BULLETS, NICK!
START THE CAR!
CLUFF
CUNNNT!
...MR. BLUE WILL HAVE YOU FUCKING FLAYED.
HE GOT RIGHT PAST ME.
BASTARD'S LIKE THAT.
LEFT!
WOHH!
LEFT!
NO, RIGHT!
RIGHT!
Uhh
Oh, HOME, HOME ON THE STRANGE!
WHAT A TEAM!

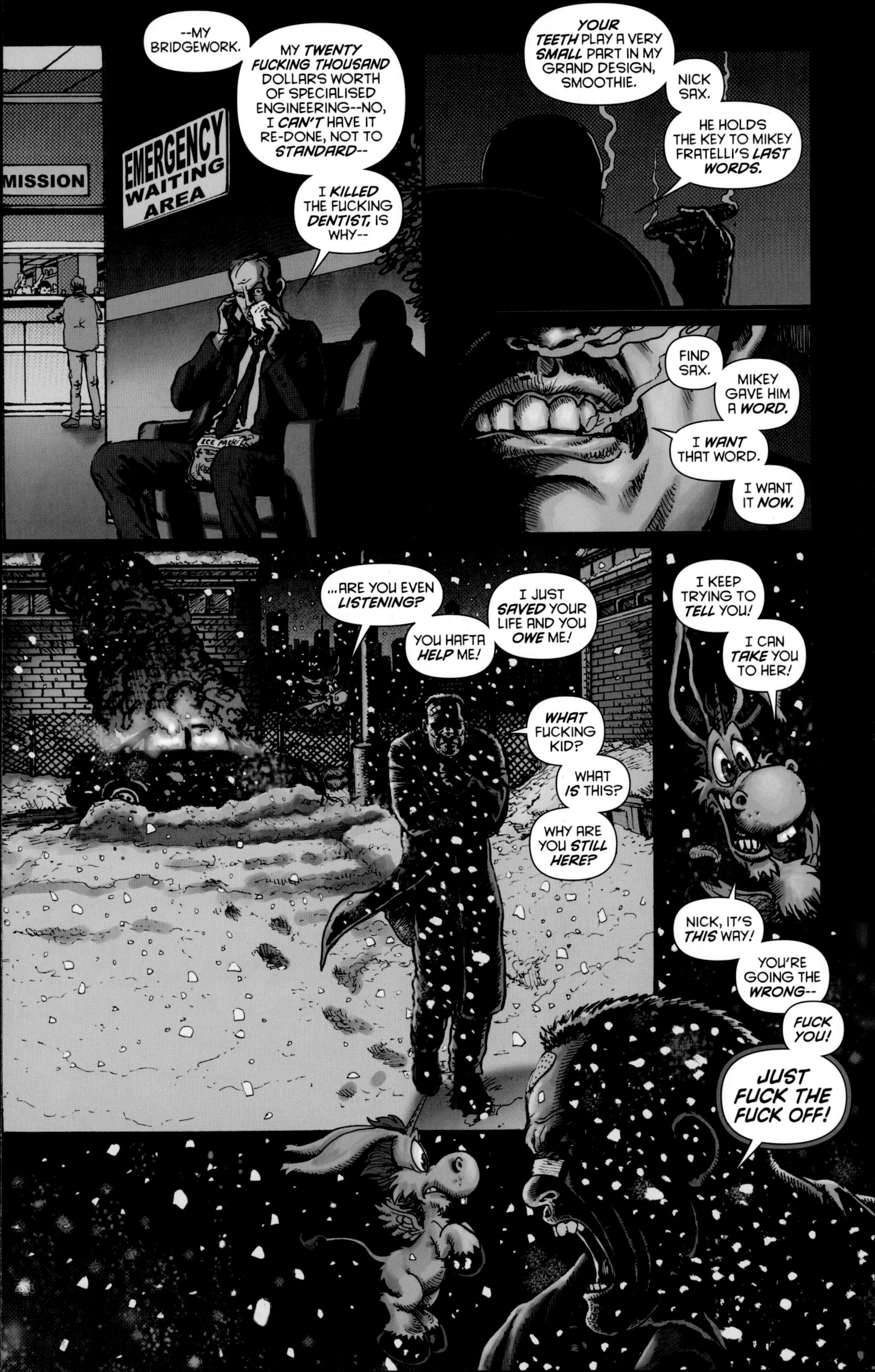
--MY BRIDGEWORK.
MY TWENTY FUCKING THOUSAND DOLLARS WORTH OF SPECIALISED ENGINEERING--NO, I CAN'T HAVE IT RE-DONE, NOT TO STANDARD--
I KILLED THE FUCKING DENTIST, IS WHY--
MISSION
EMERGENCY WAITING AREA
ICE PACK
YOUR TEETH PLAY A VERY SMALL PART IN MY GRAND DESIGN, SMOOTHIE.
NICK SAX.
HE HOLDS THE KEY TO MIKEY FRATELLI'S LAST WORDS.
FIND SAX.
MIKEY GAVE HIM A WORD.
I WANT THAT WORD.
I WANT IT NOW.
...ARE YOU EVEN LISTENING?
YOU HAFTA HELP ME!
I JUST SAVED YOUR LIFE AND YOU OWE ME!
I KEEP TRYING TO TELL YOU!
I CAN TAKE YOU TO HER!
WHAT FUCKING KID?
WHAT IS THIS?
WHY ARE YOU STILL HERE?
NICK, IT'S THIS WAY!
YOU'RE GOING THE WRONG--
FUCK YOU!
JUST FUCK THE FUCK OFF!

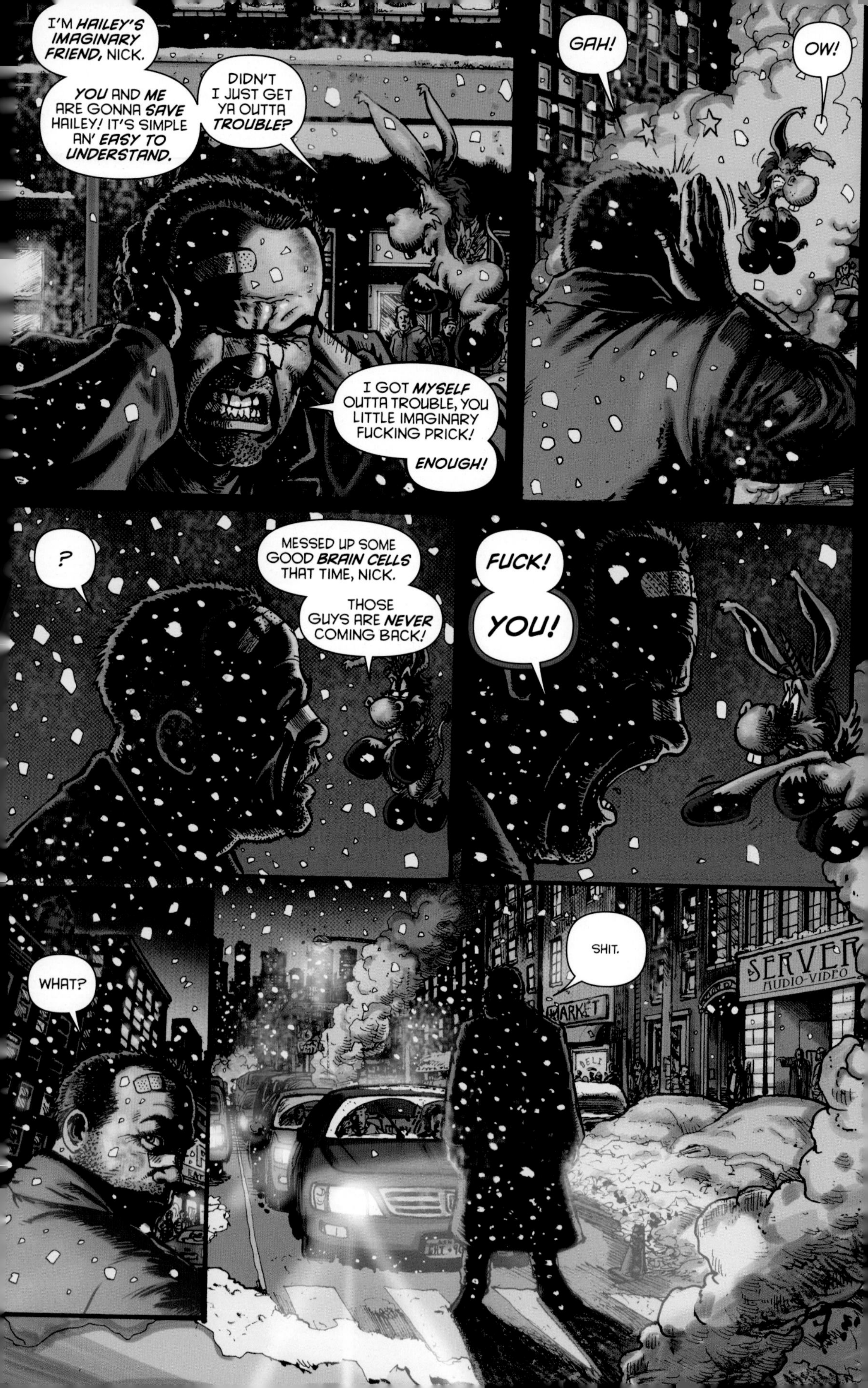

I'M HAILEY'S IMAGINARY FRIEND, NICK.
YOU AND ME ARE GONNA SAVE HAILEY! IT'S SIMPLE AN' EASY TO UNDERSTAND.
DIDN'T I JUST GET YA OUTTA TROUBLE?
I GOT MYSELF OUTTA TROUBLE, YOU LITTLE IMAGINARY FUCKING PRICK!
ENOUGH!
GAH!
OW!
?
MESSED UP SOME GOOD BRAIN CELLS THAT TIME, NICK.
THOSE GUYS ARE NEVER COMING BACK!
FUCK!
YOU!
WHAT?
SHIT.
MARKET
SERVER
AUDIO-VIDEO
DELI

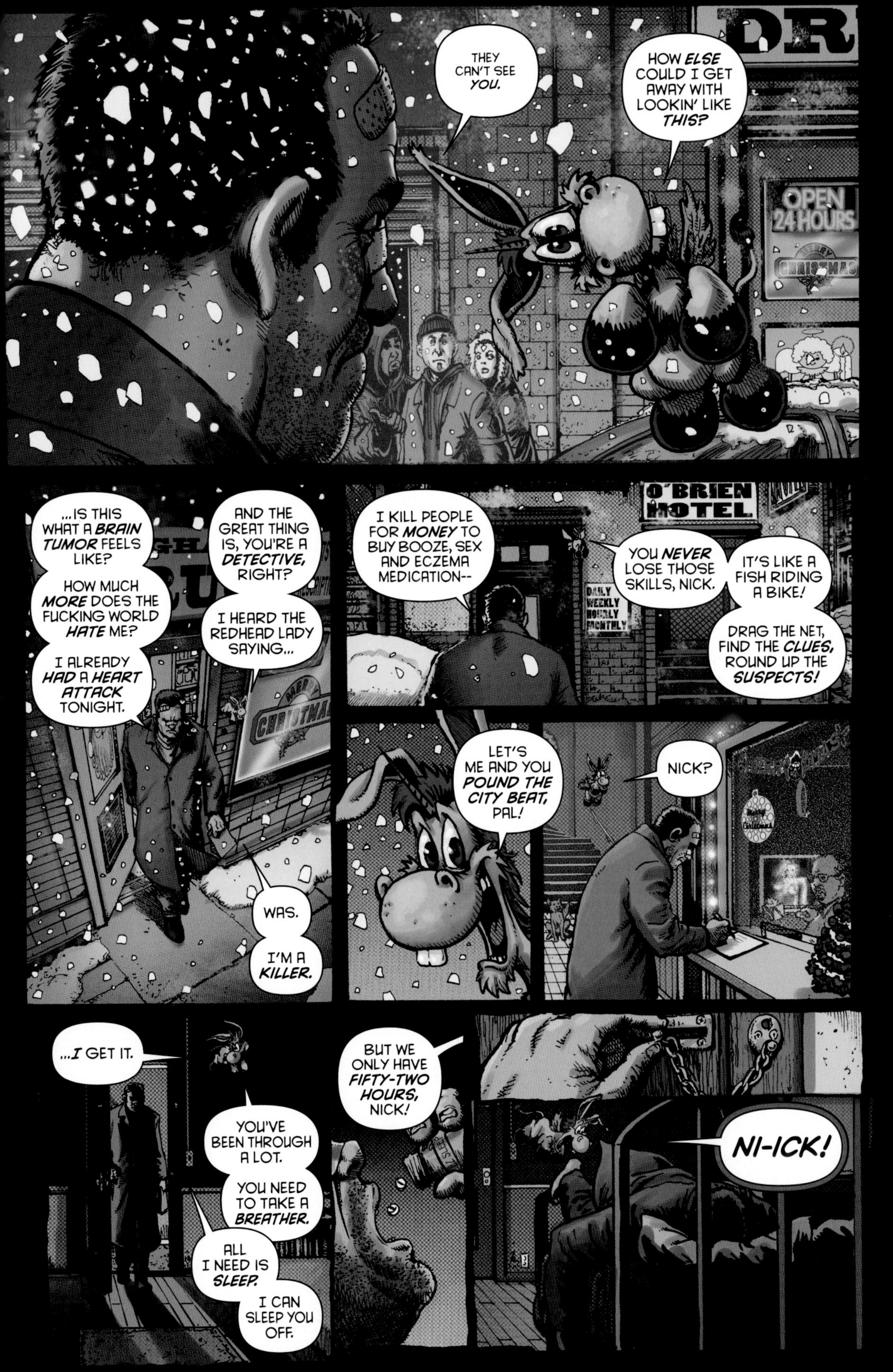
DR
THEY CAN'T SEE *YOU.*
HOW *ELSE* COULD I GET AWAY WITH LOOKIN' LIKE *THIS?*
OPEN 24 HOURS
MERRY CHRISTMAS
...IS THIS WHAT A *BRAIN TUMOR* FEELS LIKE?
HOW MUCH *MORE* DOES THE FUCKING WORLD *HATE* ME?
I ALREADY *HAD A HEART ATTACK* TONIGHT.
AND THE GREAT THING IS, YOU'RE A *DETECTIVE,* RIGHT?
I HEARD THE REDHEAD LADY SAYING...
MERRY CHRISTMAS
WAS.
I'M A *KILLER.*
O'BRIEN HOTEL
I KILL PEOPLE FOR *MONEY* TO BUY BOOZE, SEX AND ECZEMA MEDICATION--
DAILY WEEKLY HOURLY MONTHLY
YOU *NEVER* LOSE THOSE SKILLS, NICK.
IT'S LIKE A FISH RIDING A BIKE!
DRAG THE NET, FIND THE *CLUES,* ROUND UP THE *SUSPECTS!*
LET'S ME AND YOU *POUND THE CITY BEAT,* PAL!
NICK?
...*I* GET IT.
YOU'VE BEEN THROUGH A LOT.
YOU NEED TO TAKE A *BREATHER.*
ALL I NEED IS *SLEEP.*
I CAN SLEEP YOU OFF.
BUT WE ONLY HAVE *FIFTY-TWO HOURS,* NICK!
NI-ICK!

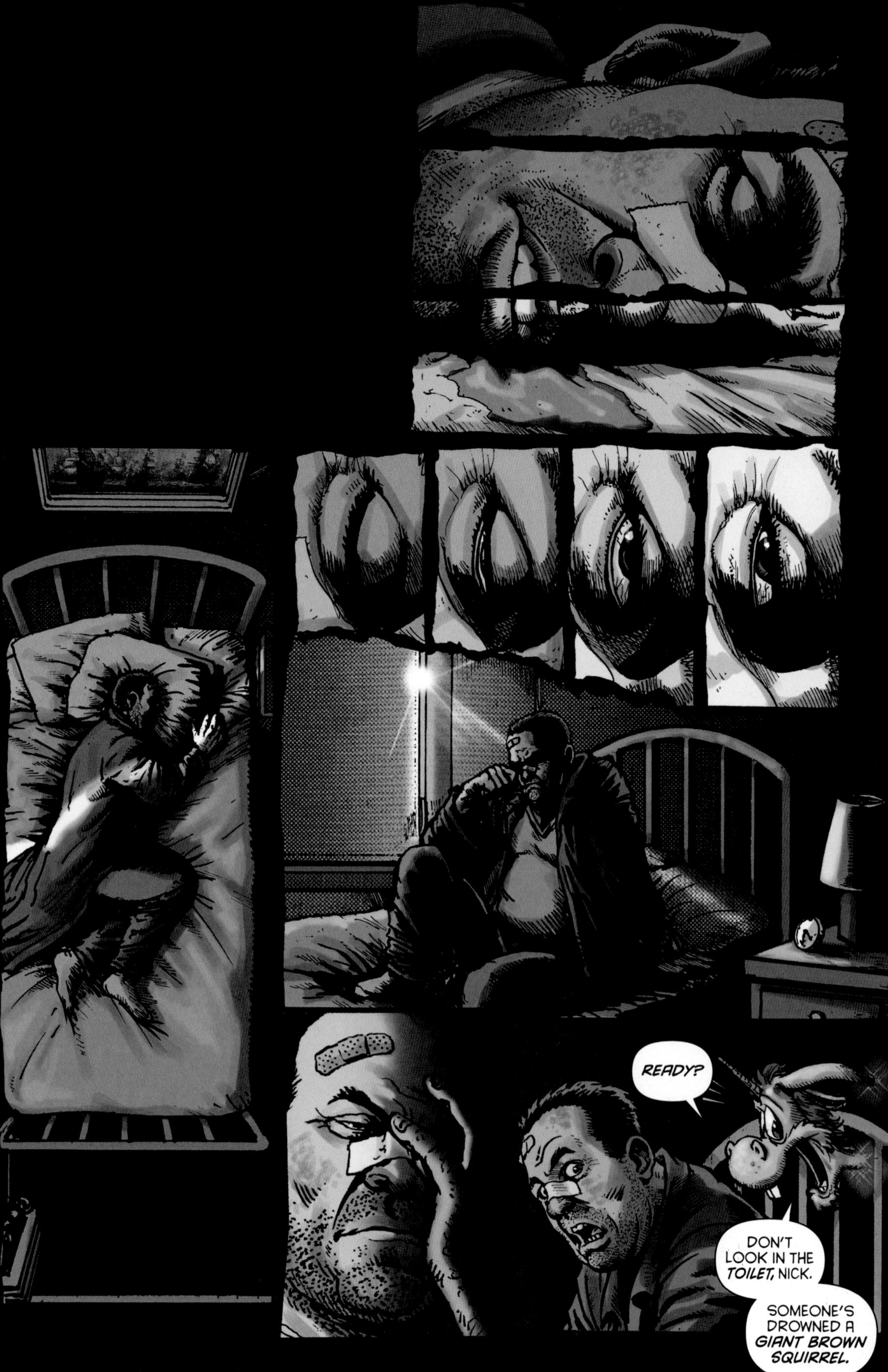
READY?
DON'T LOOK IN THE TOILET, NICK.
SOMEONE'S DROWNED A GIANT BROWN SQUIRREL.

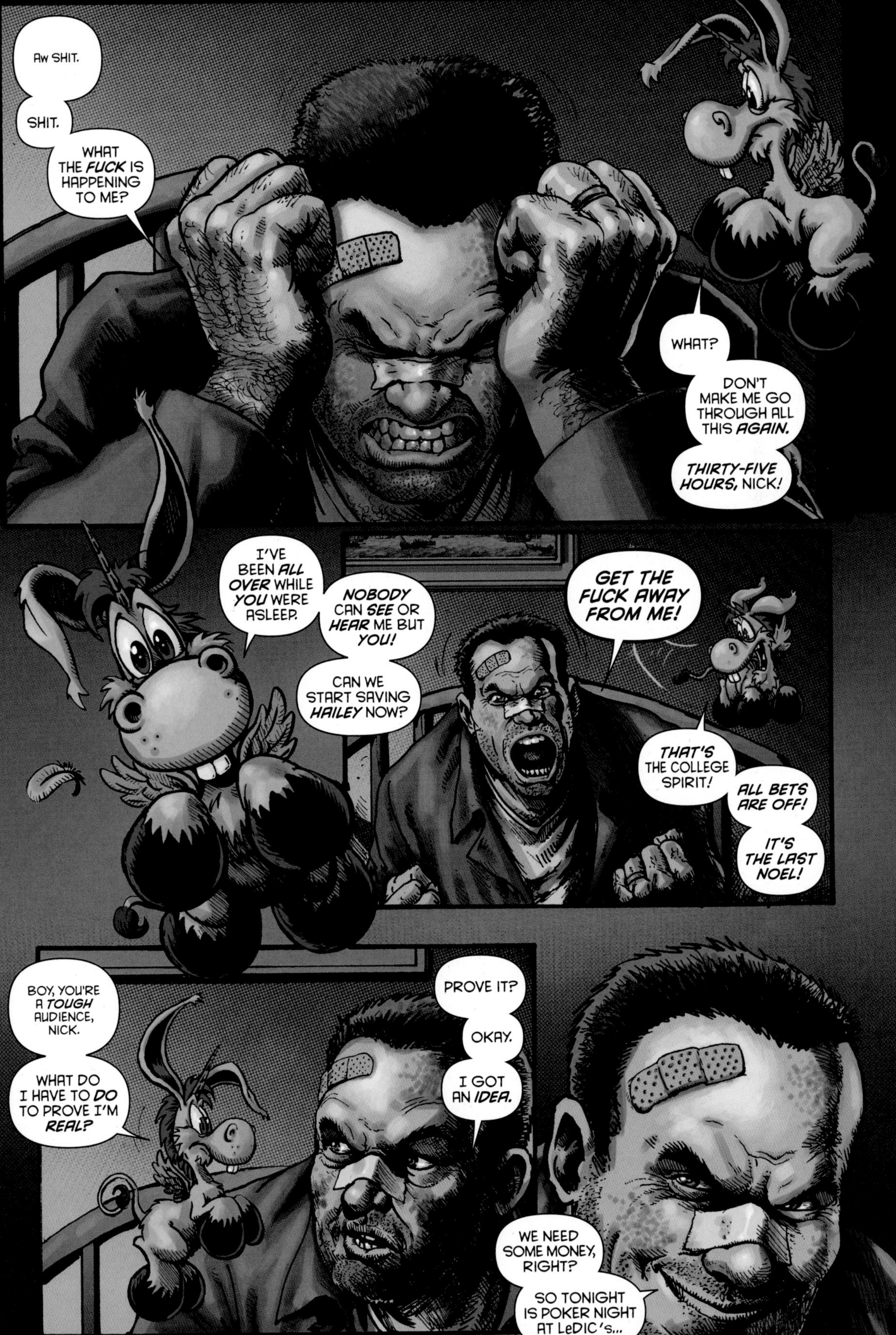
AW SHIT.
SHIT.
WHAT THE FUCK IS HAPPENING TO ME?
WHAT?
DON'T MAKE ME GO THROUGH ALL THIS AGAIN.
THIRTY-FIVE HOURS, NICK!
I'VE BEEN ALL OVER WHILE YOU WERE ASLEEP.
NOBODY CAN SEE OR HEAR ME BUT YOU!
CAN WE START SAVING HAILEY NOW?
GET THE FUCK AWAY FROM ME!
THAT'S THE COLLEGE SPIRIT!
ALL BETS ARE OFF!
IT'S THE LAST NOEL!
BOY, YOU'RE A TOUGH AUDIENCE, NICK.
WHAT DO I HAVE TO DO TO PROVE I'M REAL?
PROVE IT?
OKAY.
I GOT AN IDEA.
WE NEED SOME MONEY, RIGHT?
SO TONIGHT IS POKER NIGHT AT LeDIC's...

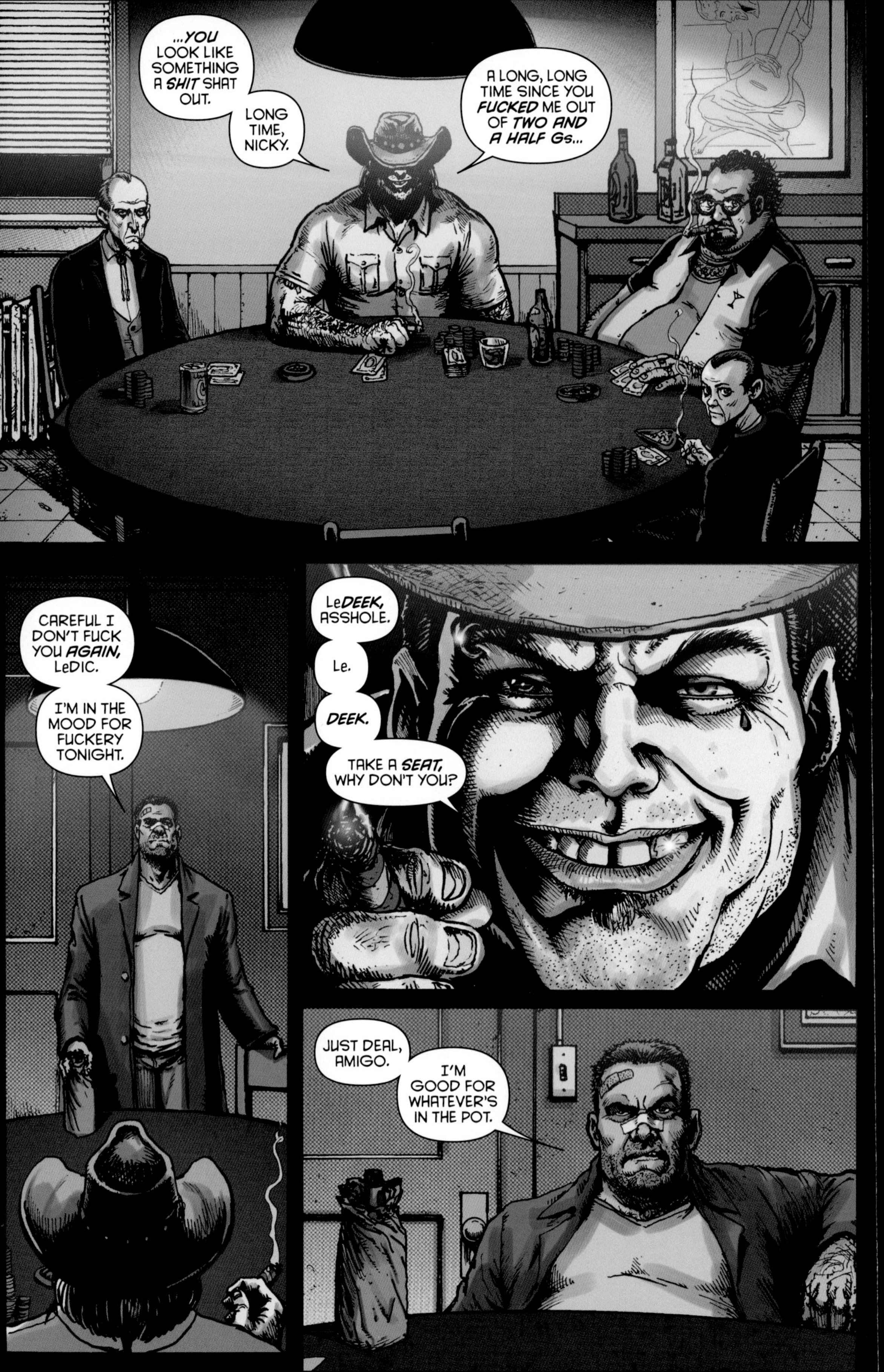
...YOU LOOK LIKE SOMETHING A SHIT SHAT OUT.
LONG TIME, NICKY.
A LONG, LONG TIME SINCE YOU FUCKED ME OUT OF TWO AND A HALF Gs...
CAREFUL I DON'T FUCK YOU AGAIN, LeDIC.
I'M IN THE MOOD FOR FUCKERY TONIGHT.
LeDEEK, ASSHOLE.
Le.
DEEK.
TAKE A SEAT, WHY DON'T YOU?
JUST DEAL, AMIGO.
I'M GOOD FOR WHATEVER'S IN THE POT.

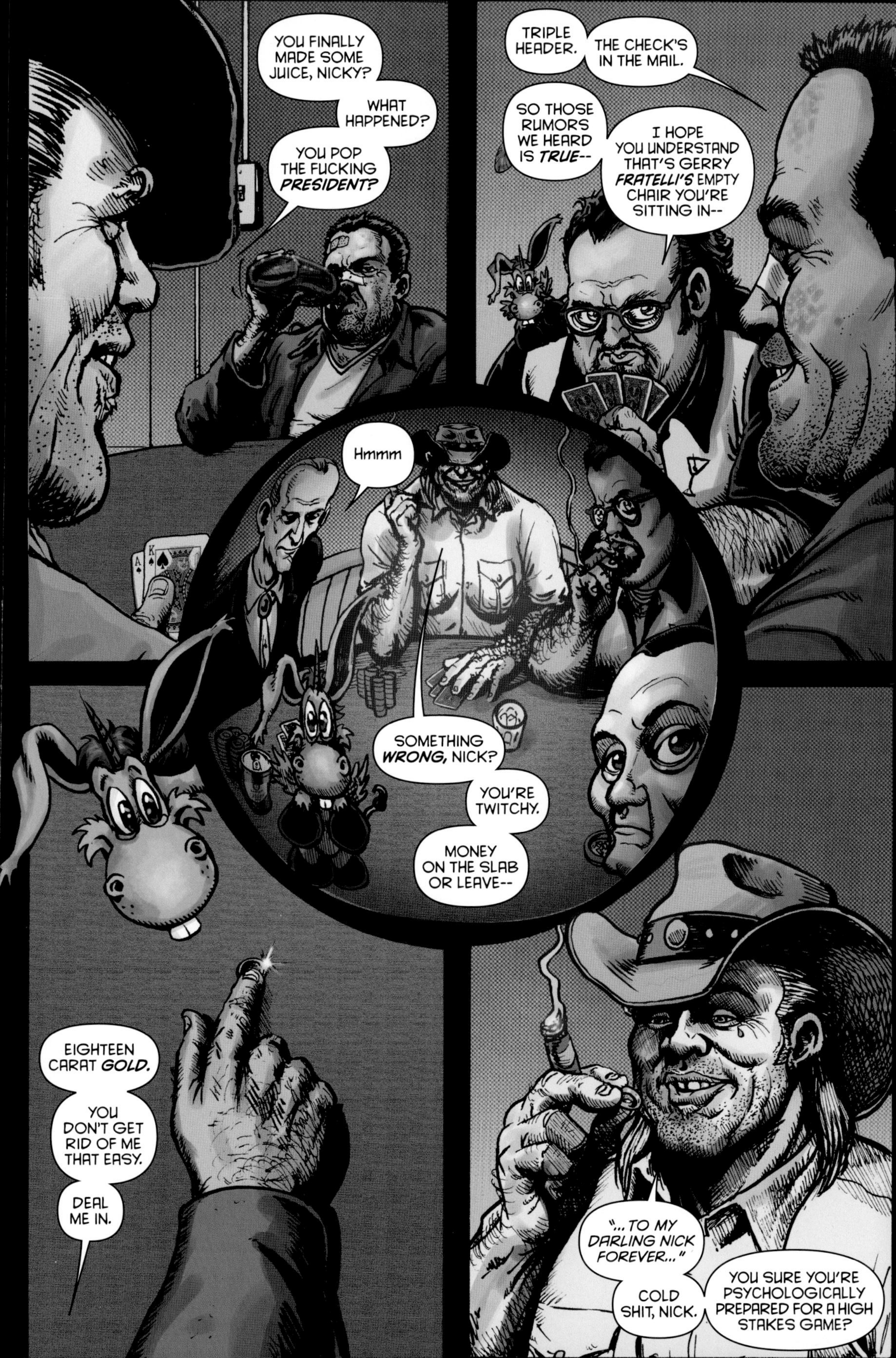
YOU FINALLY MADE SOME JUICE, NICKY?
WHAT HAPPENED?
YOU POP THE FUCKING *PRESIDENT?*
TRIPLE HEADER.
THE CHECK'S IN THE MAIL.
SO THOSE RUMORS WE HEARD IS *TRUE*--
I HOPE YOU UNDERSTAND THAT'S GERRY *FRATELLI'S* EMPTY CHAIR YOU'RE SITTING IN--
Hmmm
SOMETHING *WRONG,* NICK?
YOU'RE TWITCHY.
MONEY ON THE SLAB OR LEAVE--
EIGHTEEN CARAT *GOLD.*
YOU DON'T GET RID OF ME THAT EASY.
DEAL ME IN.
"...TO MY DARLING NICK FOREVER..."
COLD SHIT, NICK.
YOU SURE YOU'RE PSYCHOLOGICALLY PREPARED FOR A HIGH STAKES GAME?

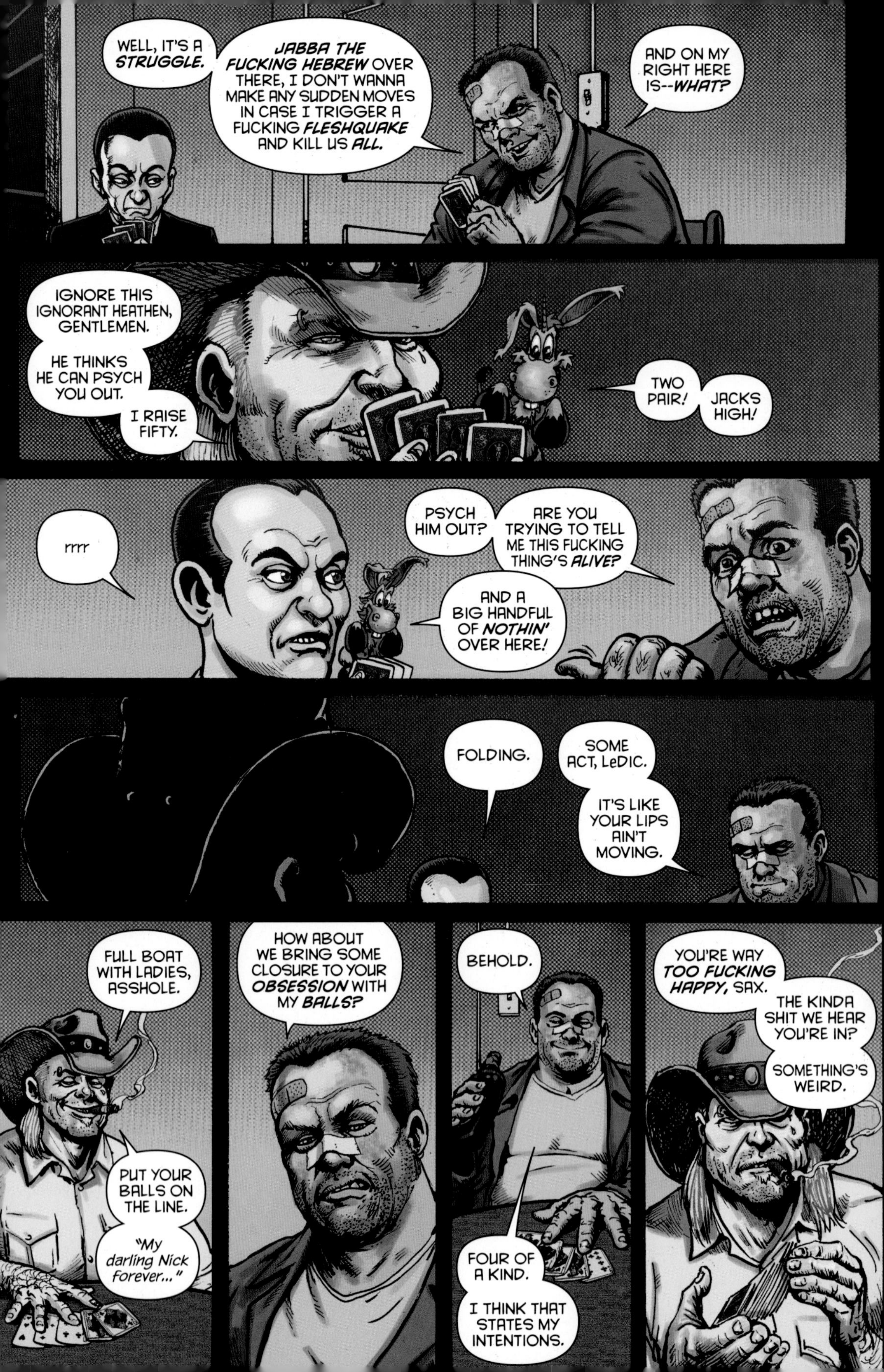
WELL, IT'S A *STRUGGLE.*
JABBA THE FUCKING HEBREW OVER THERE, I DON'T WANNA MAKE ANY SUDDEN MOVES IN CASE I TRIGGER A FUCKING ***FLESHQUAKE*** AND KILL US ***ALL.***
AND ON MY RIGHT HERE IS--***WHAT?***
IGNORE THIS IGNORANT HEATHEN, GENTLEMEN.
HE THINKS HE CAN PSYCH YOU OUT.
I RAISE FIFTY.
TWO PAIR!
JACKS HIGH!
rrrr
PSYCH HIM OUT?
ARE YOU TRYING TO TELL ME THIS FUCKING THING'S ***ALIVE?***
AND A BIG HANDFUL OF ***NOTHIN'*** OVER HERE!
FOLDING.
SOME ACT, LeDIC.
IT'S LIKE YOUR LIPS AIN'T MOVING.
FULL BOAT WITH LADIES, ASSHOLE.
PUT YOUR BALLS ON THE LINE.
"My darling Nick Forever..."
HOW ABOUT WE BRING SOME CLOSURE TO YOUR ***OBSESSION*** WITH MY ***BALLS?***
BEHOLD.
FOUR OF A KIND.
I THINK THAT STATES MY INTENTIONS.
YOU'RE WAY ***TOO FUCKING HAPPY,*** SAX.
THE KINDA SHIT WE HEAR YOU'RE IN?
SOMETHING'S WEIRD.

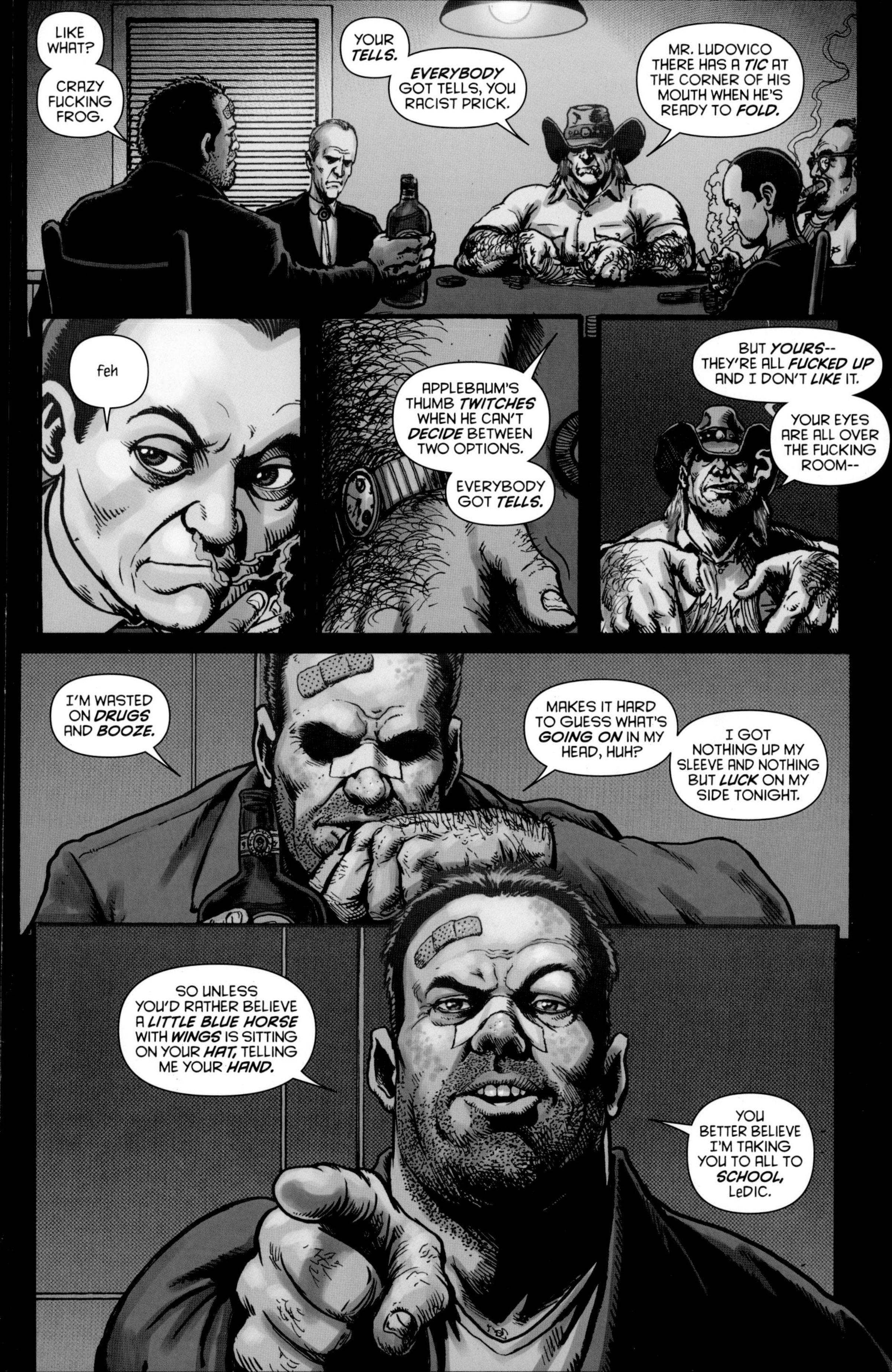
LIKE WHAT?
CRAZY FUCKING FROG.
YOUR TELLS.
EVERYBODY GOT TELLS, YOU RACIST PRICK.
MR. LUDOVICO THERE HAS A TIC AT THE CORNER OF HIS MOUTH WHEN HE'S READY TO FOLD.
feh
APPLEBAUM'S THUMB TWITCHES WHEN HE CAN'T DECIDE BETWEEN TWO OPTIONS.
EVERYBODY GOT TELLS.
BUT YOURS-- THEY'RE ALL FUCKED UP AND I DON'T LIKE IT.
YOUR EYES ARE ALL OVER THE FUCKING ROOM--
I'M WASTED ON DRUGS AND BOOZE.
MAKES IT HARD TO GUESS WHAT'S GOING ON IN MY HEAD, HUH?
I GOT NOTHING UP MY SLEEVE AND NOTHING BUT LUCK ON MY SIDE TONIGHT.
SO UNLESS YOU'D RATHER BELIEVE A LITTLE BLUE HORSE WITH WINGS IS SITTING ON YOUR HAT, TELLING ME YOUR HAND.
YOU BETTER BELIEVE I'M TAKING YOU TO ALL TO SCHOOL, LeDIC.

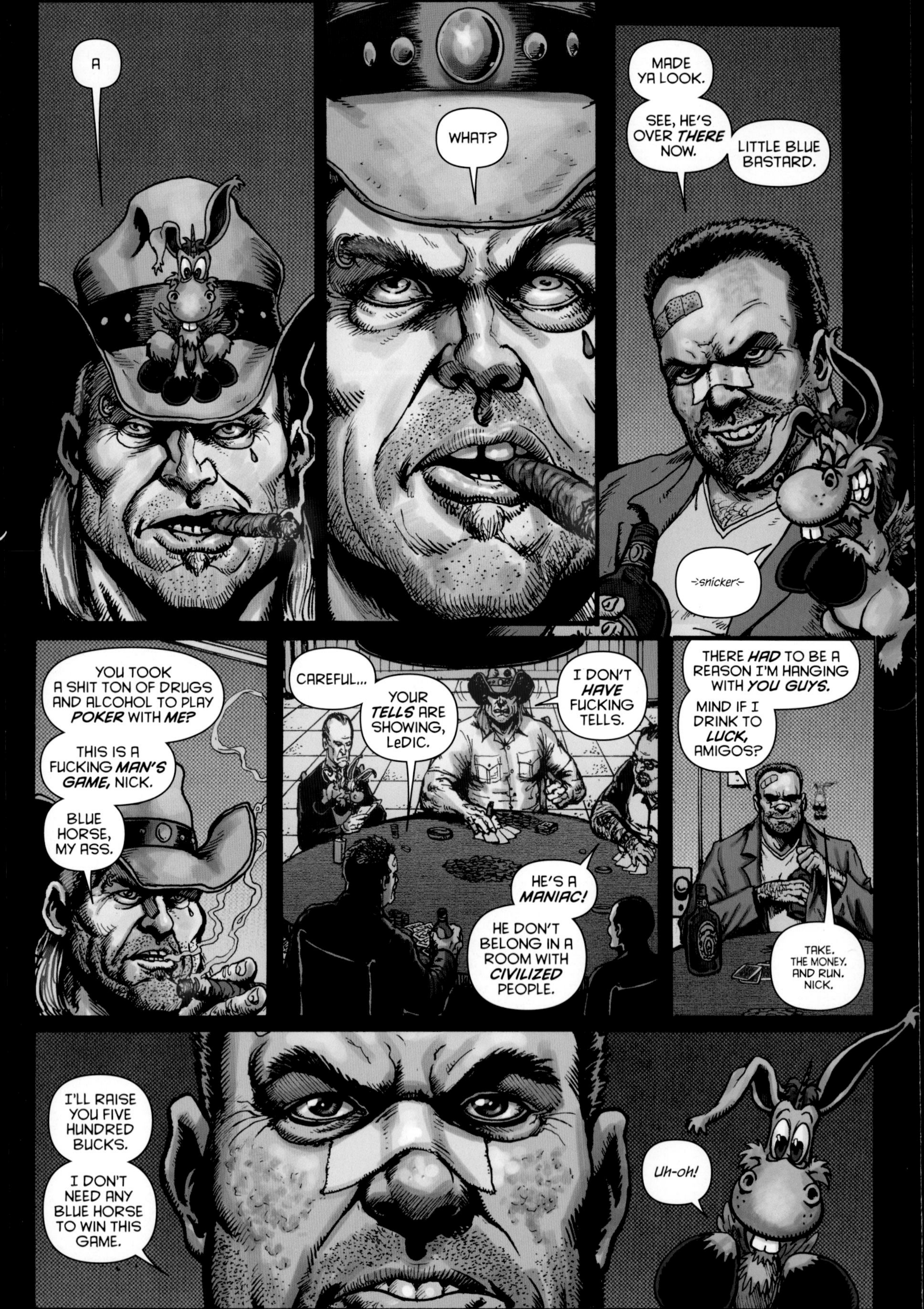
A
WHAT?
MADE YA LOOK.
SEE, HE'S OVER THERE NOW.
LITTLE BLUE BASTARD.
snicker
YOU TOOK A SHIT TON OF DRUGS AND ALCOHOL TO PLAY POKER WITH ME?
THIS IS A FUCKING MAN'S GAME, NICK.
BLUE HORSE, MY ASS.
CAREFUL...
YOUR TELLS ARE SHOWING, LeDIC.
I DON'T HAVE FUCKING TELLS.
HE'S A MANIAC!
HE DON'T BELONG IN A ROOM WITH CIVILIZED PEOPLE.
THERE HAD TO BE A REASON I'M HANGING WITH YOU GUYS.
MIND IF I DRINK TO LUCK, AMIGOS?
TAKE. THE MONEY. AND RUN. NICK.
I'LL RAISE YOU FIVE HUNDRED BUCKS.
I DON'T NEED ANY BLUE HORSE TO WIN THIS GAME.
Uh-oh!

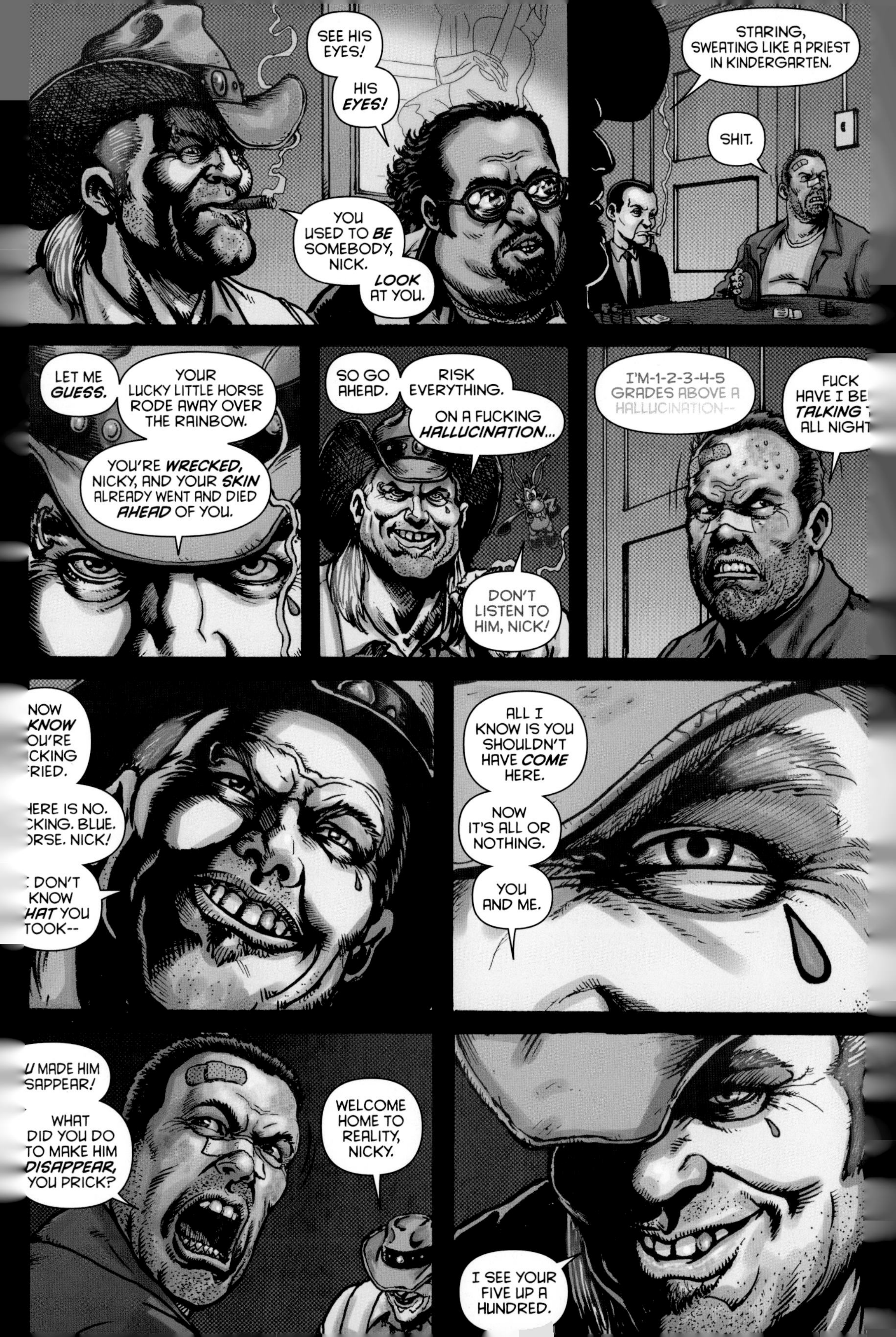
SEE HIS EYES!
HIS *EYES!*
YOU USED TO *BE* SOMEBODY, NICK.
LOOK AT YOU.
STARING, SWEATING LIKE A PRIEST IN KINDERGARTEN.
SHIT.
LET ME *GUESS.*
YOUR LUCKY LITTLE HORSE RODE AWAY OVER THE RAINBOW.
YOU'RE *WRECKED,* NICKY, AND YOUR *SKIN* ALREADY WENT AND DIED *AHEAD* OF YOU.
SO GO AHEAD.
RISK EVERYTHING.
ON A FUCKING *HALLUCINATION...*
DON'T LISTEN TO HIM, NICK!
I'M-1-2-3-4-5 GRADES ABOVE A HALLUCINATION--
FUCK HAVE I BE *TALKING* ALL NIGHT
NOW *KNOW* OU'RE CKING FRIED.
HERE IS NO. CKING. BLUE. ORSE. NICK!
DON'T KNOW *HAT* YOU TOOK--
ALL I KNOW IS YOU SHOULDN'T HAVE *COME* HERE.
NOW IT'S ALL OR NOTHING.
YOU AND ME.
U MADE HIM SAPPEAR!
WHAT DID YOU DO TO MAKE HIM *DISAPPEAR,* YOU PRICK?
WELCOME HOME TO REALITY, NICKY.
I SEE YOUR FIVE UP A HUNDRED.

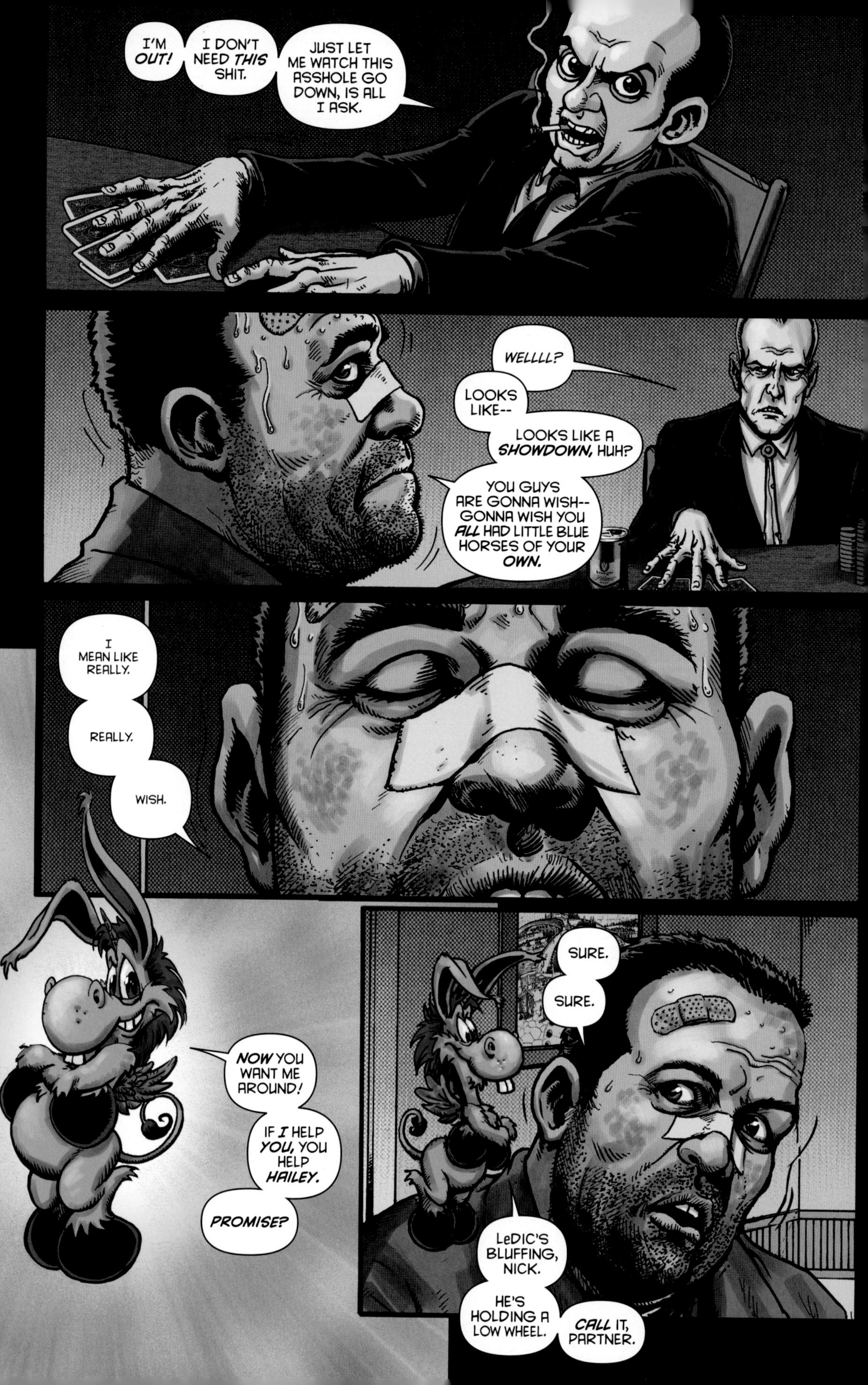
I'M *OUT!*
I DON'T NEED *THIS* SHIT.
JUST LET ME WATCH THIS ASSHOLE GO DOWN, IS ALL I ASK.
WELLLL?
LOOKS LIKE--
LOOKS LIKE A *SHOWDOWN,* HUH?
YOU GUYS ARE GONNA WISH-- GONNA WISH YOU *ALL* HAD LITTLE BLUE HORSES OF YOUR *OWN.*
I MEAN LIKE REALLY.
REALLY.
WISH.
NOW YOU WANT ME AROUND!
IF *I* HELP *YOU,* YOU HELP *HAILEY.*
PROMISE?
SURE.
SURE.
LeDIC'S BLUFFING, NICK.
HE'S HOLDING A LOW WHEEL.
CALL IT, PARTNER.

THE FUCK.

I JUST WANT YOU TO KNOW I WON THIS FAIR AND SQUARE.

YOU'VE NEVER BEEN LUCKY IN YOUR LIFE.

WHAT THE FUCK DID YOU JUST *PULL?*

YOU SAID IT YOURSELF.

GOTTA WATCH THOSE *TELLS.*

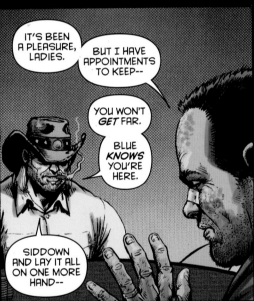

IT'S BEEN A PLEASURE, LADIES.

BUT I HAVE APPOINTMENTS TO KEEP--

YOU WON'T *GET* FAR.

BLUE *KNOWS* YOU'RE HERE.

SIDDOWN AND LAY IT ALL ON ONE MORE HAND--

SAX.

I INSIST.

REACH FOR A WEAPON, I PUT YOU DOWN.

WHAT KINDA WEAPON IS A *PEN?*

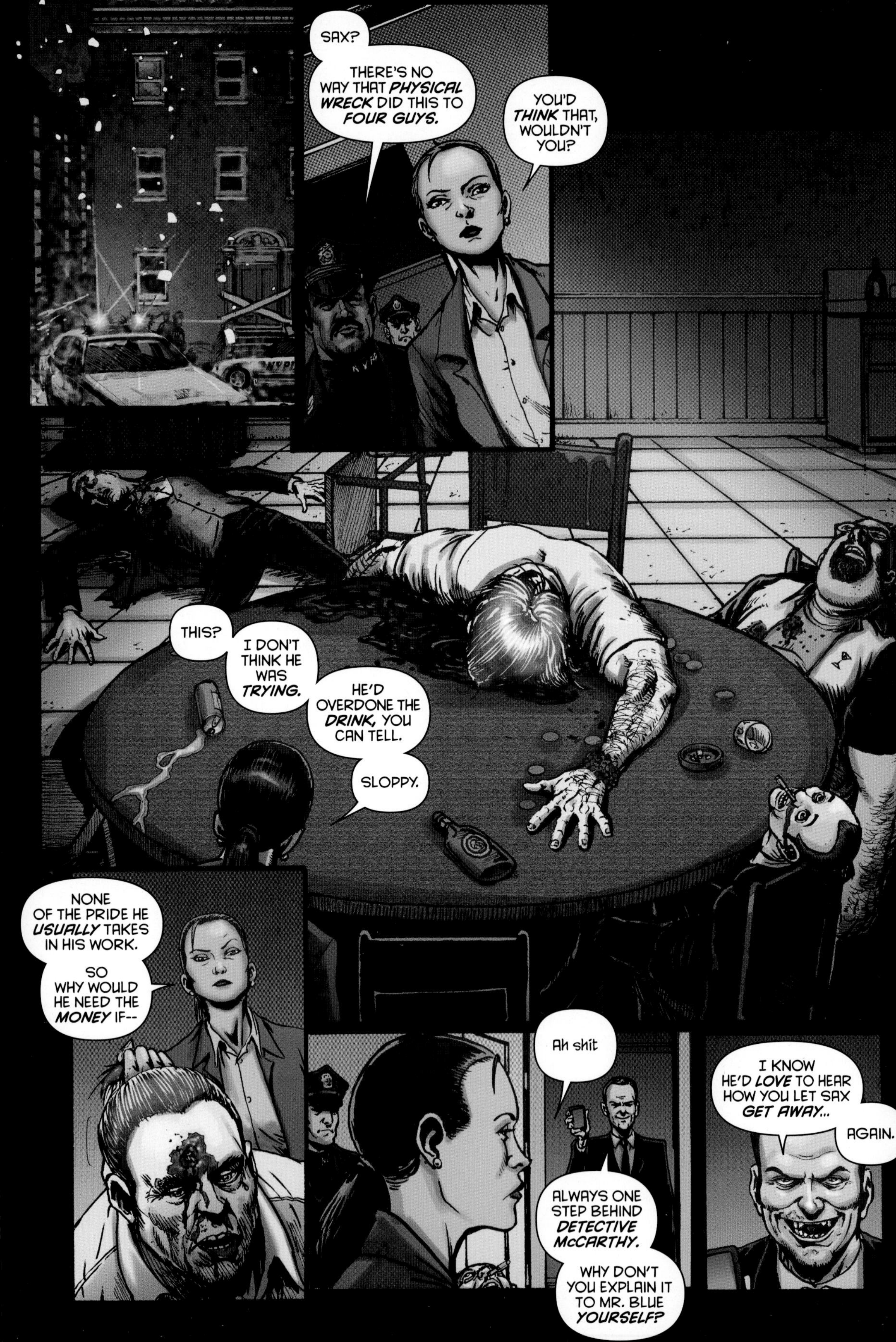
SAX?
THERE'S NO WAY THAT PHYSICAL WRECK DID THIS TO FOUR GUYS.
YOU'D THINK THAT, WOULDN'T YOU?
THIS?
I DON'T THINK HE WAS TRYING.
HE'D OVERDONE THE DRINK, YOU CAN TELL.
SLOPPY.
NONE OF THE PRIDE HE USUALLY TAKES IN HIS WORK.
SO WHY WOULD HE NEED THE MONEY IF--
Ah shit
ALWAYS ONE STEP BEHIND DETECTIVE McCARTHY.
WHY DON'T YOU EXPLAIN IT TO MR. BLUE YOURSELF?
I KNOW HE'D LOVE TO HEAR HOW YOU LET SAX GET AWAY...
AGAIN.

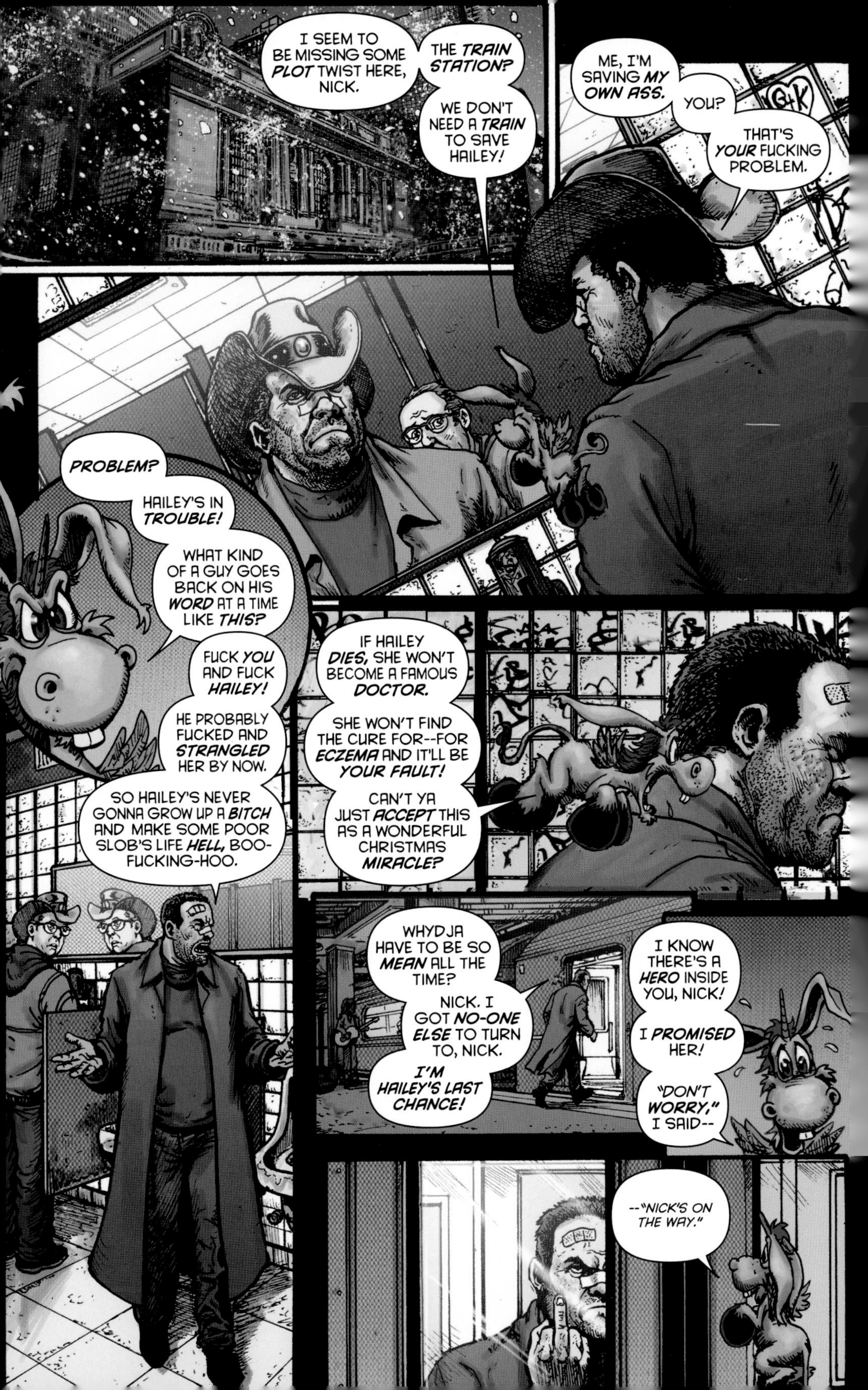

I SEEM TO BE MISSING SOME PLOT TWIST HERE, NICK.
THE TRAIN STATION?
WE DON'T NEED A TRAIN TO SAVE HAILEY!
ME, I'M SAVING MY OWN ASS.
YOU?
THAT'S YOUR FUCKING PROBLEM.
PROBLEM?
HAILEY'S IN TROUBLE!
WHAT KIND OF A GUY GOES BACK ON HIS WORD AT A TIME LIKE THIS?
FUCK YOU AND FUCK HAILEY!
HE PROBABLY FUCKED AND STRANGLED HER BY NOW.
SO HAILEY'S NEVER GONNA GROW UP A BITCH AND MAKE SOME POOR SLOB'S LIFE HELL, BOO-FUCKING-HOO.
IF HAILEY DIES, SHE WON'T BECOME A FAMOUS DOCTOR.
SHE WON'T FIND THE CURE FOR--FOR ECZEMA AND IT'LL BE YOUR FAULT!
CAN'T YA JUST ACCEPT THIS AS A WONDERFUL CHRISTMAS MIRACLE?
WHYDJA HAVE TO BE SO MEAN ALL THE TIME?
NICK. I GOT NO-ONE ELSE TO TURN TO, NICK.
I'M HAILEY'S LAST CHANCE!
I KNOW THERE'S A HERO INSIDE YOU, NICK!
I PROMISED HER!
"DON'T WORRY," I SAID--
--"NICK'S ON THE WAY."

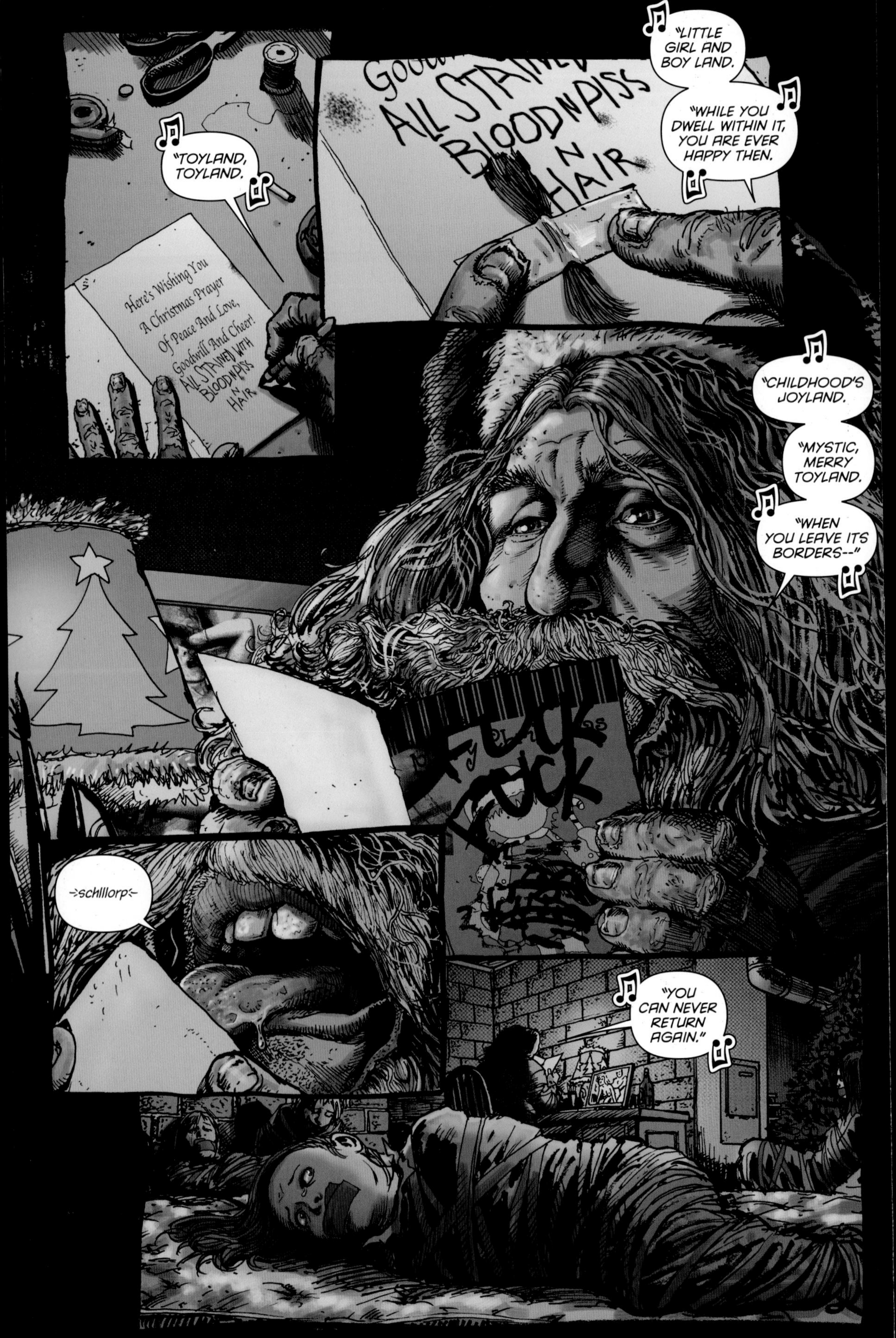
"TOYLAND, TOYLAND.
Here's Wishing You A Christmas Prayer Of Peace And Love, Goodwill And Cheer! ALL STAINED WITH BLOODNPISS N HAIR
ALL STAINED BLOODNPISS N HAIR
"LITTLE GIRL AND BOY LAND.
"WHILE YOU DWELL WITHIN IT, YOU ARE EVER HAPPY THEN.
"CHILDHOOD'S JOYLAND.
"MYSTIC, MERRY TOYLAND.
"WHEN YOU LEAVE ITS BORDERS--"
FUCK FUCK
-schlllorp-
"YOU CAN NEVER RETURN AGAIN."

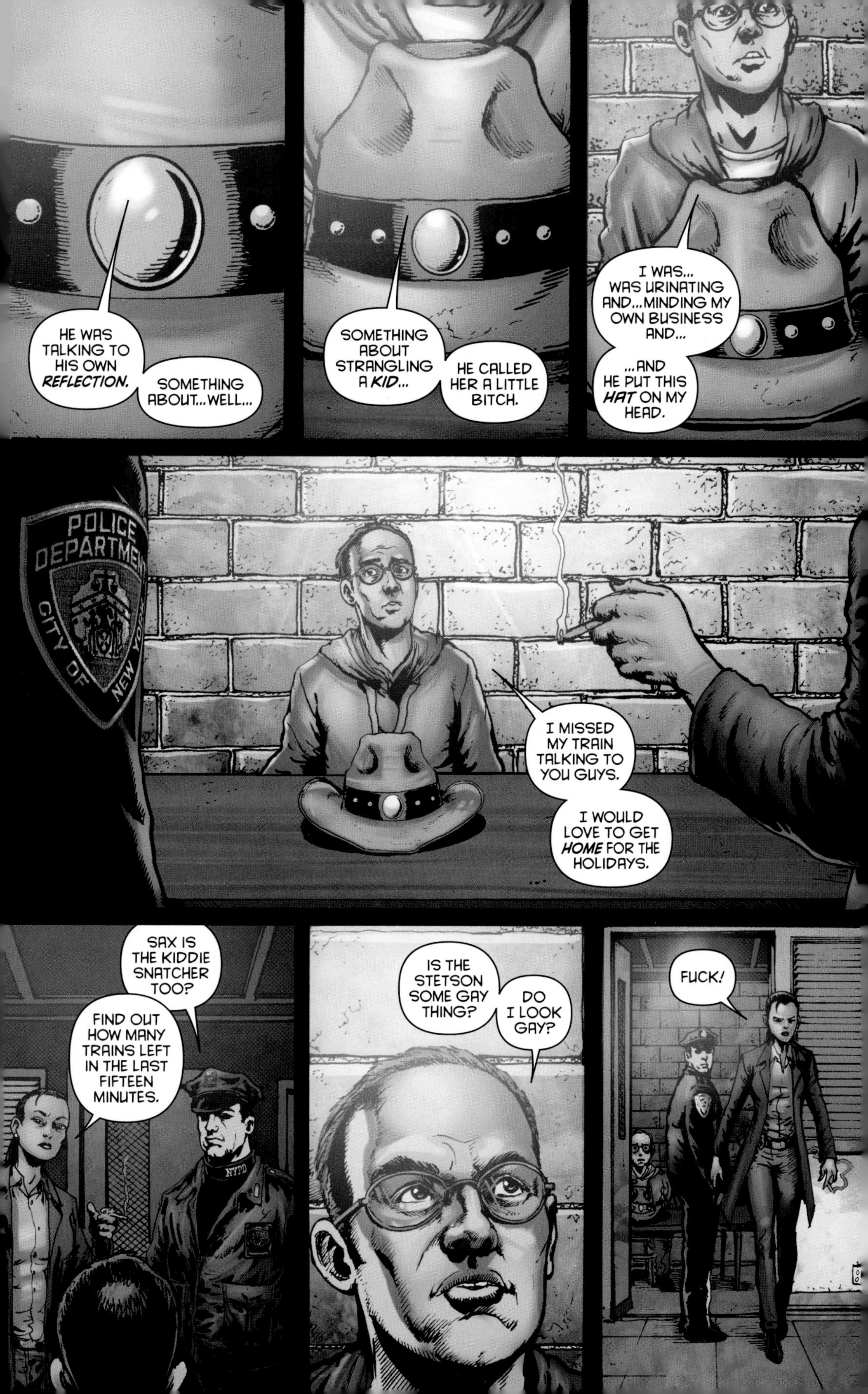
HE WAS TALKING TO HIS OWN *REFLECTION.*
SOMETHING ABOUT...WELL...
SOMETHING ABOUT STRANGLING A *KID*...
HE CALLED HER A LITTLE BITCH.
I WAS... WAS URINATING AND...MINDING MY OWN BUSINESS AND...
...AND HE PUT THIS *HAT* ON MY HEAD.
POLICE DEPARTMENT CITY OF NEW YORK
I MISSED MY TRAIN TALKING TO YOU GUYS.
I WOULD LOVE TO GET *HOME* FOR THE HOLIDAYS.
SAX IS THE KIDDIE SNATCHER TOO?
FIND OUT HOW MANY TRAINS LEFT IN THE LAST FIFTEEN MINUTES.
NYPD
IS THE STETSON SOME GAY THING?
DO I LOOK GAY?
FUCK!

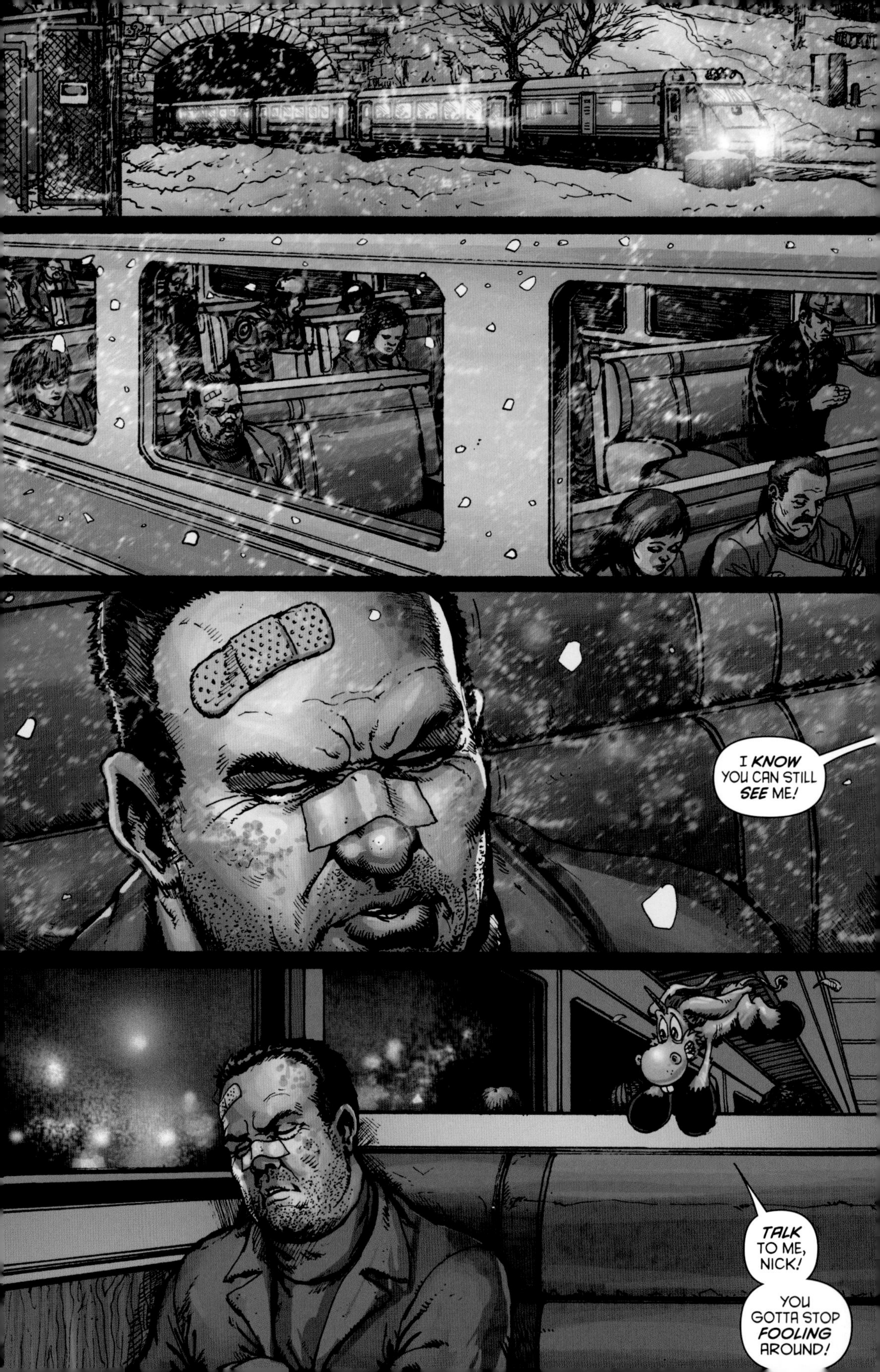
I KNOW YOU CAN STILL SEE ME!
TALK TO ME, NICK!
YOU GOTTA STOP FOOLING AROUND!

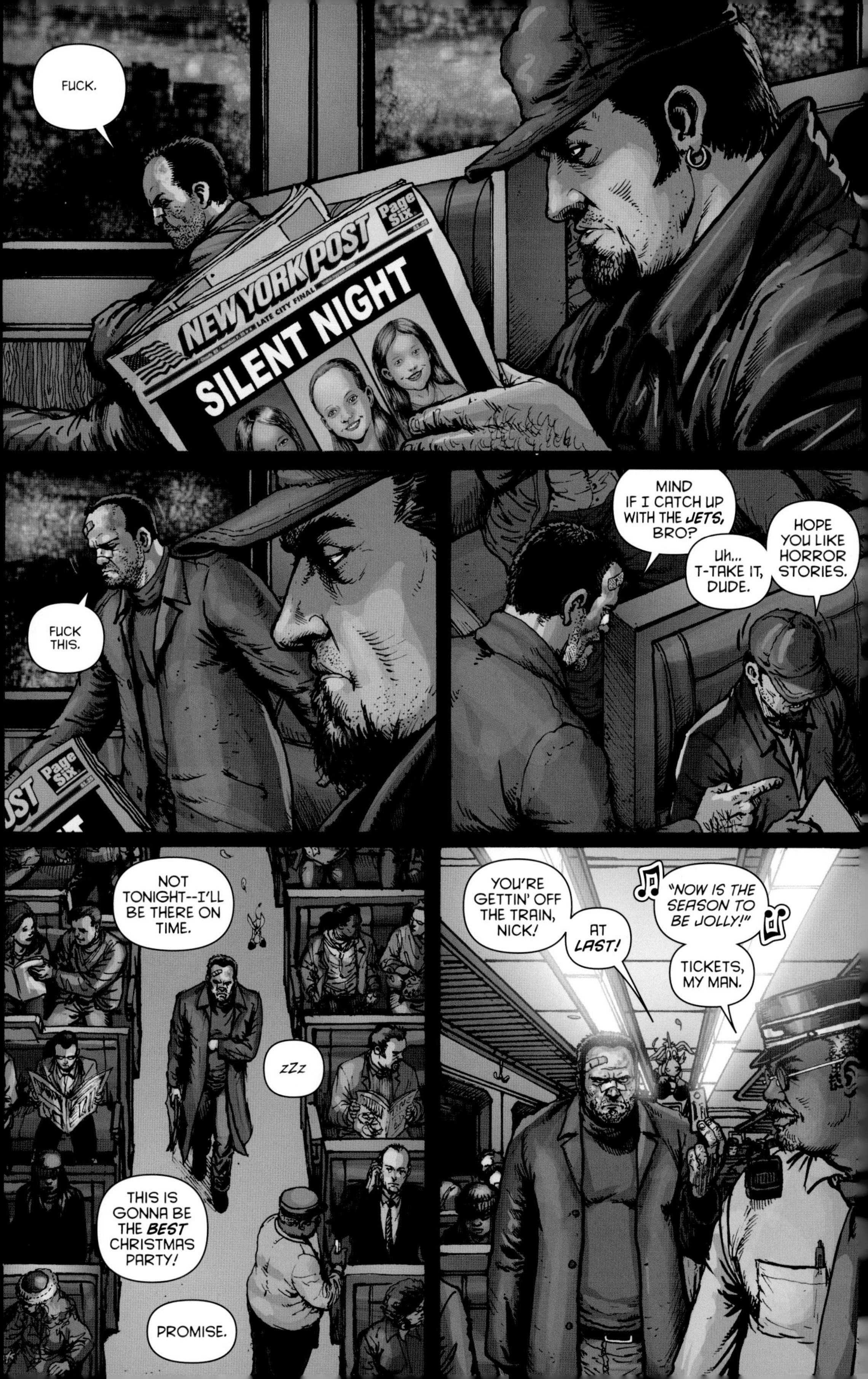
FUCK.
NEW YORK POST
LATE CITY FINAL
Page Six
SILENT NIGHT
FUCK THIS.
MIND IF I CATCH UP WITH THE *JETS,* BRO?
UH... T-TAKE IT, DUDE.
HOPE YOU LIKE HORROR STORIES.
NOT TONIGHT--I'LL BE THERE ON TIME.
zZz
THIS IS GONNA BE THE *BEST* CHRISTMAS PARTY!
PROMISE.
YOU'RE GETTIN' OFF THE TRAIN, NICK!
AT *LAST!*
"NOW IS THE SEASON TO BE JOLLY!"
TICKETS, MY MAN.

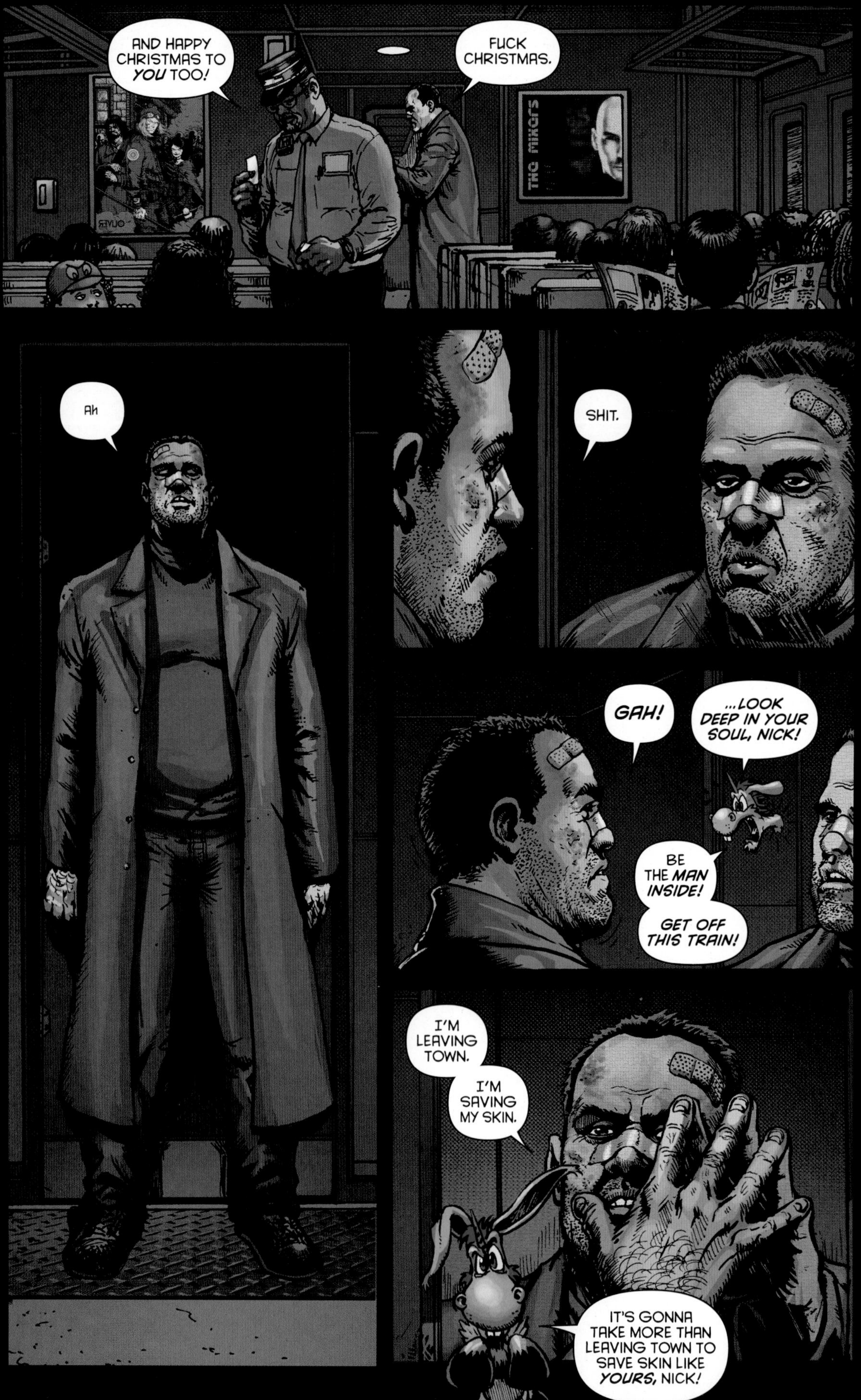
AND HAPPY CHRISTMAS TO *YOU* TOO!
FUCK CHRISTMAS.
THE MIKERS
OLIVER
Ah
SHIT.
GAH!
...LOOK DEEP IN YOUR SOUL, NICK!
BE THE *MAN* INSIDE!
GET OFF THIS TRAIN!
I'M LEAVING TOWN.
I'M SAVING MY SKIN.
IT'S GONNA TAKE MORE THAN LEAVING TOWN TO SAVE SKIN LIKE *YOURS*, NICK!

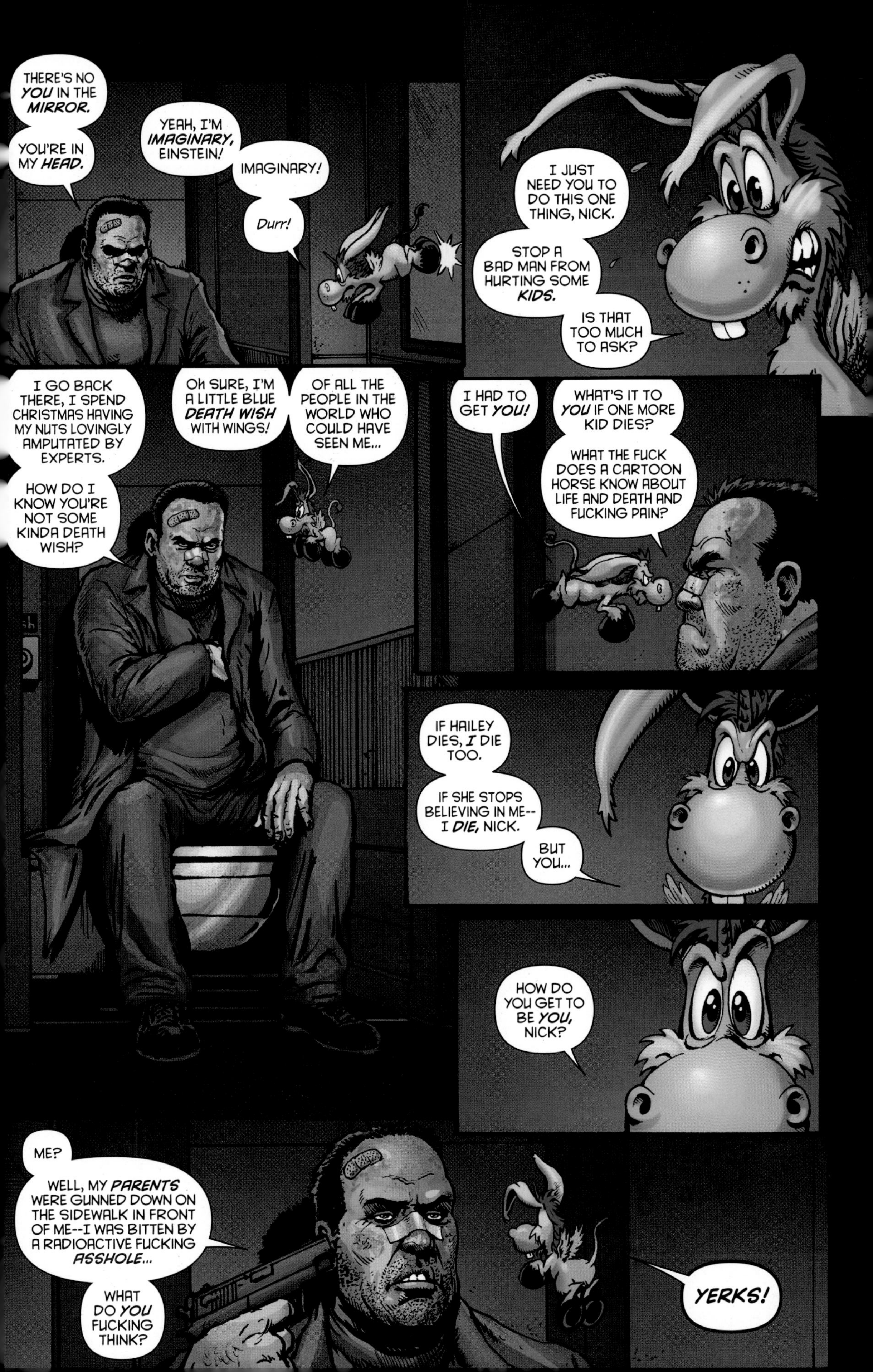

THERE'S NO YOU IN THE MIRROR.
YOU'RE IN MY HEAD.
YEAH, I'M IMAGINARY, EINSTEIN!
IMAGINARY!
Durr!
I JUST NEED YOU TO DO THIS ONE THING, NICK.
STOP A BAD MAN FROM HURTING SOME KIDS.
IS THAT TOO MUCH TO ASK?
I GO BACK THERE, I SPEND CHRISTMAS HAVING MY NUTS LOVINGLY AMPUTATED BY EXPERTS.
HOW DO I KNOW YOU'RE NOT SOME KINDA DEATH WISH?
Oh SURE, I'M A LITTLE BLUE DEATH WISH WITH WINGS!
OF ALL THE PEOPLE IN THE WORLD WHO COULD HAVE SEEN ME...
I HAD TO GET YOU!
WHAT'S IT TO YOU IF ONE MORE KID DIES?
WHAT THE FUCK DOES A CARTOON HORSE KNOW ABOUT LIFE AND DEATH AND FUCKING PAIN?
IF HAILEY DIES, I DIE TOO.
IF SHE STOPS BELIEVING IN ME-- I DIE, NICK.
BUT YOU...
HOW DO YOU GET TO BE YOU, NICK?
ME?
WELL, MY PARENTS WERE GUNNED DOWN ON THE SIDEWALK IN FRONT OF ME--I WAS BITTEN BY A RADIOACTIVE FUCKING ASSHOLE...
WHAT DO YOU FUCKING THINK?
YERKS!

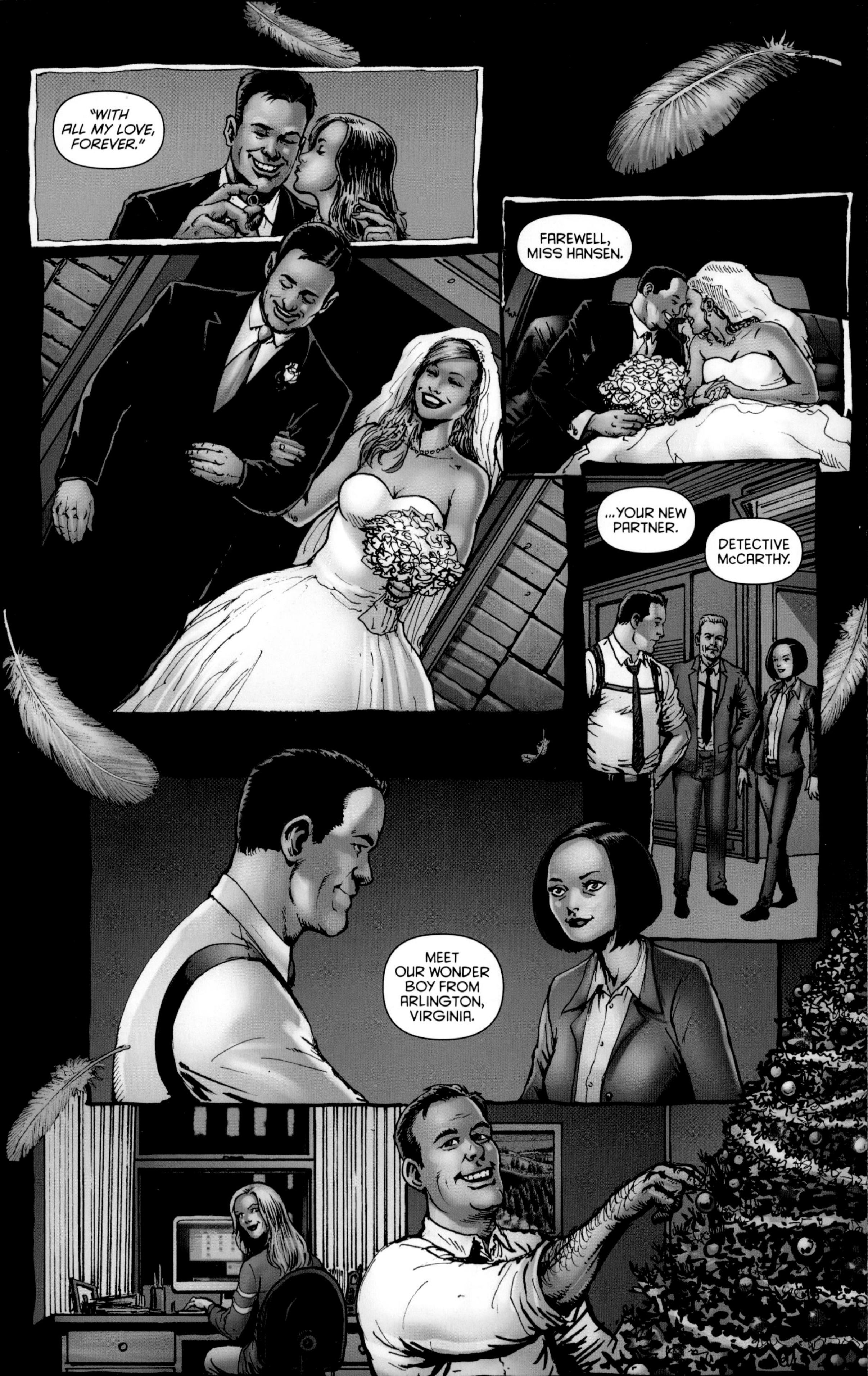
"WITH ALL MY LOVE, FOREVER."
FAREWELL, MISS HANSEN.
...YOUR NEW PARTNER.
DETECTIVE McCARTHY.
MEET OUR WONDER BOY FROM ARLINGTON, VIRGINIA.

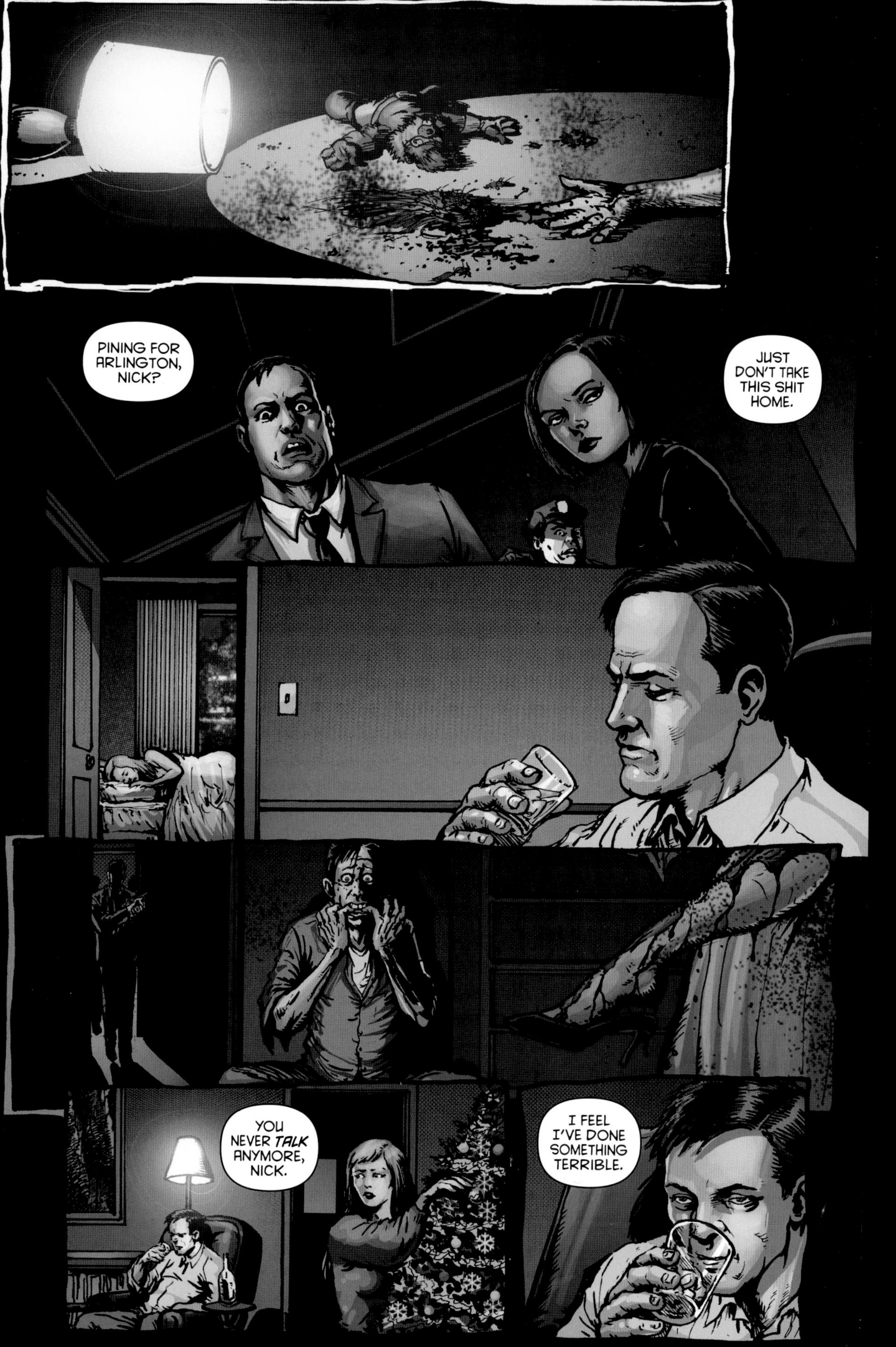
PINING FOR ARLINGTON, NICK?
JUST DON'T TAKE THIS SHIT HOME.
YOU NEVER TALK ANYMORE, NICK.
I FEEL I'VE DONE SOMETHING TERRIBLE.

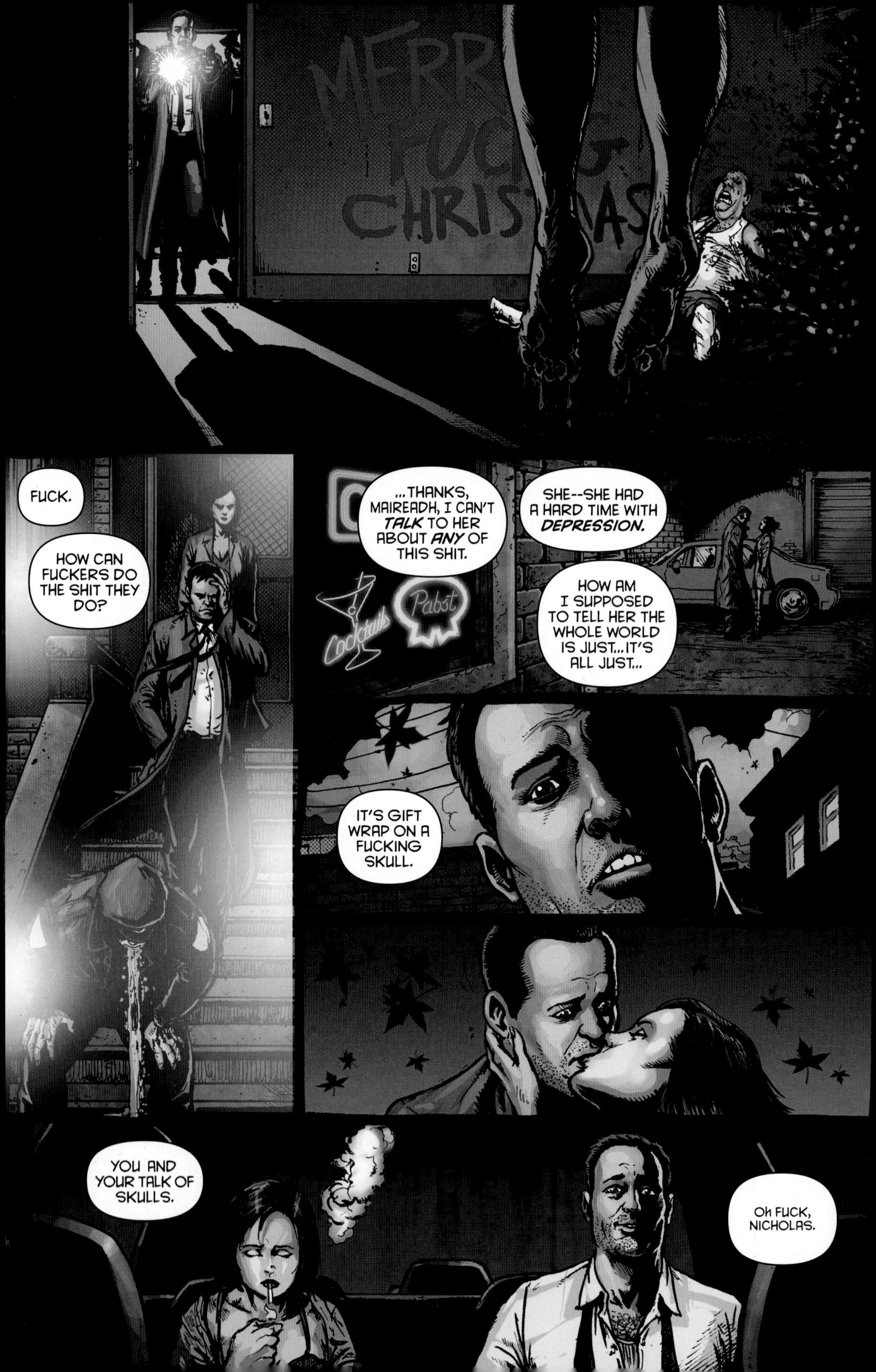
MERRY FUCKING CHRISTMAS
FUCK.
HOW CAN FUCKERS DO THE SHIT THEY DO?
...THANKS, MAIREADH, I CAN'T TALK TO HER ABOUT ANY OF THIS SHIT.
Cocktails
Pabst
SHE--SHE HAD A HARD TIME WITH DEPRESSION.
HOW AM I SUPPOSED TO TELL HER THE WHOLE WORLD IS JUST...IT'S ALL JUST...
IT'S GIFT WRAP ON A FUCKING SKULL.
YOU AND YOUR TALK OF SKULLS.
Oh FUCK, NICHOLAS.

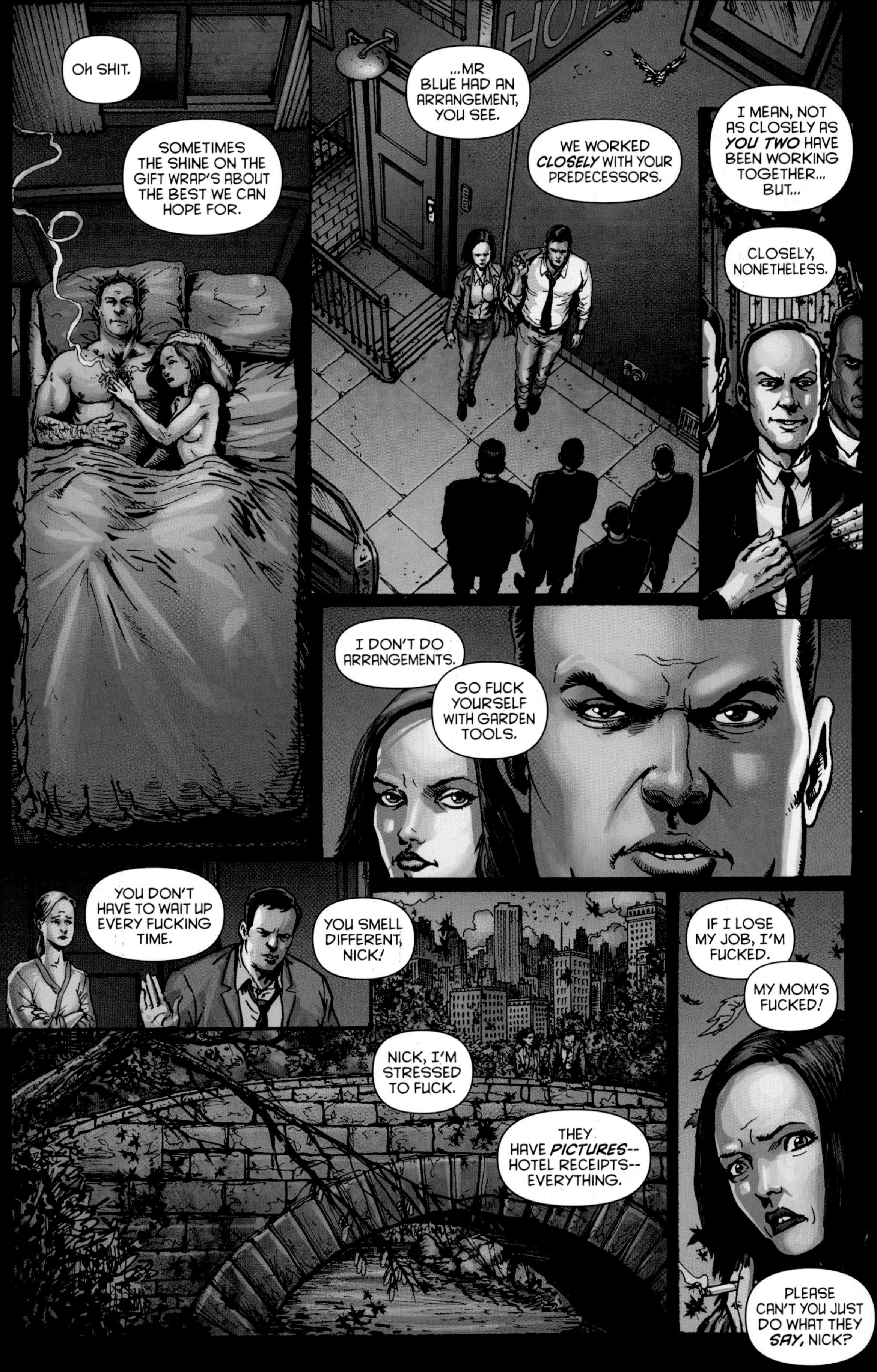
Oh SHIT.
SOMETIMES THE SHINE ON THE GIFT WRAP'S ABOUT THE BEST WE CAN HOPE FOR.
...MR BLUE HAD AN ARRANGEMENT, YOU SEE.
WE WORKED *CLOSELY* WITH YOUR PREDECESSORS.
I MEAN, NOT AS CLOSELY AS *YOU TWO* HAVE BEEN WORKING TOGETHER... BUT...
CLOSELY, NONETHELESS.
I DON'T DO ARRANGEMENTS.
GO FUCK YOURSELF WITH GARDEN TOOLS.
YOU DON'T HAVE TO WAIT UP EVERY FUCKING TIME.
YOU SMELL DIFFERENT, NICK!
NICK, I'M STRESSED TO FUCK.
THEY HAVE *PICTURES*-- HOTEL RECEIPTS-- EVERYTHING.
IF I LOSE MY JOB, I'M FUCKED.
MY MOM'S FUCKED!
PLEASE CAN'T YOU JUST DO WHAT THEY *SAY,* NICK?

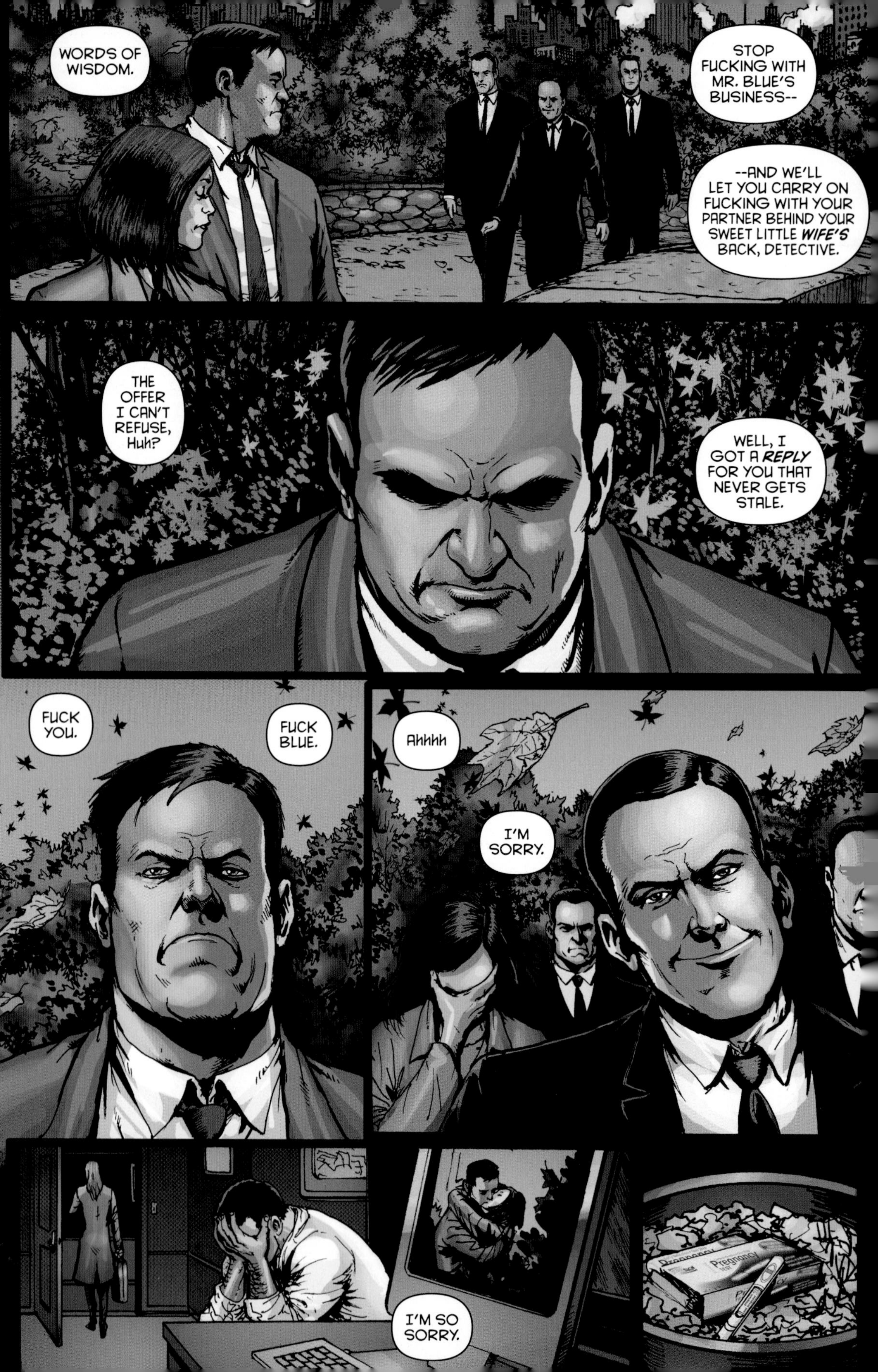
WORDS OF WISDOM.
STOP FUCKING WITH MR. BLUE'S BUSINESS--
--AND WE'LL LET YOU CARRY ON FUCKING WITH YOUR PARTNER BEHIND YOUR SWEET LITTLE *WIFE'S* BACK, DETECTIVE.
THE OFFER I CAN'T REFUSE, Huh?
WELL, I GOT A *REPLY* FOR YOU THAT NEVER GETS STALE.
FUCK YOU.
FUCK BLUE.
Ahhhh
I'M SORRY.
I'M SO SORRY.

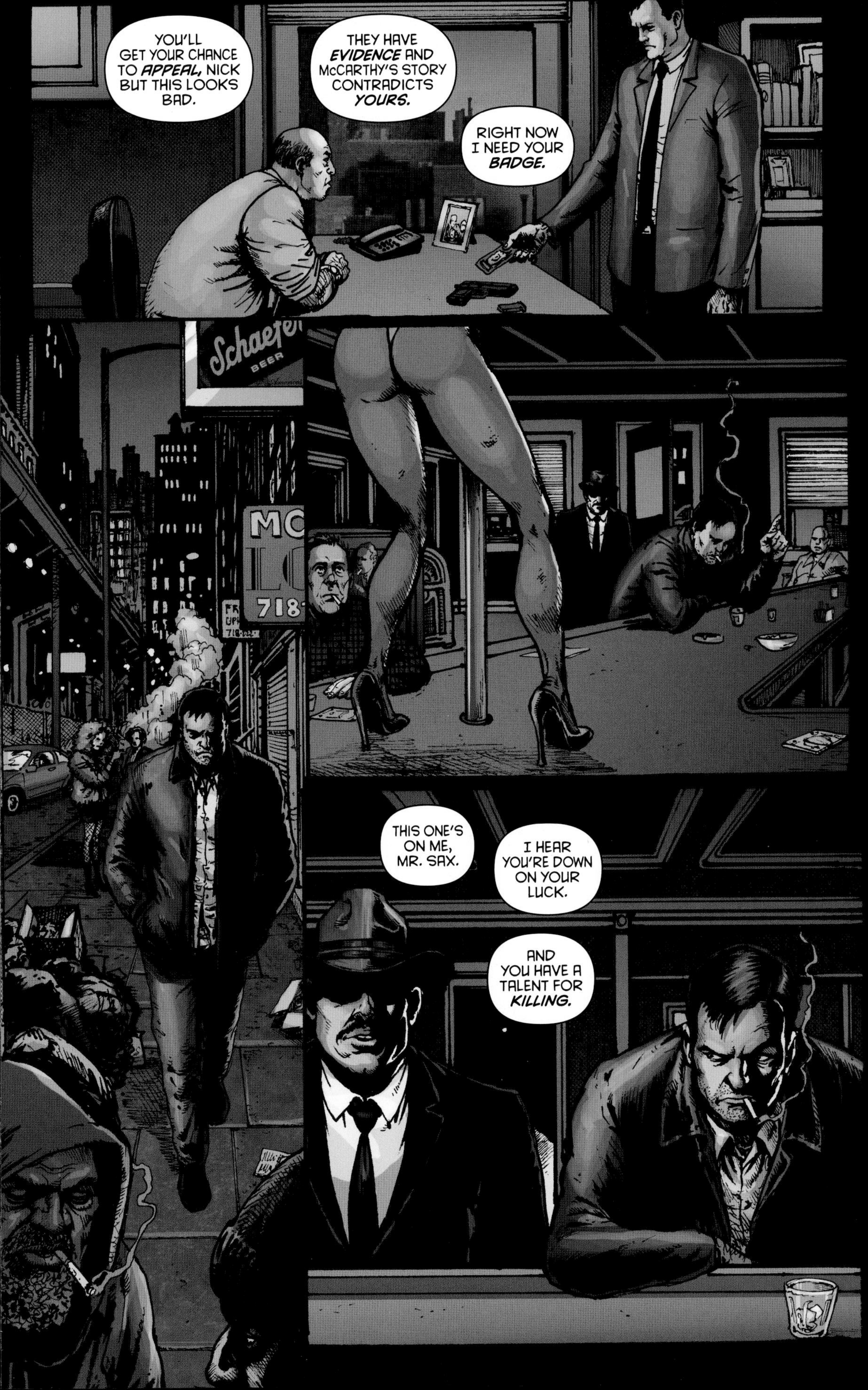
YOU'LL GET YOUR CHANCE TO *APPEAL,* NICK BUT THIS LOOKS BAD.
THEY HAVE *EVIDENCE* AND McCARTHY'S STORY CONTRADICTS *YOURS.*
RIGHT NOW I NEED YOUR *BADGE.*
THIS ONE'S ON ME, MR. SAX.
I HEAR YOU'RE DOWN ON YOUR LUCK.
AND YOU HAVE A TALENT FOR *KILLING.*

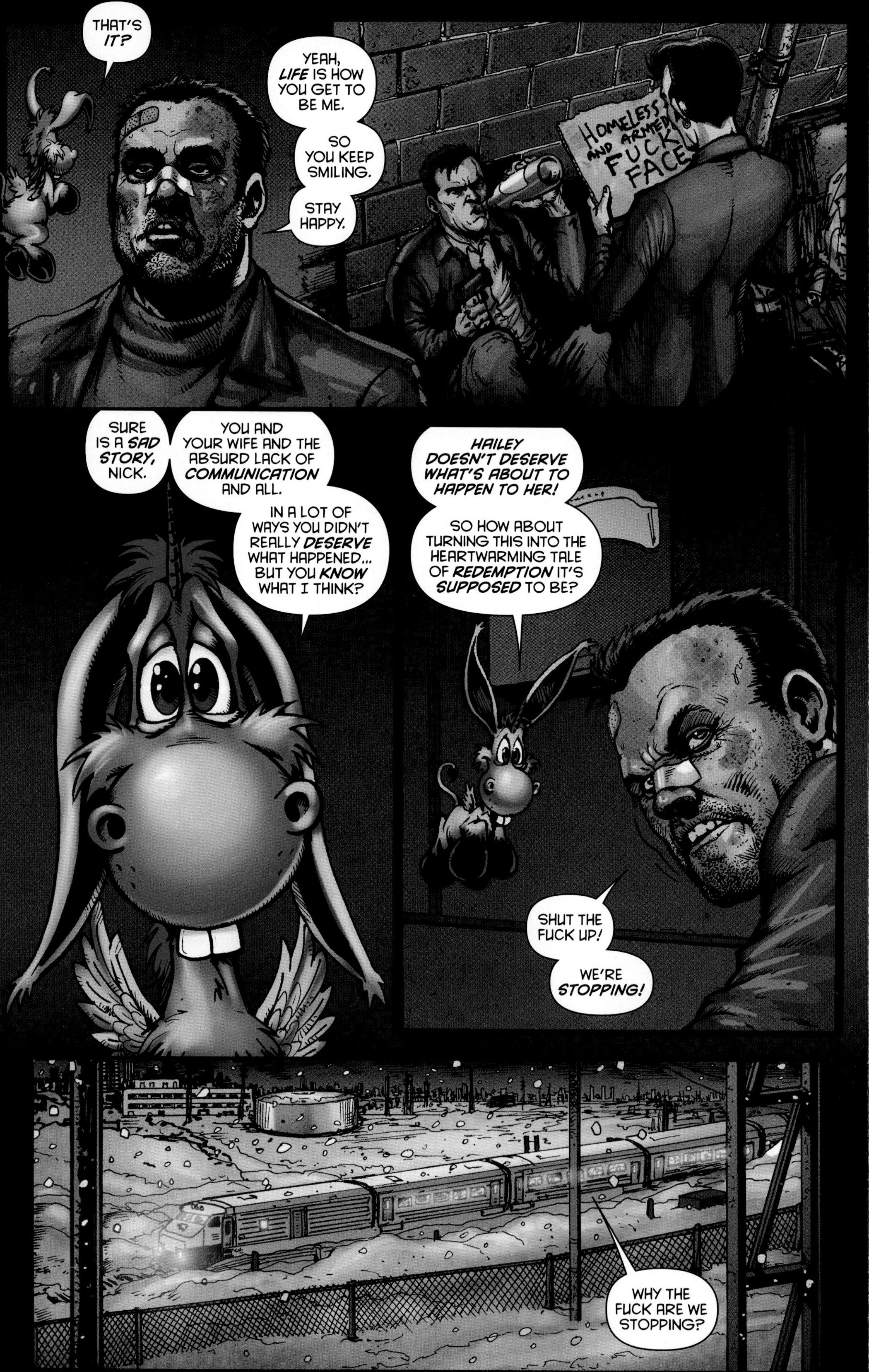
THAT'S IT?
YEAH, LIFE IS HOW YOU GET TO BE ME.
SO YOU KEEP SMILING.
STAY HAPPY.
HOMELESS AND ARMED FUCK FACE
SURE IS A SAD STORY, NICK.
YOU AND YOUR WIFE AND THE ABSURD LACK OF COMMUNICATION AND ALL.
IN A LOT OF WAYS YOU DIDN'T REALLY DESERVE WHAT HAPPENED... BUT YOU KNOW WHAT I THINK?
HAILEY DOESN'T DESERVE WHAT'S ABOUT TO HAPPEN TO HER!
SO HOW ABOUT TURNING THIS INTO THE HEARTWARMING TALE OF REDEMPTION IT'S SUPPOSED TO BE?
SHUT THE FUCK UP!
WE'RE STOPPING!
WHY THE FUCK ARE WE STOPPING?

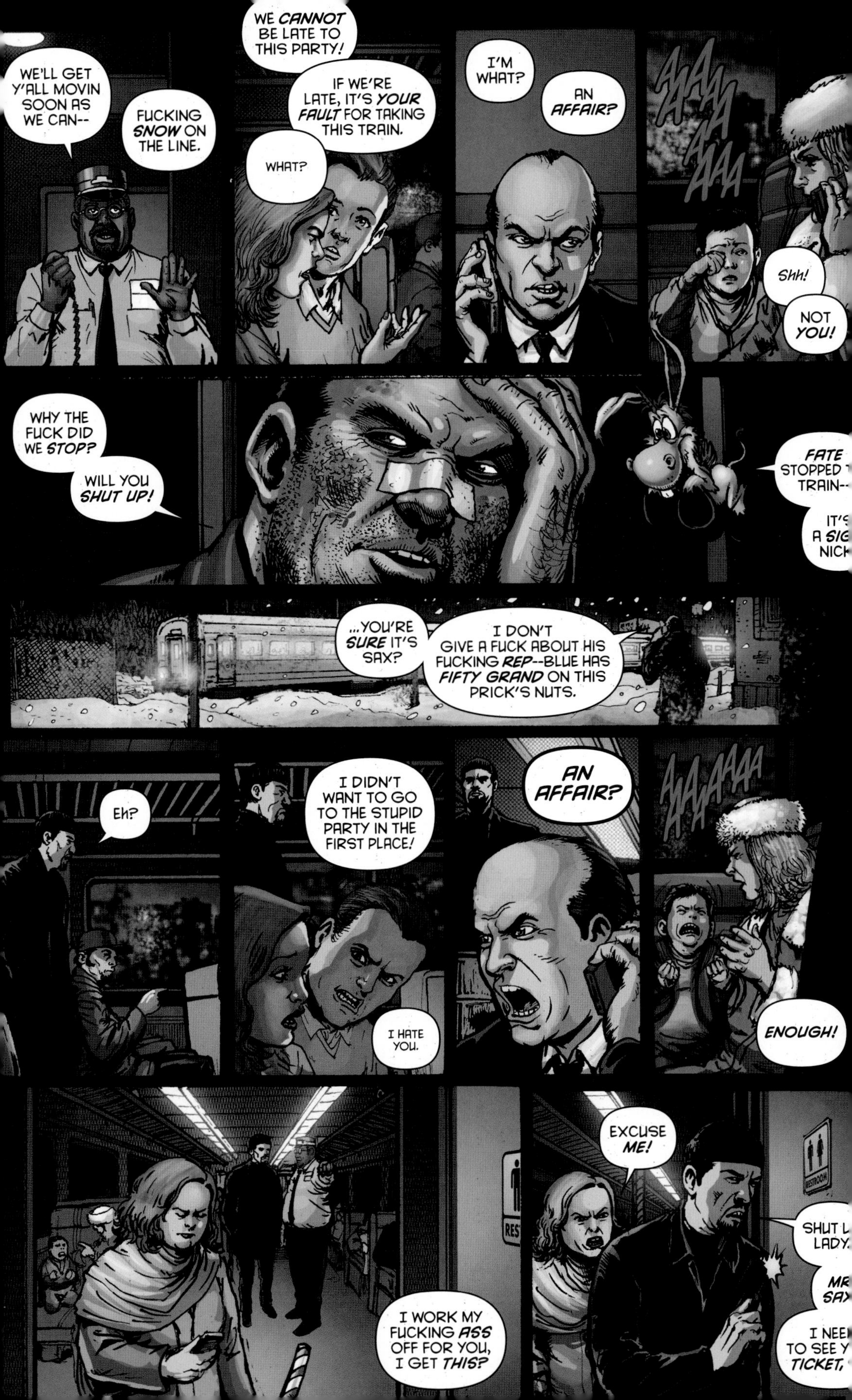
WE'LL GET Y'ALL MOVIN SOON AS WE CAN--
FUCKING SNOW ON THE LINE.
WE CANNOT BE LATE TO THIS PARTY!
IF WE'RE LATE, IT'S YOUR FAULT FOR TAKING THIS TRAIN.
WHAT?
I'M WHAT?
AN AFFAIR?
AAAAAAAAA
Shh!
NOT YOU!
WHY THE FUCK DID WE STOP?
WILL YOU SHUT UP!
FATE STOPPED T TRAIN--
IT'S A SIG NICK
...YOU'RE SURE IT'S SAX?
I DON'T GIVE A FUCK ABOUT HIS FUCKING REP--BLUE HAS FIFTY GRAND ON THIS PRICK'S NUTS.
Eh?
I DIDN'T WANT TO GO TO THE STUPID PARTY IN THE FIRST PLACE!
I HATE YOU.
AN AFFAIR?
AAAAAAAA
ENOUGH!
I WORK MY FUCKING ASS OFF FOR YOU, I GET THIS?
EXCUSE ME!
SHUT L LADY.
MR SAX
I NEE TO SEE Y TICKET,

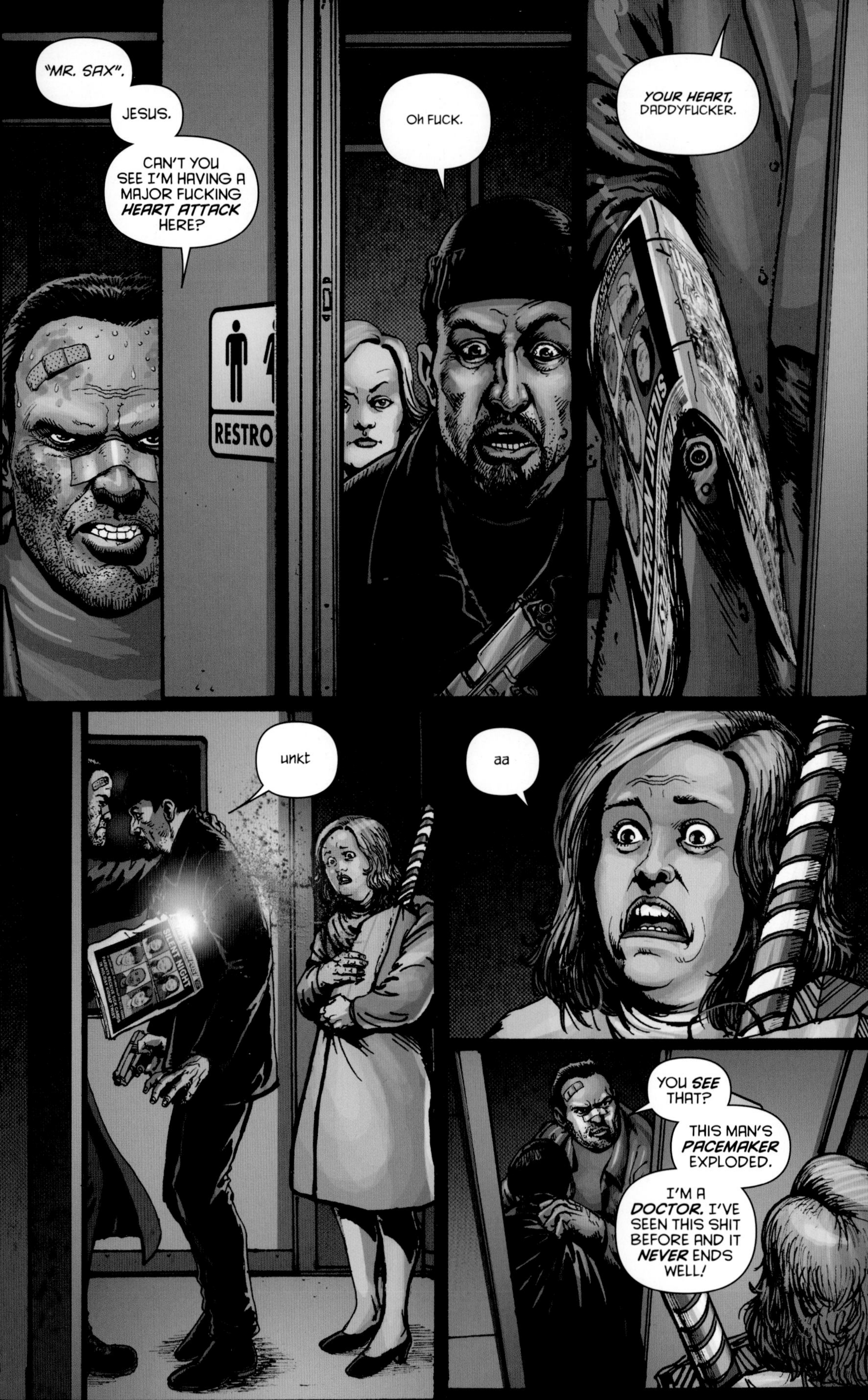

"MR. SAX".
JESUS.
CAN'T YOU SEE I'M HAVING A MAJOR FUCKING HEART ATTACK HERE?
RESTRO
Oh FUCK.
YOUR HEART, DADDYFUCKER.
unkt
SILENT NIGHT
aa
YOU SEE THAT?
THIS MAN'S PACEMAKER EXPLODED.
I'M A DOCTOR. I'VE SEEN THIS SHIT BEFORE AND IT NEVER ENDS WELL!

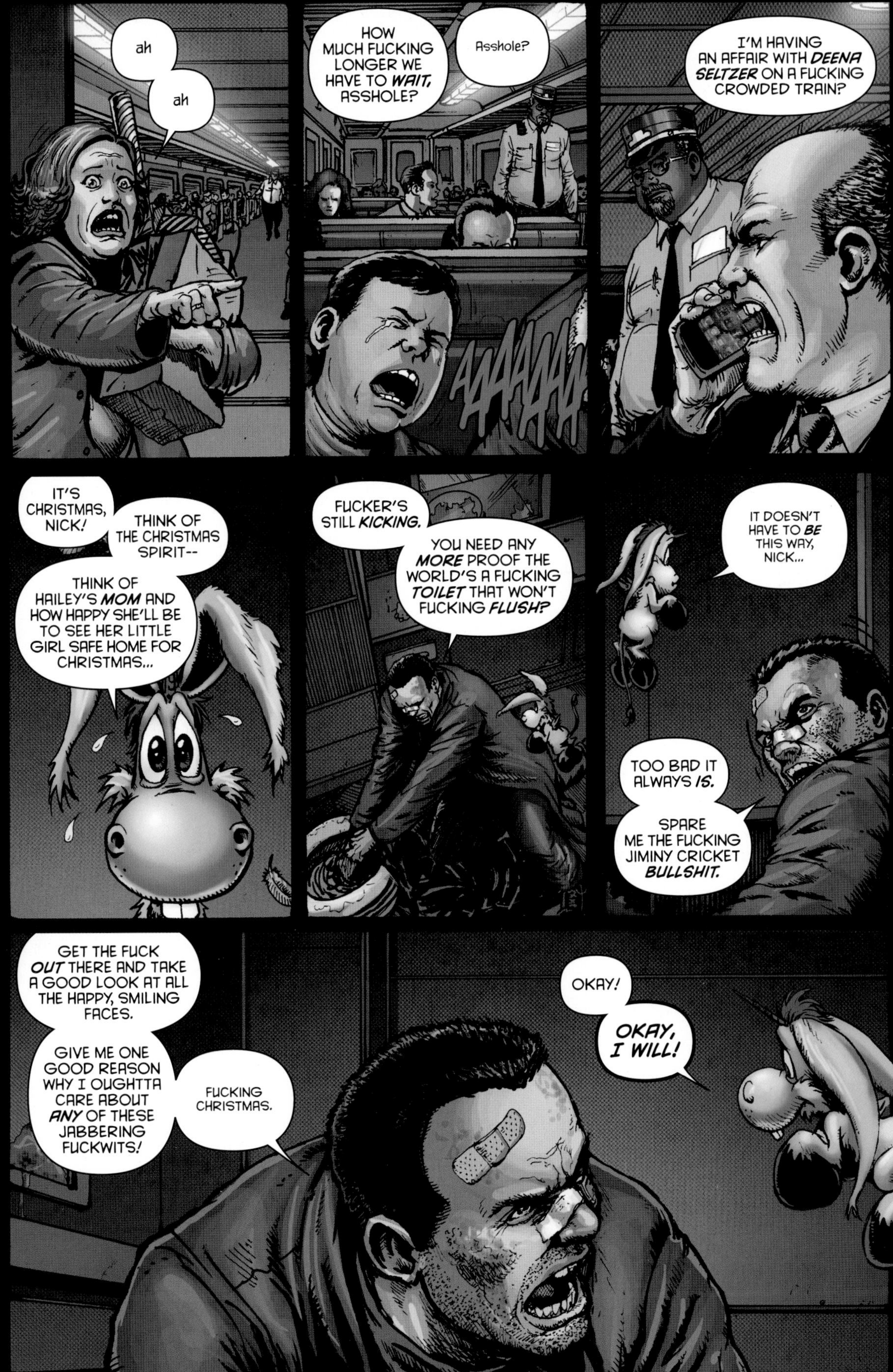
ah
ah
HOW MUCH FUCKING LONGER WE HAVE TO WAIT, ASSHOLE?
Asshole?
AAAAAAAA
I'M HAVING AN AFFAIR WITH DEENA SELTZER ON A FUCKING CROWDED TRAIN?
IT'S CHRISTMAS, NICK!
THINK OF THE CHRISTMAS SPIRIT--
THINK OF HAILEY'S MOM AND HOW HAPPY SHE'LL BE TO SEE HER LITTLE GIRL SAFE HOME FOR CHRISTMAS...
FUCKER'S STILL KICKING.
YOU NEED ANY MORE PROOF THE WORLD'S A FUCKING TOILET THAT WON'T FUCKING FLUSH?
IT DOESN'T HAVE TO BE THIS WAY, NICK...
TOO BAD IT ALWAYS IS.
SPARE ME THE FUCKING JIMINY CRICKET BULLSHIT.
GET THE FUCK OUT THERE AND TAKE A GOOD LOOK AT ALL THE HAPPY, SMILING FACES.
GIVE ME ONE GOOD REASON WHY I OUGHTTA CARE ABOUT ANY OF THESE JABBERING FUCKWITS!
FUCKING CHRISTMAS.
OKAY!
OKAY, I WILL!

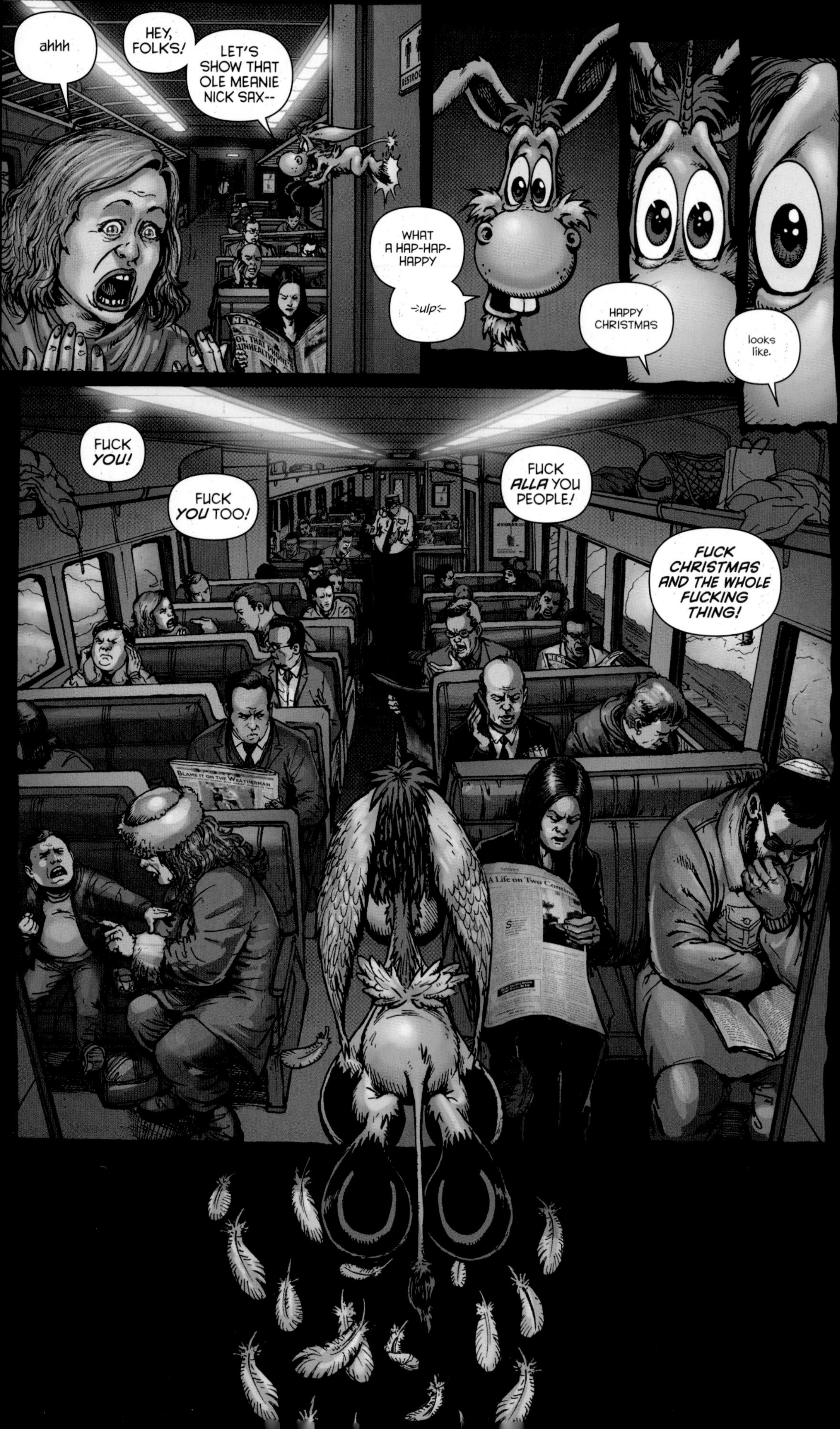
ahhh
HEY, FOLKS!
LET'S SHOW THAT OLE MEANIE NICK SAX--
RESTROOM
WHAT A HAP-HAP-HAPPY
~ulp~
HAPPY CHRISTMAS
looks like.
FUCK YOU!
FUCK YOU TOO!
FUCK ALLA YOU PEOPLE!
FUCK CHRISTMAS AND THE WHOLE FUCKING THING!
BLAME IT ON THE WEATHERMAN
A Life on Two Contin

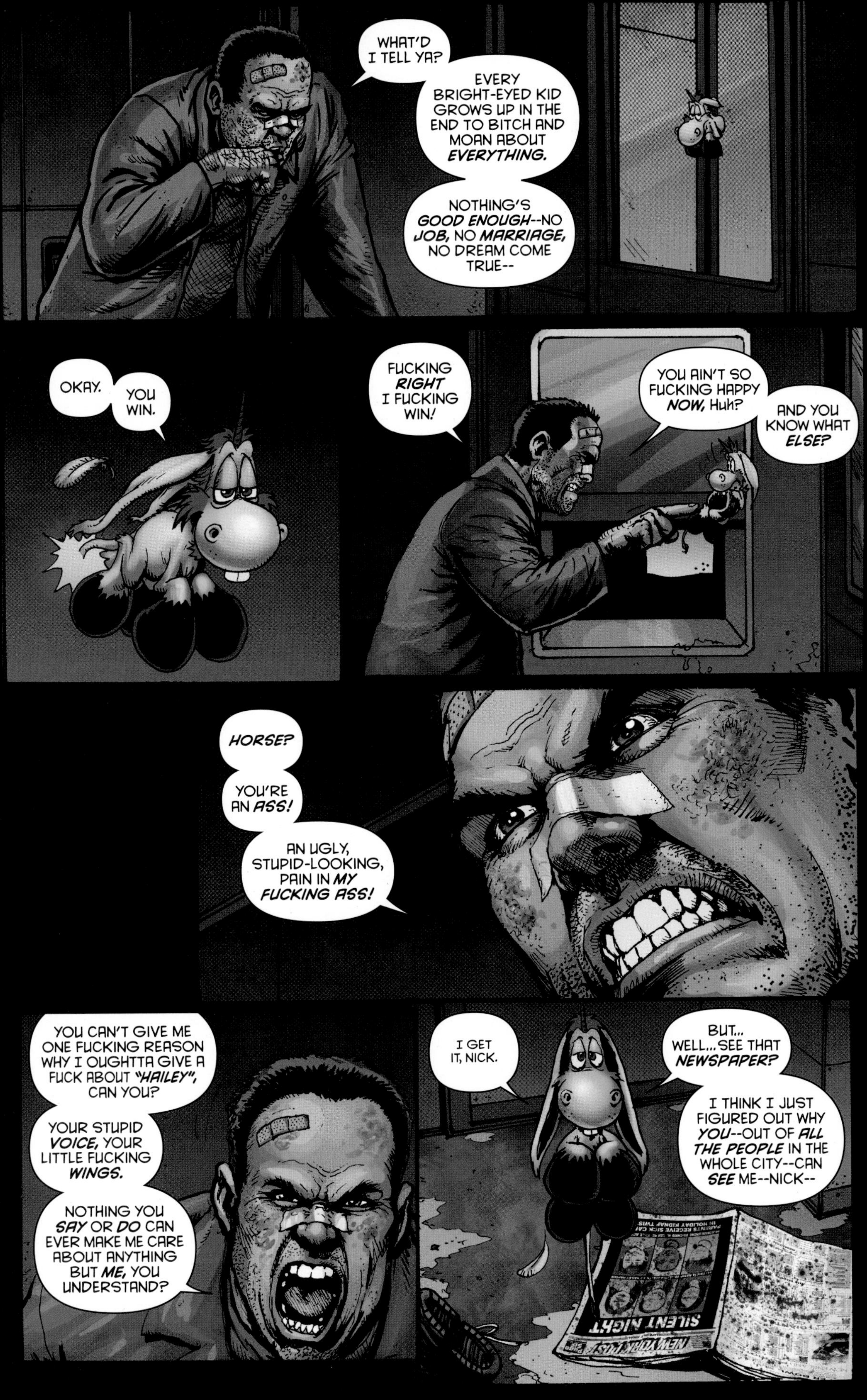
WHAT'D I TELL YA?
EVERY BRIGHT-EYED KID GROWS UP IN THE END TO BITCH AND MOAN ABOUT *EVERYTHING.*
NOTHING'S *GOOD ENOUGH*--NO *JOB,* NO *MARRIAGE,* NO DREAM COME TRUE--
OKAY.
YOU WIN.
FUCKING *RIGHT* I FUCKING WIN!
YOU AIN'T SO FUCKING HAPPY *NOW,* Huh?
AND YOU KNOW WHAT *ELSE?*
HORSE?
YOU'RE AN *ASS!*
AN UGLY, STUPID-LOOKING, PAIN IN *MY FUCKING ASS!*
YOU CAN'T GIVE ME ONE FUCKING REASON WHY I OUGHTTA GIVE A FUCK ABOUT "HAILEY", CAN YOU?
YOUR STUPID *VOICE,* YOUR LITTLE FUCKING *WINGS.*
NOTHING YOU *SAY* OR *DO* CAN EVER MAKE ME CARE ABOUT ANYTHING BUT *ME,* YOU UNDERSTAND?
I GET IT, NICK.
BUT... WELL... SEE THAT *NEWSPAPER?*
I THINK I JUST FIGURED OUT WHY *YOU*--OUT OF *ALL THE PEOPLE* IN THE WHOLE CITY--CAN *SEE* ME--NICK--
NEW YORK POST
SILENT NIGHT

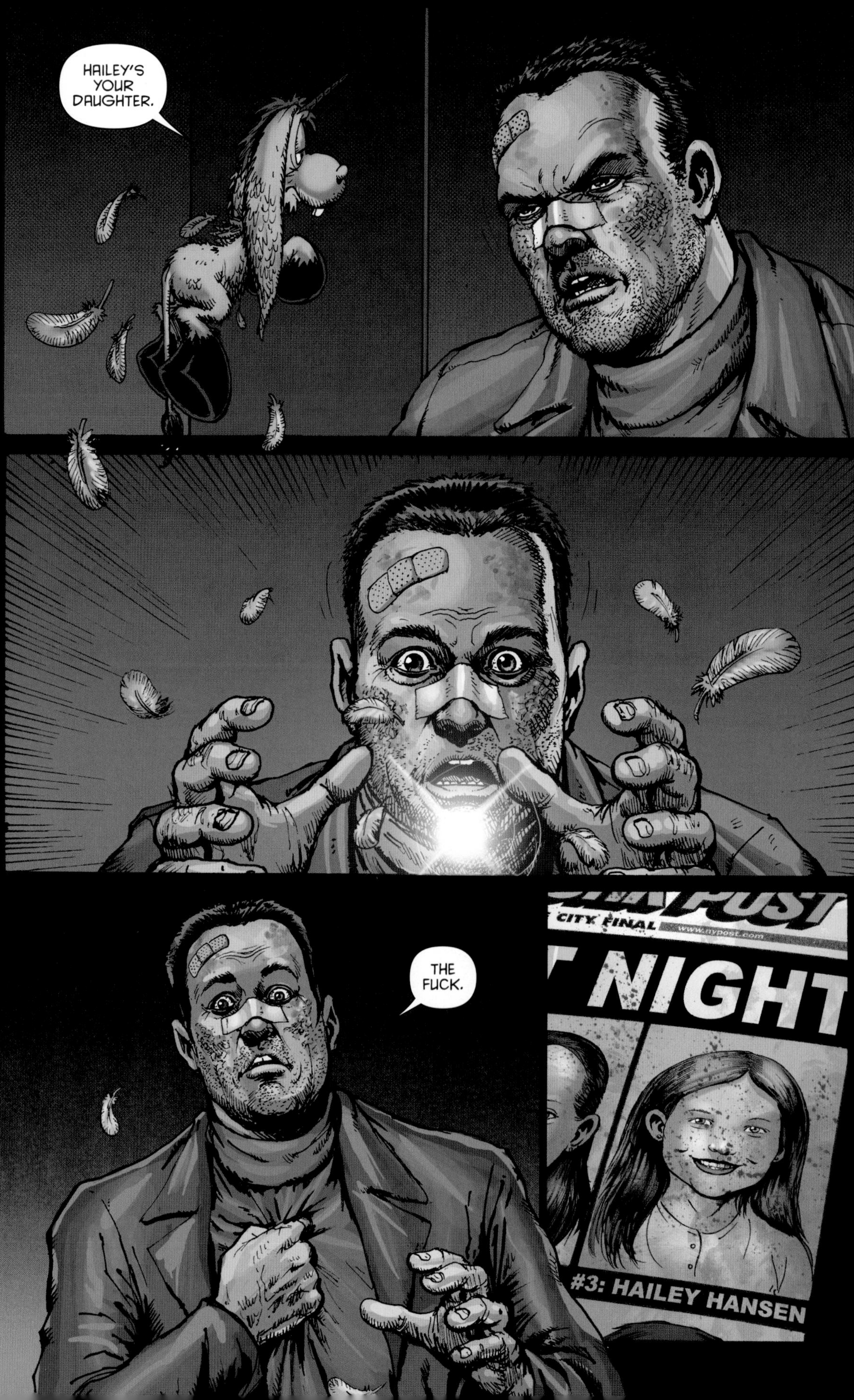
HAILEY'S YOUR DAUGHTER.
CITY FINAL
www.nypost.com
NIGHT
#3: HAILEY HANSEN
THE FUCK.

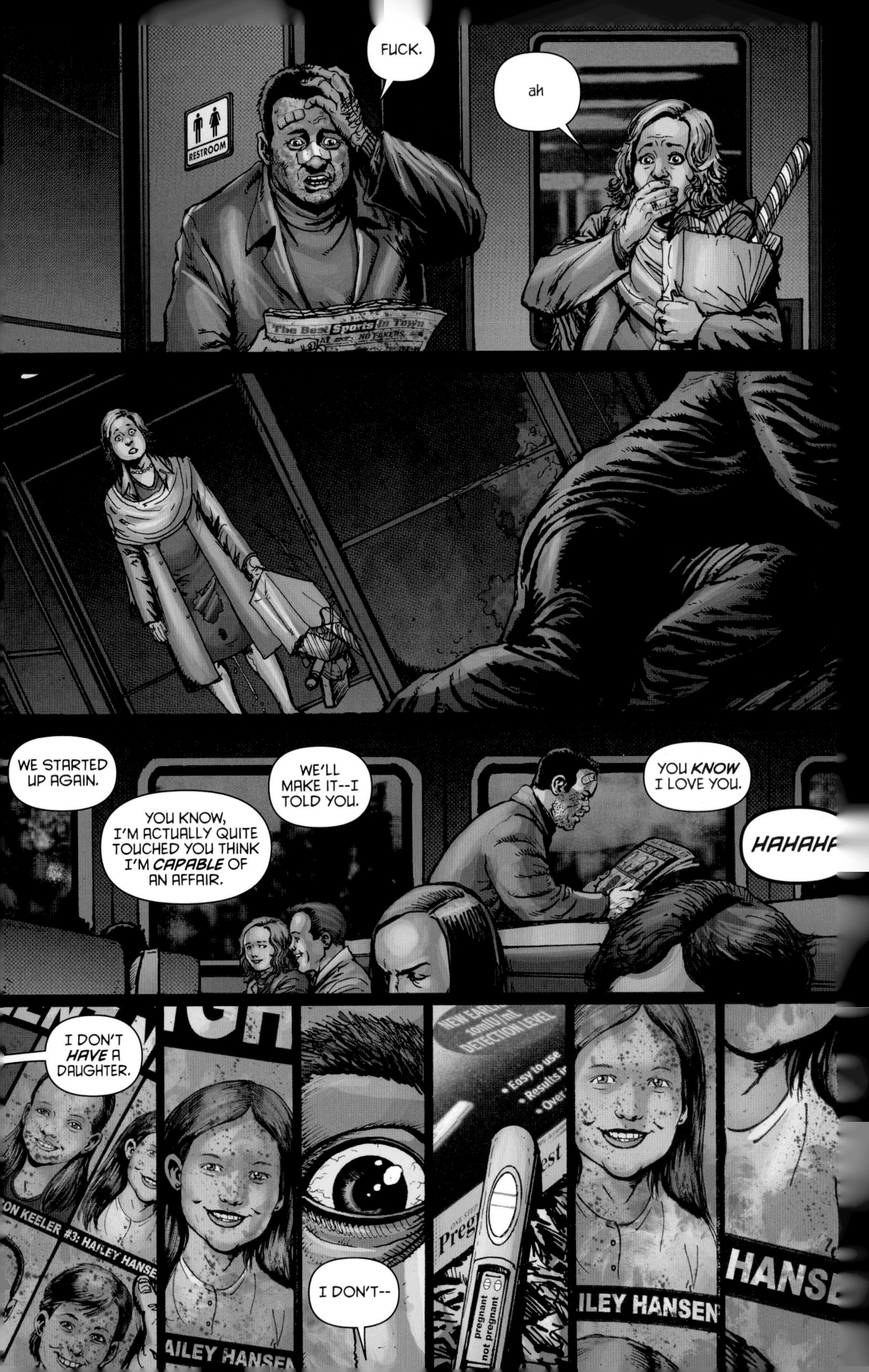
FUCK.
ah
The Best Sports In Town
NO TAKERS
WE STARTED UP AGAIN.
YOU KNOW, I'M ACTUALLY QUITE TOUCHED YOU THINK I'M *CAPABLE* OF AN AFFAIR.
WE'LL MAKE IT--I TOLD YOU.
YOU *KNOW* I LOVE YOU.
HAHAHA
I DON'T *HAVE* A DAUGHTER.
#3: HAILEY HANSE
AILEY HANSEN
I DON'T--
NEW EARLY
10mIU/mL
DETECTION LEVEL
Easy to use
pregnant
not pregnant
ILEY HANSEN
HANSE

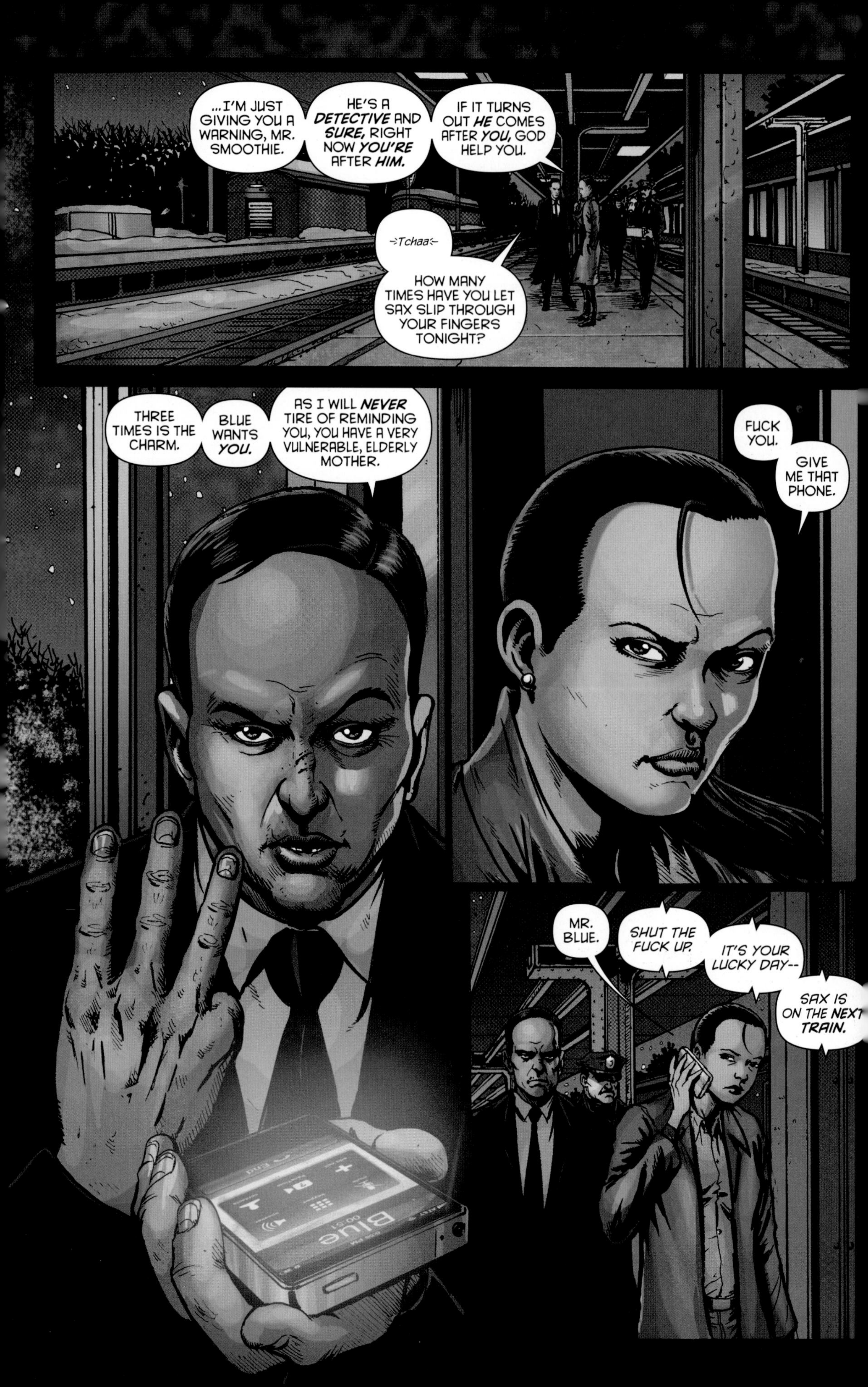
...I'M JUST GIVING YOU A WARNING, MR. SMOOTHIE.
HE'S A DETECTIVE AND SURE, RIGHT NOW YOU'RE AFTER HIM.
IF IT TURNS OUT HE COMES AFTER YOU, GOD HELP YOU.
Tchaa
HOW MANY TIMES HAVE YOU LET SAX SLIP THROUGH YOUR FINGERS TONIGHT?
THREE TIMES IS THE CHARM.
BLUE WANTS YOU.
AS I WILL NEVER TIRE OF REMINDING YOU, YOU HAVE A VERY VULNERABLE, ELDERLY MOTHER.
FUCK YOU.
GIVE ME THAT PHONE.
MR. BLUE.
SHUT THE FUCK UP.
IT'S YOUR LUCKY DAY--
SAX IS ON THE NEXT TRAIN.

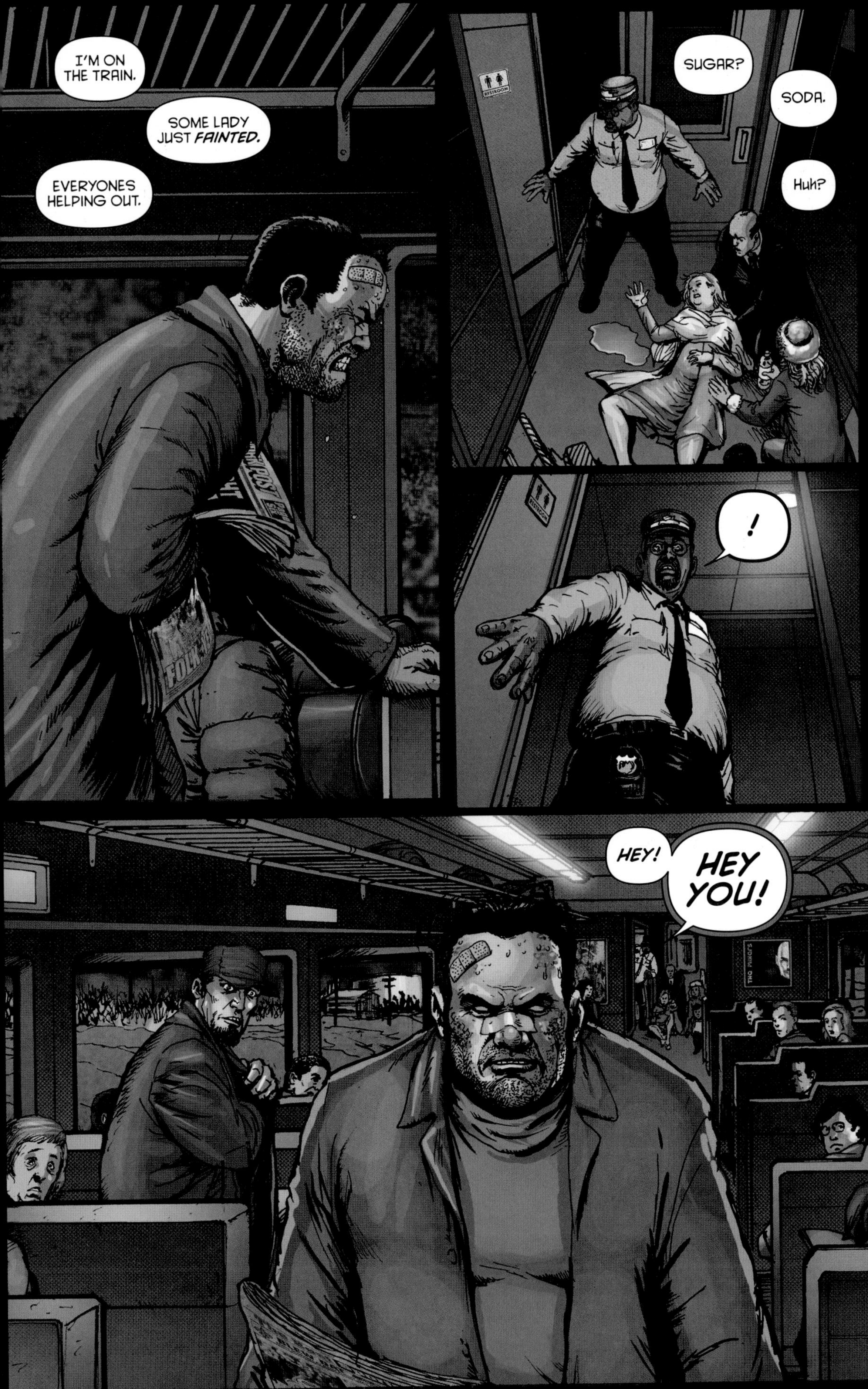
I'M ON THE TRAIN.
SOME LADY JUST *FAINTED.*
EVERYONES HELPING OUT.
SUGAR?
SODA.
Huh?
!
HEY!
HEY YOU!

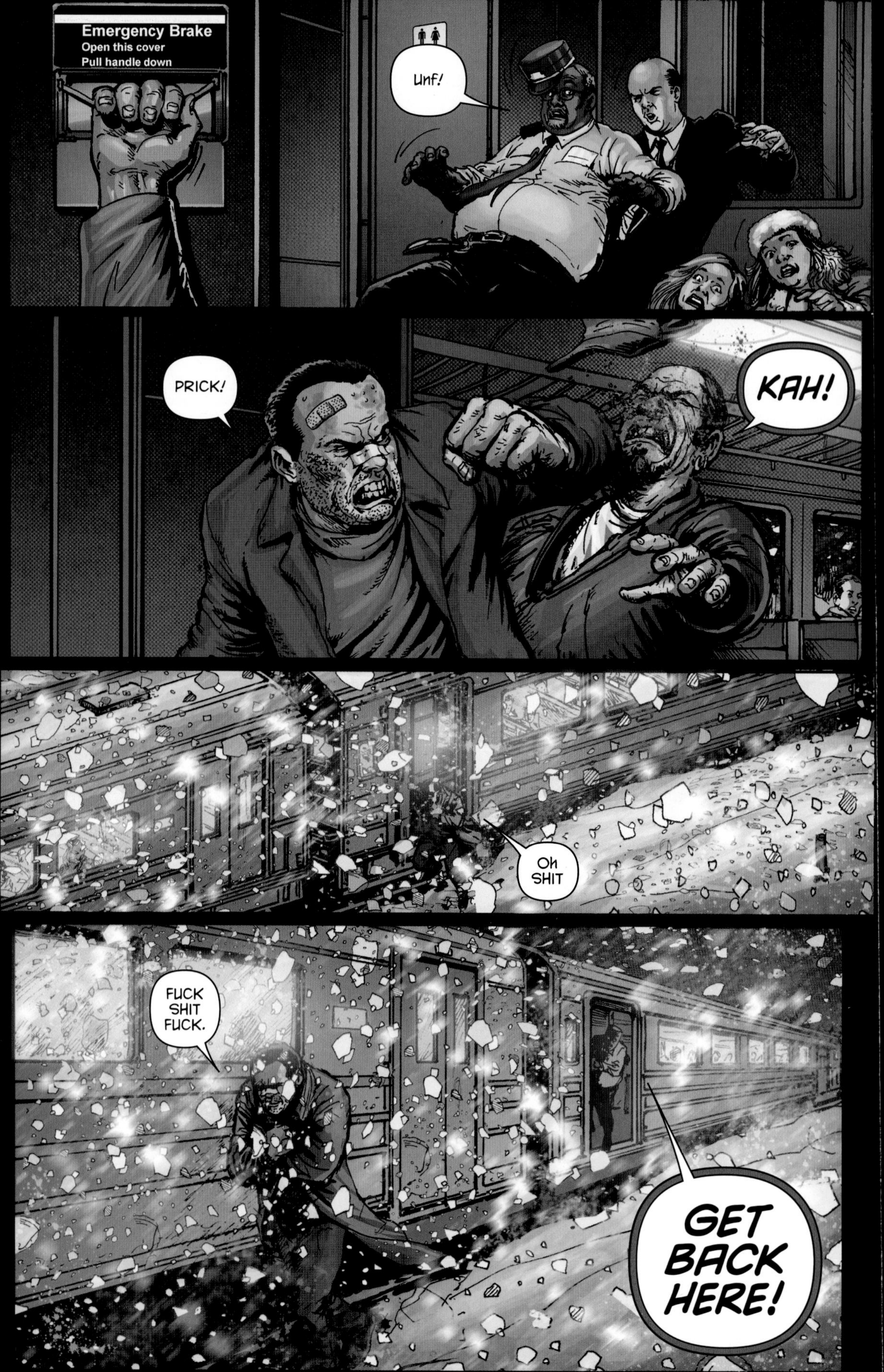
Emergency Brake
Open this cover
Pull handle down
Unf!
PRICK!
KAH!
Oh SHIT
FUCK SHIT FUCK.
GET BACK HERE!

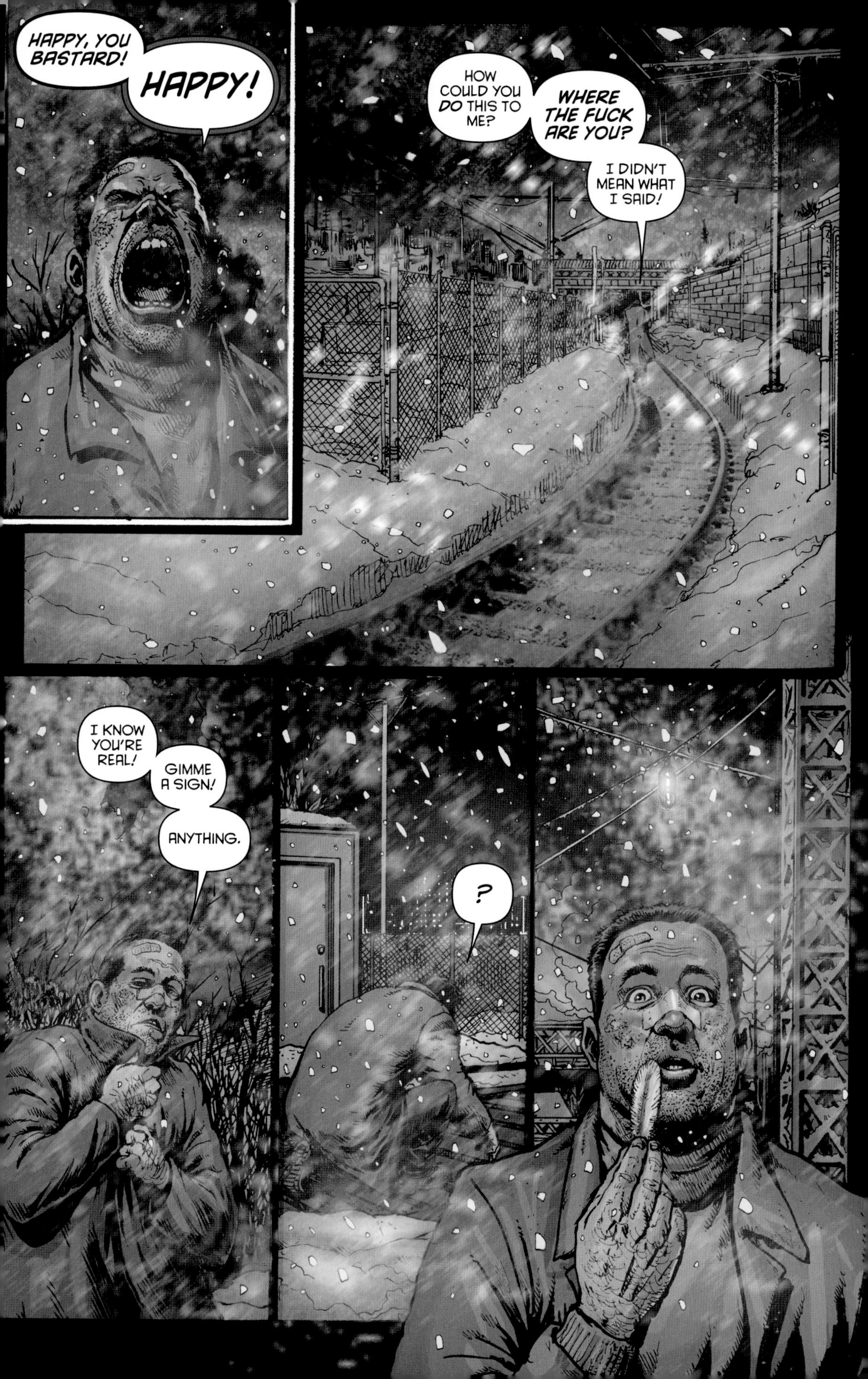
HAPPY, YOU BASTARD!
HAPPY!
HOW COULD YOU DO THIS TO ME?
WHERE THE FUCK ARE YOU?
I DIDN'T MEAN WHAT I SAID!
I KNOW YOU'RE REAL!
GIMME A SIGN!
ANYTHING.
?

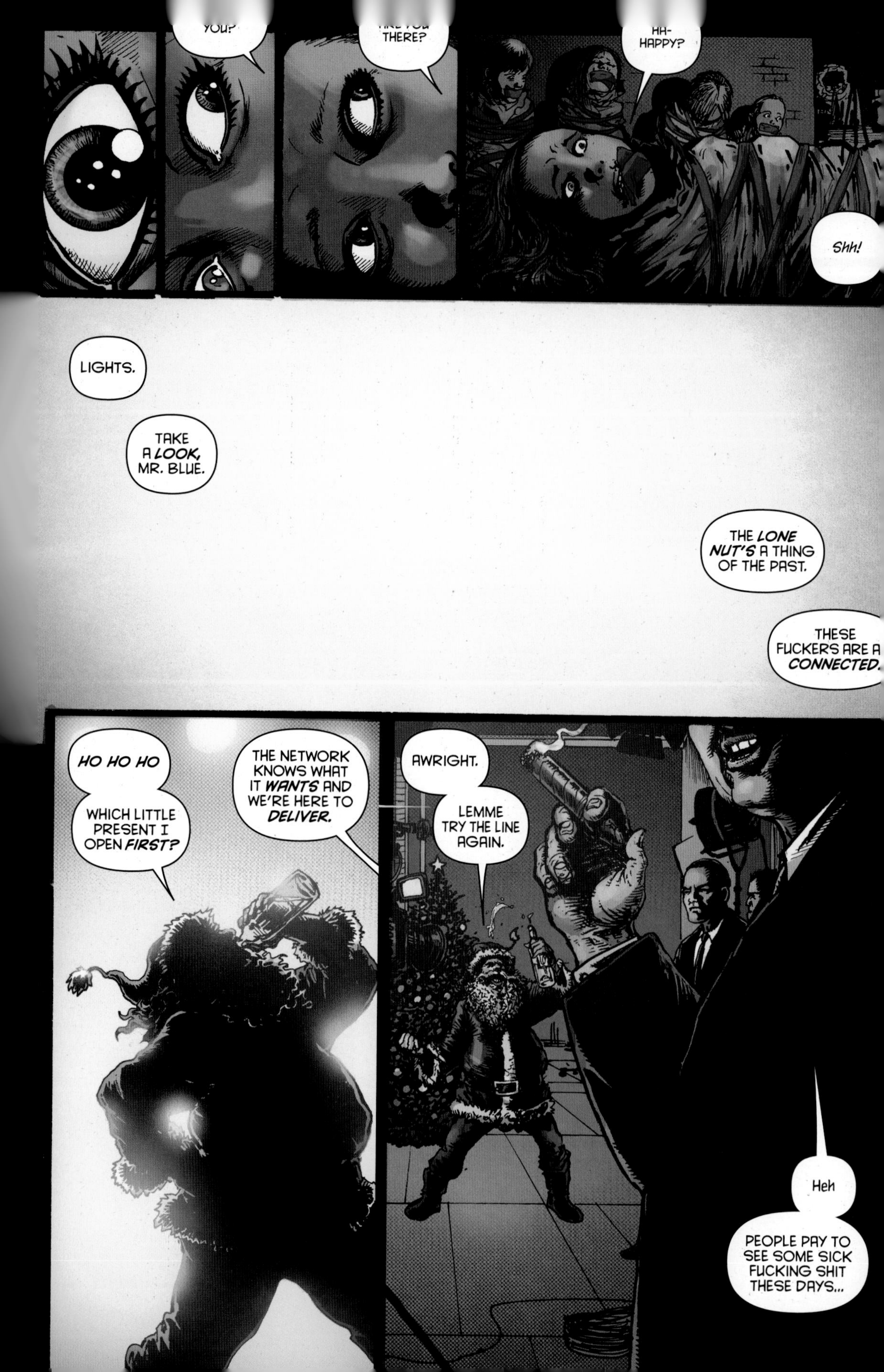
YOU?
THERE?
HH- HAPPY?
Shh!
LIGHTS.
TAKE A LOOK, MR. BLUE.
THE LONE NUT'S A THING OF THE PAST.
THESE FUCKERS ARE A CONNECTED.
HO HO HO
WHICH LITTLE PRESENT I OPEN FIRST?
THE NETWORK KNOWS WHAT IT WANTS AND WE'RE HERE TO DELIVER.
AWRIGHT.
LEMME TRY THE LINE AGAIN.
Heh
PEOPLE PAY TO SEE SOME SICK FUCKING SHIT THESE DAYS...

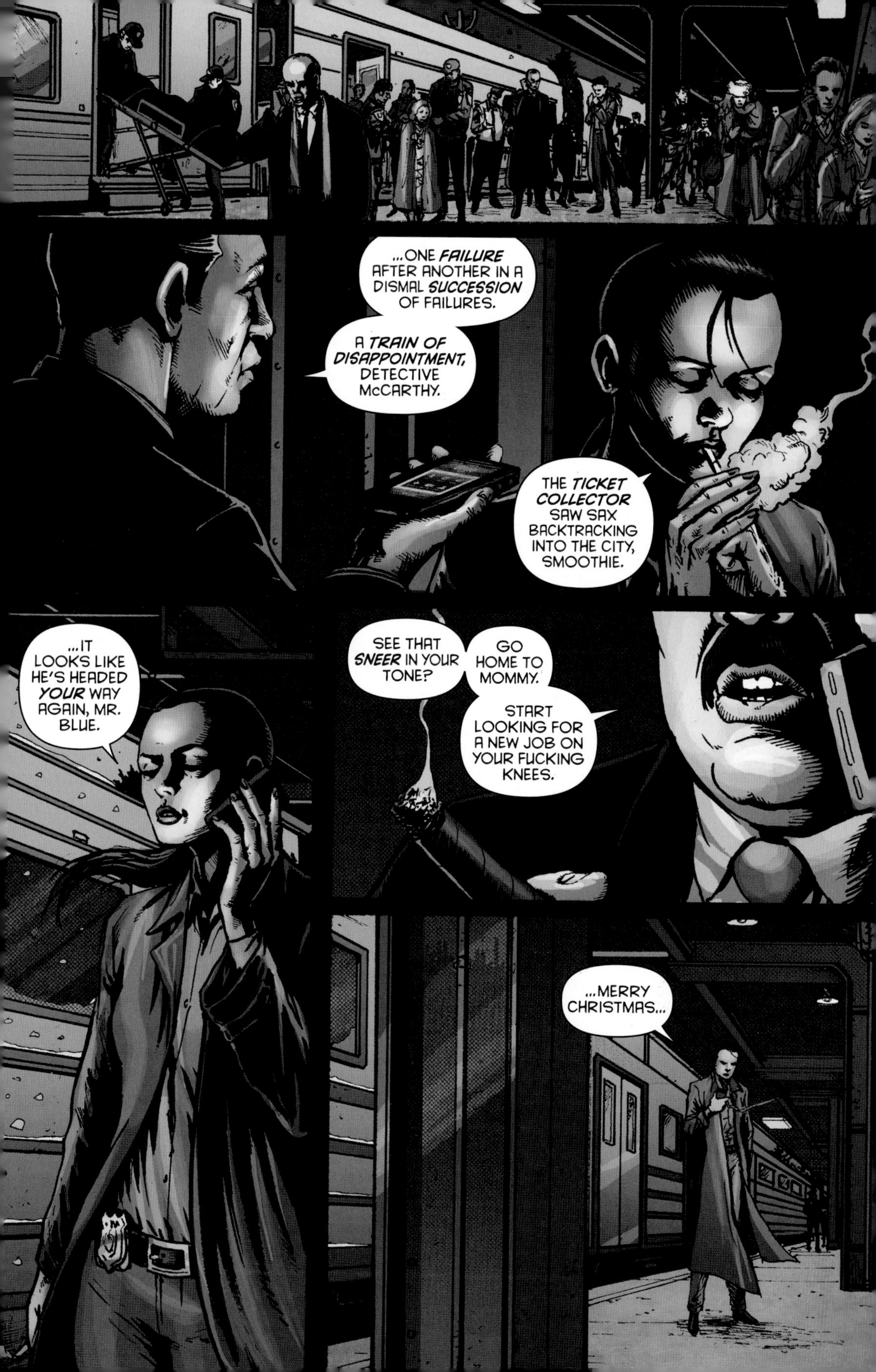
...ONE FAILURE AFTER ANOTHER IN A DISMAL SUCCESSION OF FAILURES.
A TRAIN OF DISAPPOINTMENT, DETECTIVE McCARTHY.
THE TICKET COLLECTOR SAW SAX BACKTRACKING INTO THE CITY, SMOOTHIE.
...IT LOOKS LIKE HE'S HEADED YOUR WAY AGAIN, MR. BLUE.
SEE THAT SNEER IN YOUR TONE?
GO HOME TO MOMMY.
START LOOKING FOR A NEW JOB ON YOUR FUCKING KNEES.
...MERRY CHRISTMAS...

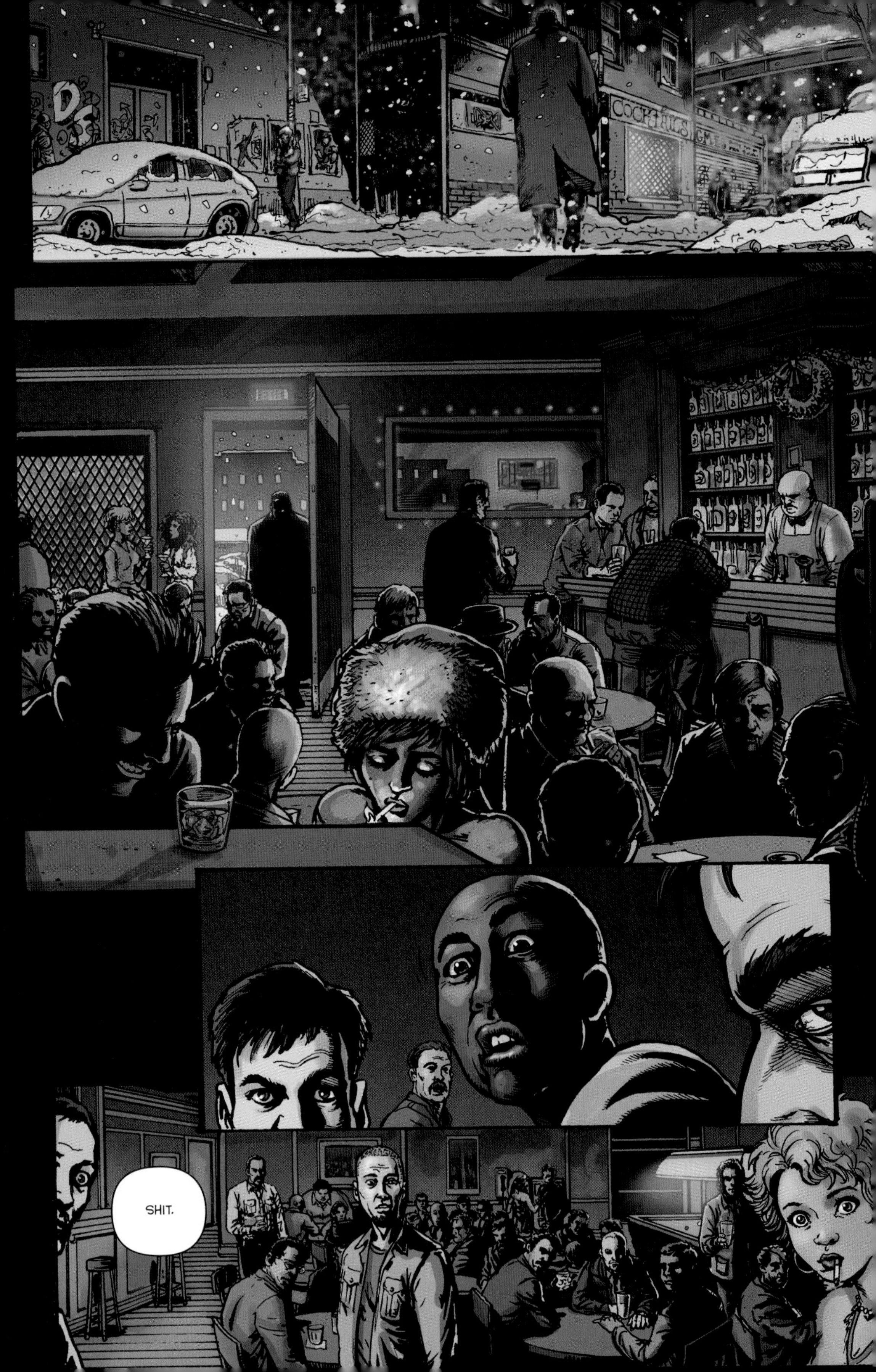
SHIT.

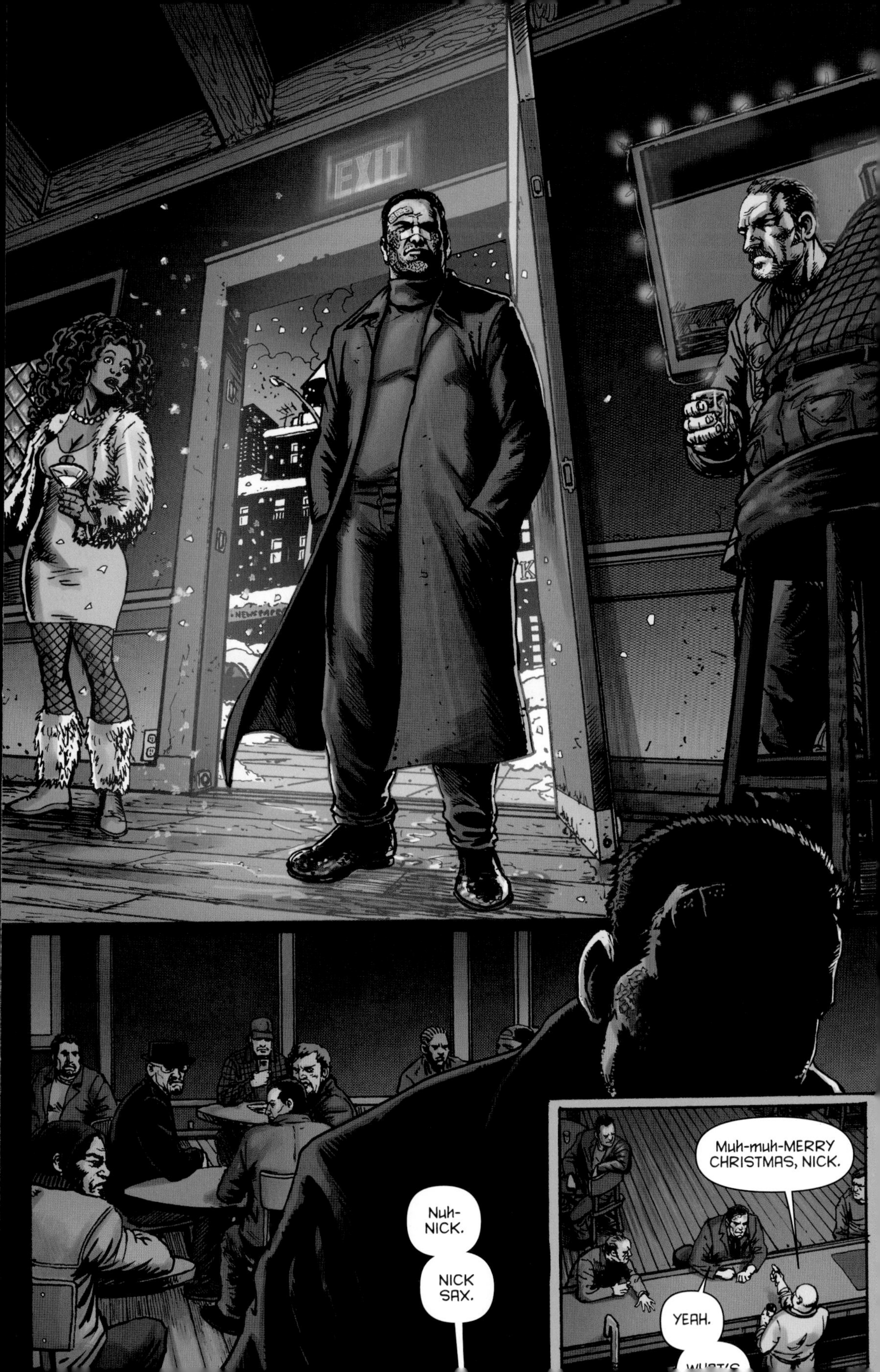
EXIT
Nuh-NICK.
NICK SAX.
Muh-muh-MERRY CHRISTMAS, NICK.
YEAH.

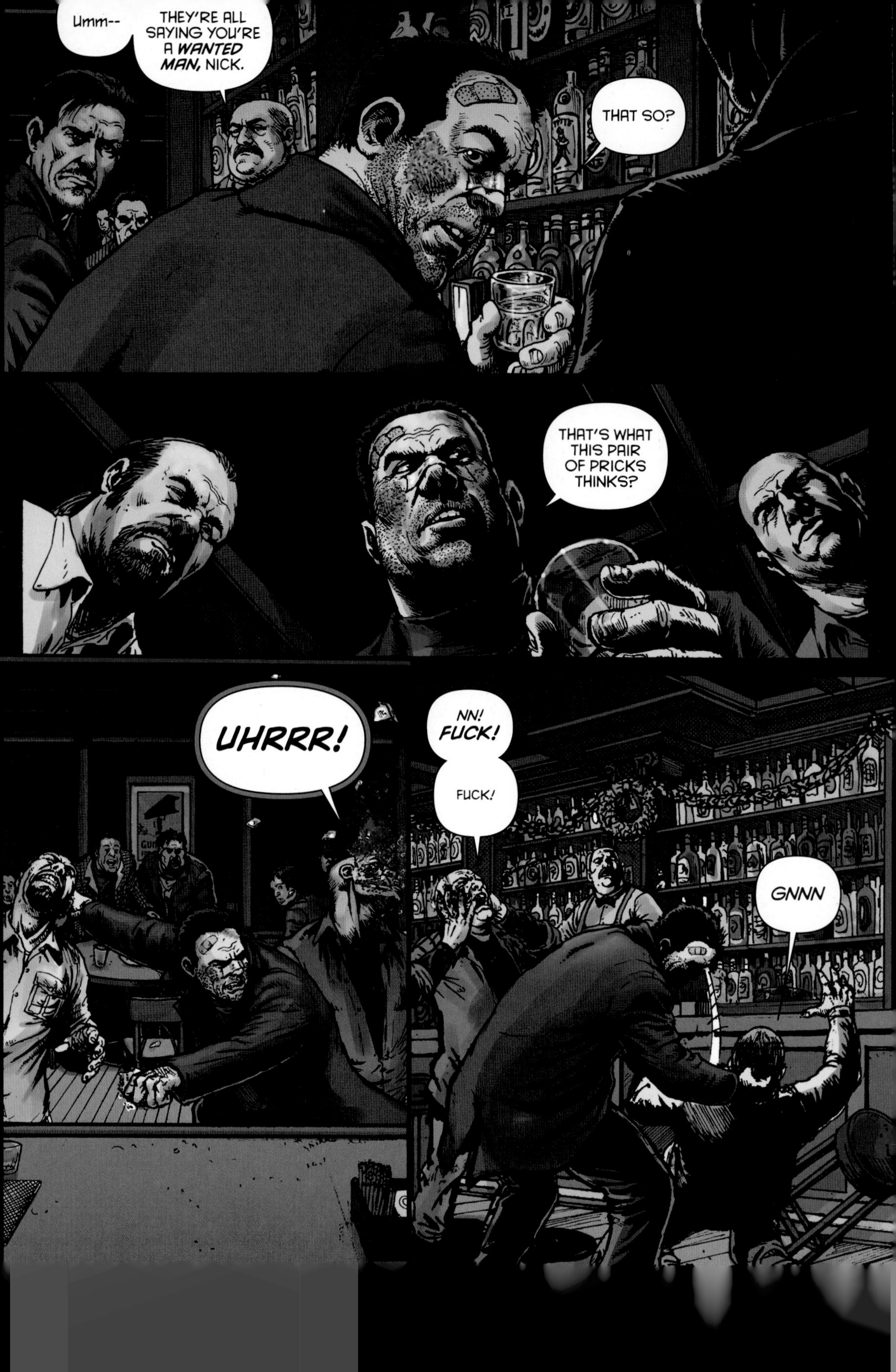
Umm--
THEY'RE ALL SAYING YOU'RE A WANTED MAN, NICK.
THAT SO?
THAT'S WHAT THIS PAIR OF PRICKS THINKS?
UHRRR!
NN! FUCK!
FUCK!
GNNN

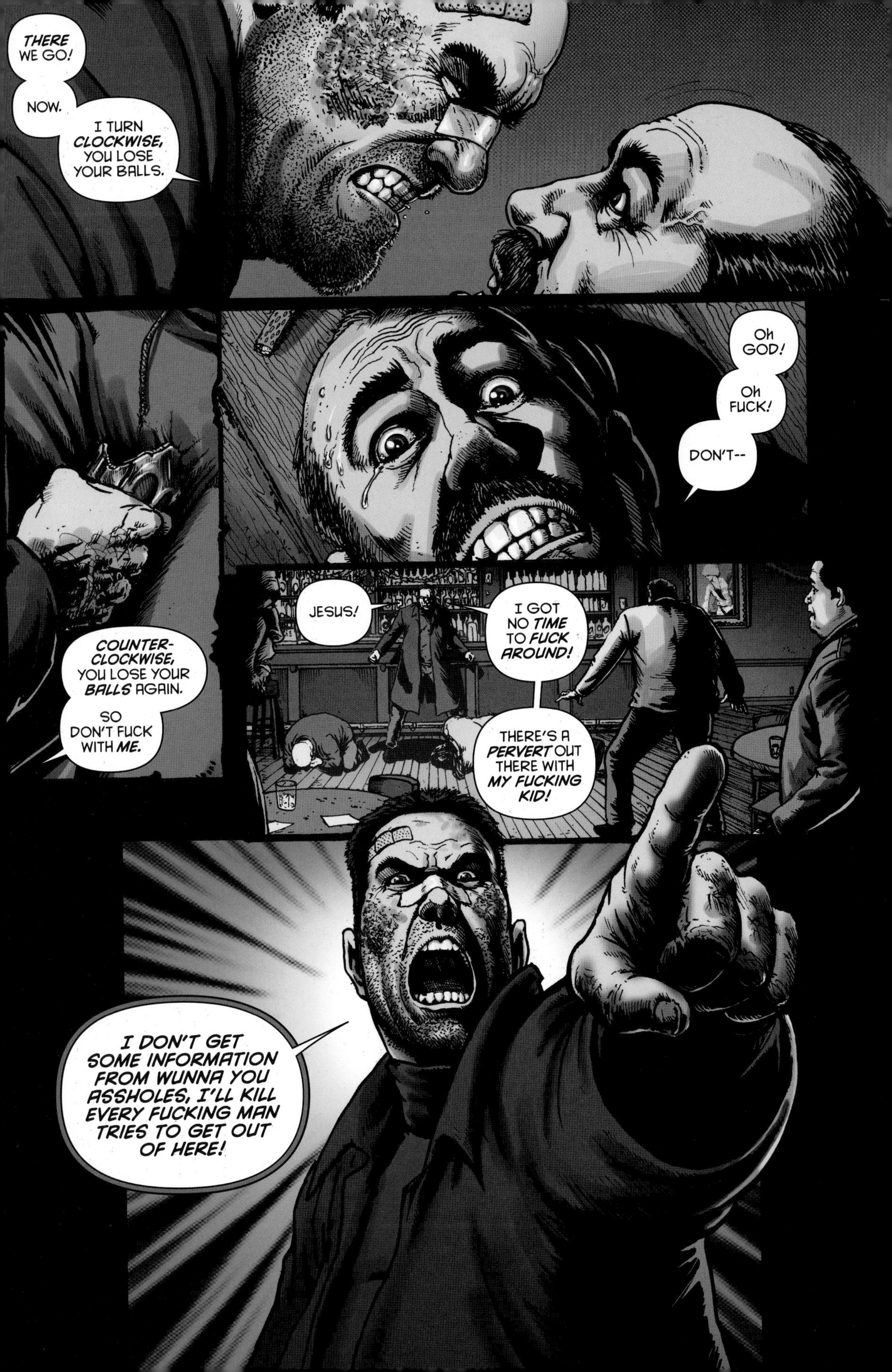
THERE WE GO!
NOW.
I TURN CLOCKWISE, YOU LOSE YOUR BALLS.
OH GOD!
OH FUCK!
DON'T--
COUNTER-CLOCKWISE, YOU LOSE YOUR BALLS AGAIN.
SO DON'T FUCK WITH ME.
JESUS!
I GOT NO TIME TO FUCK AROUND!
THERE'S A PERVERT OUT THERE WITH MY FUCKING KID!
I DON'T GET SOME INFORMATION FROM WUNNA YOU ASSHOLES, I'LL KILL EVERY FUCKING MAN TRIES TO GET OUT OF HERE!

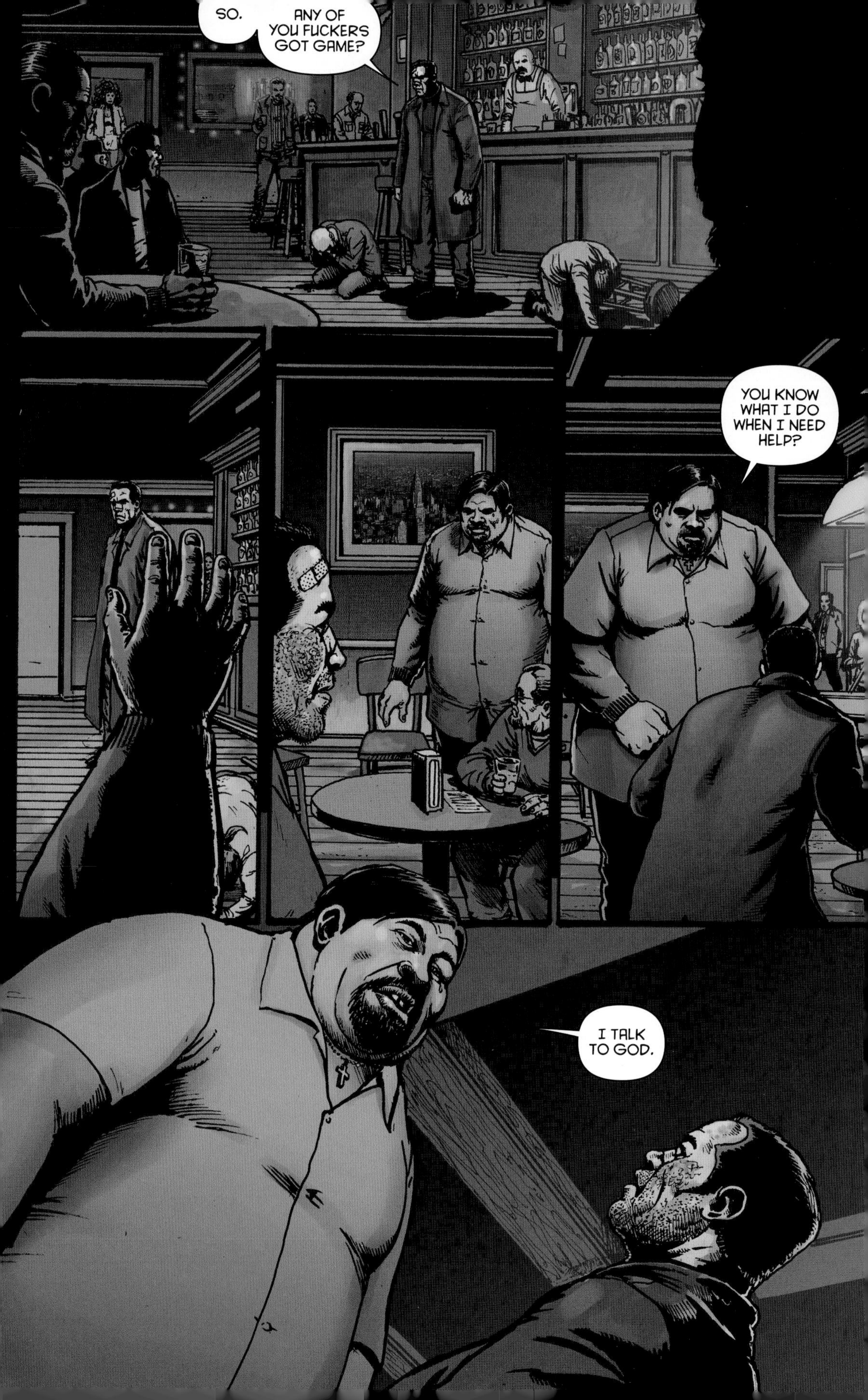
SO.
ANY OF YOU FUCKERS GOT GAME?
YOU KNOW WHAT I DO WHEN I NEED HELP?
I TALK TO GOD.

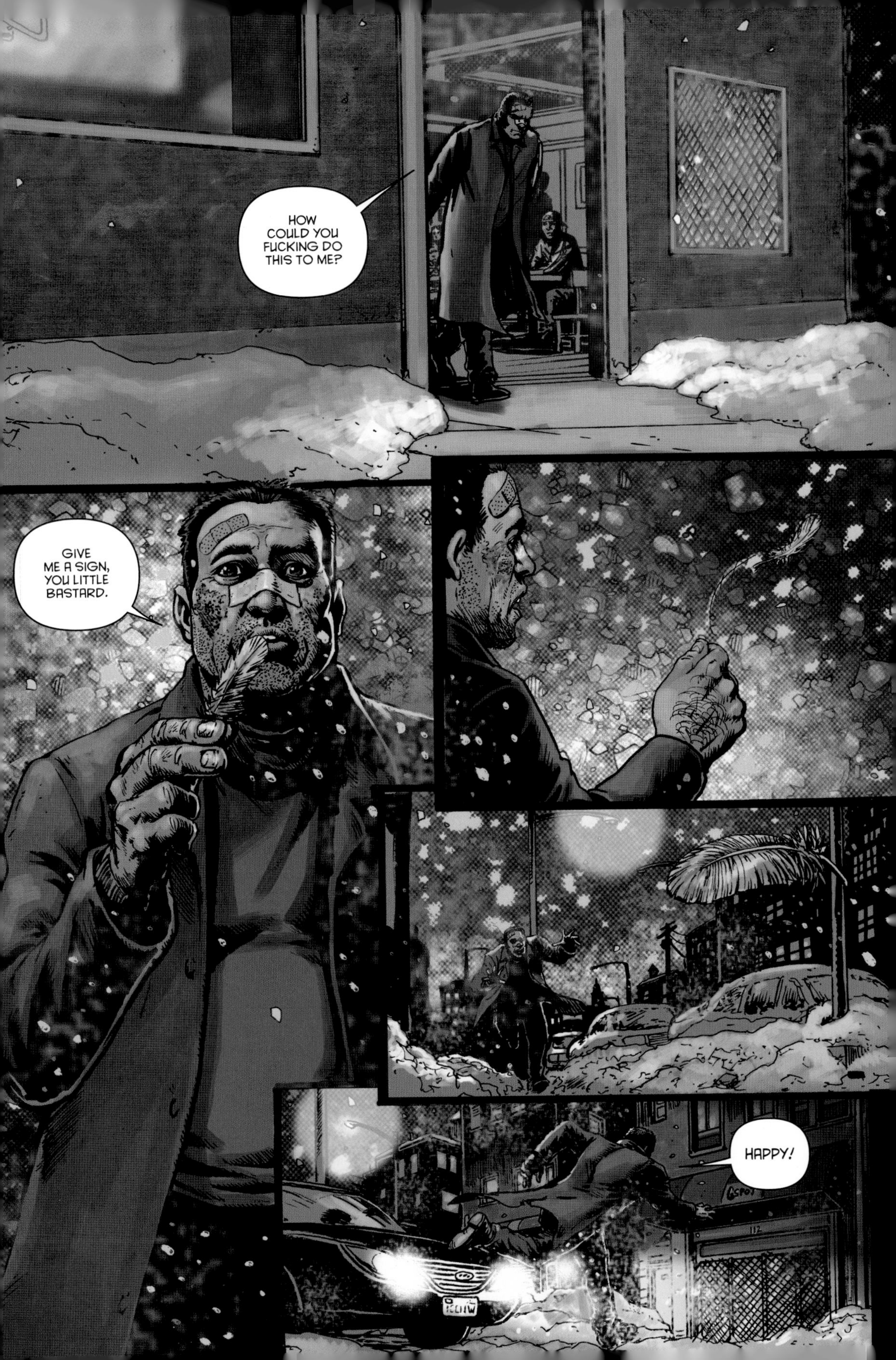
HOW COULD YOU FUCKING DO THIS TO ME?
GIVE ME A SIGN, YOU LITTLE BASTARD.
HAPPY!

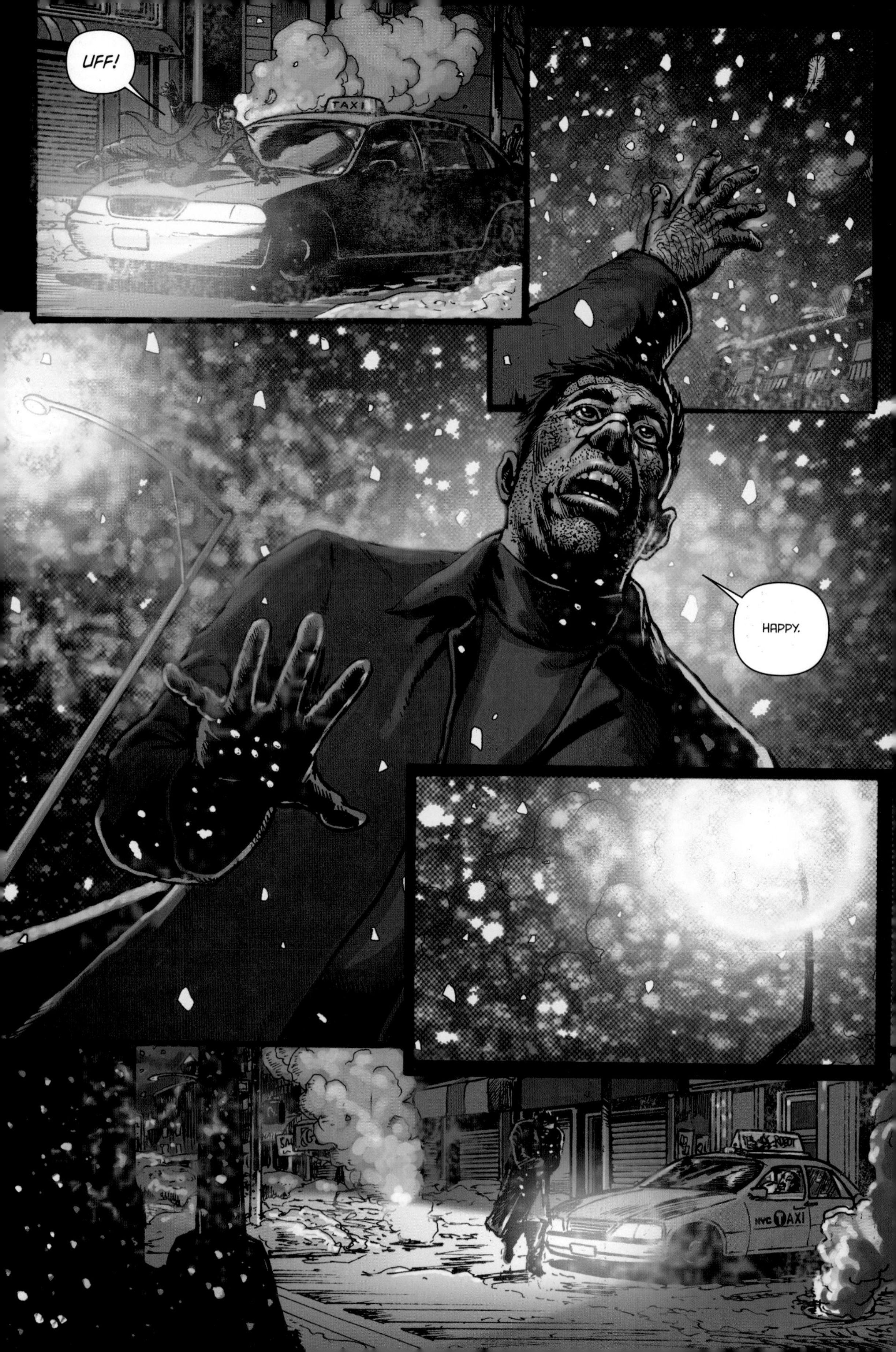
UFF!
TAXI
HAPPY.
NYC TAXI

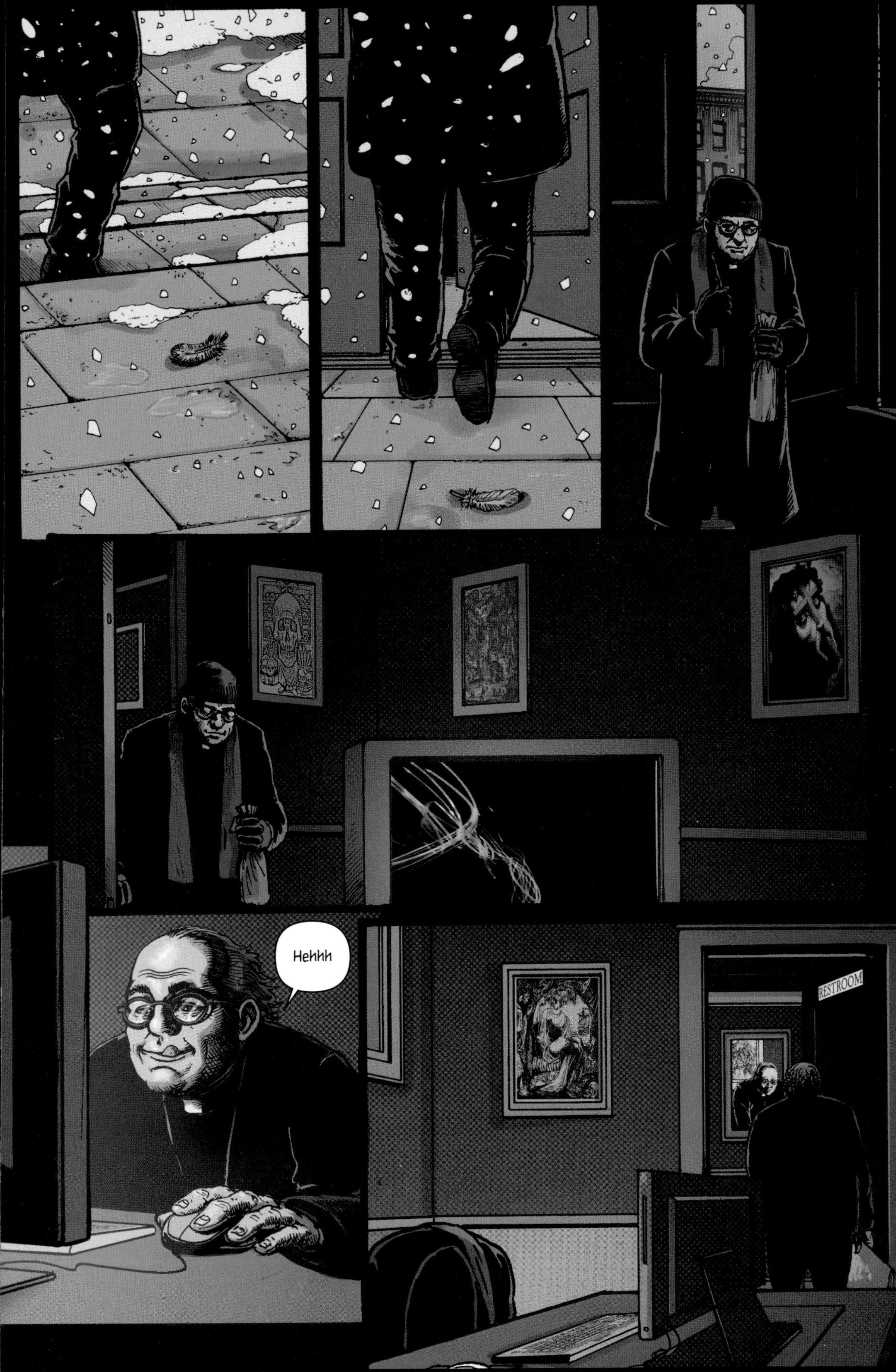
Hehhh
RESTROOM

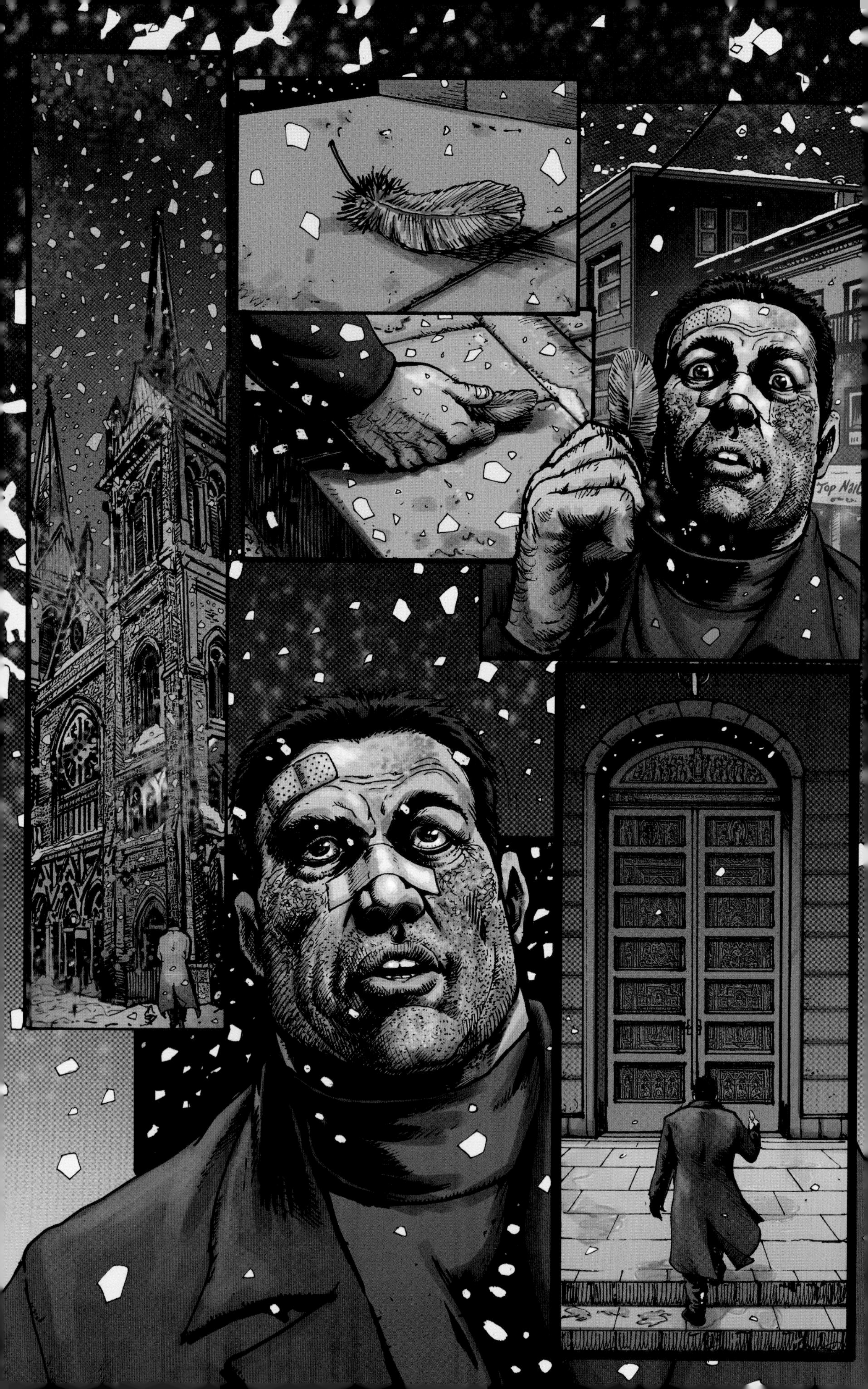

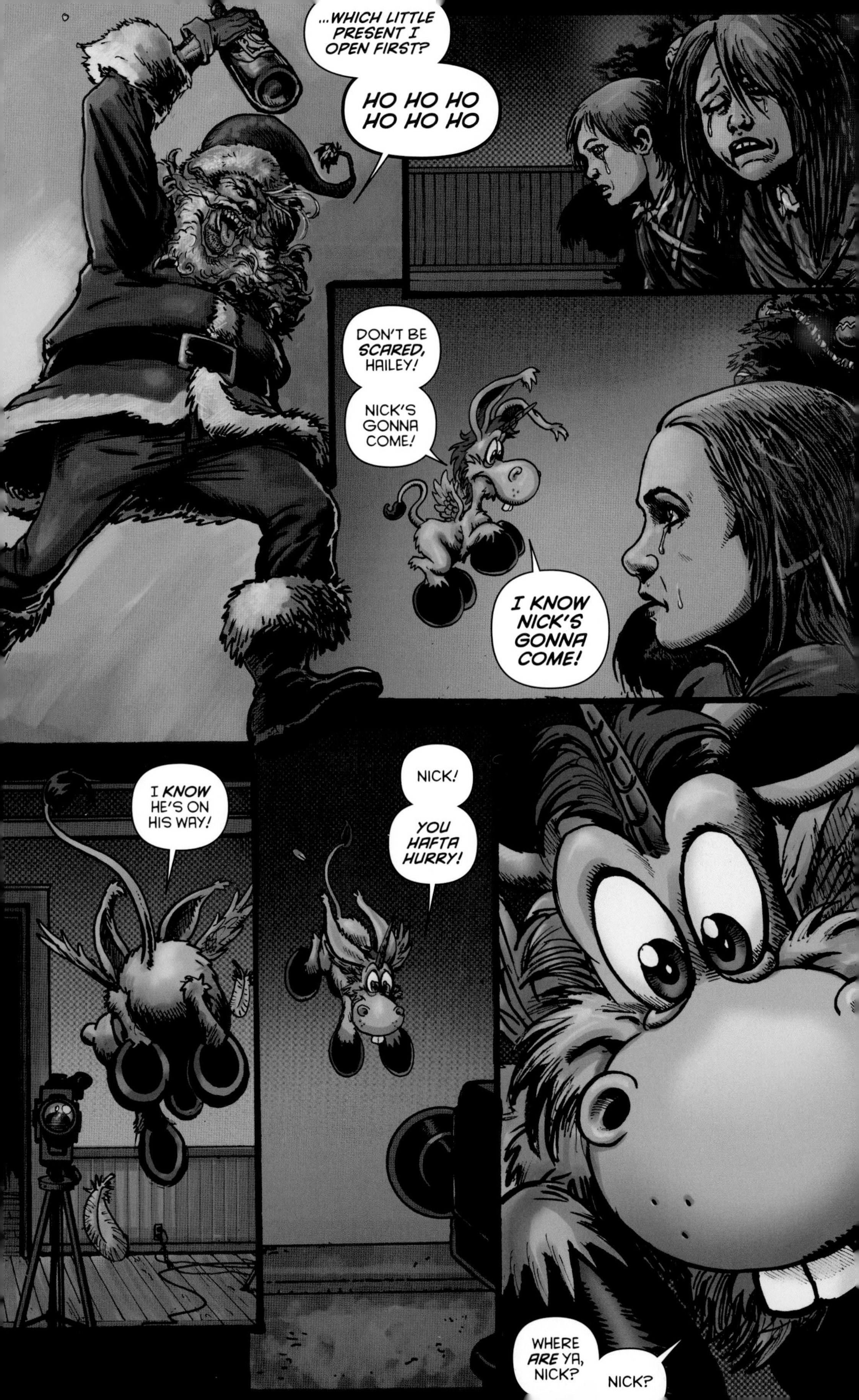
...WHICH LITTLE PRESENT I OPEN FIRST?
HO HO HO HO HO HO
DON'T BE SCARED, HAILEY!
NICK'S GONNA COME!
I KNOW NICK'S GONNA COME!
I KNOW HE'S ON HIS WAY!
NICK!
YOU HAFTA HURRY!
WHERE ARE YA, NICK?
NICK?

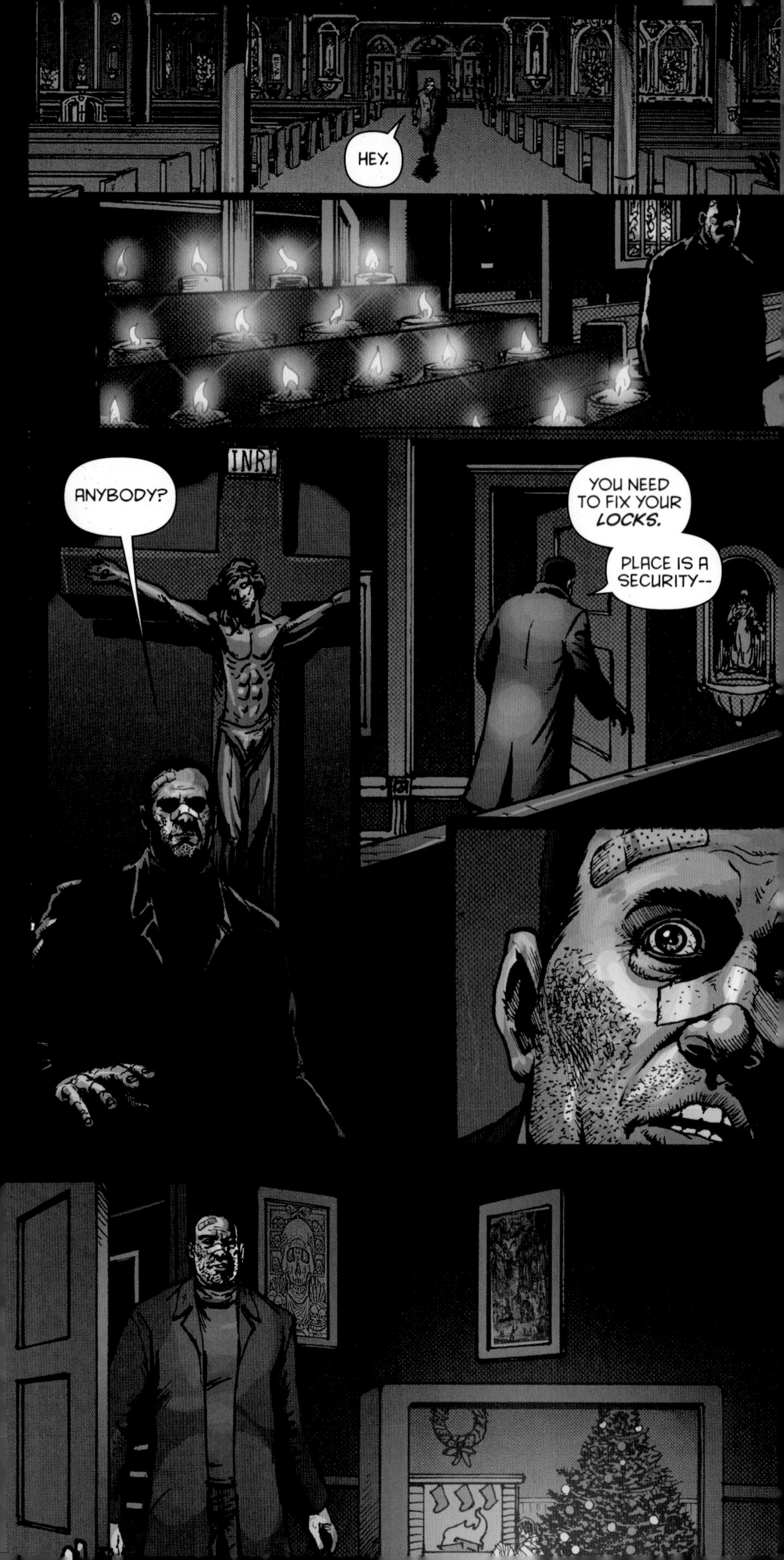
HEY.
ANYBODY?
INRI
YOU NEED TO FIX YOUR LOCKS.
PLACE IS A SECURITY--

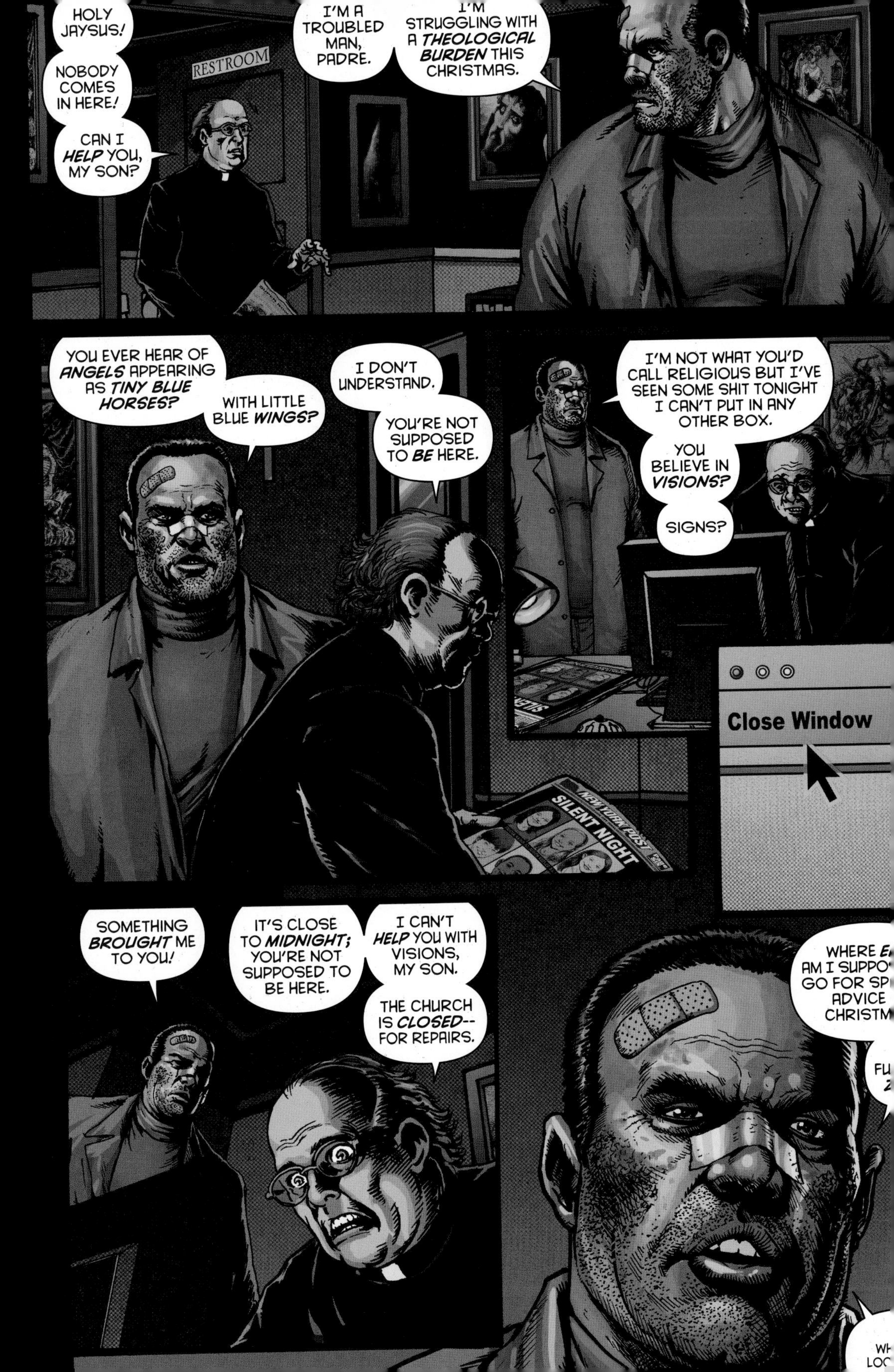
HOLY JAYSUS!
NOBODY COMES IN HERE!
CAN I HELP YOU, MY SON?
RESTROOM
I'M A TROUBLED MAN, PADRE.
I'M STRUGGLING WITH A THEOLOGICAL BURDEN THIS CHRISTMAS.
YOU EVER HEAR OF ANGELS APPEARING AS TINY BLUE HORSES?
WITH LITTLE BLUE WINGS?
I DON'T UNDERSTAND.
YOU'RE NOT SUPPOSED TO BE HERE.
NEW YORK POST
SILENT NIGHT
I'M NOT WHAT YOU'D CALL RELIGIOUS BUT I'VE SEEN SOME SHIT TONIGHT I CAN'T PUT IN ANY OTHER BOX.
YOU BELIEVE IN VISIONS?
SIGNS?
Close Window
SOMETHING BROUGHT ME TO YOU!
IT'S CLOSE TO MIDNIGHT; YOU'RE NOT SUPPOSED TO BE HERE.
I CAN'T HELP YOU WITH VISIONS, MY SON.
THE CHURCH IS CLOSED-- FOR REPAIRS.
WHERE E
AM I SUPPO
GO FOR SP
ADVICE
CHRISTM
FU
WH
LOC

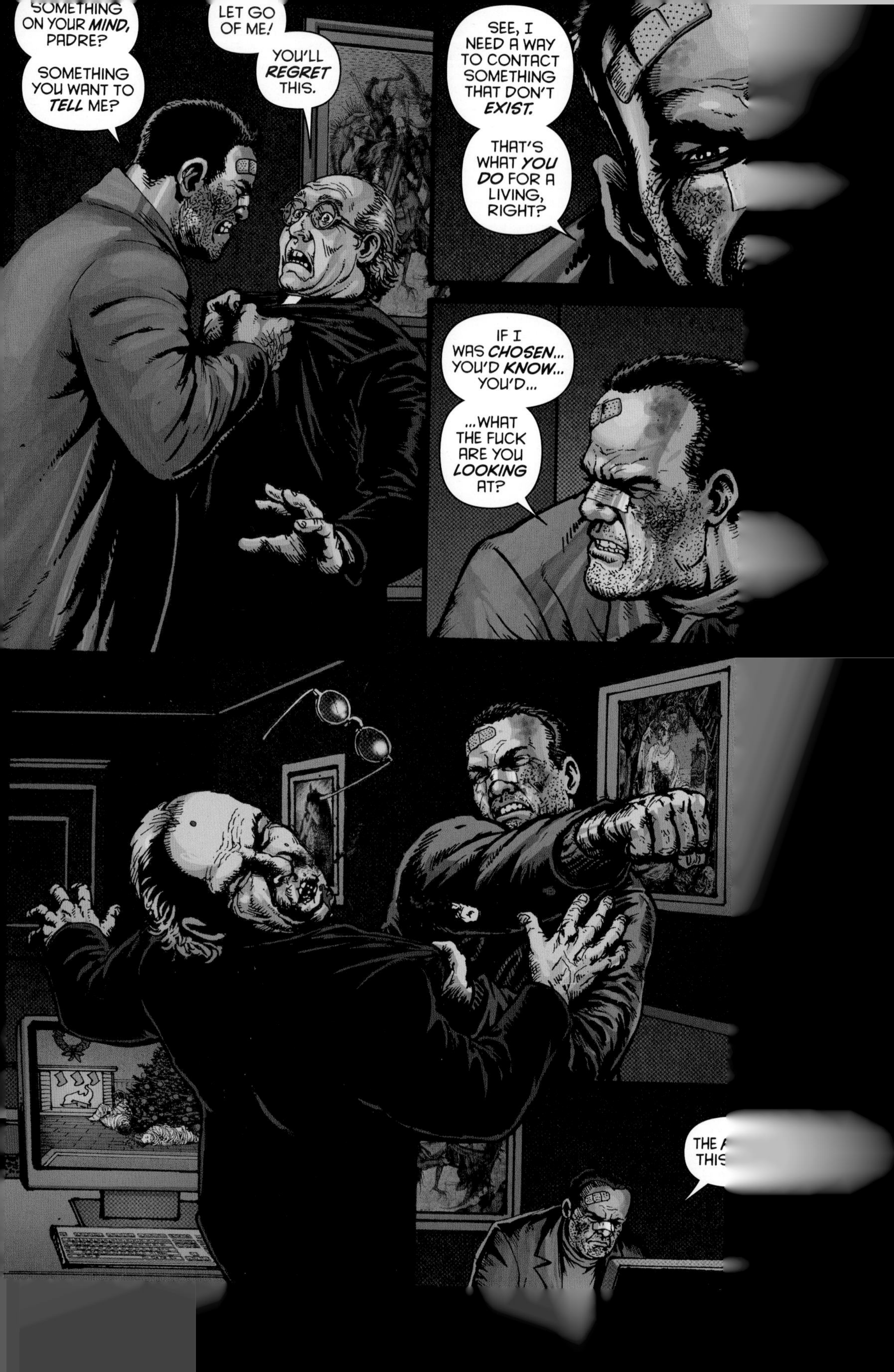

SOMETHING ON YOUR MIND, PADRE?
SOMETHING YOU WANT TO TELL ME?
LET GO OF ME!
YOU'LL REGRET THIS.
SEE, I NEED A WAY TO CONTACT SOMETHING THAT DON'T EXIST.
THAT'S WHAT YOU DO FOR A LIVING, RIGHT?
IF I WAS CHOSEN... YOU'D KNOW... YOU'D...
...WHAT THE FUCK ARE YOU LOOKING AT?

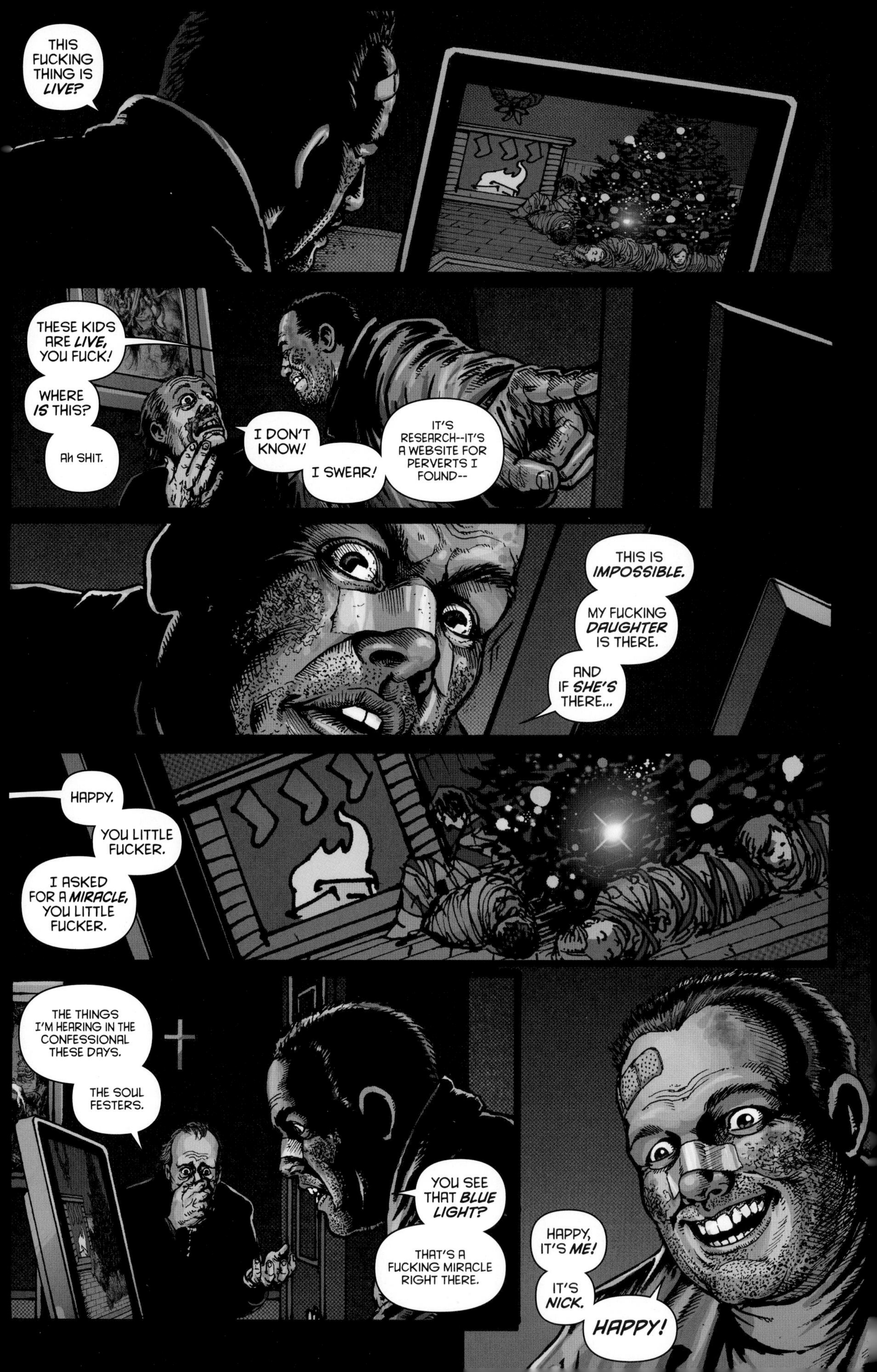
THIS FUCKING THING IS *LIVE?*
THESE KIDS ARE *LIVE,* YOU FUCK!
WHERE *IS* THIS?
Ah SHIT.
I DON'T KNOW!
I SWEAR!
IT'S RESEARCH--IT'S A WEBSITE FOR PERVERTS I FOUND--
THIS IS *IMPOSSIBLE.*
MY FUCKING *DAUGHTER* IS THERE.
AND IF *SHE'S* THERE...
HAPPY.
YOU LITTLE FUCKER.
I ASKED FOR A *MIRACLE,* YOU LITTLE FUCKER.
THE THINGS I'M HEARING IN THE CONFESSIONAL THESE DAYS.
THE SOUL FESTERS.
YOU SEE THAT *BLUE LIGHT?*
THAT'S A FUCKING MIRACLE RIGHT THERE.
HAPPY, IT'S *ME!*
IT'S *NICK.*
HAPPY!

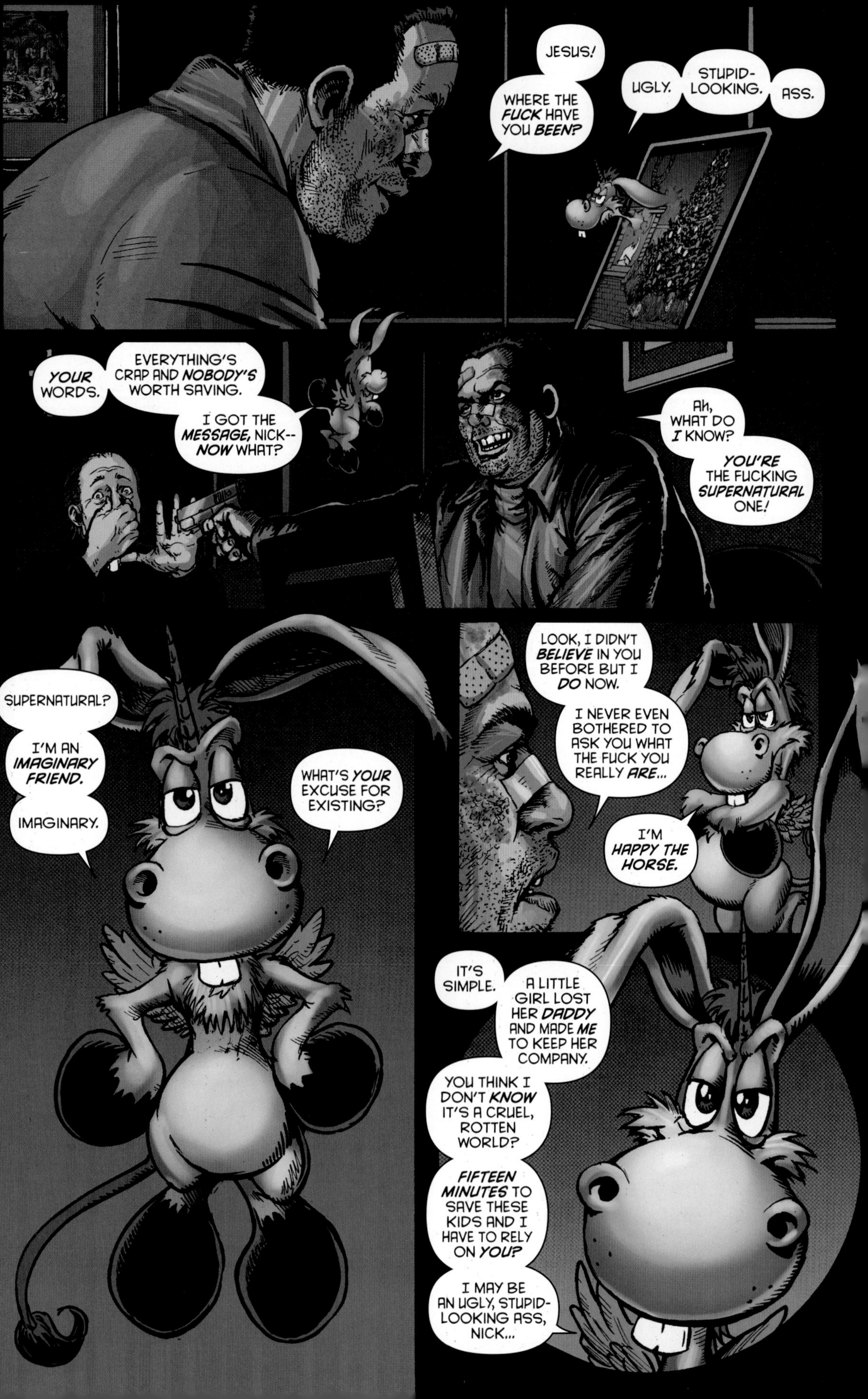
JESUS!
WHERE THE FUCK HAVE YOU BEEN?
UGLY.
STUPID-LOOKING.
ASS.
YOUR WORDS.
EVERYTHING'S CRAP AND NOBODY'S WORTH SAVING.
I GOT THE MESSAGE, NICK-- NOW WHAT?
AH, WHAT DO I KNOW?
YOU'RE THE FUCKING SUPERNATURAL ONE!
SUPERNATURAL?
I'M AN IMAGINARY FRIEND.
IMAGINARY.
WHAT'S YOUR EXCUSE FOR EXISTING?
LOOK, I DIDN'T BELIEVE IN YOU BEFORE BUT I DO NOW.
I NEVER EVEN BOTHERED TO ASK YOU WHAT THE FUCK YOU REALLY ARE...
I'M HAPPY THE HORSE.
IT'S SIMPLE.
A LITTLE GIRL LOST HER DADDY AND MADE ME TO KEEP HER COMPANY.
YOU THINK I DON'T KNOW IT'S A CRUEL, ROTTEN WORLD?
FIFTEEN MINUTES TO SAVE THESE KIDS AND I HAVE TO RELY ON YOU?
I MAY BE AN UGLY, STUPID-LOOKING ASS, NICK...

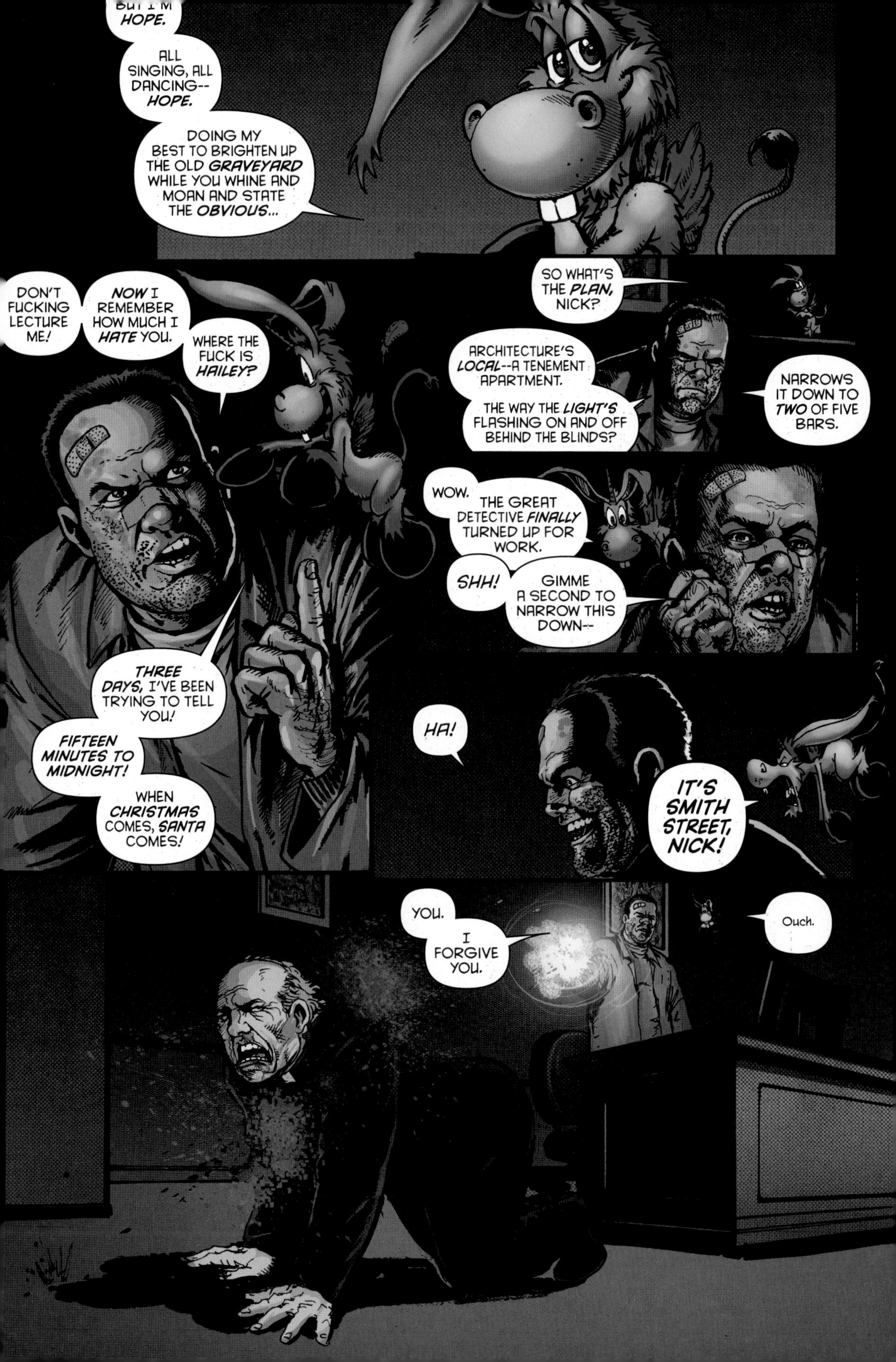
BUT I'M HOPE.
ALL SINGING, ALL DANCING-- HOPE.
DOING MY BEST TO BRIGHTEN UP THE OLD GRAVEYARD WHILE YOU WHINE AND MOAN AND STATE THE OBVIOUS...
DON'T FUCKING LECTURE ME!
NOW I REMEMBER HOW MUCH I HATE YOU.
WHERE THE FUCK IS HAILEY?
THREE DAYS, I'VE BEEN TRYING TO TELL YOU!
FIFTEEN MINUTES TO MIDNIGHT!
WHEN CHRISTMAS COMES, SANTA COMES!
SO WHAT'S THE PLAN, NICK?
ARCHITECTURE'S LOCAL--A TENEMENT APARTMENT.
THE WAY THE LIGHT'S FLASHING ON AND OFF BEHIND THE BLINDS?
NARROWS IT DOWN TO TWO OF FIVE BARS.
WOW. THE GREAT DETECTIVE FINALLY TURNED UP FOR WORK.
SHH!
GIMME A SECOND TO NARROW THIS DOWN--
HA!
IT'S SMITH STREET, NICK!
YOU.
I FORGIVE YOU.
Ouch.

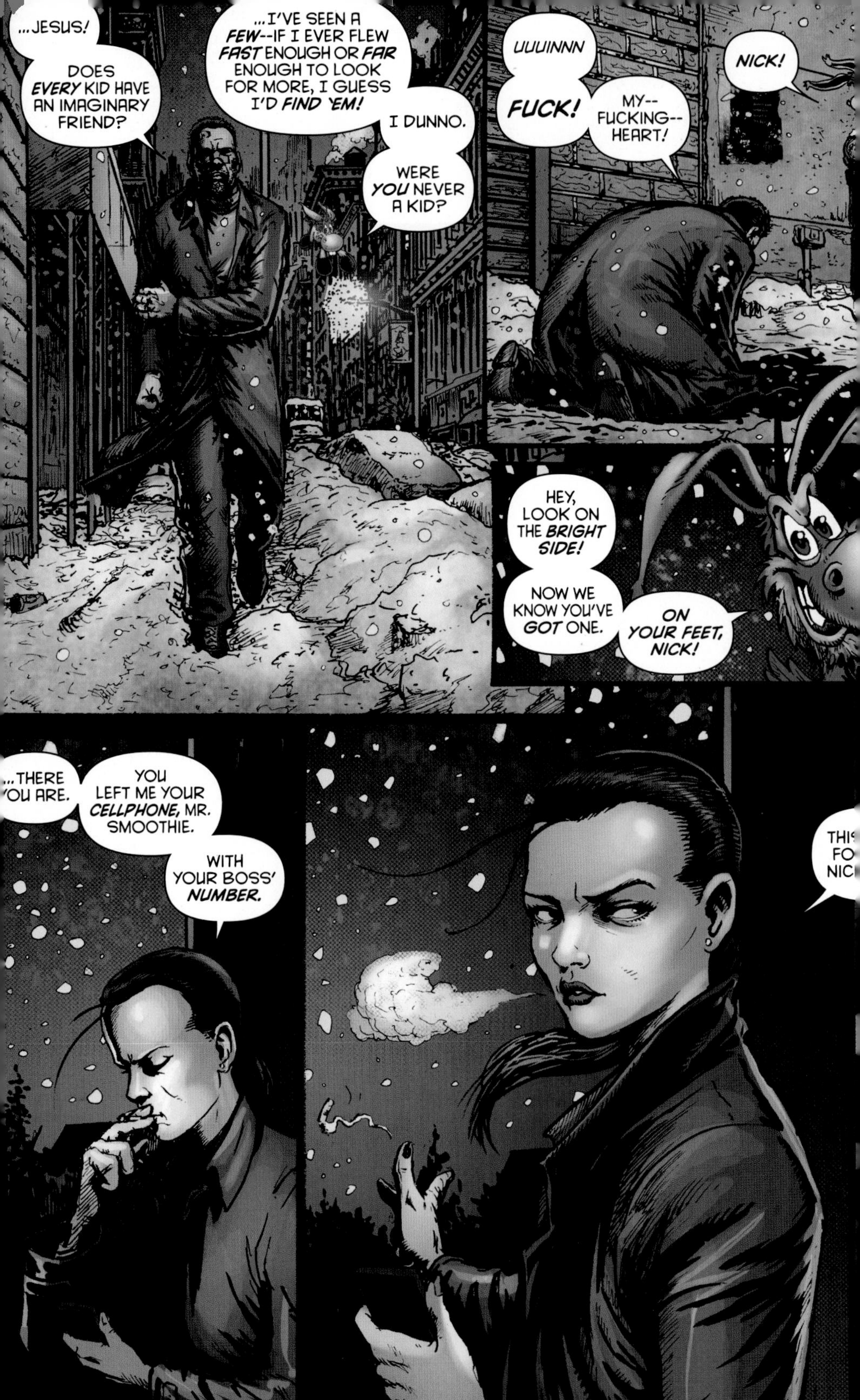
...JESUS!
DOES EVERY KID HAVE AN IMAGINARY FRIEND?
...I'VE SEEN A FEW--IF I EVER FLEW FAST ENOUGH OR FAR ENOUGH TO LOOK FOR MORE, I GUESS I'D FIND 'EM!
I DUNNO.
WERE YOU NEVER A KID?
UUUINNN
FUCK!
MY-- FUCKING-- HEART!
NICK!
HEY, LOOK ON THE BRIGHT SIDE!
NOW WE KNOW YOU'VE GOT ONE.
ON YOUR FEET, NICK!
...THERE YOU ARE.
YOU LEFT ME YOUR CELLPHONE, MR. SMOOTHIE.
WITH YOUR BOSS' NUMBER.

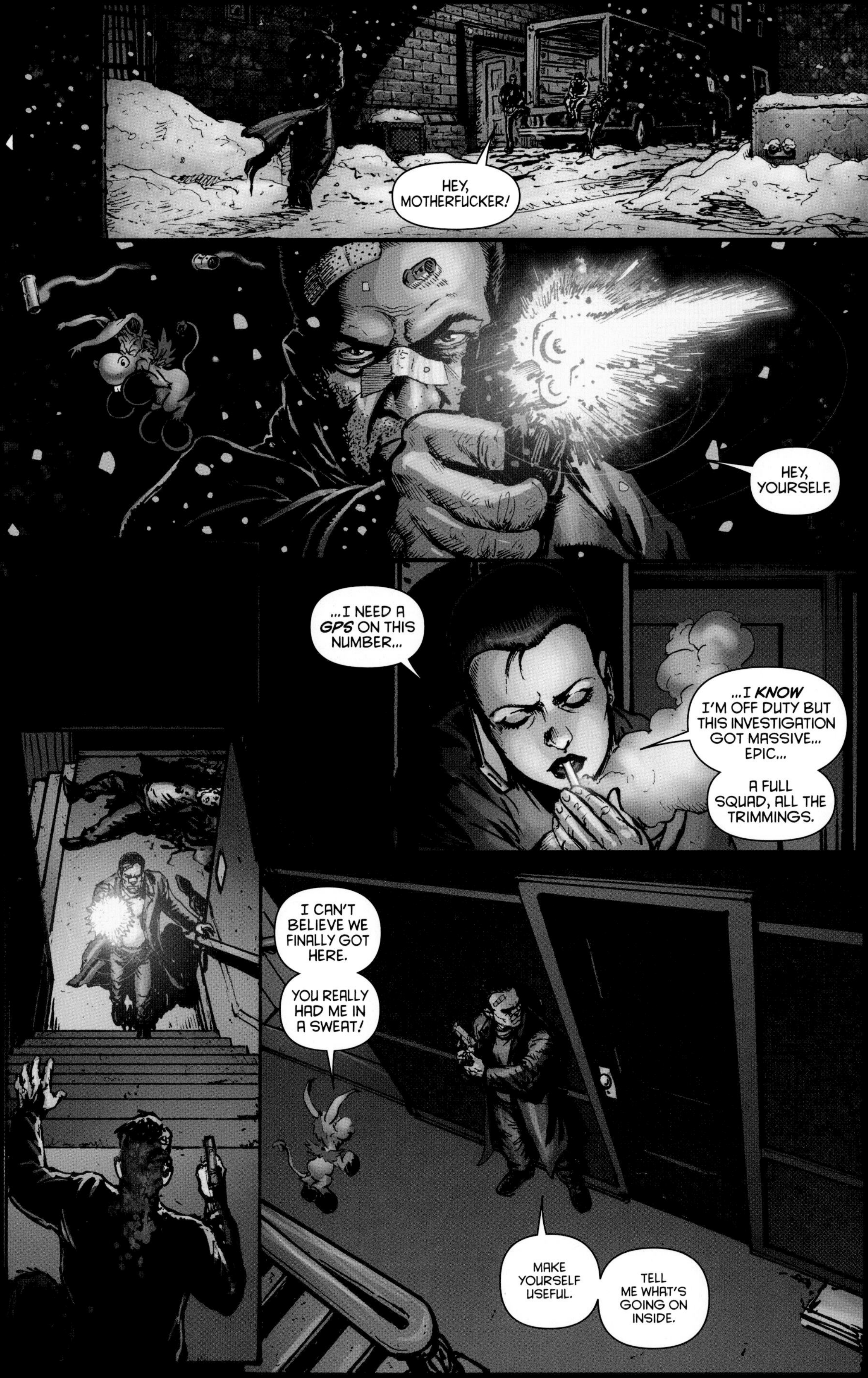
HEY, MOTHERFUCKER!
HEY, YOURSELF.
...I NEED A GPS ON THIS NUMBER...
...I KNOW I'M OFF DUTY BUT THIS INVESTIGATION GOT MASSIVE... EPIC...
A FULL SQUAD, ALL THE TRIMMINGS.
I CAN'T BELIEVE WE FINALLY GOT HERE.
YOU REALLY HAD ME IN A SWEAT!
MAKE YOURSELF USEFUL.
TELL ME WHAT'S GOING ON INSIDE.

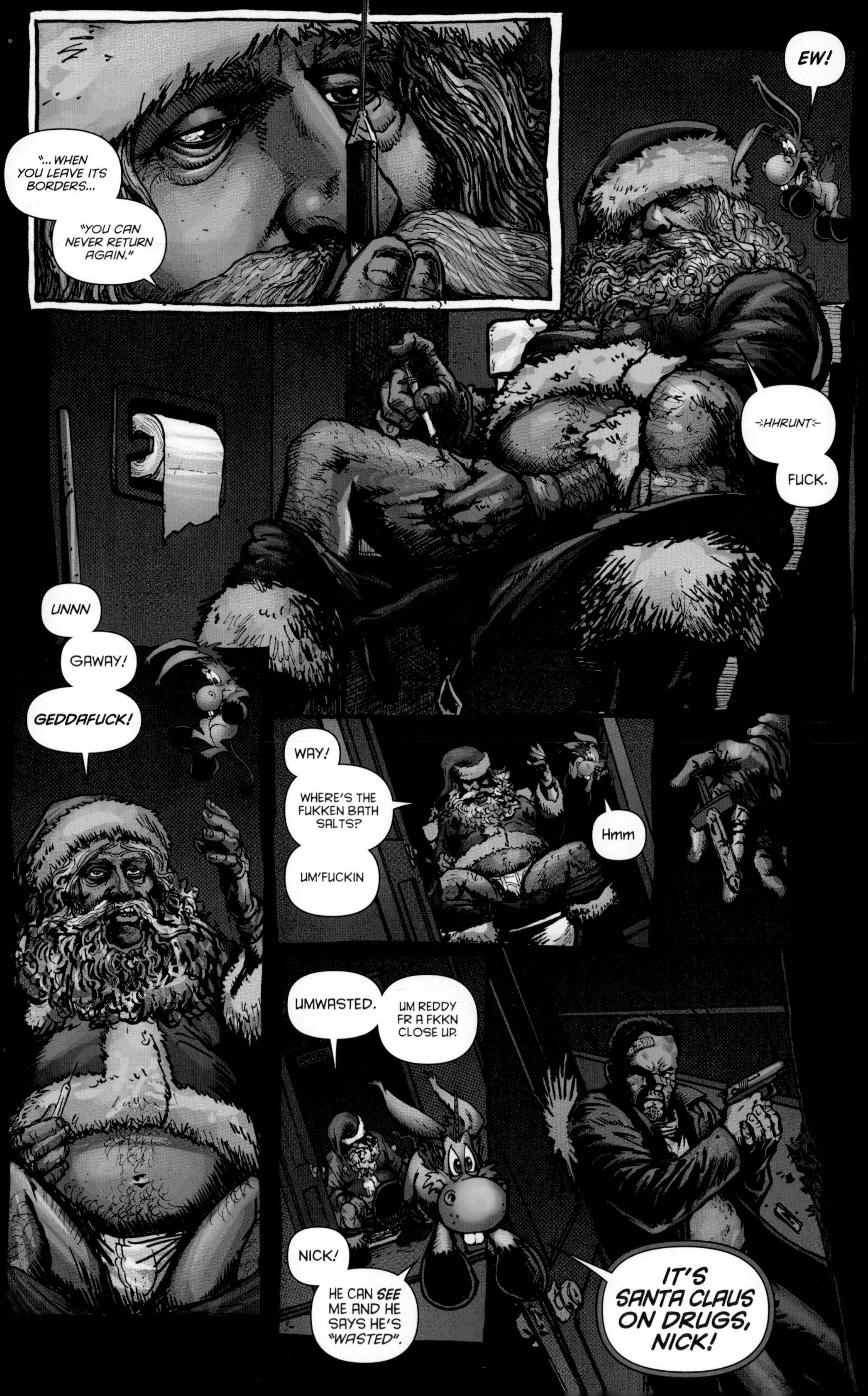
"...WHEN YOU LEAVE ITS BORDERS...
"YOU CAN NEVER RETURN AGAIN."
EW!
HHRUNT
FUCK.
UNNN
GAWAY!
GEDDAFUCK!
WAY!
WHERE'S THE FUKKEN BATH SALTS?
UM'FUCKIN
Hmm
UMWASTED.
UM REDDY FR A FKKN CLOSE UP.
NICK!
HE CAN SEE ME AND HE SAYS HE'S "WASTED".
IT'S SANTA CLAUS ON DRUGS, NICK!

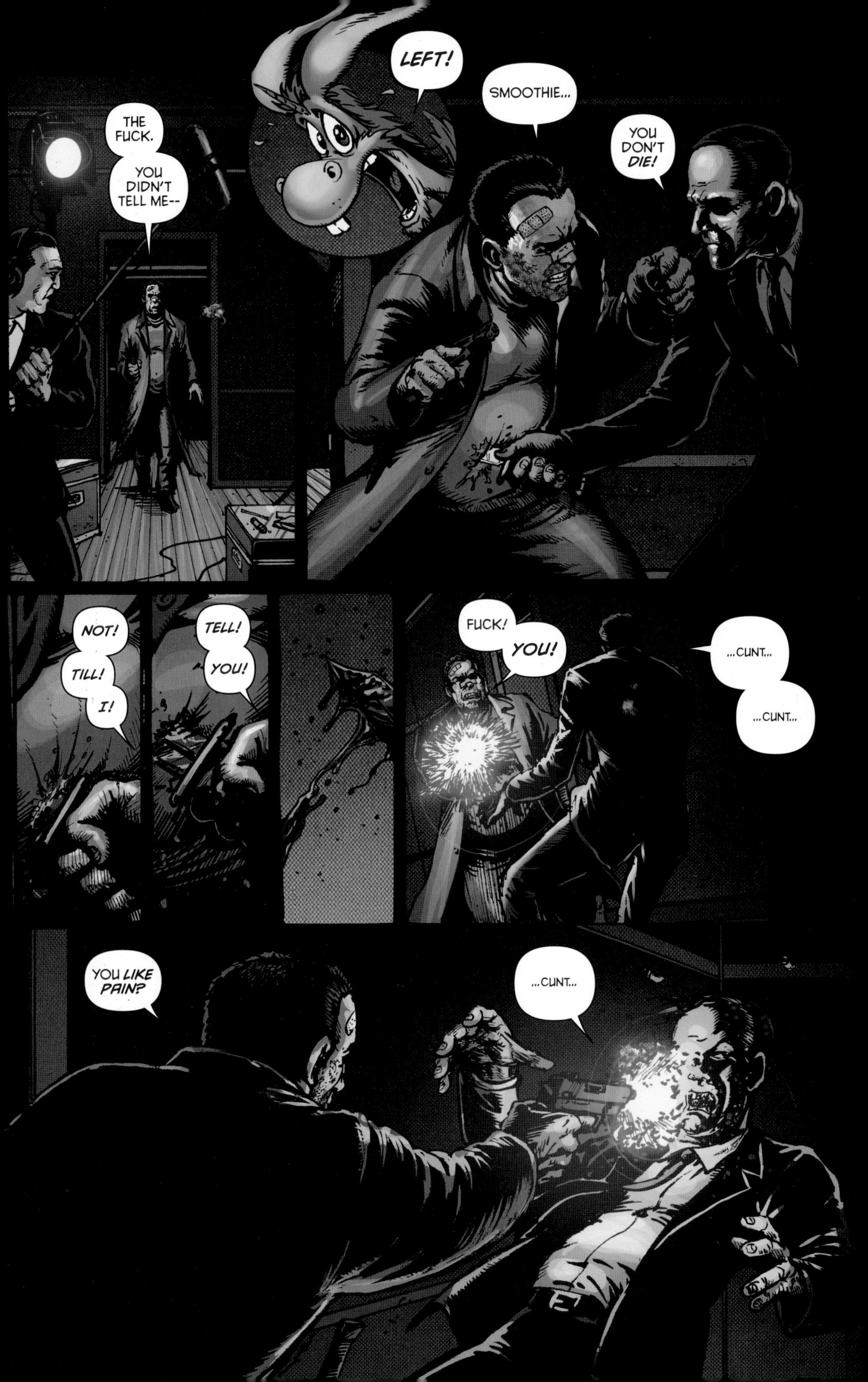
THE FUCK.
YOU DIDN'T TELL ME--
LEFT!
SMOOTHIE...
YOU DON'T DIE!
NOT!
TILL!
I!
TELL!
YOU!
FUCK!
YOU!
...CUNT...
...CUNT...
YOU LIKE PAIN?
...CUNT...

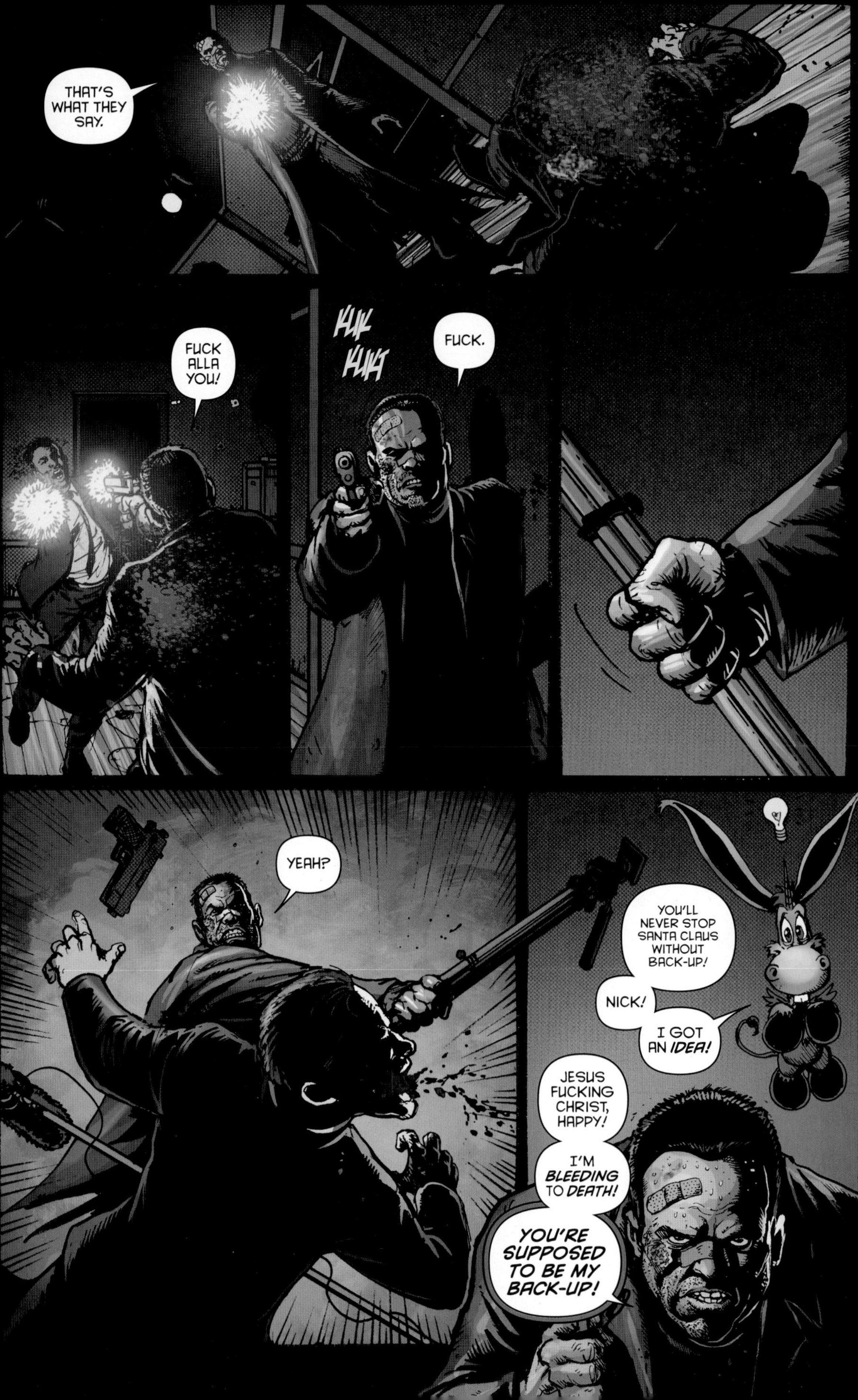
THAT'S WHAT THEY SAY.
FUCK ALLA YOU!
KLIK KLIKT
FUCK.
YEAH?
YOU'LL NEVER STOP SANTA CLAUS WITHOUT BACK-UP!
NICK!
I GOT AN *IDEA!*
JESUS FUCKING CHRIST, HAPPY!
I'M *BLEEDING* TO *DEATH!*
YOU'RE SUPPOSED TO BE MY BACK-UP!

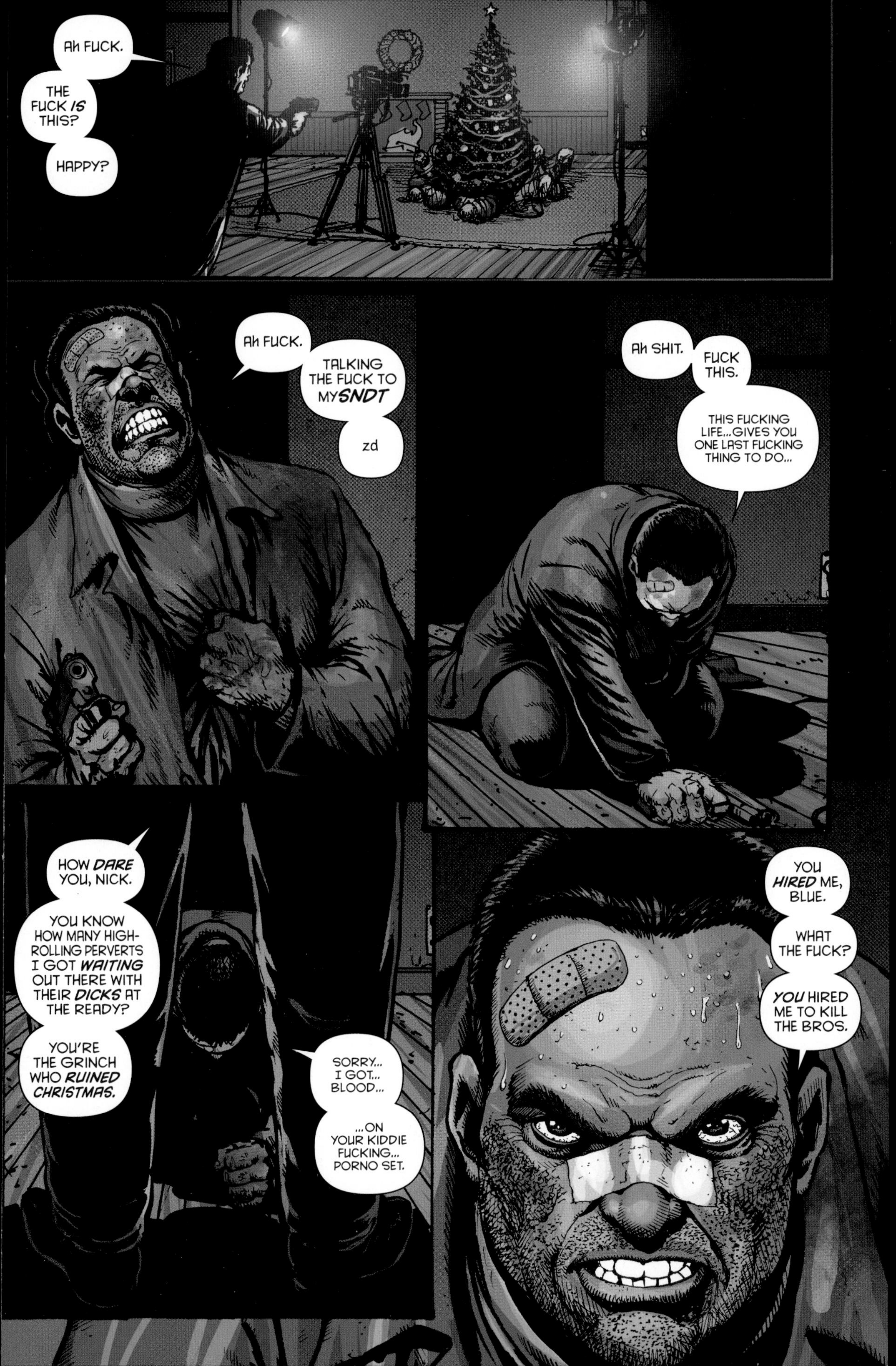

Ah FUCK.
THE FUCK *IS* THIS?
HAPPY?
Ah FUCK.
TALKING THE FUCK TO MY *SNDT*
zd
Ah SHIT.
FUCK THIS.
THIS FUCKING LIFE...GIVES YOU ONE LAST FUCKING THING TO DO...
HOW *DARE* YOU, NICK.
YOU KNOW HOW MANY HIGH-ROLLING PERVERTS I GOT *WAITING* OUT THERE WITH THEIR *DICKS* AT THE READY?
YOU'RE THE GRINCH WHO *RUINED CHRISTMAS.*
SORRY... I GOT... BLOOD...
...ON YOUR KIDDIE FUCKING... PORNO SET.
YOU *HIRED* ME, BLUE.
WHAT THE FUCK?
YOU HIRED ME TO KILL THE BROS.

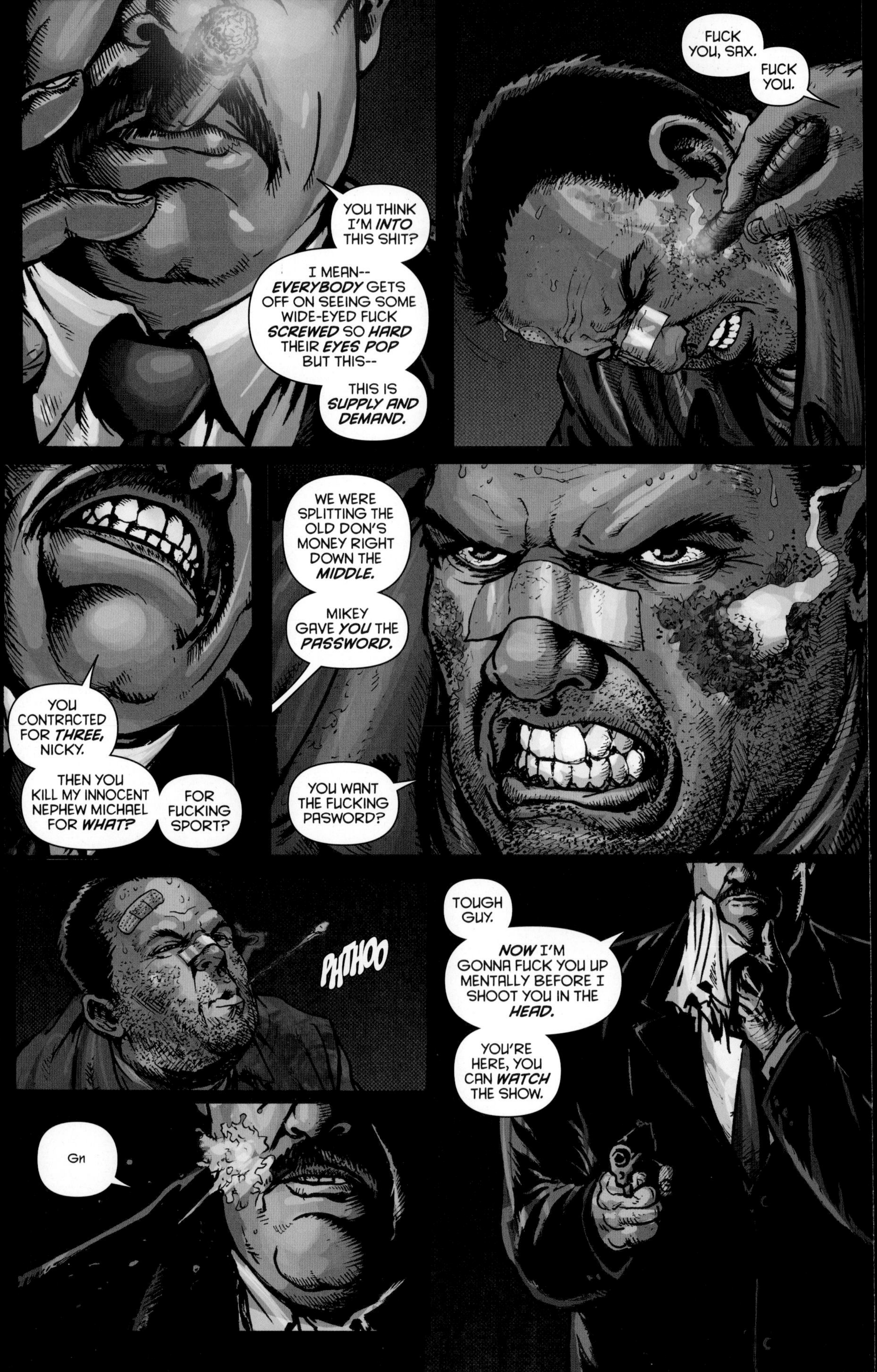
YOU THINK I'M INTO THIS SHIT?
I MEAN-- EVERYBODY GETS OFF ON SEEING SOME WIDE-EYED FUCK SCREWED SO HARD THEIR EYES POP BUT THIS--
THIS IS SUPPLY AND DEMAND.
FUCK YOU, SAX.
FUCK YOU.
YOU CONTRACTED FOR THREE, NICKY.
THEN YOU KILL MY INNOCENT NEPHEW MICHAEL FOR WHAT?
FOR FUCKING SPORT?
WE WERE SPLITTING THE OLD DON'S MONEY RIGHT DOWN THE MIDDLE.
MIKEY GAVE YOU THE PASSWORD.
YOU WANT THE FUCKING PASWORD?
PHTHOO
Gn
TOUGH GUY.
NOW I'M GONNA FUCK YOU UP MENTALLY BEFORE I SHOOT YOU IN THE HEAD.
YOU'RE HERE, YOU CAN WATCH THE SHOW.

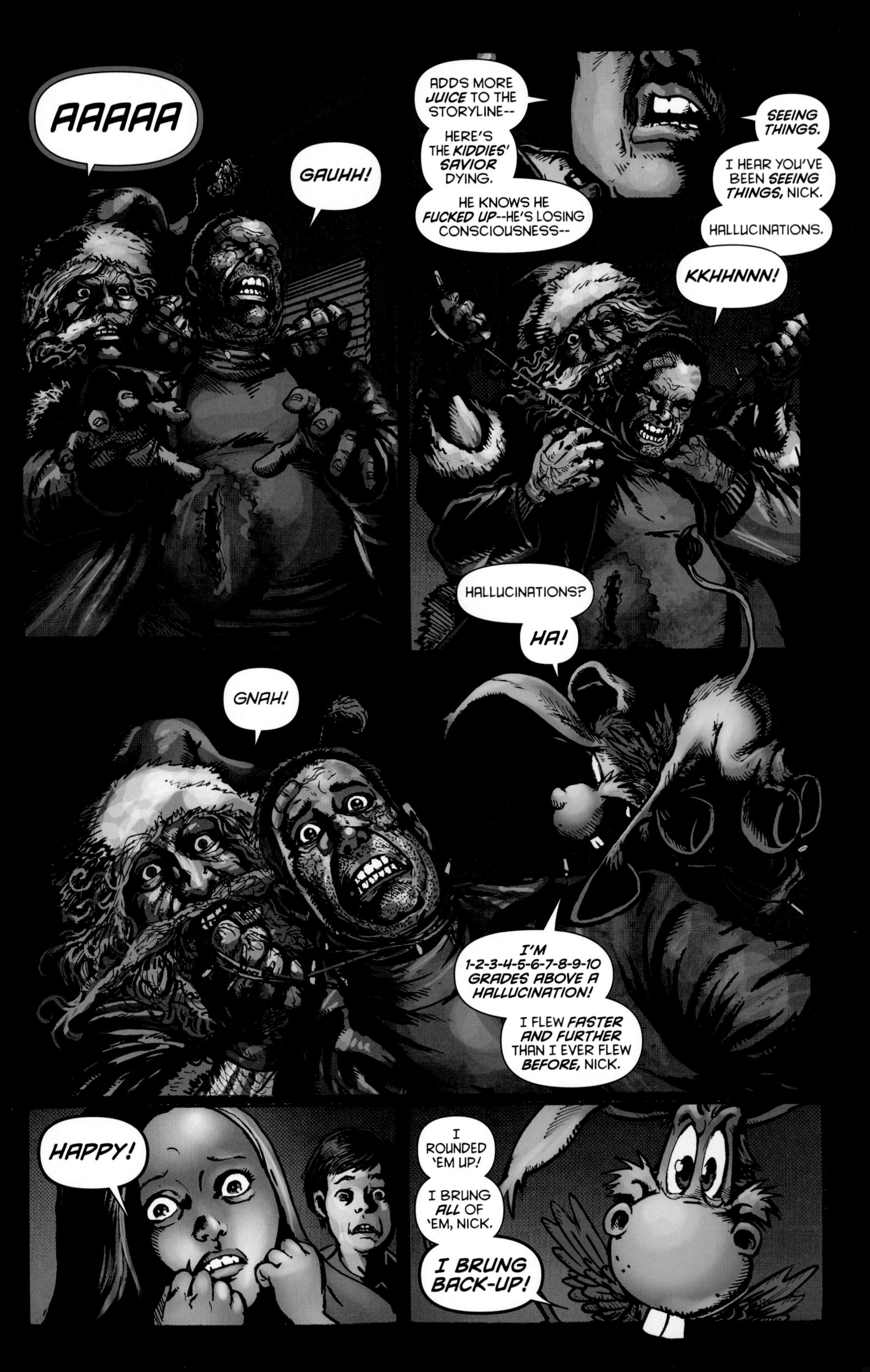
AAAAA
GAUHH!
ADD'S MORE JUICE TO THE STORYLINE--
HERE'S THE KIDDIES' SAVIOR DYING.
HE KNOWS HE FUCKED UP--HE'S LOSING CONSCIOUSNESS--
SEEING THINGS.
I HEAR YOU'VE BEEN SEEING THINGS, NICK.
HALLUCINATIONS.
KKHHNNN!
HALLUCINATIONS?
HA!
GNAH!
I'M 1-2-3-4-5-6-7-8-9-10 GRADES ABOVE A HALLUCINATION!
I FLEW FASTER AND FURTHER THAN I EVER FLEW BEFORE, NICK.
HAPPY!
I ROUNDED 'EM UP!
I BRUNG ALL OF 'EM, NICK.
I BRUNG BACK-UP!

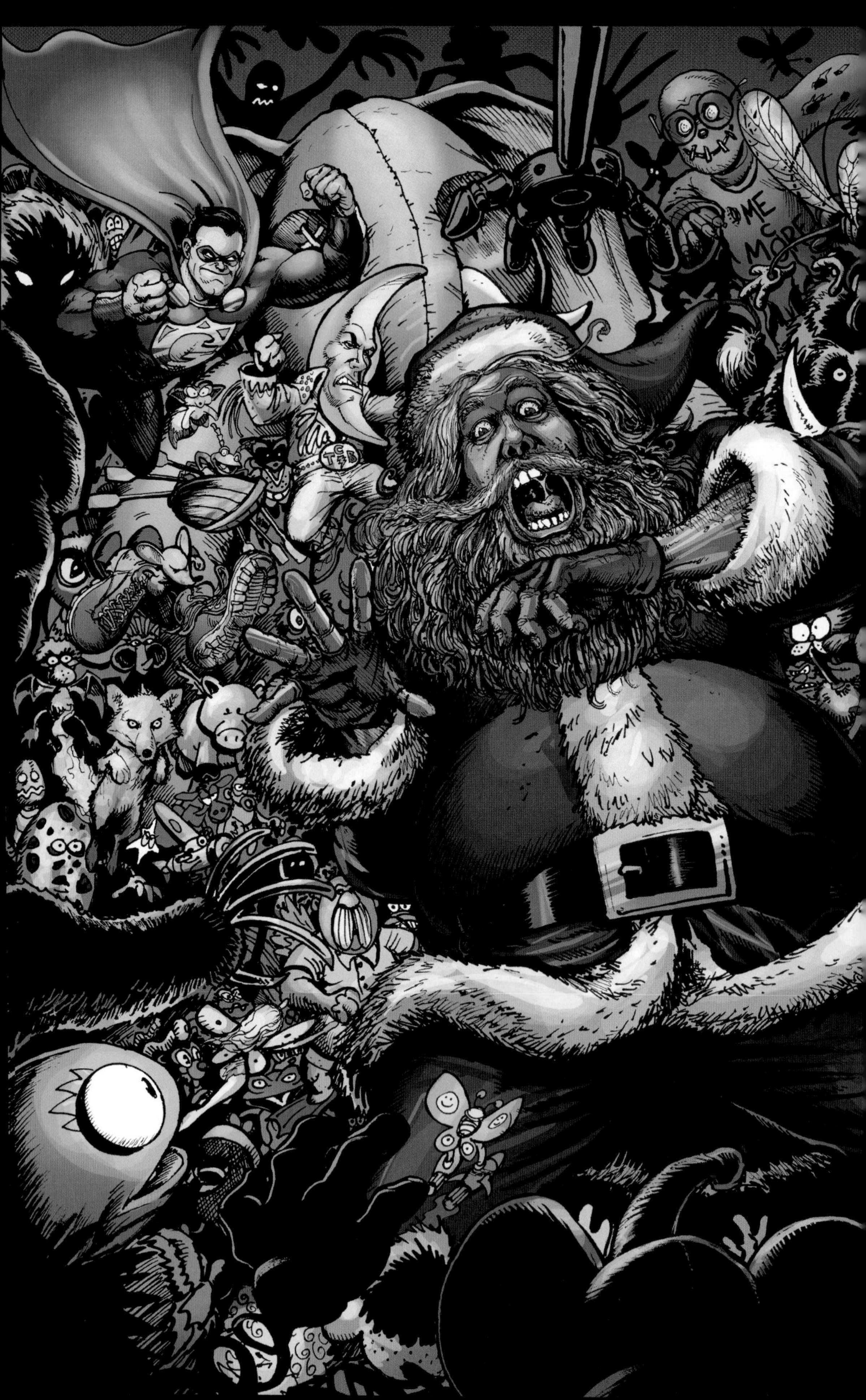

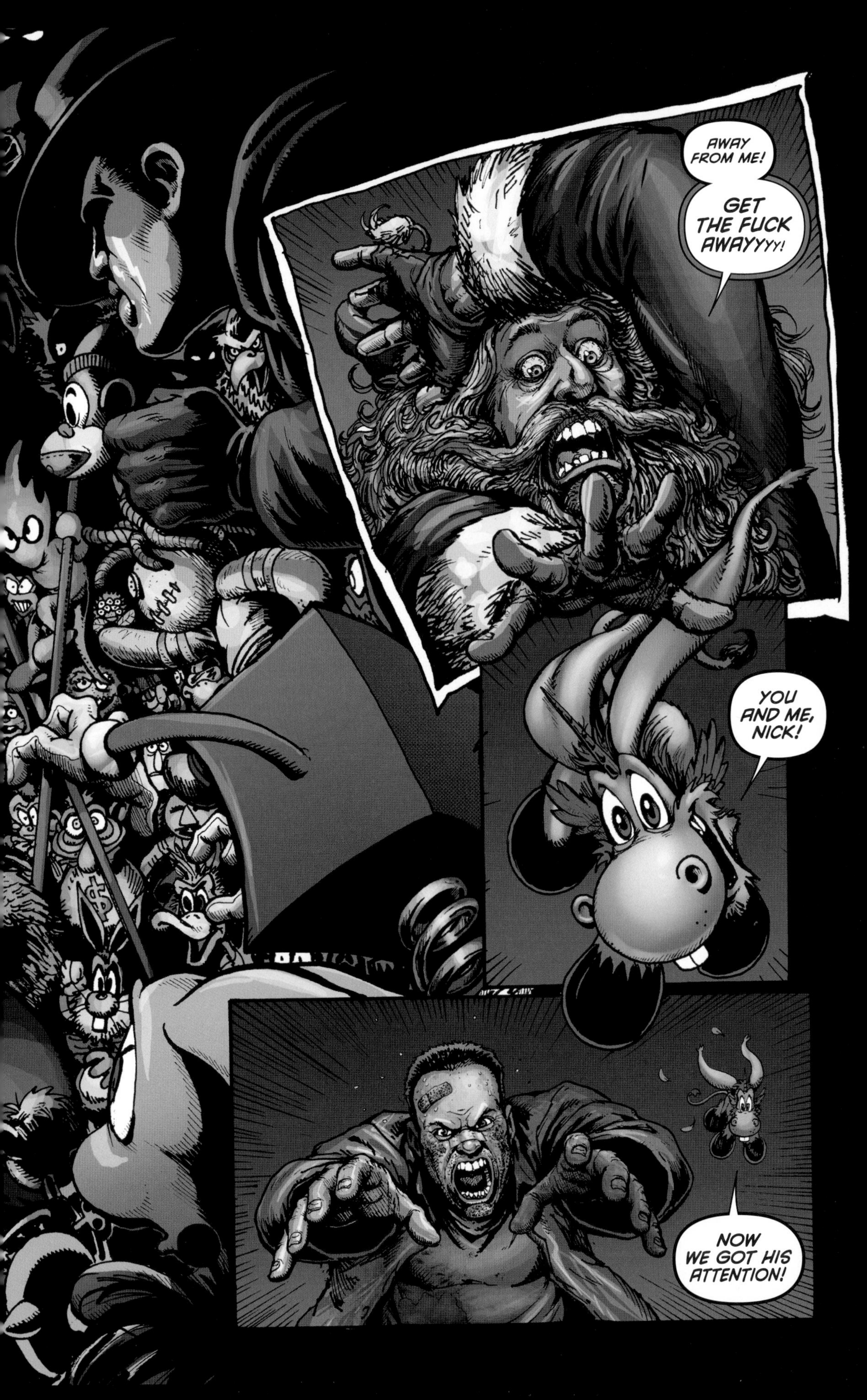
AWAY FROM ME!
GET THE FUCK AWAYYYY!
YOU AND ME, NICK!
NOW WE GOT HIS ATTENTION!

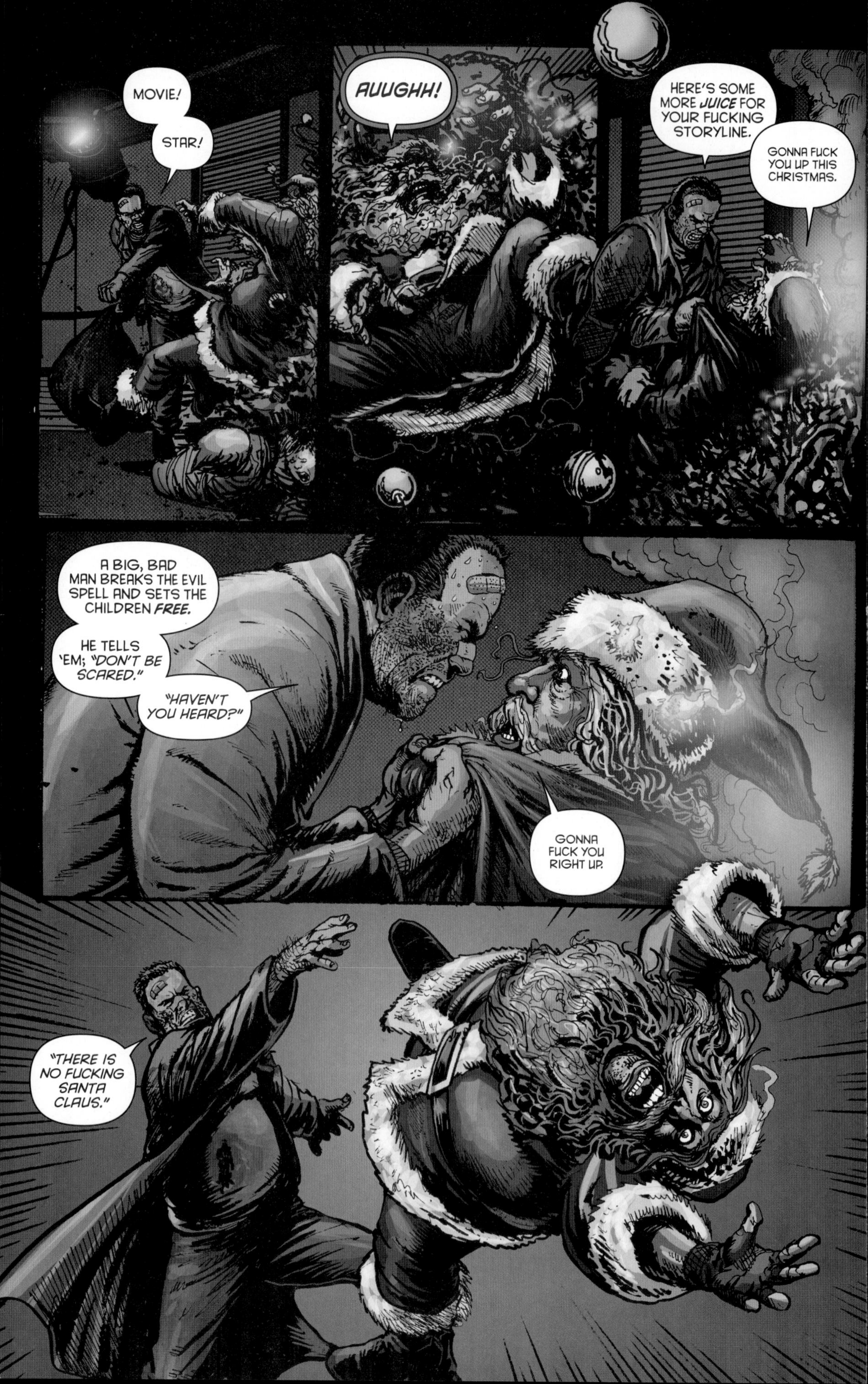
MOVIE!
STAR!
AUUGHH!
HERE'S SOME MORE JUICE FOR YOUR FUCKING STORYLINE.
GONNA FUCK YOU UP THIS CHRISTMAS.
A BIG, BAD MAN BREAKS THE EVIL SPELL AND SETS THE CHILDREN FREE.
HE TELLS 'EM; "DON'T BE SCARED."
"HAVEN'T YOU HEARD?"
GONNA FUCK YOU RIGHT UP.
"THERE IS NO FUCKING SANTA CLAUS."

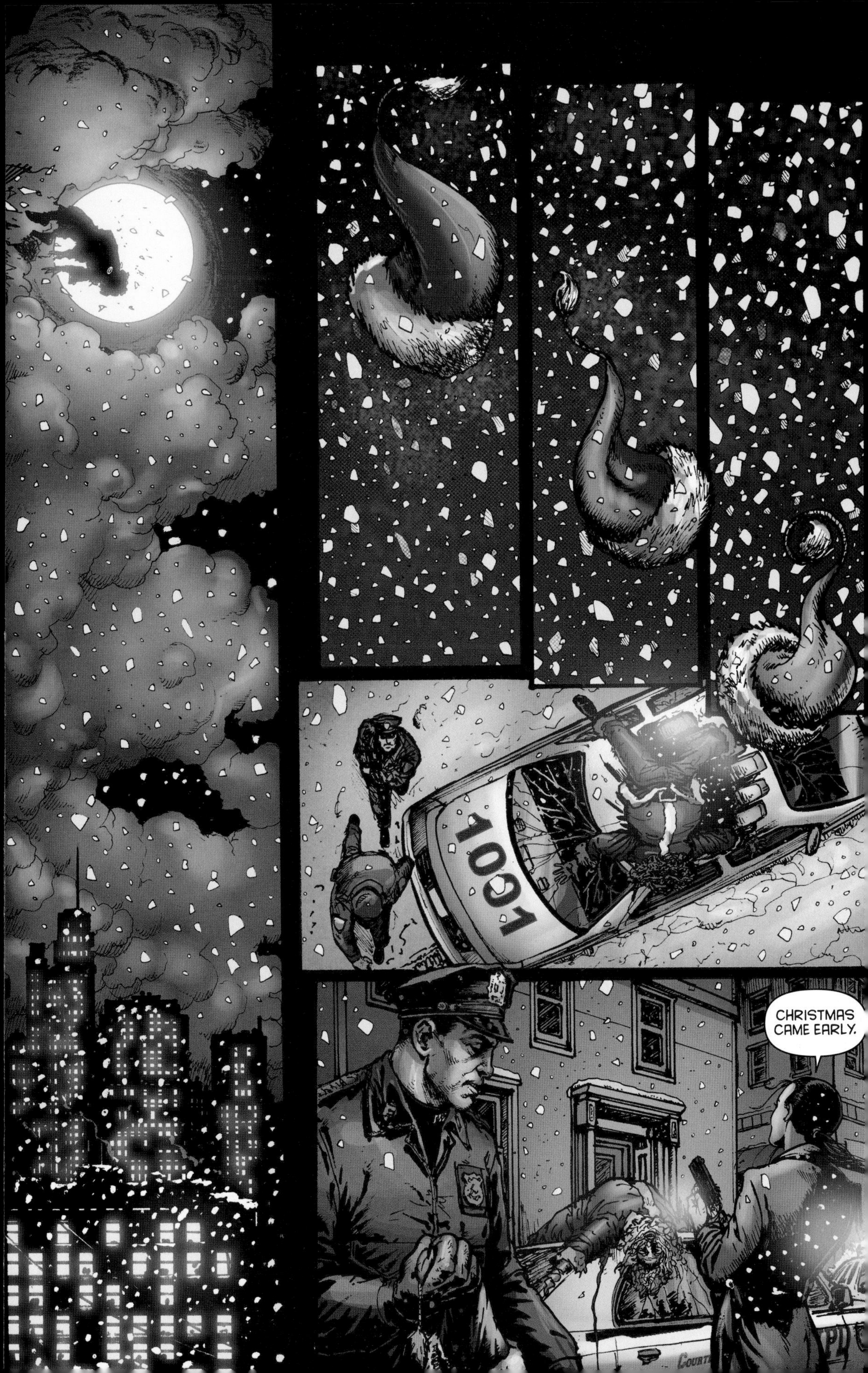
CHRISTMAS CAME EARLY.
1001

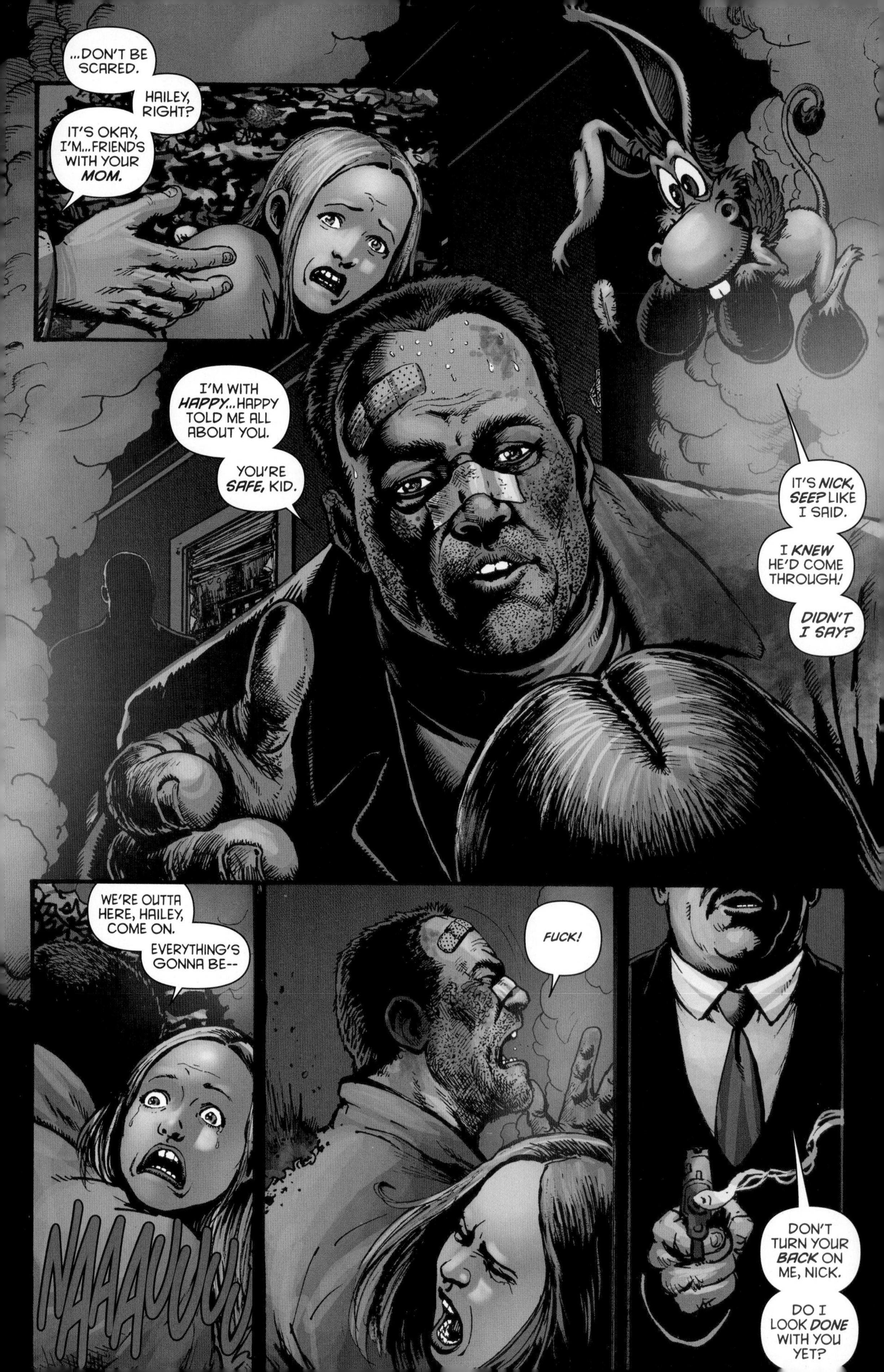
...DON'T BE SCARED.
HAILEY, RIGHT?
IT'S OKAY, I'M...FRIENDS WITH YOUR *MOM.*
I'M WITH *HAPPY*...HAPPY TOLD ME ALL ABOUT YOU.
YOU'RE *SAFE,* KID.
IT'S *NICK, SEE?* LIKE I SAID.
I *KNEW* HE'D COME THROUGH!
DIDN'T I SAY?
WE'RE OUTTA HERE, HAILEY, COME ON.
EVERYTHING'S GONNA BE--
NAAAUUUU
FUCK!
DON'T TURN YOUR *BACK* ON ME, NICK.
DO I LOOK *DONE* WITH YOU YET?

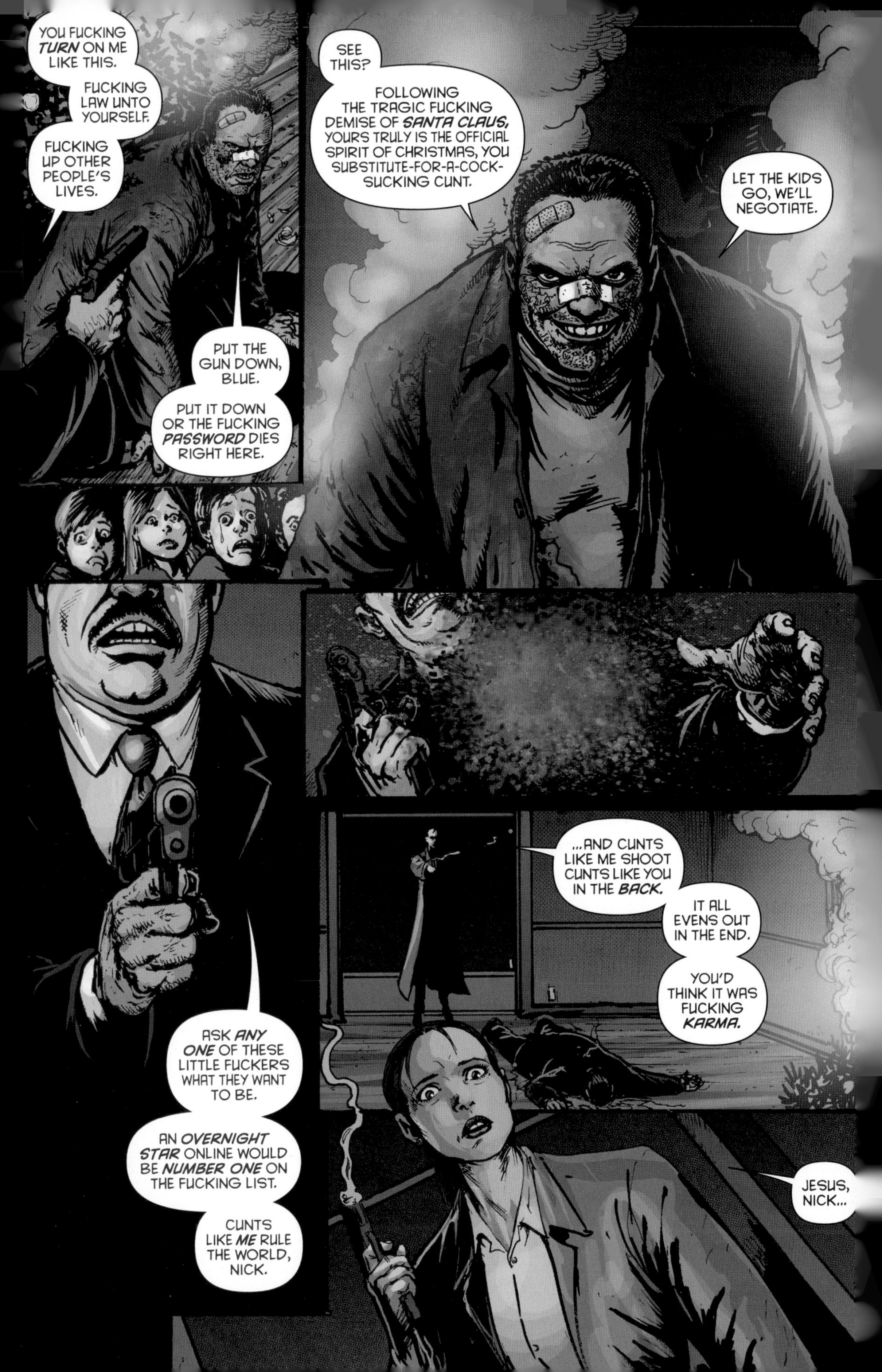
YOU FUCKING TURN ON ME LIKE THIS.
FUCKING LAW UNTO YOURSELF.
FUCKING UP OTHER PEOPLE'S LIVES.
PUT THE GUN DOWN, BLUE.
PUT IT DOWN OR THE FUCKING PASSWORD DIES RIGHT HERE.
SEE THIS?
FOLLOWING THE TRAGIC FUCKING DEMISE OF SANTA CLAUS, YOURS TRULY IS THE OFFICIAL SPIRIT OF CHRISTMAS, YOU SUBSTITUTE-FOR-A-COCK-SUCKING CUNT.
LET THE KIDS GO, WE'LL NEGOTIATE.
ASK ANY ONE OF THESE LITTLE FUCKERS WHAT THEY WANT TO BE.
AN OVERNIGHT STAR ONLINE WOULD BE NUMBER ONE ON THE FUCKING LIST.
CUNTS LIKE ME RULE THE WORLD, NICK.
...AND CUNTS LIKE ME SHOOT CUNTS LIKE YOU IN THE BACK.
IT ALL EVENS OUT IN THE END.
YOU'D THINK IT WAS FUCKING KARMA.
JESUS, NICK...

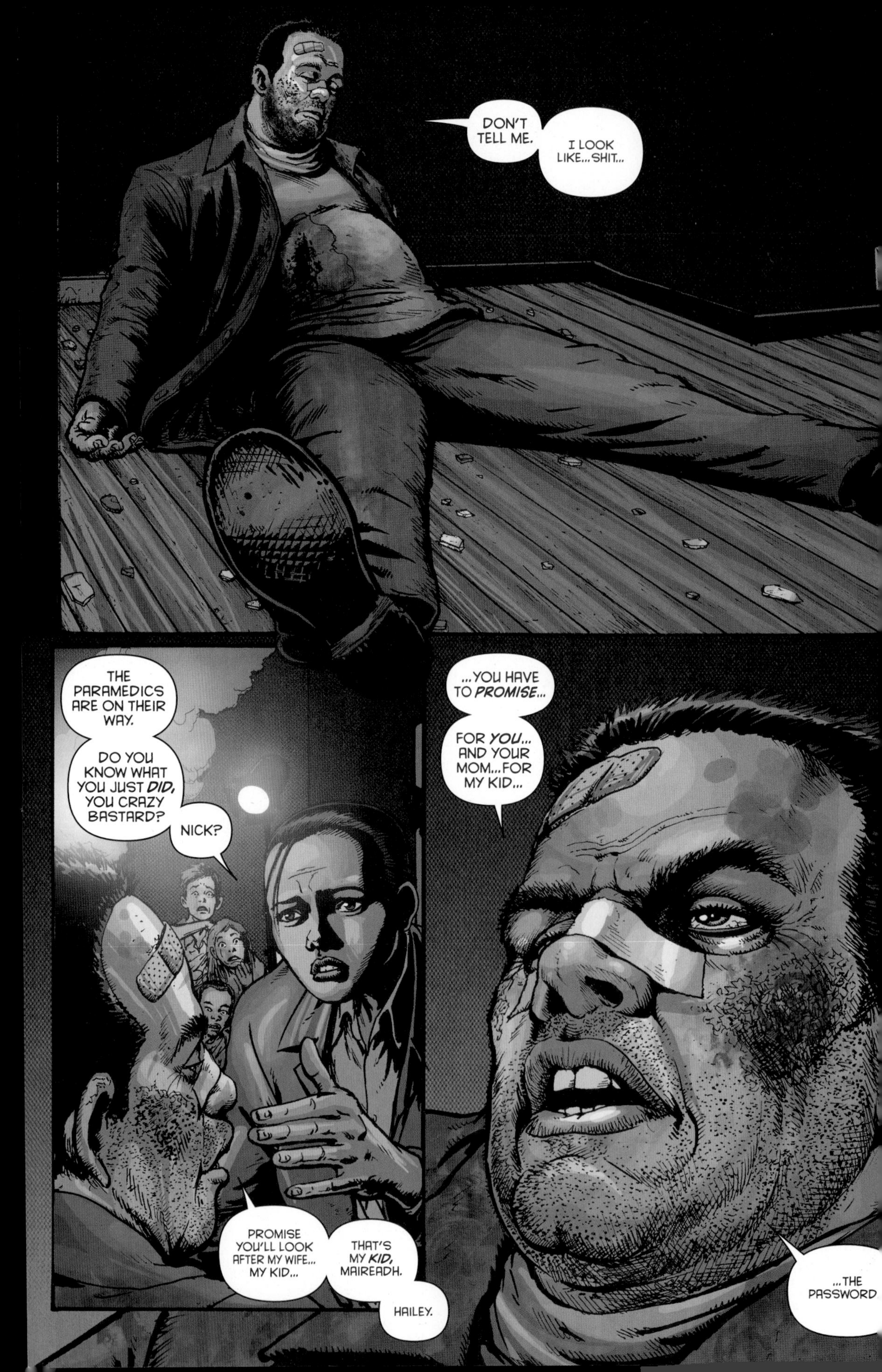

DON'T TELL ME.
I LOOK LIKE... SHIT...
THE PARAMEDICS ARE ON THEIR WAY.
DO YOU KNOW WHAT YOU JUST *DID*, YOU CRAZY BASTARD?
NICK?
PROMISE YOU'LL LOOK AFTER MY WIFE... MY KID...
THAT'S MY *KID*, MAIREADH.
HAILEY.
...YOU HAVE TO *PROMISE*...
FOR *YOU*... AND YOUR MOM... FOR MY KID...
...THE PASSWORD

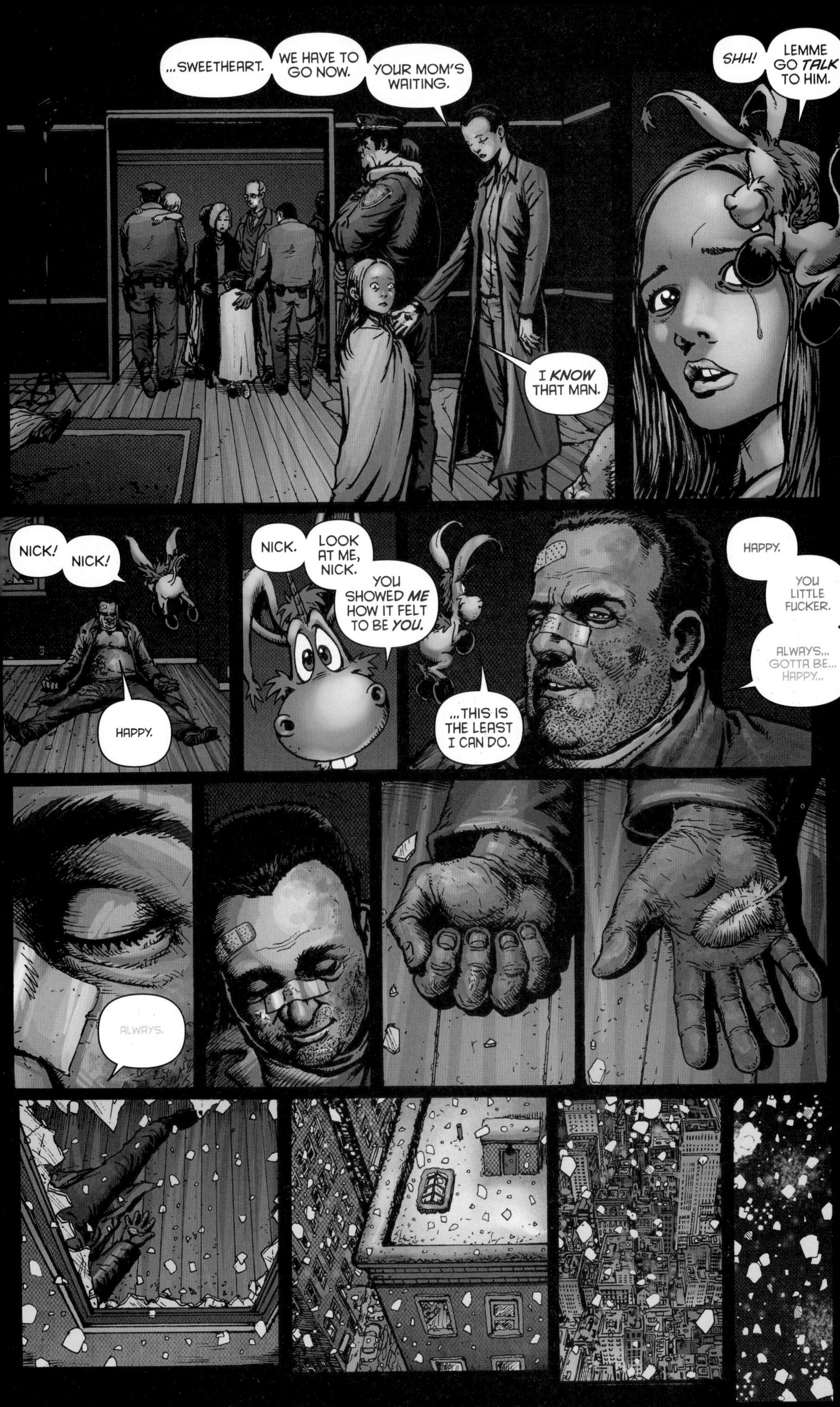
...SWEETHEART.
WE HAVE TO GO NOW.
YOUR MOM'S WAITING.
I KNOW THAT MAN.
SHH!
LEMME GO TALK TO HIM.
NICK!
NICK!
HAPPY.
NICK.
LOOK AT ME, NICK.
YOU SHOWED ME HOW IT FELT TO BE YOU.
...THIS IS THE LEAST I CAN DO.
HAPPY.
YOU LITTLE FUCKER.
ALWAYS... GOTTA BE... HAPPY...
ALWAYS.

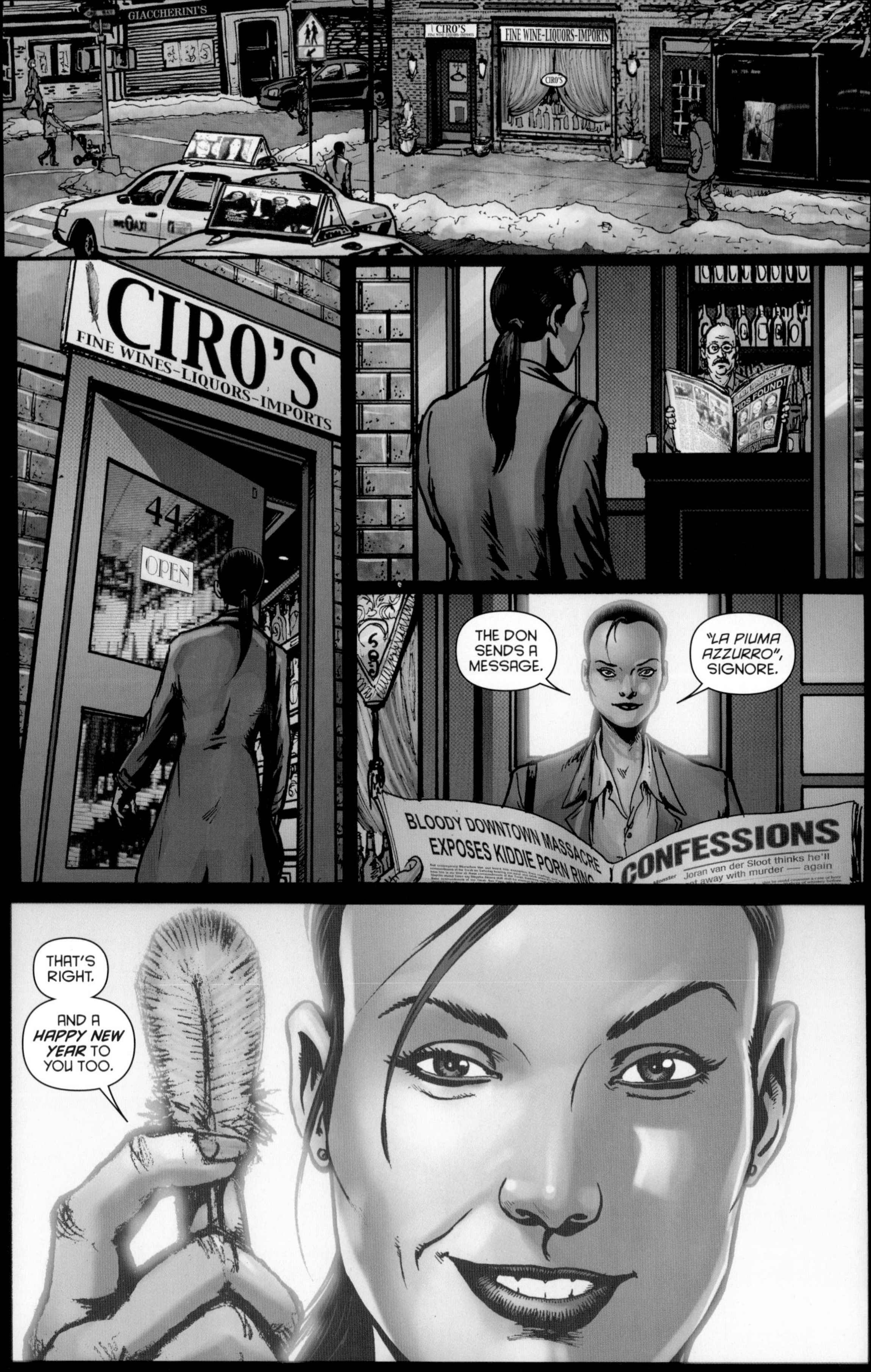
GIACCHERINI'S
CIRO'S
FINE WINE-LIQUORS-IMPORTS
CIRO'S
CIRO'S
FINE WINES-LIQUORS-IMPORTS
44
OPEN
KIDS FOUND!
THE DON SENDS A MESSAGE.
"LA PIUMA AZZURRO", SIGNORE.
BLOODY DOWNTOWN MASSACRE
EXPOSES KIDDIE PORN RING
CONFESSIONS
Joran van der Sloot thinks he'll
THAT'S RIGHT.
AND A *HAPPY NEW YEAR* TO YOU TOO.

THE END

BECOMING HAPPY!

HAPPY!

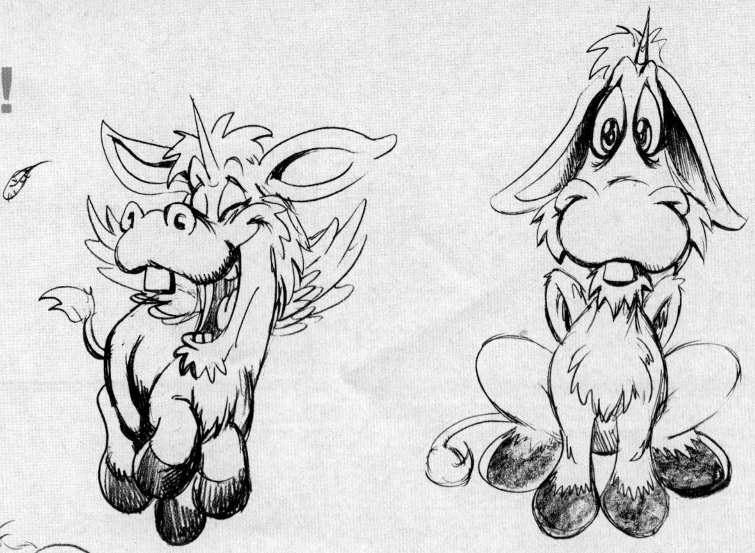

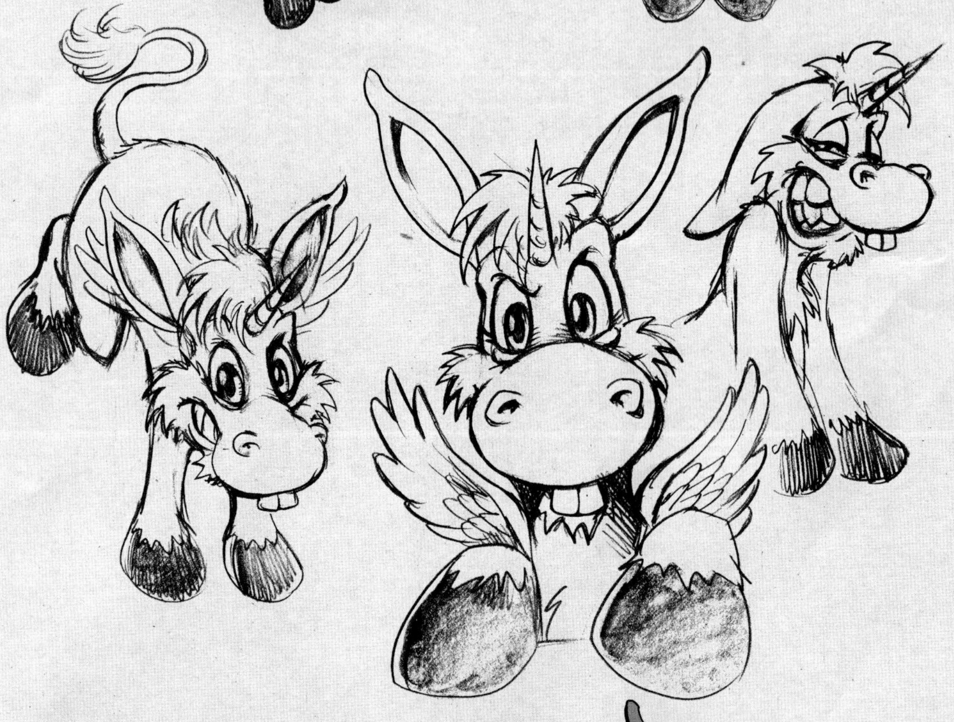

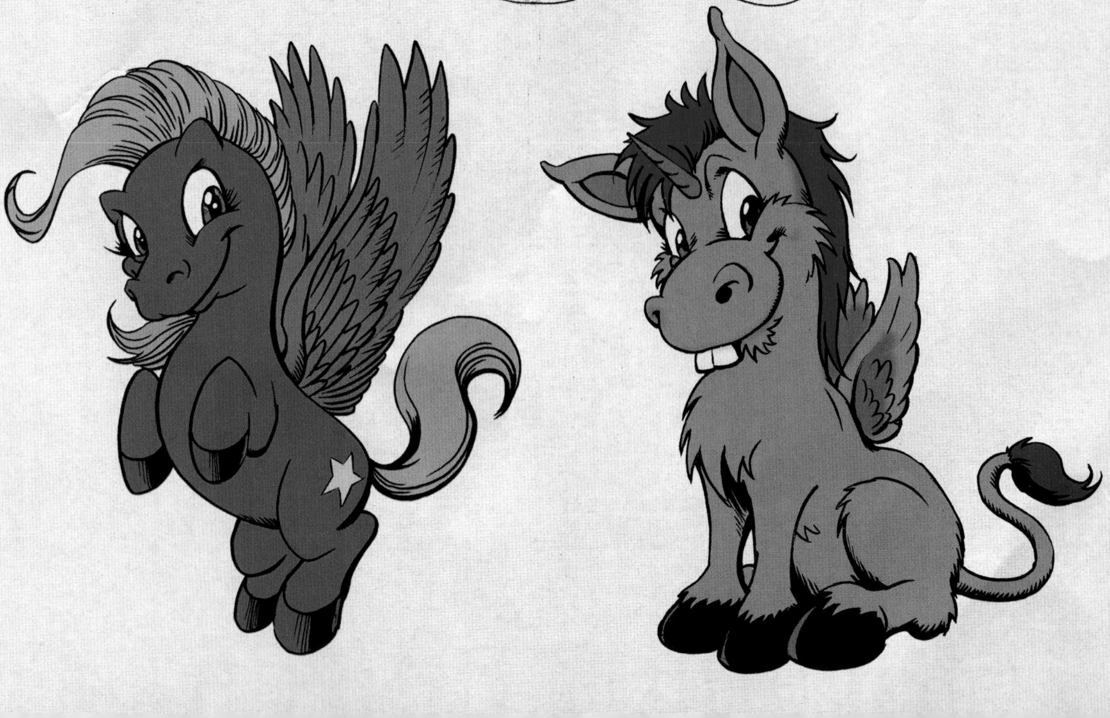

NICK SAX

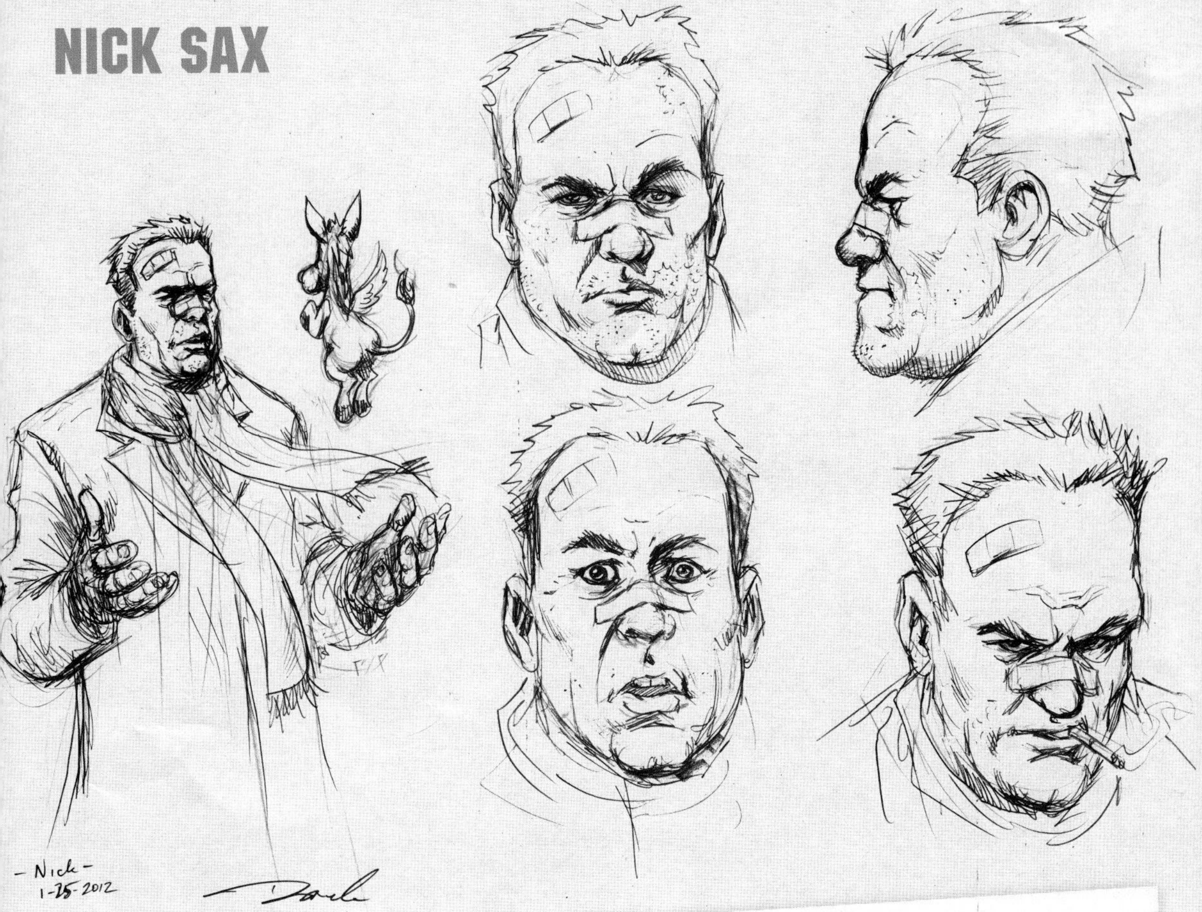
-Nick-
1-25-2012

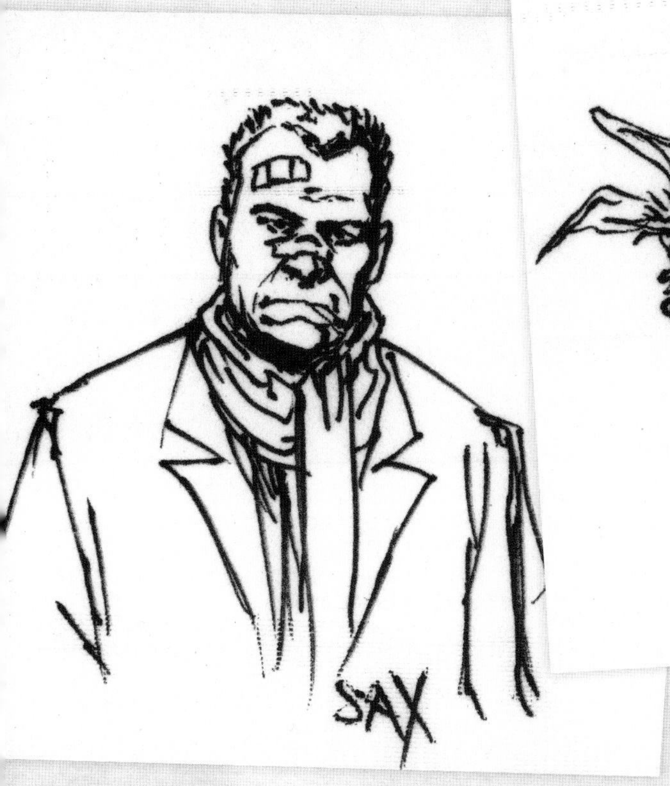
SAX

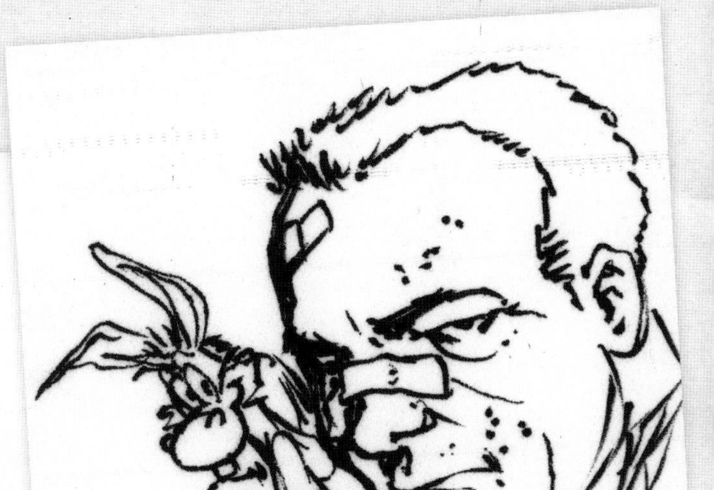

FROM SCRIPT TO INK

PAGE 2

Frame 1   Gerry and Mikey enter the scene from the left – we see them in foreground from chest or waist up. Dominating this title image, however, is the central figure lumbering out of the METHADONE CLINIC (maybe even the church is now the methadone clinic).

It's a disgusting Santa Claus with a filthy sack. His vile torn suit is stained with god knows what –especially around the crotch. It's clear his ungainly progress is going to take him smack into the two hitmen, wrapped up in conversation and trying to keep warm in the sleeting snow. Santa's eyes are fixed on empty air and he paws something away.

(At the end of the story Happy rounds up all the imaginary friends in the city to descend on Santa's lair – so we want to establish him here as a crazy alcoholic man who sees things. Here we want him to comes across as one more seedy detail in the picture we're painting, rather than the primary element he will become.)

Snow continues to spat down across the outdoor scenes throughout the book.

GERRY: THE BALLS ARE ALL YOURS, BRO, BUT JESUS...
MIKEY: EVERYBODY HAS TO LEARN ABOUT REAL LIFE SOMETIME.
MIKEY: RIGHT?

Frame 2   Santa collides with Gerry as he makes a swipe at something that's not there.

SANTA: NNRN!
GERRY: THE FUCK, YOU!

Frame 3   A moment of impending trouble – Mikey grabs Gerry's shoulder to pull him away – Gerry is squaring up to Santa. Santa simply glares at him.

GERRY: HOW 'BOUT SOME BASIC FUCKING RESPECT?
GERRY: FUCKING ASSHOLE!
MIKEY: JESUS CHRIST, IT'S SANNACLAUS, FOR FUCK'S SAKE!

Frame 4   Close up low angle on pedo Santa – the most nightmarish vision of Santa Claus ever conceived by human imagination, Darick. This is the ultimate pedophile monster – low angle shot as he turns to look at us past his shoulder – it's as if this monster has just noticed us for the first time.

SANTA: YOU WANT THE LITTLE KIDDIES GET NONE?
         (cracked whispery lettering)

Frame 5   The hitmen carry on across the road arguing about what just happened. Hitman is yelling, pointing at Santa who chops at the air, caught up in his own shambling drama as he heads offstage through the snow.

GERRY: ...I WOULDN'T LET MY KIDS WITHIN A HUNDRED FUCKING MILES OF THAT PERVERT FUCK!
GERRY: FUCK SHOWS HIS FACE AT MY FUCKING CHIMNEY, HE DIES.
GERRY: SANTA FUCKING DIES!

Frame 6   Now we're looking down the dark corridor of a tenement as the assassins approach. They walk past some nuns – Mikey smiling, trying to calm Gerry who's hyper, drunk and speeding.

GERRY: EH?
MIKEY: YOU DON'T HAVE A FUCKING CHIMNEY.
MIKEY: TONE IT THE FUCK DOWN, WILLYA?
MIKEY: WE CAN DO THIS WITHOUT ALL THE FUCKING LANGUAGE.

Frame 7   Up the tenement stairs.

MIKEY: LIGHTEN UP, FOR FUCK'S SAKE.

MIKEY: IT'S CHRISTMAS, FOR CRYING OUT LOUD.
MIKEY: IT'S A TIME FOR GIVING.

PAGE 3

Frame 1   The top half of the page has four vertical panels that zoom out on an ordinary looking middle class suburban man – except he's wearing some kind of weird garish pink suit. Begin with a close up on the man glaring down – in the throes of a blow job. He wears glasses.

PRAWN-MAN: ...THAT'S IT.
PRAWN-MAN: THAT'S THE WAY.
PRAWN-MAN: THEY PROVED USING RESEARCH – DETAILED FIGURES - HOOKERS LIKE YOU, SEASONAL - WHORES - WORKING PEAK PERIODS -

Frame 2   Pull back to see more of him – his chest, the top of is stomach, so we still don't see the girl on her knees below. His arm is extended down off panel where he's holding the hooker's head. To add a curious note to the scene, the man is dressed in a PRAWN costume - see reference to be provided!

The guy is reaching into his pocket to pull something out of there. We're in a cheap and sleazy hotel room.

PRAWN-MAN: >fffp<

Frame 3   Pull back – the man raises a hammer – he holds the hooker's head down tilts his head back, taking an almighty puff on the reefer. She's dressed as an angel – in a white gown and those strap-on wings with a little motor that you can buy in party stores (for those readers who choose to believe that Nick might be hallucinating Happy, there are a few cues here and there to suggest where his subconscious mind got the idea to combine wings and horses, including these little angel wings on the hooker's back).

PRAWN-MAN: FFOOOH
PRAWN-MAN: THEY PROVED WHORES WERE THE SAME AS SANTA CLAUS.
PRAWN-MAN: SO EMPTY MY FUCKING

Frame 4   Then the mood changes – he turns to look off panel –light down his side.

PRAWN-MAN: ...SACKS...
PRAWN-MAN: BITCH.

Frame 5   A bullet goes neatly through one eye and out the back of prawn-man's head. His body jerks sideways. He is presumably coming in the hooker's face as he dies but we see only the back of her head, her hands raised in horror as she feels the body snap away from her.

Frame 6   Close on the hammerspliff falling away.

Frame 7   A splash of blood.

Frame 8   Close on the prawn-man's glasses.

PAGE 4

Frame 4   NICK SAX REVEAL – this is our first in story shot of our story's grizzled anti-hero NICK SAX – broken down ex-cop turned hitman. He's suffering an attack of eczema too, brought on by the cold weather. He is an image of man, ugly, ornery and defiant at the last gasp of hope. Condense the man and his mood into this single image, Darick. A shadow across the top of his head and one shoulder as he stands in the open doorway of this seedy hotel.

SAX: NOW I'VE SEEN EVERYTHING.

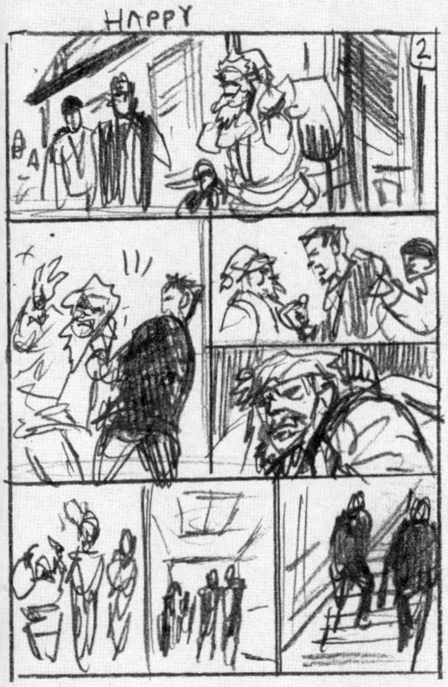
HAPPY
2
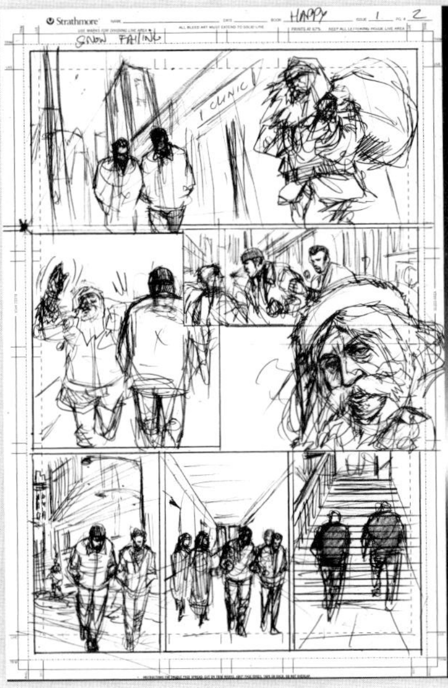
HAPPY
SNOW FALLING
CLINIC
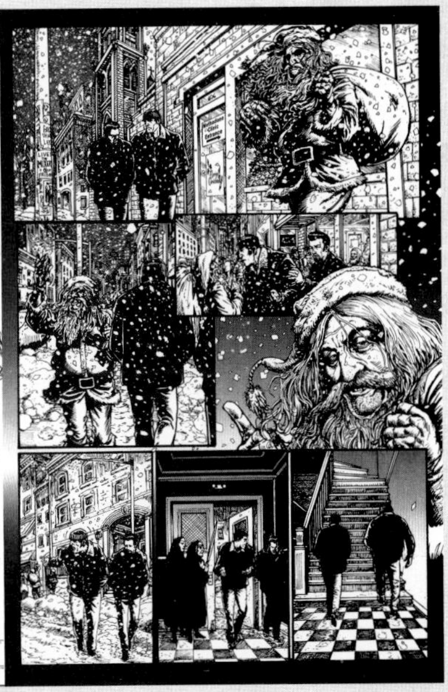
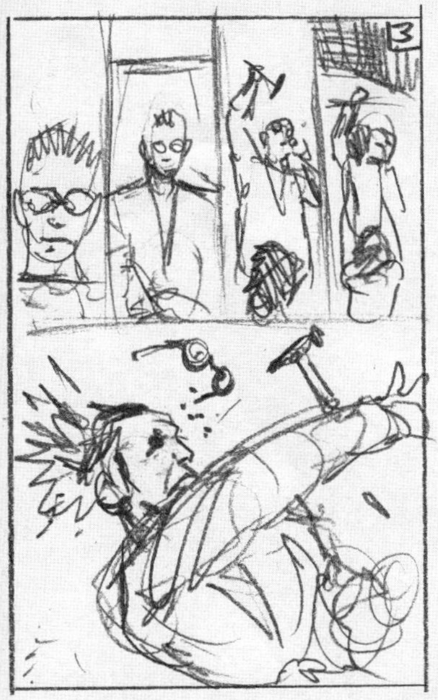
3
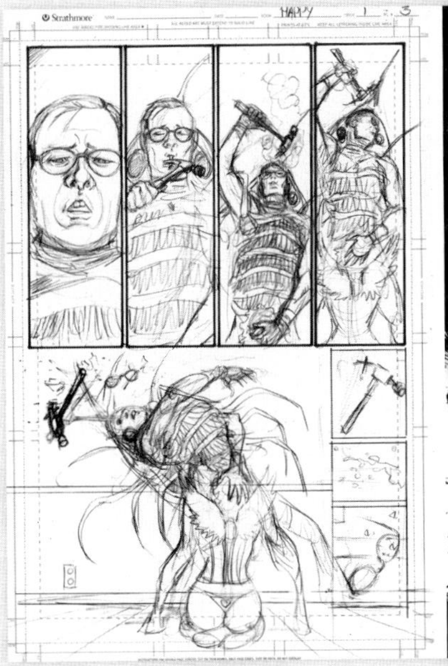
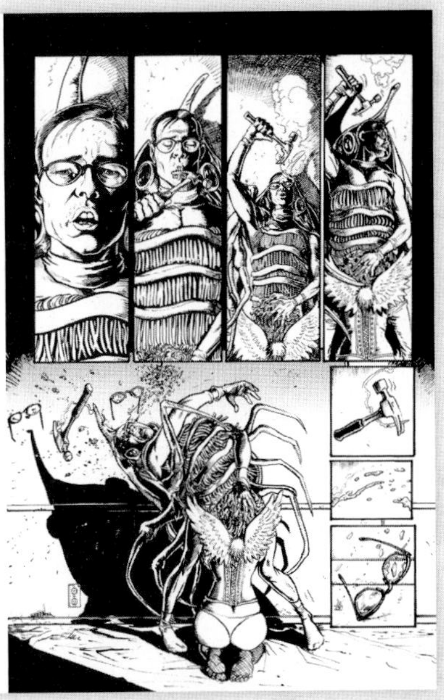
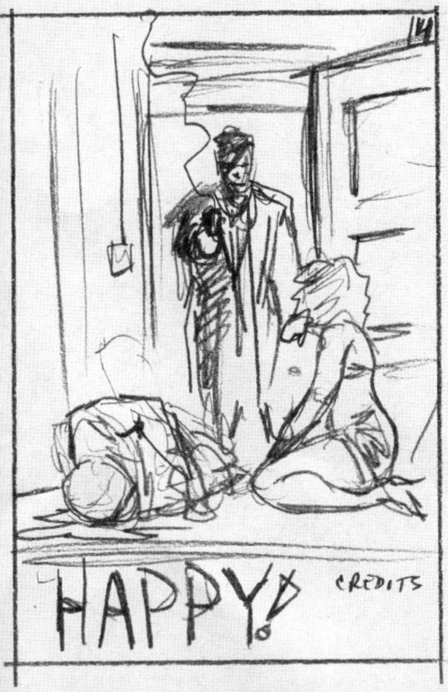
14
HAPPY!
CREDITS
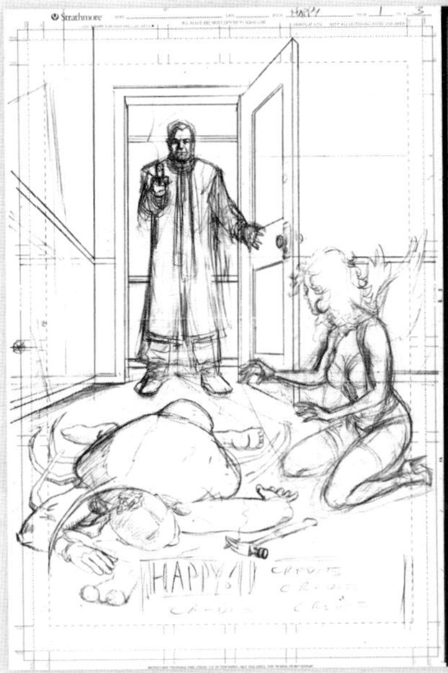
HAPPY!
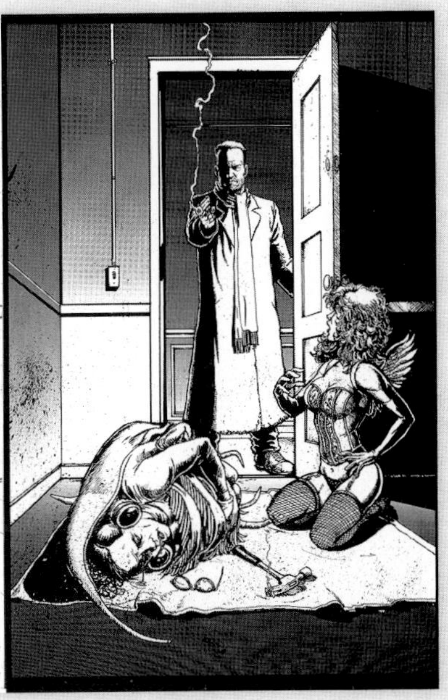

TRAIN SCENE NOTES FROM GRANT

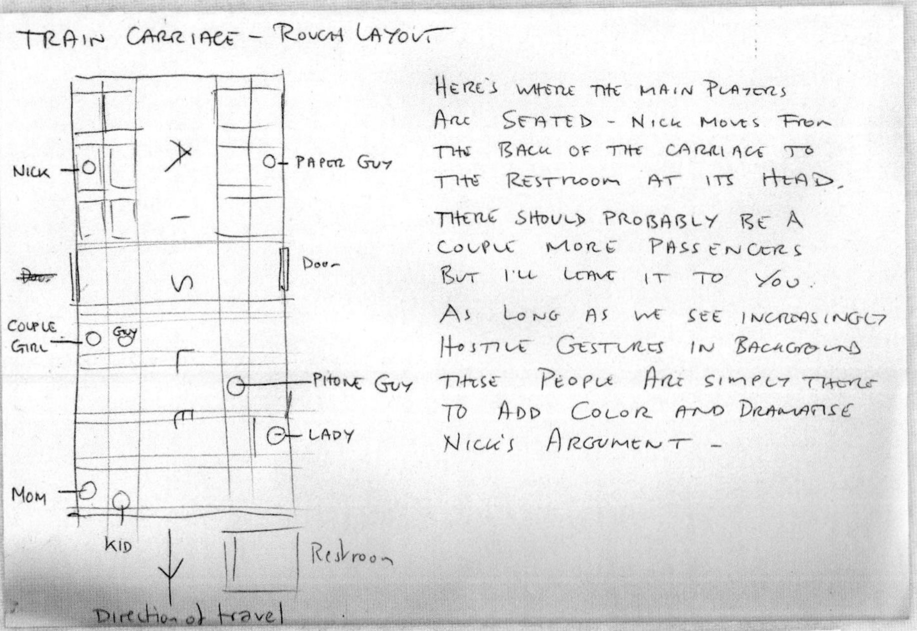
TRAIN CARRIAGE - ROUGH LAYOUT
NICK
PAPER GUY
DOOR
COUPLE GIRL
GUY
PHONE GUY
LADY
MOM
KID
Restroom
Direction of travel
HERE'S WHERE THE MAIN PLAYERS ARE SEATED - NICK MOVES FROM THE BACK OF THE CARRIAGE TO THE RESTROOM AT ITS HEAD.
THERE SHOULD PROBABLY BE A COUPLE MORE PASSENGERS BUT I'LL LEAVE IT TO YOU.
AS LONG AS WE SEE INCREASINGLY HOSTILE GESTURES IN BACKGROUND THESE PEOPLE ARE SIMPLY THERE TO ADD COLOR AND DRAMATISE NICK'S ARGUMENT -

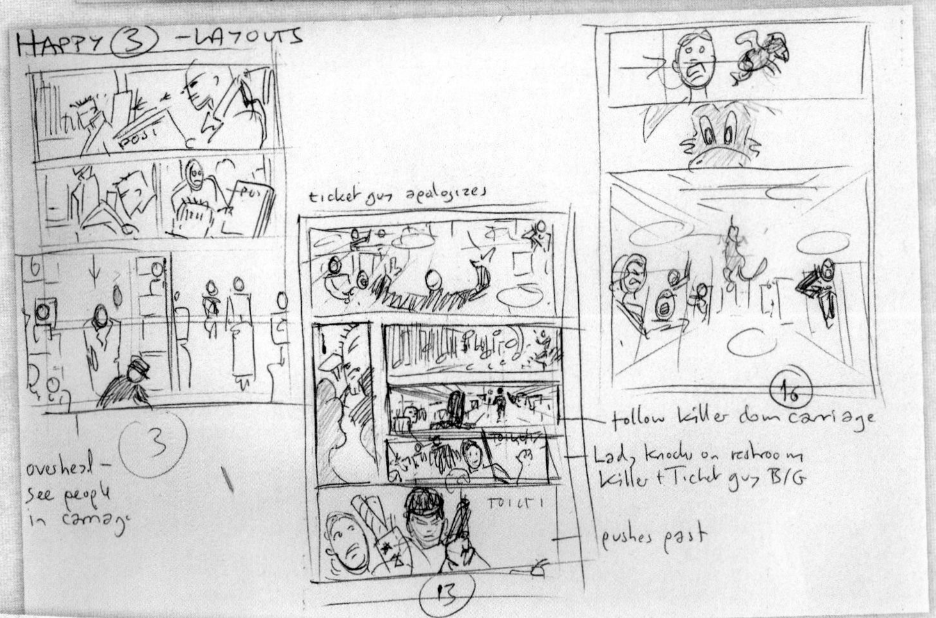
HAPPY 3 - LAYOUTS
3
overhead - see people in carriage
ticket guy apologizes
TOILET
13
16
follow killer down carriage
Lady knocks on restroom
Killer + Ticket guy B/G
pushes past

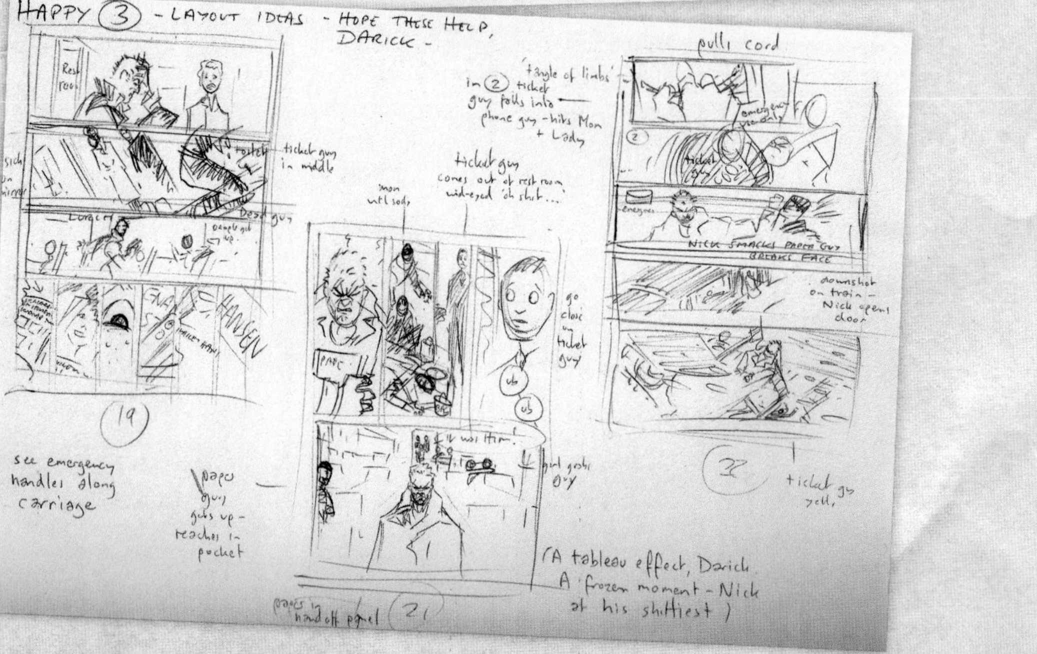
HAPPY 3 - LAYOUT IDEAS - HOPE THESE HELP, DARICK -
19
see emergency handles along carriage
paper guy gets up - reaches in pocket
'tangle of limbs' in 2 ticket guy falls into phone guy - hits Mom + Lady
ticket guy comes out of rest room wide-eyed 'oh shit...'
go close on ticket guy
21
(A tableau effect, Darick A 'frozen moment' - Nick at his shittiest)
pulls cord
NICK SMACKS PAPER GUY BREAKS FACE
downshot on train - Nick opens door
ticket guy yells

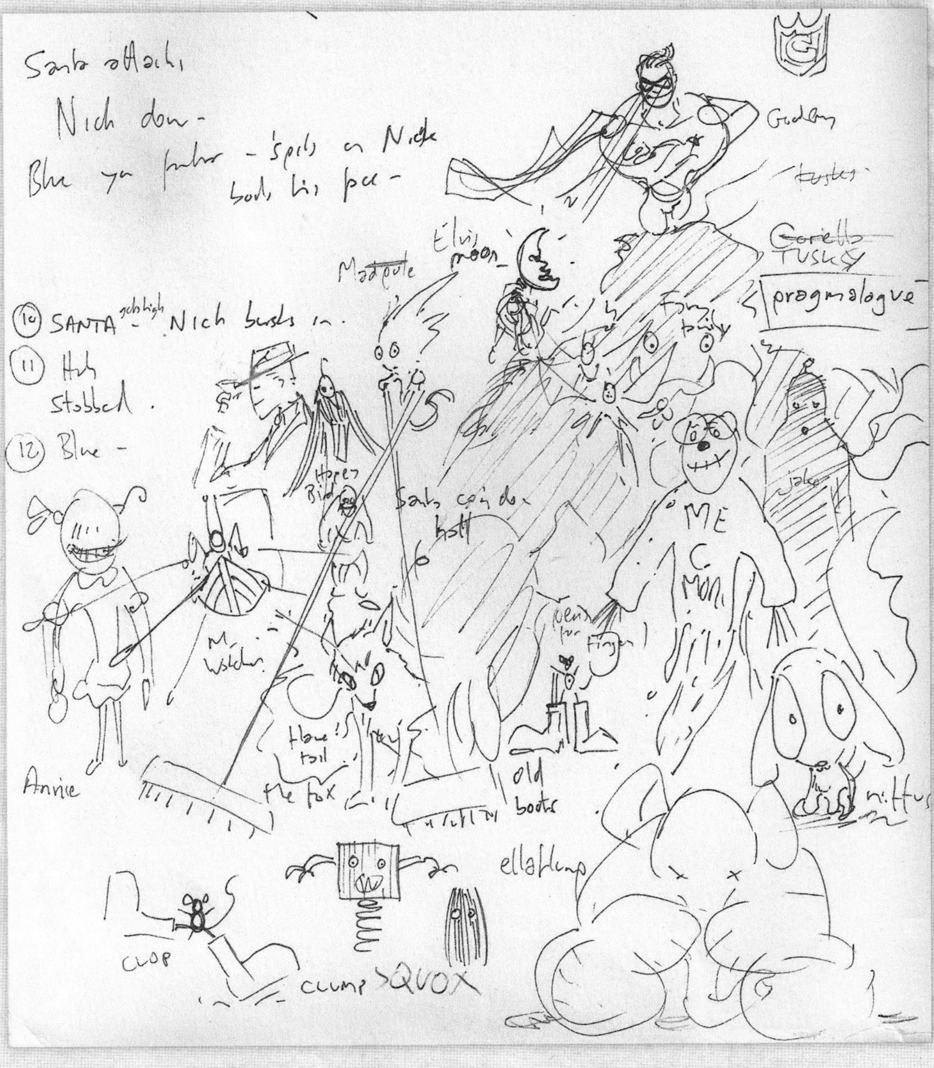
SANTA - Nich busts in.
Annie
Madpole
Elvis moon
TUSKY
Flame tail
the fox
old boots
ellaflump
SQUOX
Jake
ME C MOR

THE IMAGINARY FRIENDS

OLE BOOTS – a tiny cartoon mouse, like Ignatz, from 'Krazy Kat', wearing enormous work boots.

GOOD GUY – a cartoonish Mr. Incredible/masked Superman character with a 'G' shield on his chest.

NIFFUS – a droopy sad-looking cloth dog with a huge head and eyes.

ANNIE – a little girl-thing with only smiley smudges for a face and a little handbag in her hand. A kid's drawing come to life.

ME C. MORE – a pillow-head with a stitched smiley face and button eyes. Colored felt-tipped pens for fingers emerge from the flapping arms of a ghostly trailing sweater filled with holes and the words 'ME C. MORE' written on the front.

MADPOLE – a weird little Doctor Seuss tadpole creature walking with the aid of two brooms.

FLAME TAIL – a luminous, wise and ghostly fox with a tail of fire.

FAIRY FAMILY – a team of mom, dad, sis, bro, baby and dog fairies.

MR. WATCHER – a kindly James Stewart-looking man in '50s suit and hat – a wry gentle smile.

JAKE – a weird shadow presence with smoky tendrils.

ELVIS MOON – Elvis in Vegas white rhinestone suit and the crescent head of a Man-in-the-Moon night light.

ELLAFLUMP – a huge, soft, elephant Buddha creature.

SQUOX – a black cube with two round eyes and a spiky mouth on one face. Two arms with little Mickey Mouse three-fingered gloves at each side. And a spring below so he can bounce around.

TUSKY – a HUGE shaggy shadow creature with plaintive eyes and tusks. Otherwise a silhouette.

THINGMY – a green bug with six arms is sitting in a tiny rowboat. Each arm works a pair of oars. There are three pairs.

UNDER THE COVERS

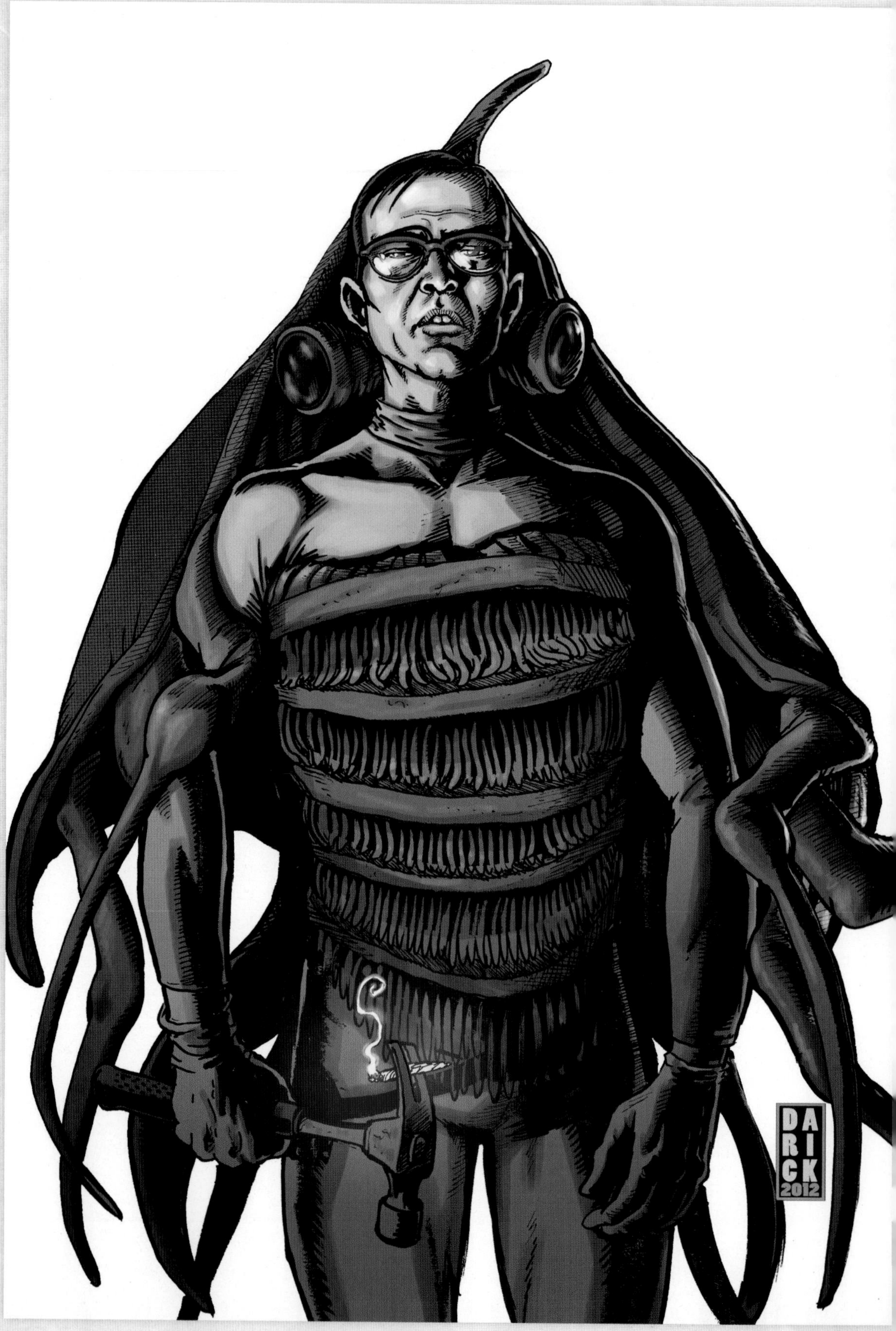
DARICK 2012

TEASER OPTIONS

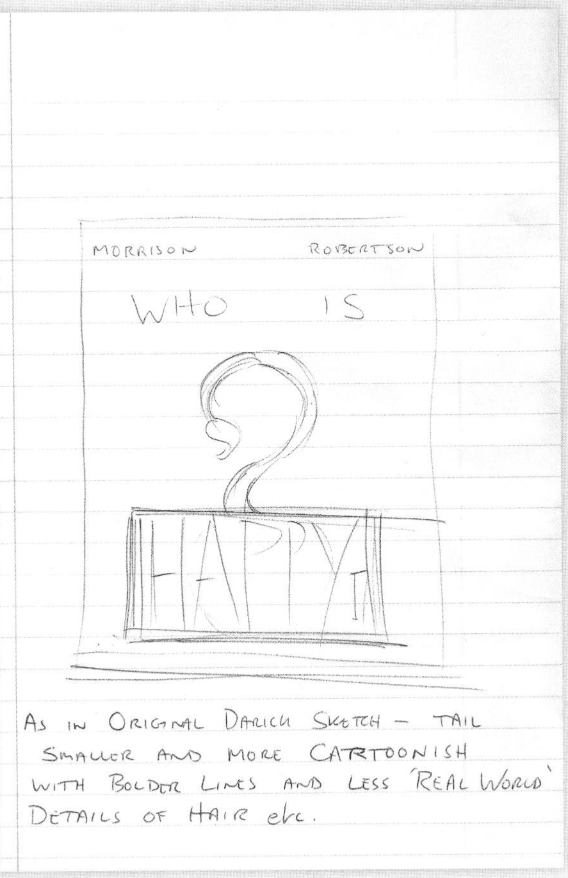
MORRISON
ROBERTSON
WHO IS
HAPPY
As in Original Darick Sketch – Tail smaller and more cartoonish with bolder lines and less 'Real World' details of hair etc.

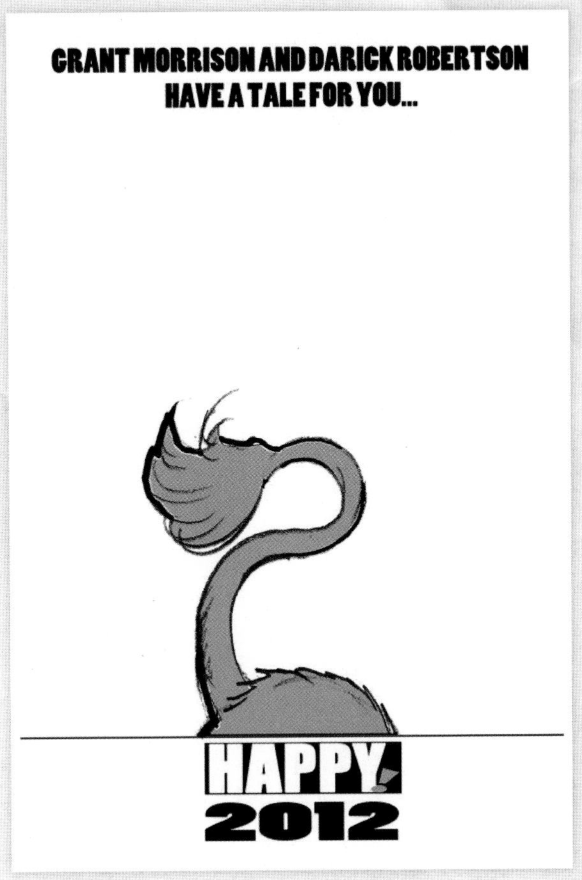
GRANT MORRISON AND DARICK ROBERTSON
HAVE A TALE FOR YOU...
HAPPY!
2012

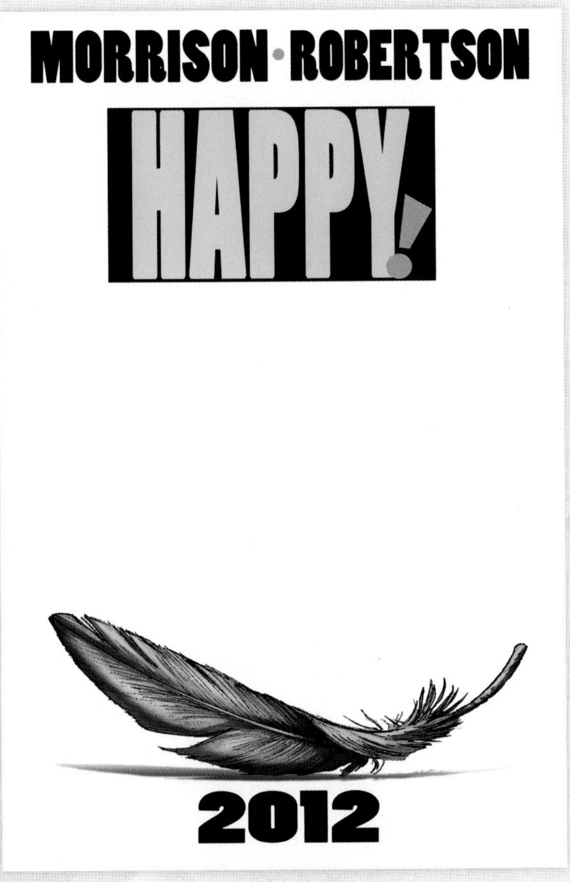
MORRISON · ROBERTSON
HAPPY!
2012

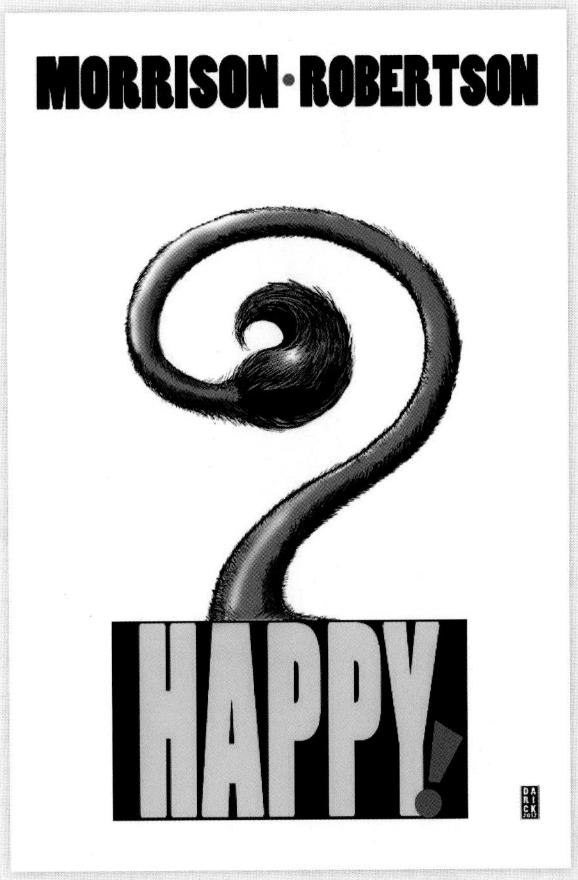
MORRISON · ROBERTSON
HAPPY!

ISSUE ONE COVER DEVELOPMENT

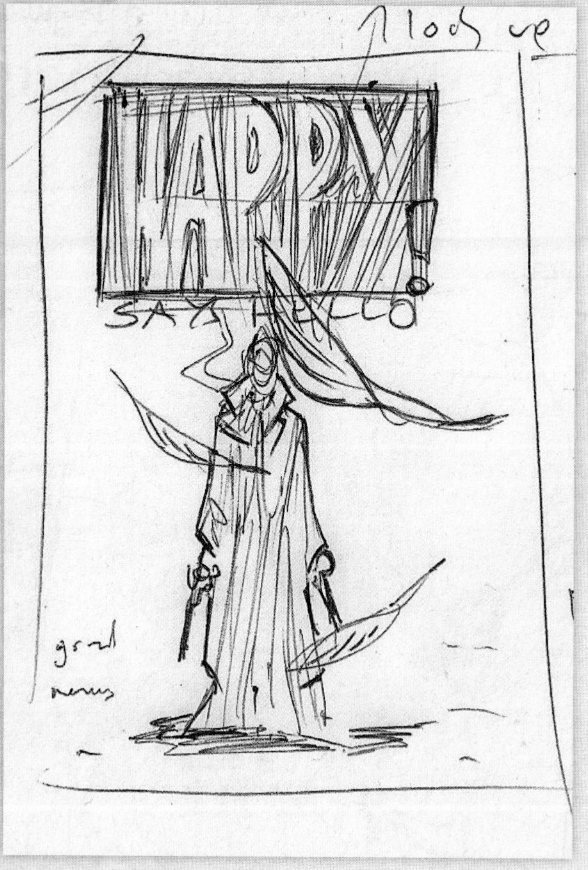
look up
HAPPY!
SAY HELLO
good news

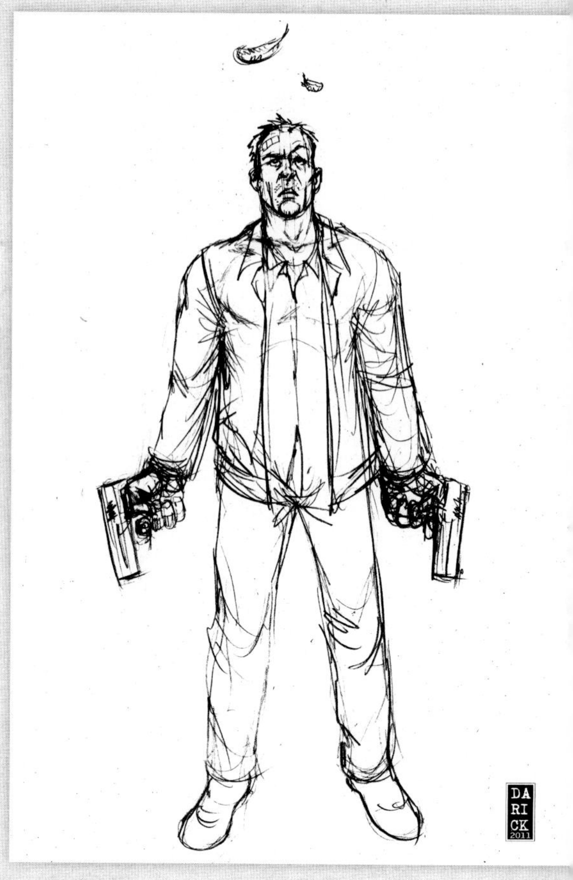
DARICK 2011

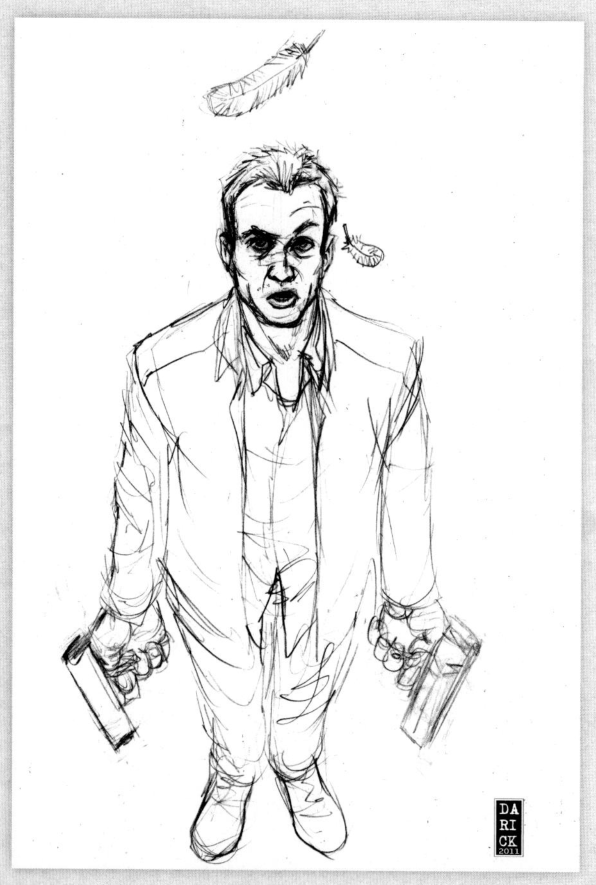
DARICK 2011

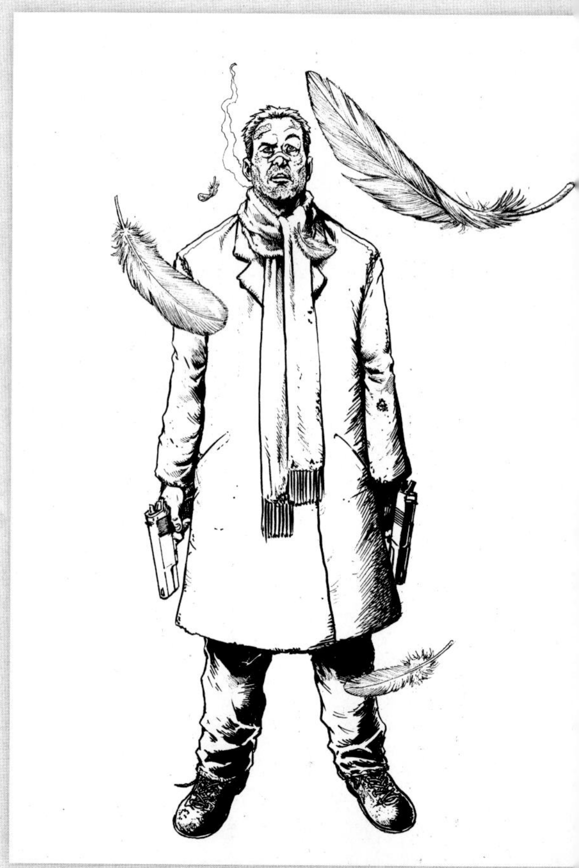

VARIANT COVER OUTTAKES AND SKETCHES

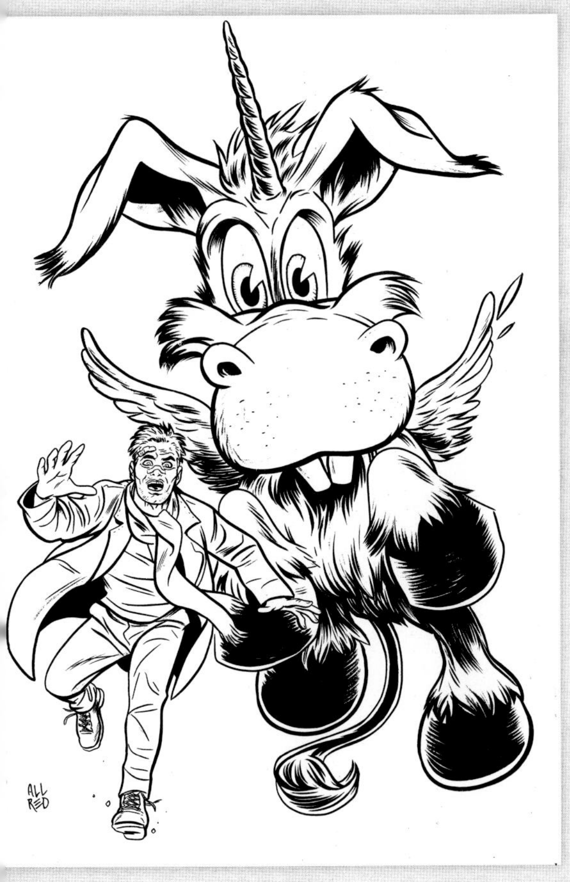
ALL
RED

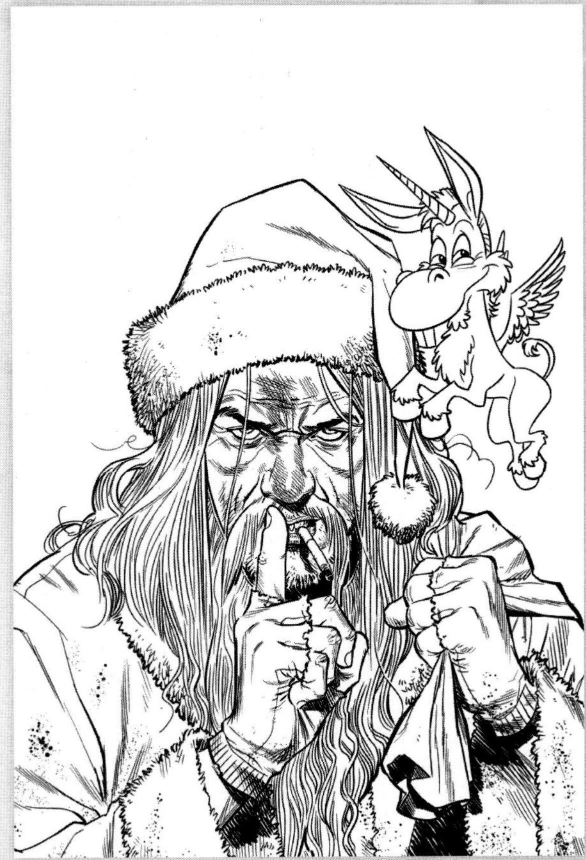

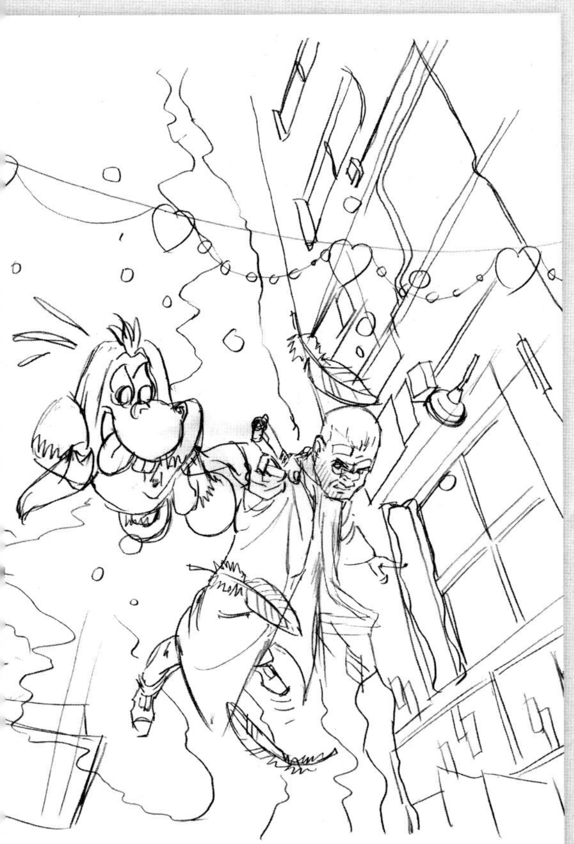

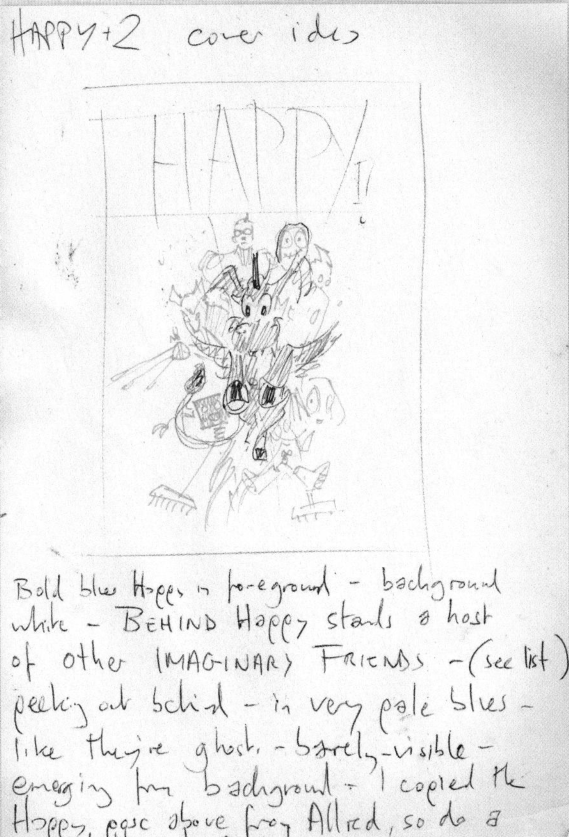
HAPPY+2 cover idea
HAPPY!!
Bold blue Happy in fore-ground - background white - BEHIND Happy stands a host of other IMAGINARY FRIENDS -(see list) peeking out behind - in very pale blues - like they're ghosts - barely-visible - emerging from background - I copied the Happy pose above from Allred, so do a different one!

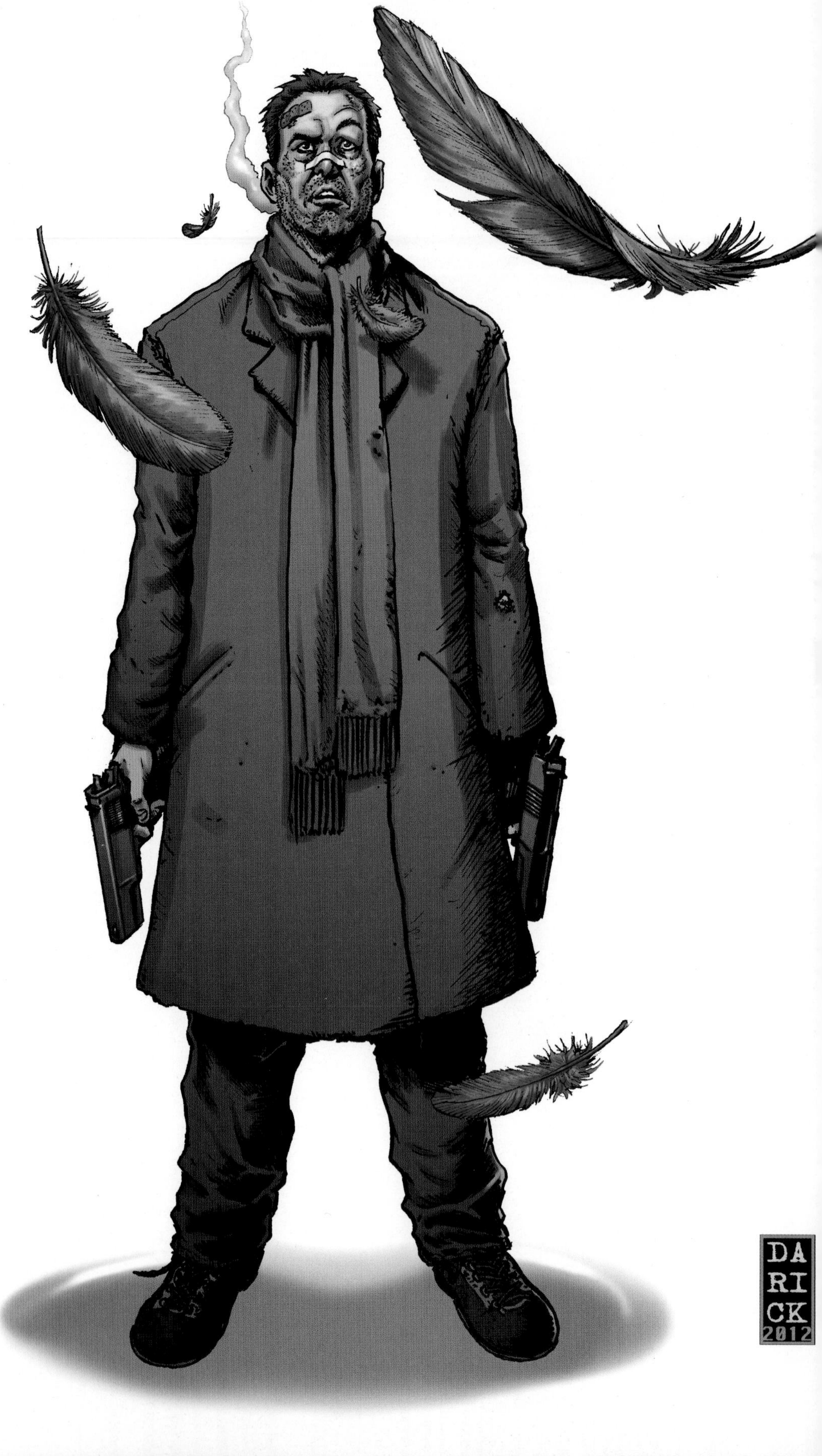
DA
RI
CK
2012

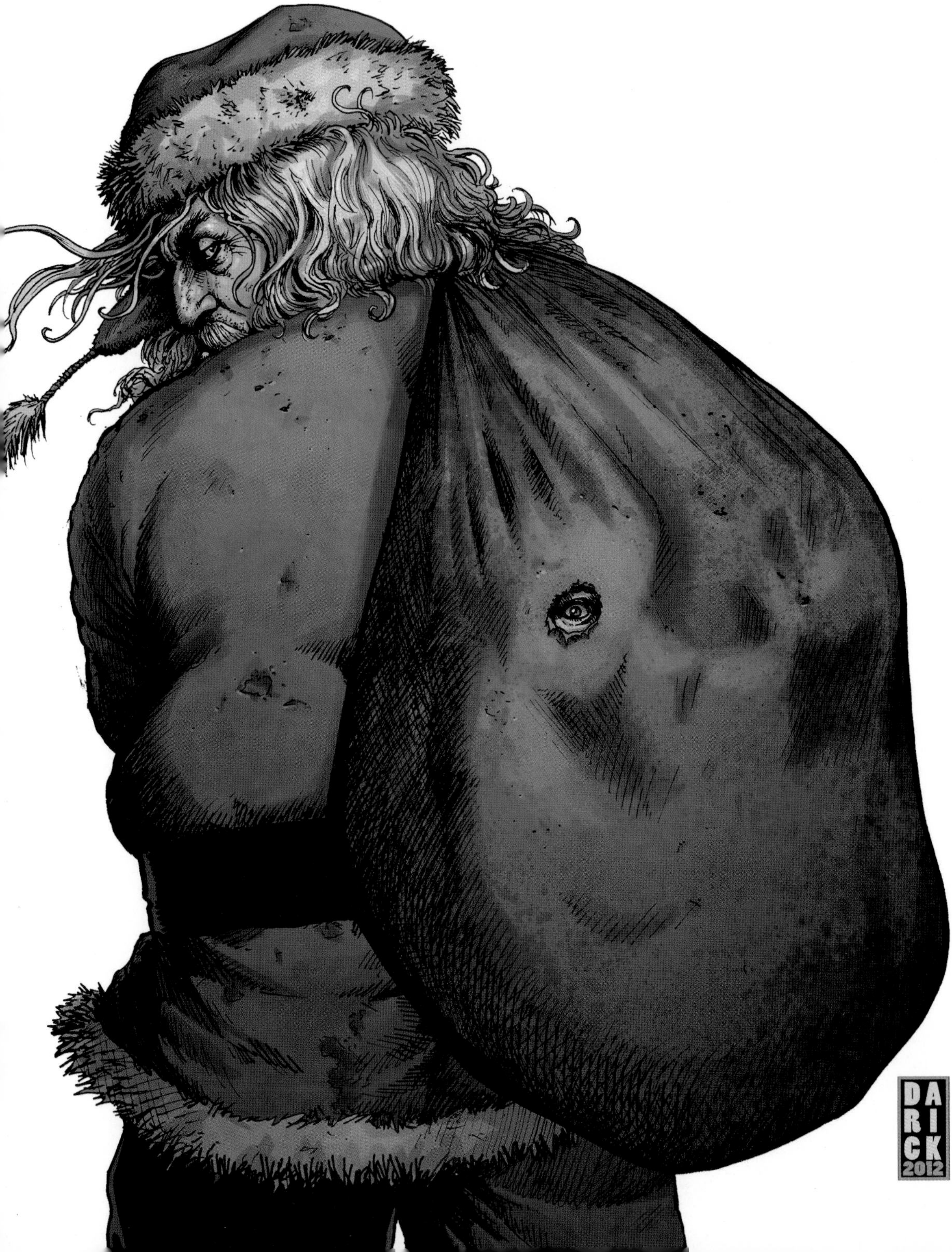
DARICK 2012

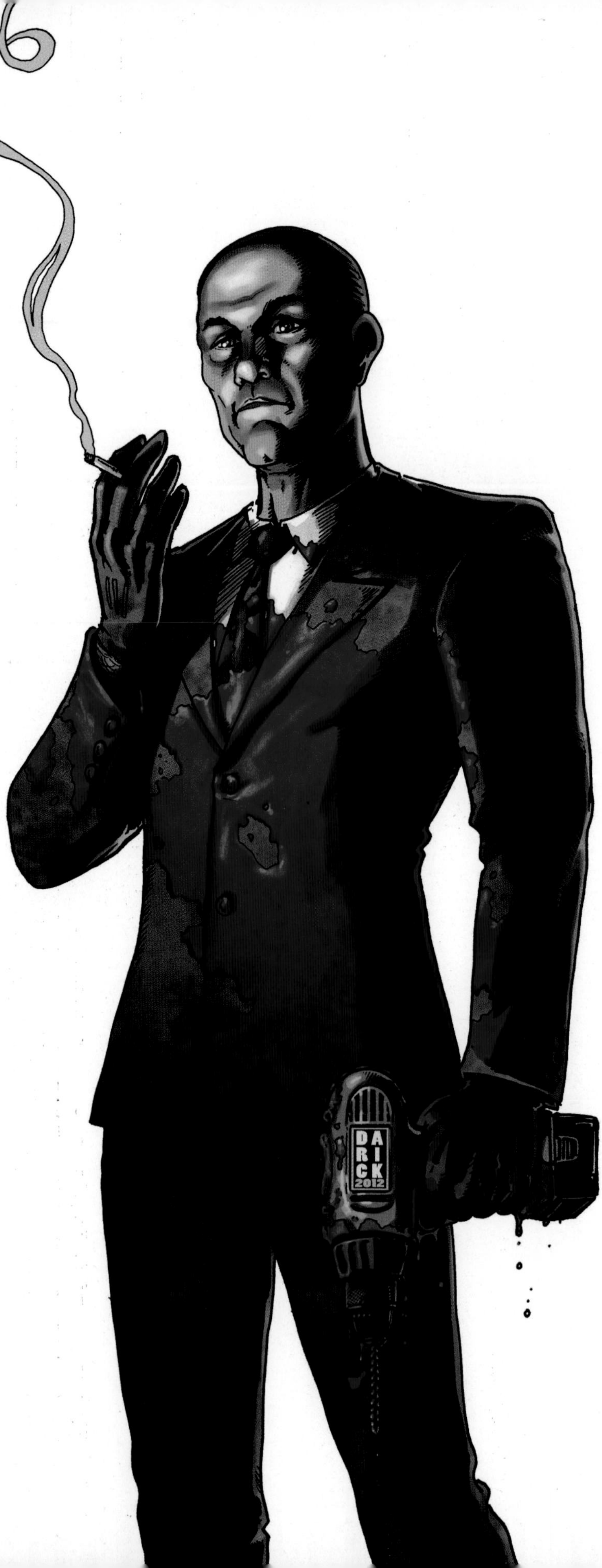
DA
RI
CK
2012

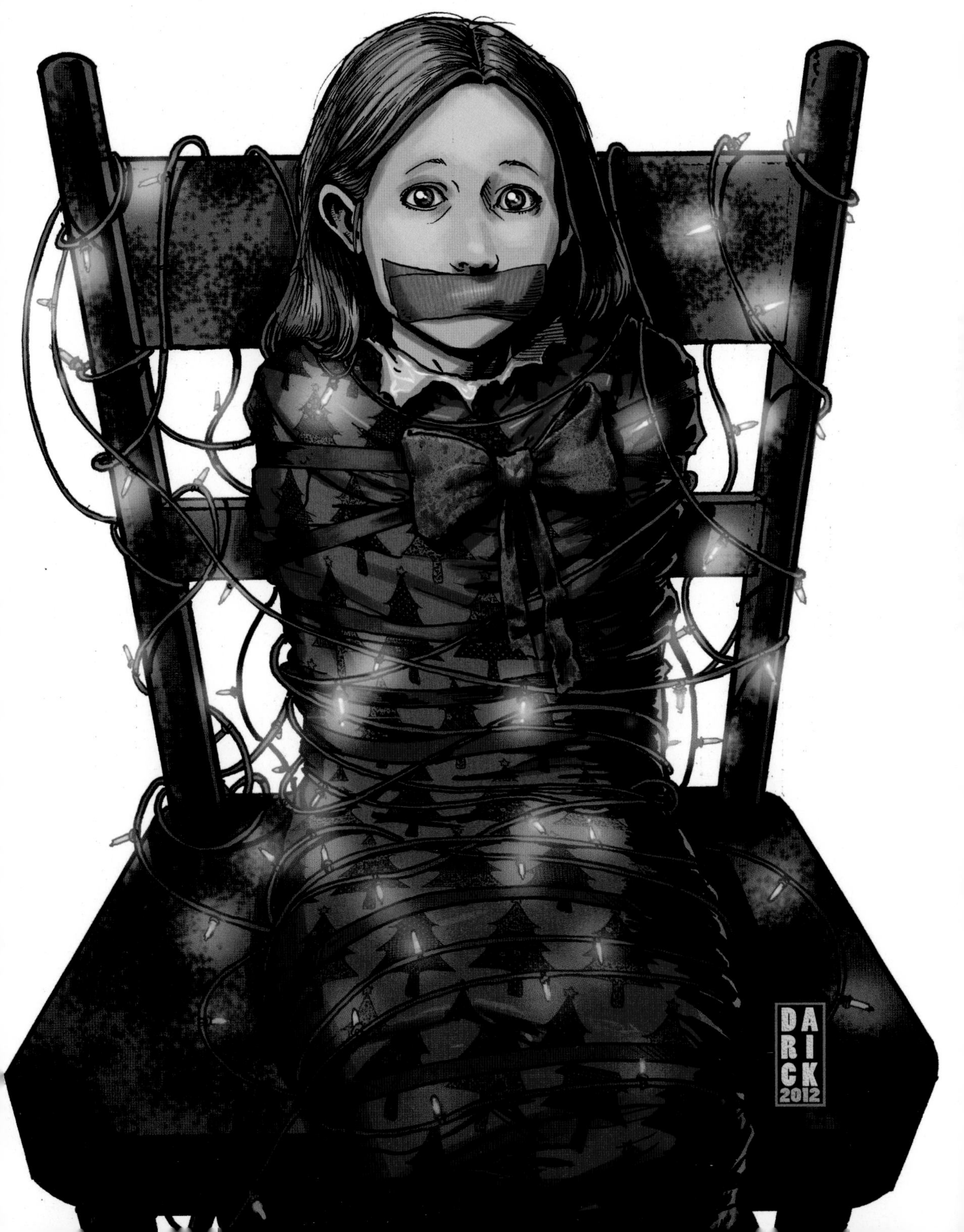
DARICK 2012

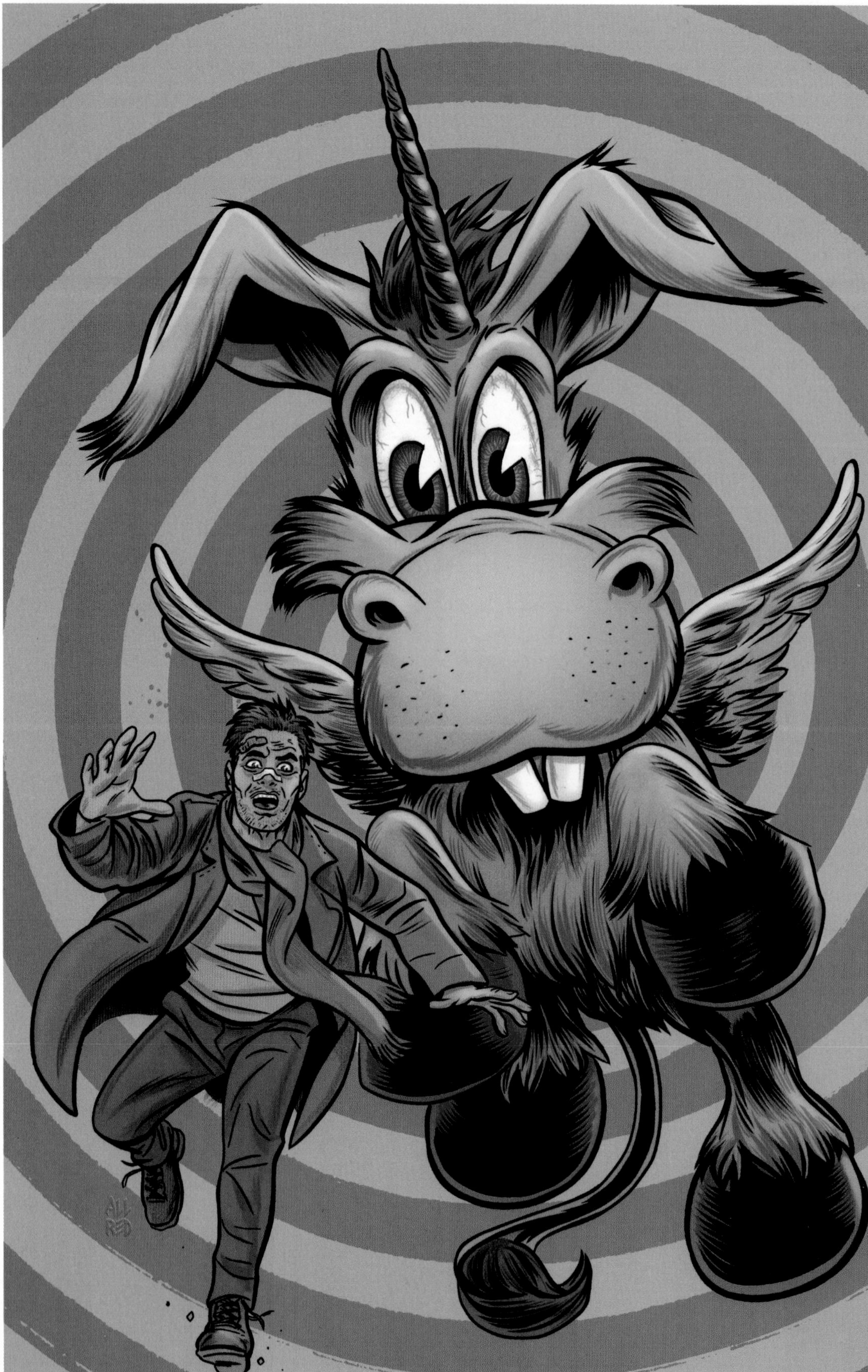
ALLRED

MICHAEL & LAURA ALLRED

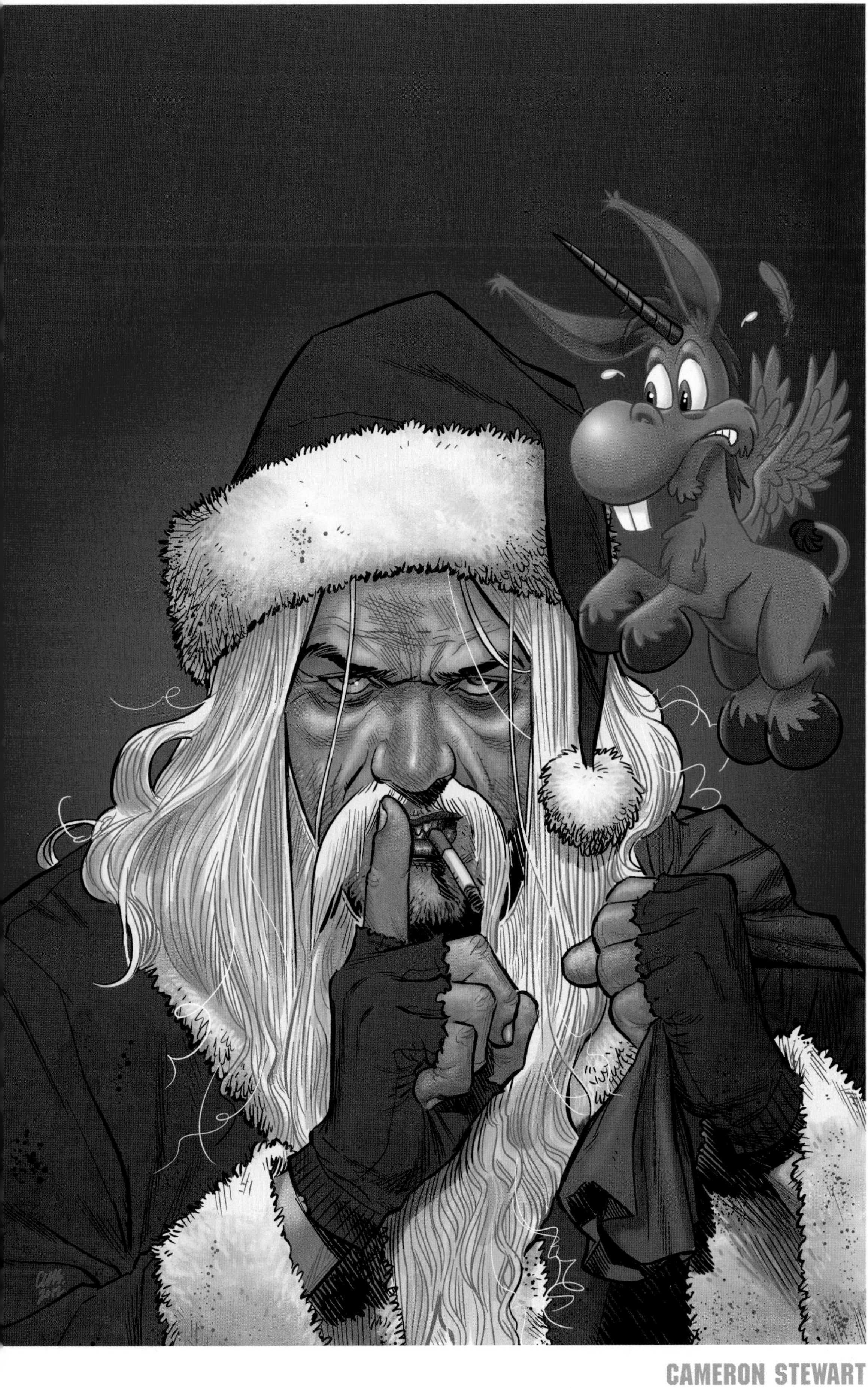

CAMERON STEWART

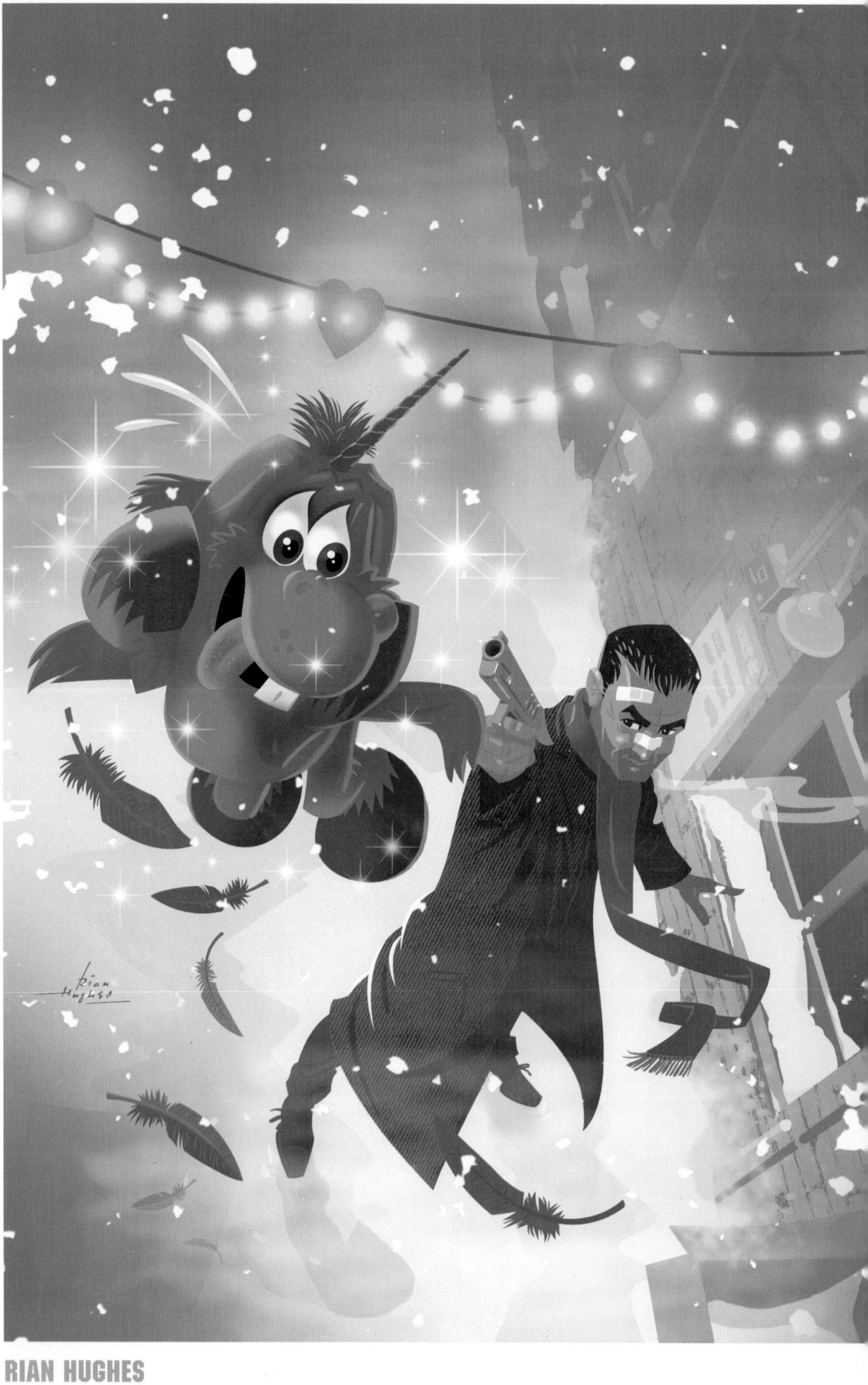

RIAN HUGHES

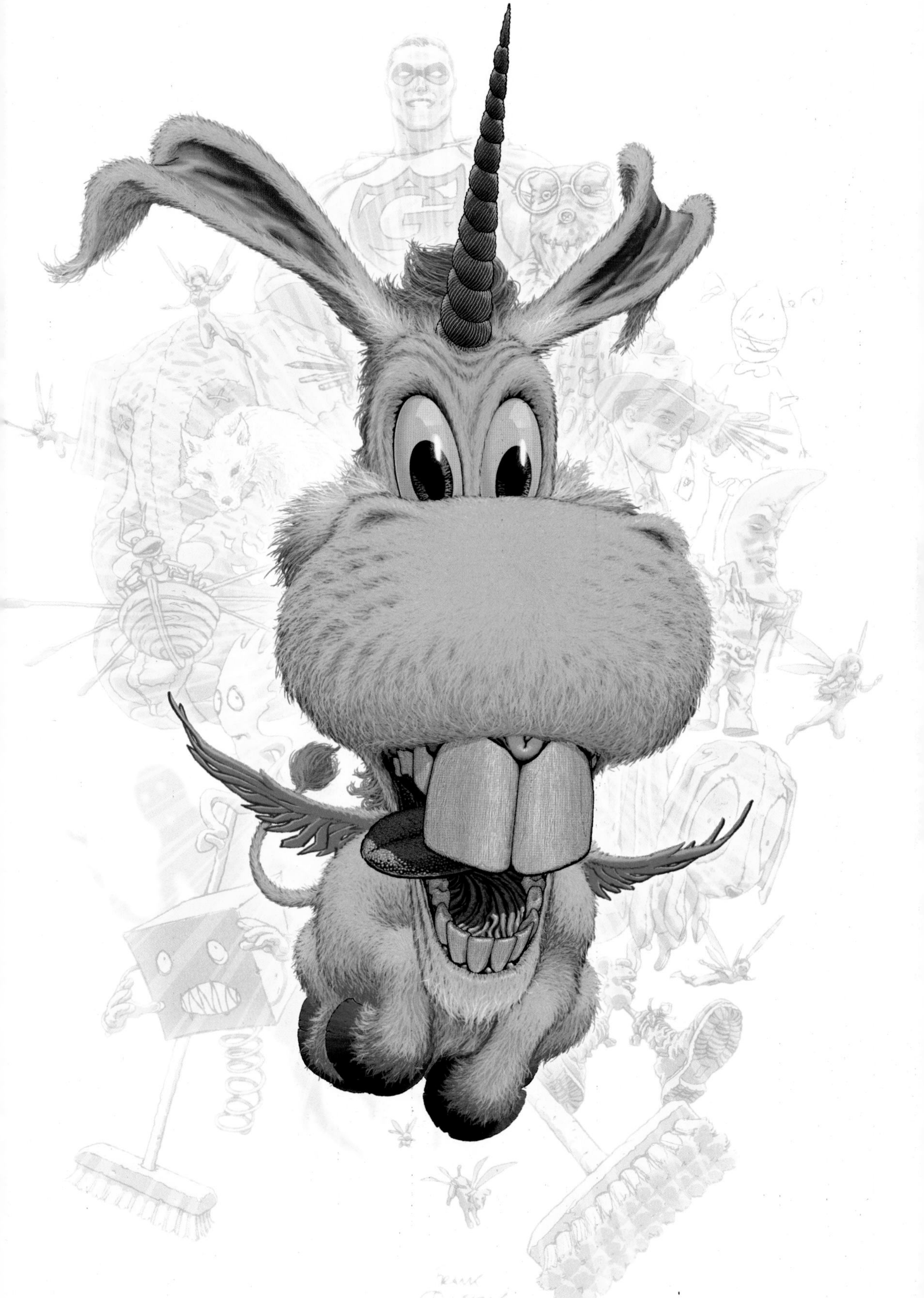

FRANK QUITELY

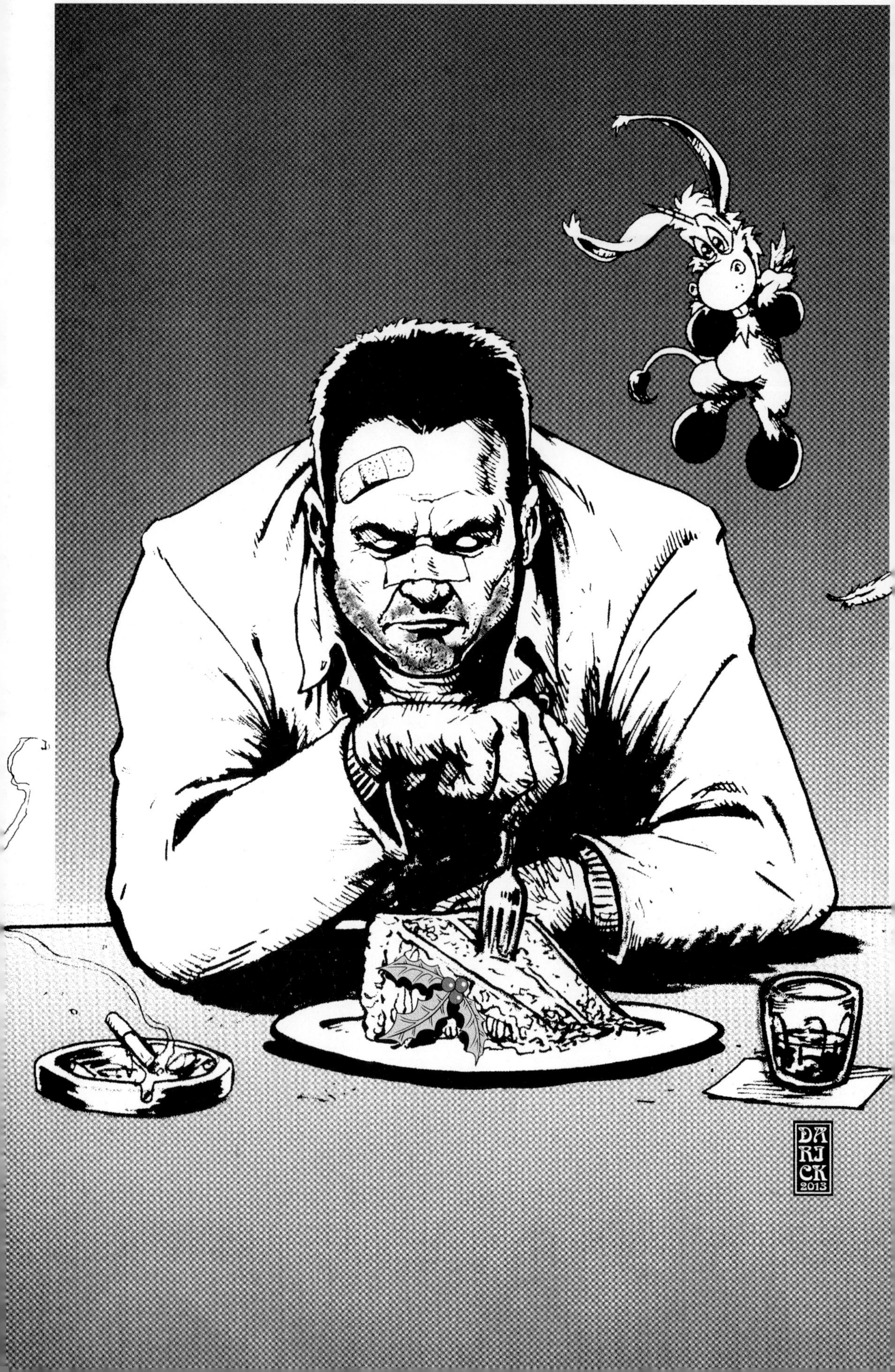
DARICK 2013